big NATE
GAME ON!

More

big NATE

adventures from

LINCOLN PEIRCE

Novels:

Big Nate: In a Class By Himself
Big Nate Strikes Again
Big Nate On a Roll
Big Nate Goes For Broke

Activity Books:

Big Nate Boredom Buster
Big Nate Fun Blaster

Comic Compilations:

Big Nate From the Top
Big Nate Out Loud
Big Nate and Friends
Big Nate: What Could Possibly Go Wrong?
Big Nate: Here Goes Nothing
Big Nate Makes the Grade
Big Nate All Work and No Play

big NATE

GAME ON!

by LINCOLN PEIRCE

**Andrews McMeel
Publishing, LLC**

Kansas City • Sydney • London

Big Nate is distributed internationally by Universal Uclick.

Andrews McMeel Publishing, LLC
an Andrews McMeel Universal company
1130 Walnut Street, Kansas City, Missouri 64106

www.andrewsmcmeel.com

13 14 15 16 17 RR2 10 9 8 7 6 5 4 3 2 1

ISBN: 978-1-4494-2777-1

Library of Congress Control Number: 2012952339

Big Nate can be viewed on the Internet at
www.comics.com/big_nate

ATTENTION: SCHOOLS AND BUSINESSES
Andrews McMeel books are available at quantity discounts with bulk purchase for educational, business, or sales promotional use. For information, please e-mail the Andrews McMeel Publishing Special Sales Department:
specialsales@amuniversal.com

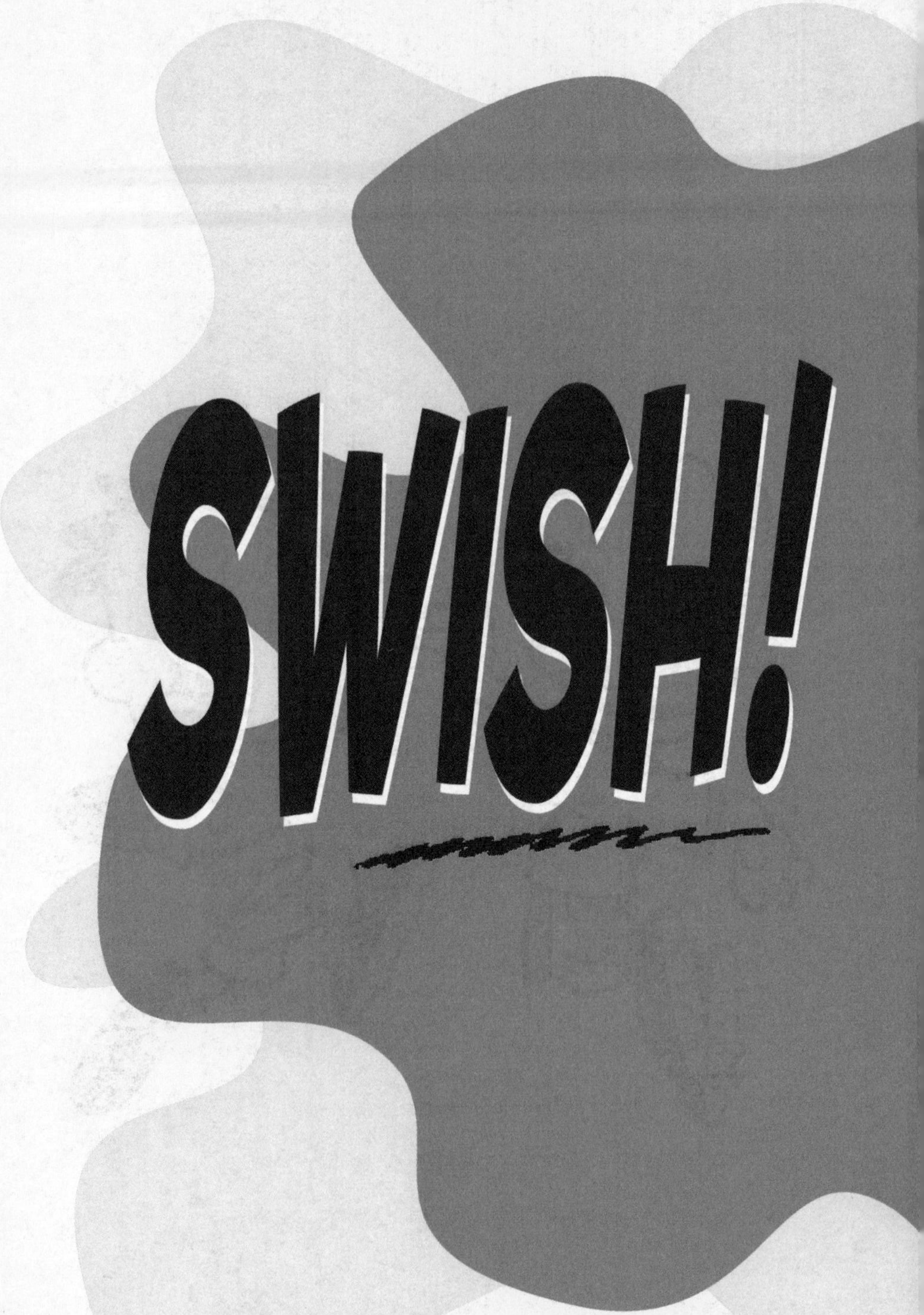
SWISH!

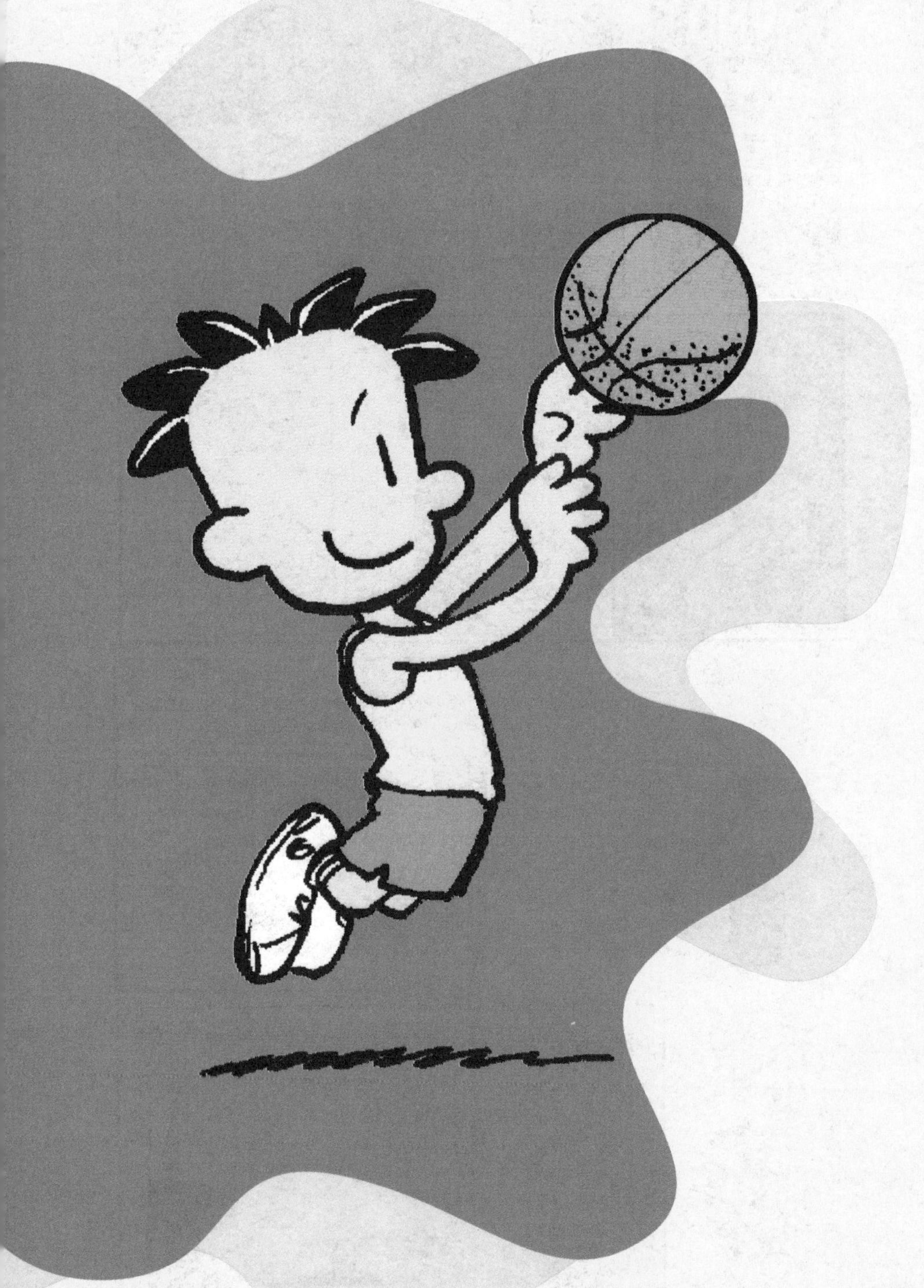

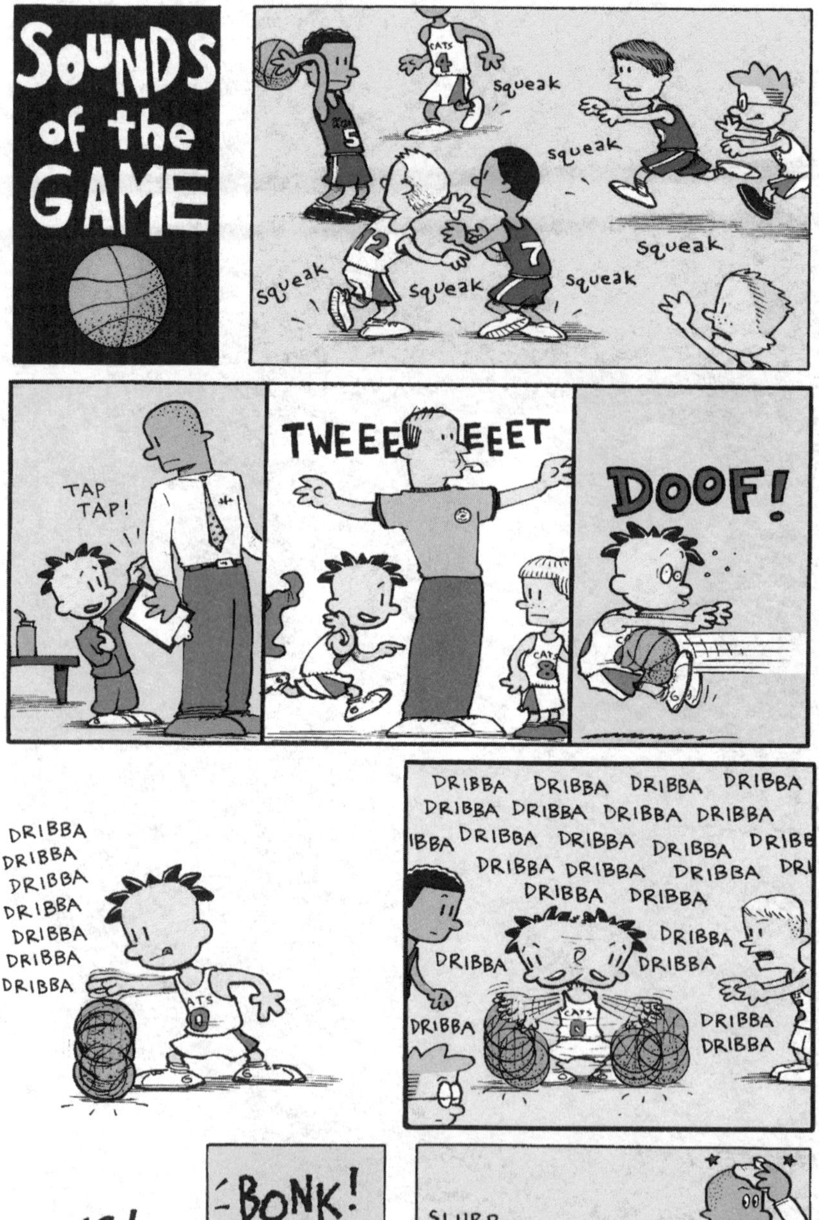
SOUNDS of the GAME
squeak
squeak
squeak
squeak
squeak
squeak
TAP TAP!
TWEEEEEEET
DOOF!
DRIBBA DRIBBA DRIBBA DRIBBA DRIBBA DRIBBA DRIBBA
DRIBBA DRIBBA DRIBBA DRIBBA
DRIBBA DRIBBA DRIBBA DRIBBA
DRIBBA DRIBBA DRIBBA DRIBBA
DRIBBA DRIBBA DRIBBA
DRIBBA DRIBBA
DRIBBA DRIBBA DRIBBA
DRIBBA
DRIBBA DRIBBA
ZING!
BONK!
SLURP

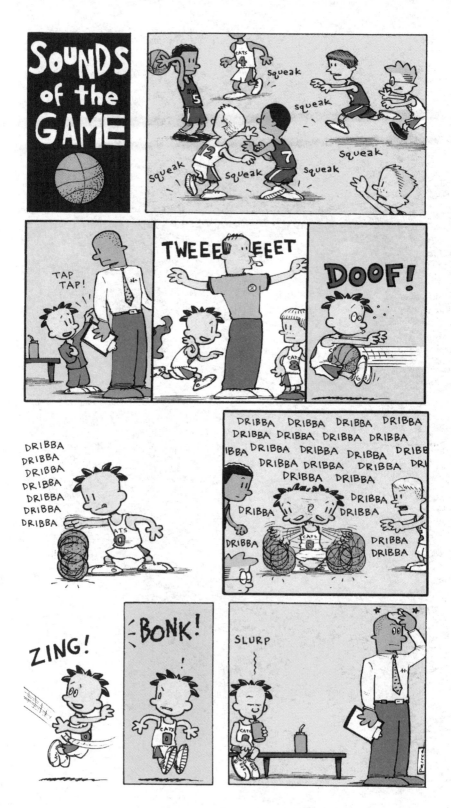

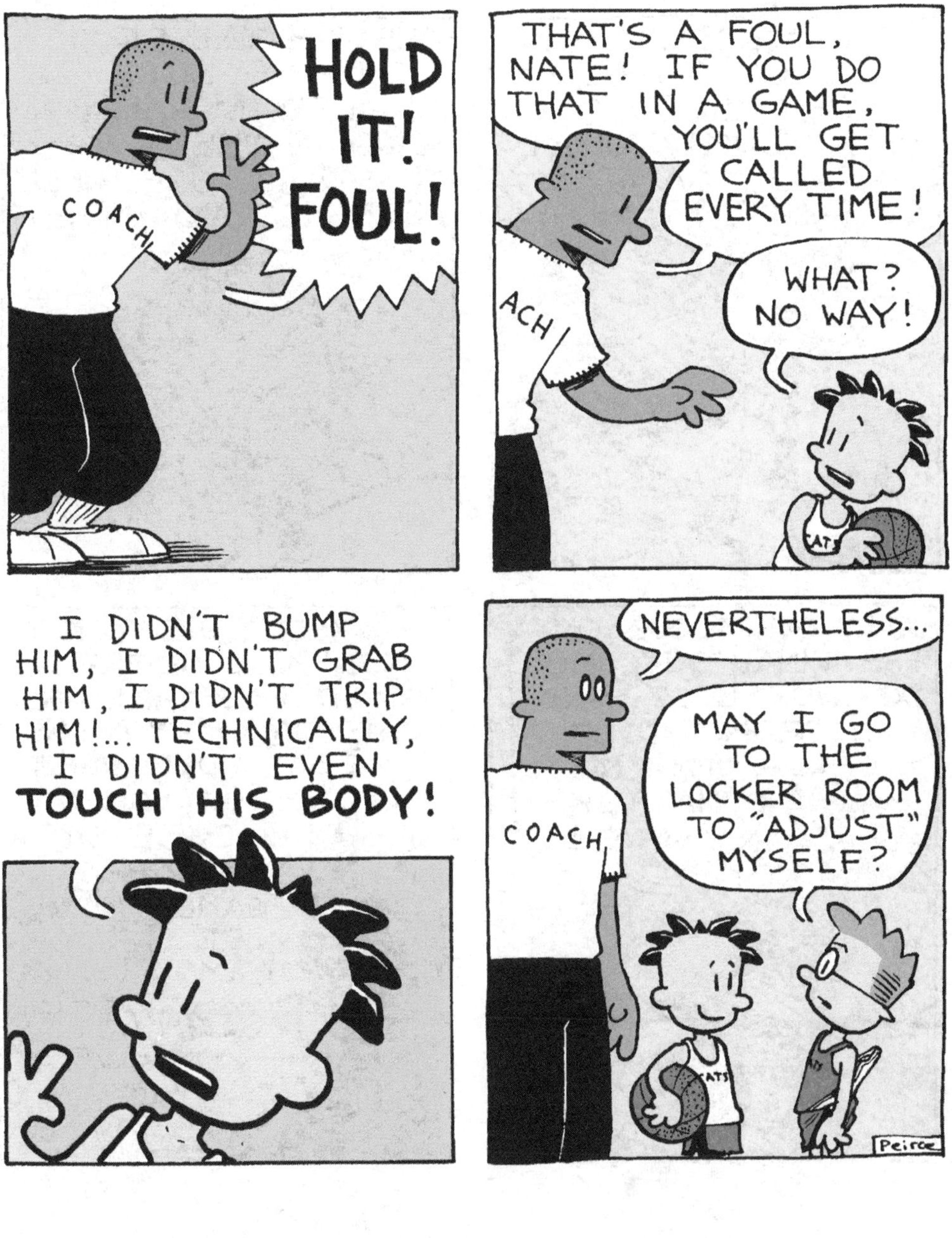
HOLD IT! FOUL!
COACH
THAT'S A FOUL, NATE! IF YOU DO THAT IN A GAME, YOU'LL GET CALLED EVERY TIME!
WHAT? NO WAY!
I DIDN'T BUMP HIM, I DIDN'T GRAB HIM, I DIDN'T TRIP HIM!... TECHNICALLY, I DIDN'T EVEN **TOUCH HIS BODY!**
NEVERTHELESS...
MAY I GO TO THE LOCKER ROOM TO "ADJUST" MYSELF?
COACH
Peirce

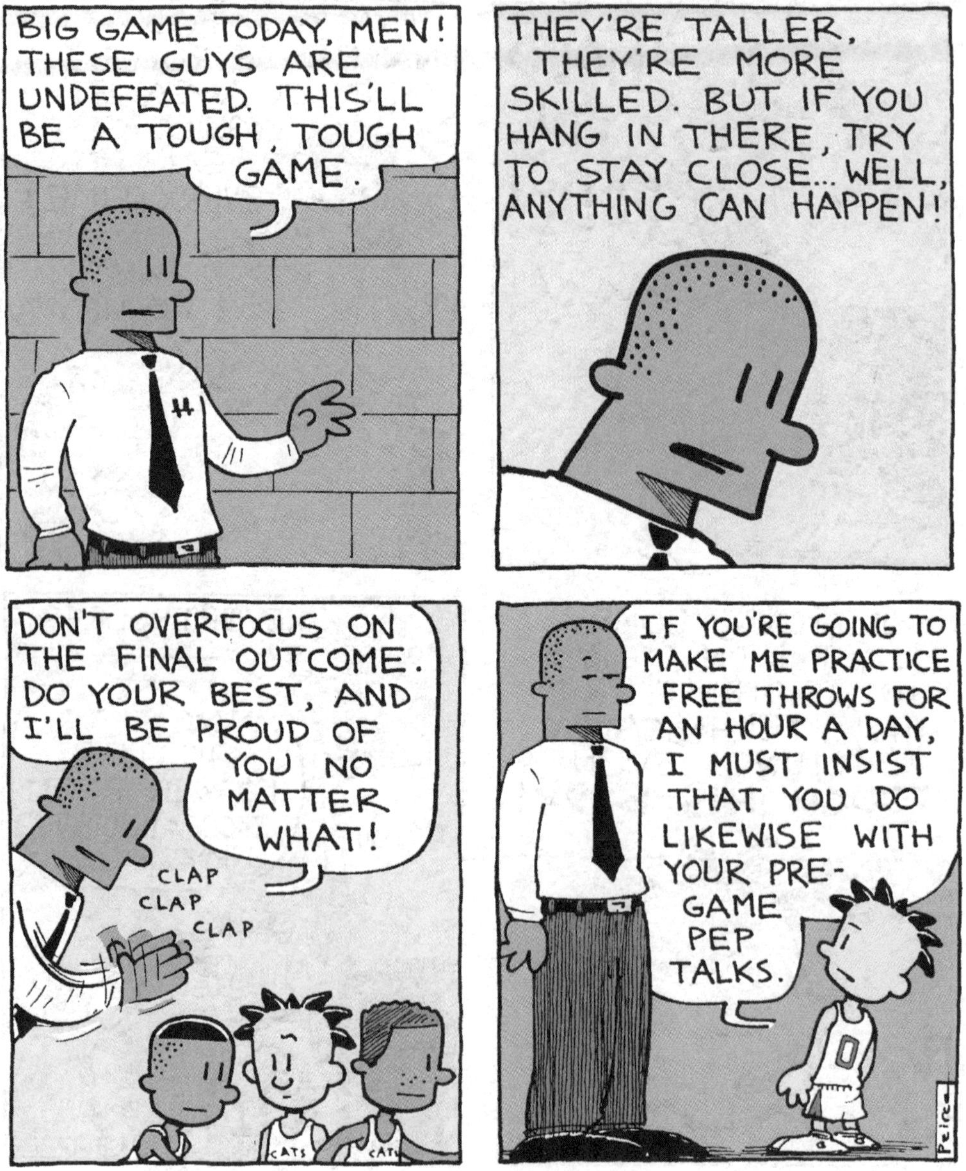
BIG GAME TODAY, MEN! THESE GUYS ARE UNDEFEATED. THIS'LL BE A TOUGH, TOUGH GAME.
THEY'RE TALLER, THEY'RE MORE SKILLED. BUT IF YOU HANG IN THERE, TRY TO STAY CLOSE... WELL, ANYTHING CAN HAPPEN!
DON'T OVERFOCUS ON THE FINAL OUTCOME. DO YOUR BEST, AND I'LL BE PROUD OF YOU NO MATTER WHAT!
CLAP
CLAP
CLAP
CATS
CATS
IF YOU'RE GOING TO MAKE ME PRACTICE FREE THROWS FOR AN HOUR A DAY, I MUST INSIST THAT YOU DO LIKEWISE WITH YOUR PRE-GAME PEP TALKS.
Peirce

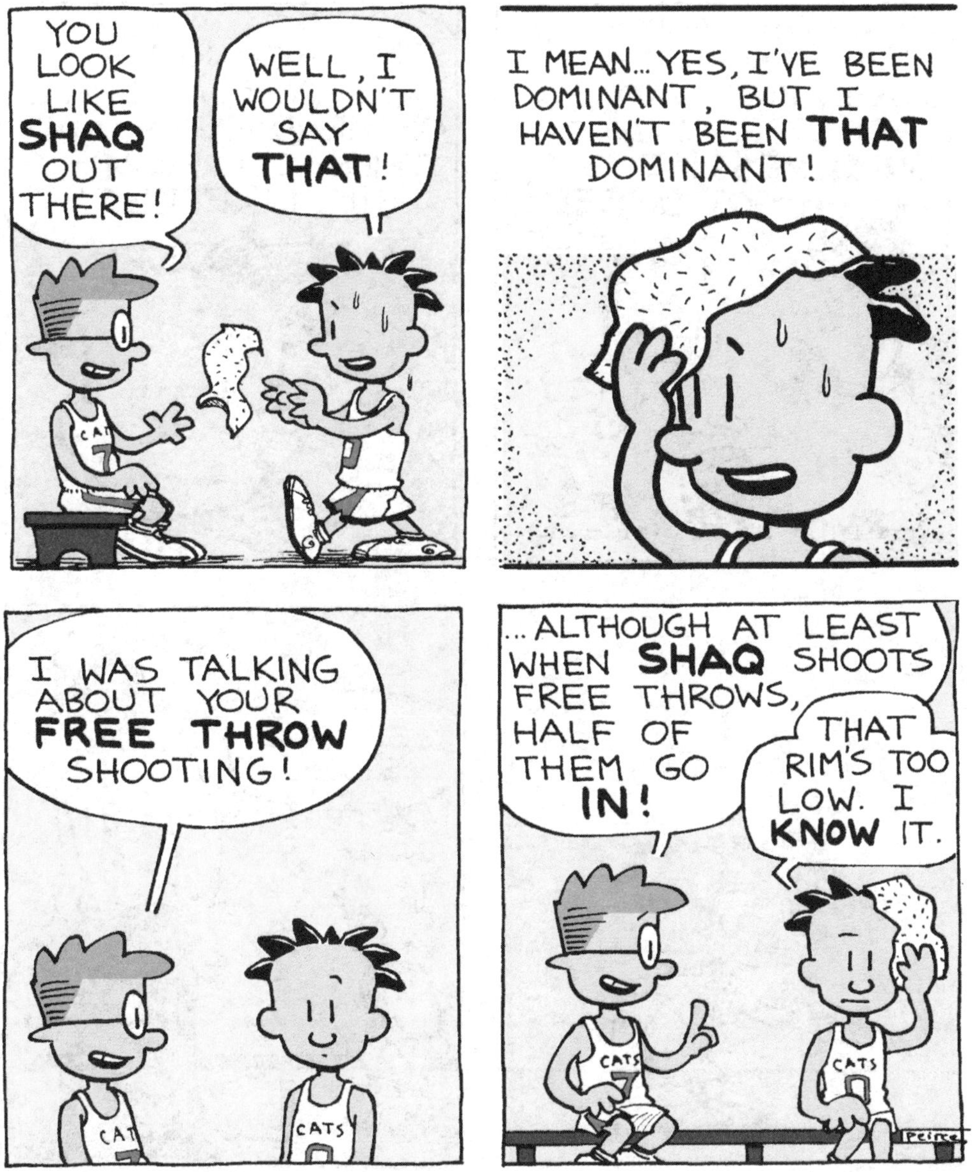

YOU LOOK LIKE **SHAQ** OUT THERE!
WELL, I WOULDN'T SAY **THAT**!
I MEAN... YES, I'VE BEEN DOMINANT, BUT I HAVEN'T BEEN **THAT** DOMINANT!
I WAS TALKING ABOUT YOUR **FREE THROW** SHOOTING!
...ALTHOUGH AT LEAST WHEN **SHAQ** SHOOTS FREE THROWS, HALF OF THEM GO **IN**!
THAT RIM'S TOO LOW. I **KNOW** IT.
CATS
CATS
Peirce

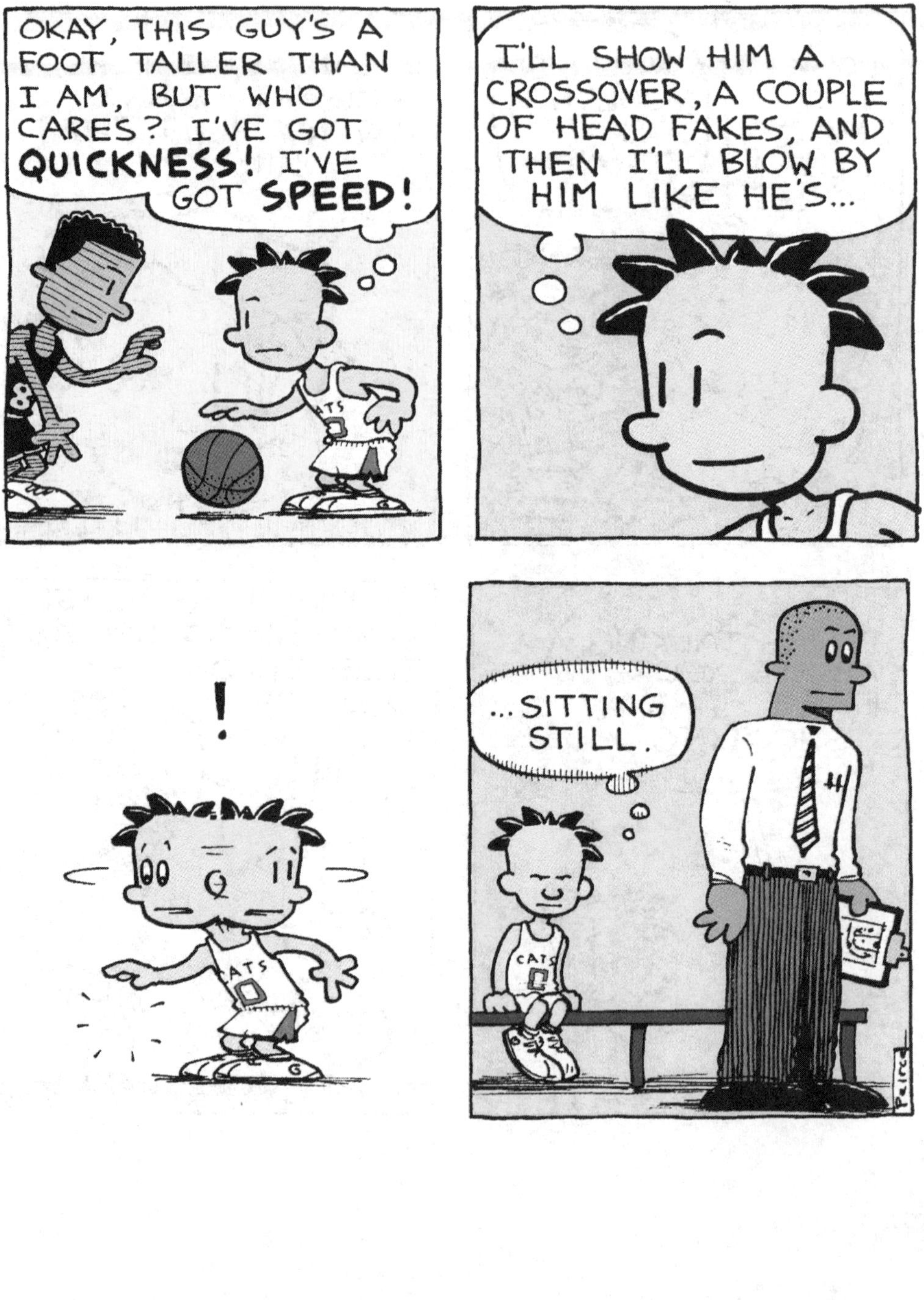
OKAY, THIS GUY'S A FOOT TALLER THAN I AM, BUT WHO CARES? I'VE GOT QUICKNESS! I'VE GOT SPEED!
I'LL SHOW HIM A CROSSOVER, A COUPLE OF HEAD FAKES, AND THEN I'LL BLOW BY HIM LIKE HE'S...
!
...SITTING STILL.

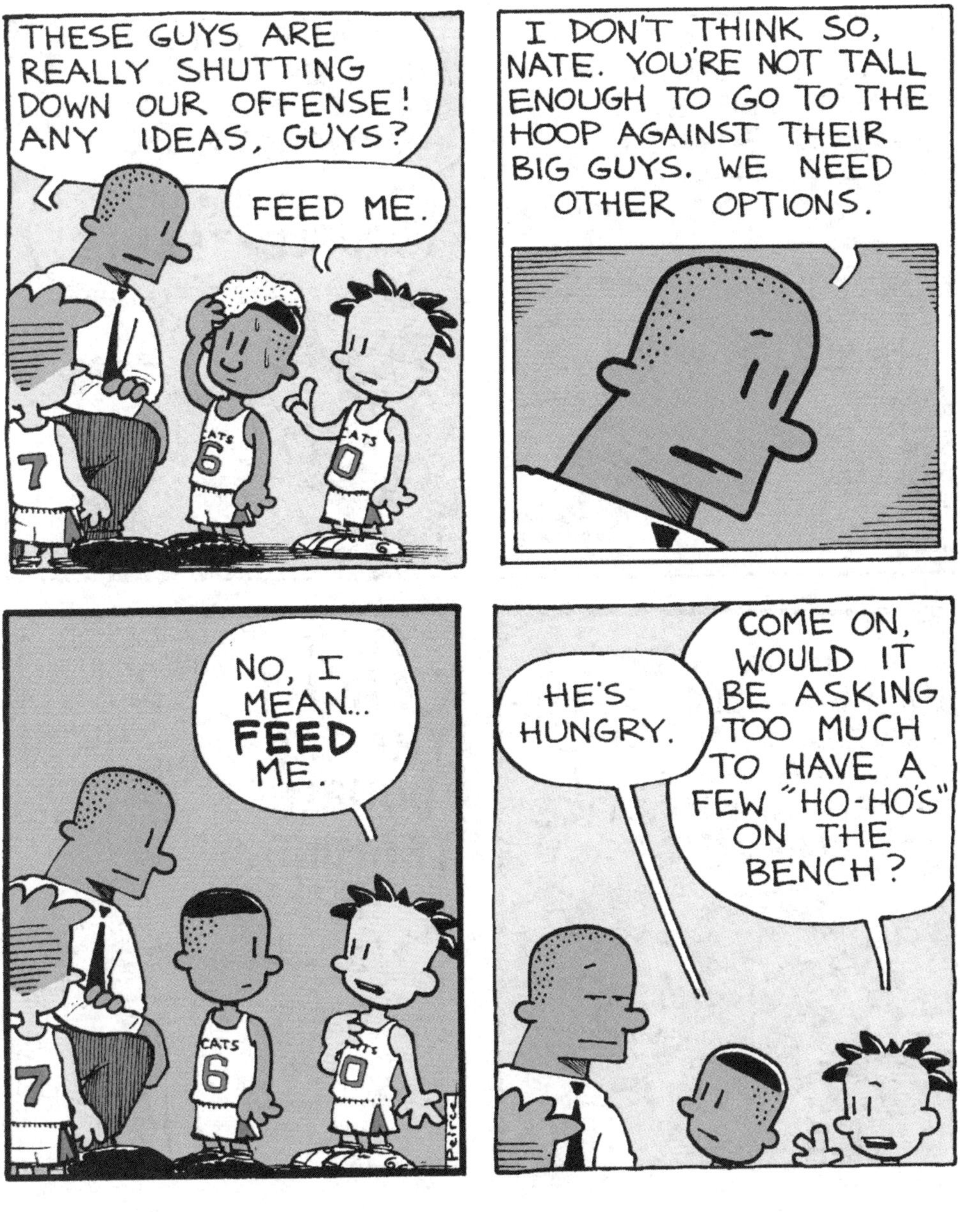
THESE GUYS ARE REALLY SHUTTING DOWN OUR OFFENSE! ANY IDEAS, GUYS?
FEED ME.
I DON'T THINK SO, NATE. YOU'RE NOT TALL ENOUGH TO GO TO THE HOOP AGAINST THEIR BIG GUYS. WE NEED OTHER OPTIONS.
NO, I MEAN... FEED ME.
HE'S HUNGRY.
COME ON, WOULD IT BE ASKING TOO MUCH TO HAVE A FEW "HO-HO'S" ON THE BENCH?

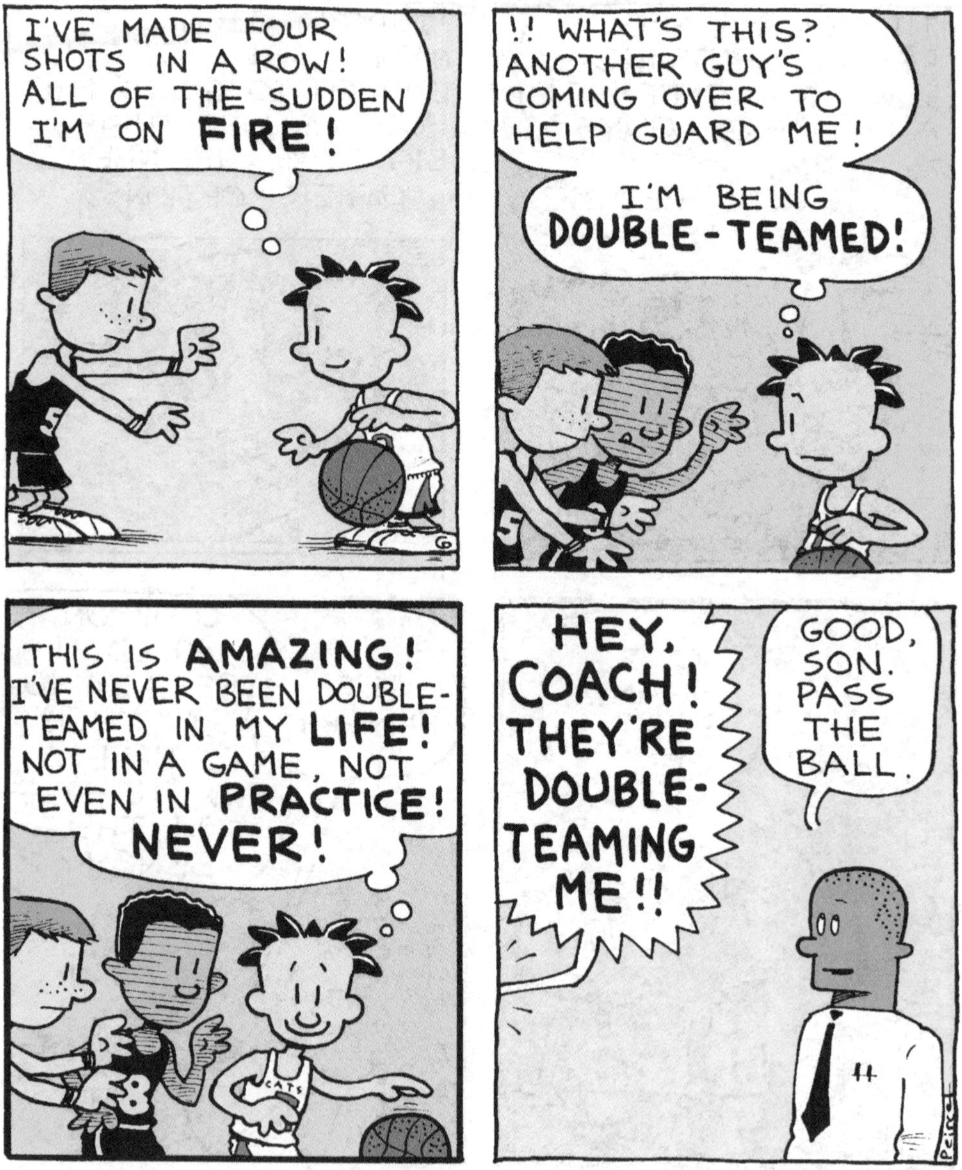
I'VE MADE FOUR SHOTS IN A ROW! ALL OF THE SUDDEN I'M ON FIRE!
!! WHAT'S THIS? ANOTHER GUY'S COMING OVER TO HELP GUARD ME!
I'M BEING DOUBLE-TEAMED!
THIS IS AMAZING! I'VE NEVER BEEN DOUBLE-TEAMED IN MY LIFE! NOT IN A GAME, NOT EVEN IN PRACTICE! NEVER!
HEY, COACH! THEY'RE DOUBLE-TEAMING ME!!
GOOD, SON. PASS THE BALL.

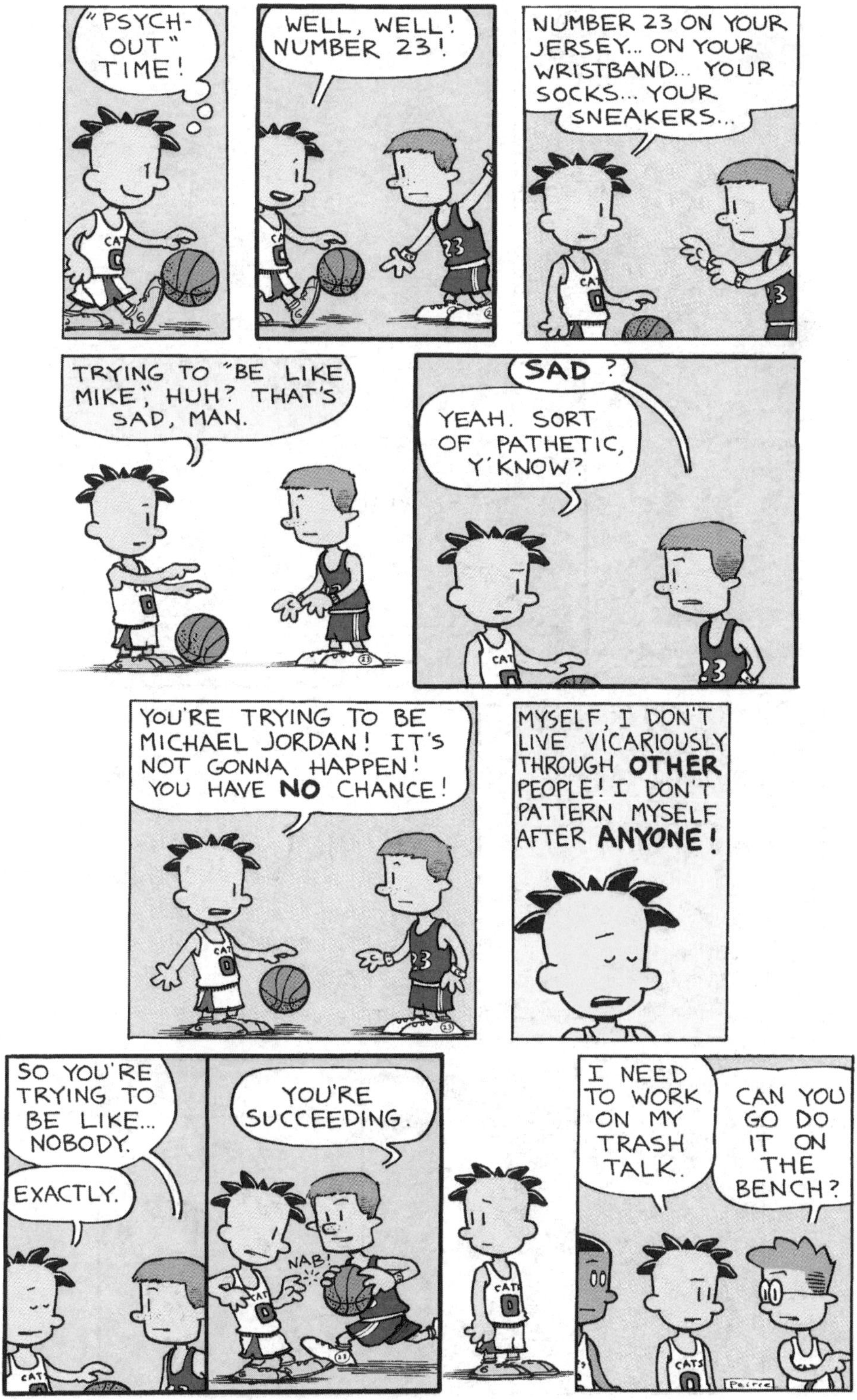
"PSYCH-OUT" TIME!
WELL, WELL! NUMBER 23!
NUMBER 23 ON YOUR JERSEY... ON YOUR WRISTBAND... YOUR SOCKS... YOUR SNEAKERS...
TRYING TO "BE LIKE MIKE," HUH? THAT'S SAD, MAN.
SAD?
YEAH. SORT OF PATHETIC, Y'KNOW?
YOU'RE TRYING TO BE MICHAEL JORDAN! IT'S NOT GONNA HAPPEN! YOU HAVE NO CHANCE!
MYSELF, I DON'T LIVE VICARIOUSLY THROUGH OTHER PEOPLE! I DON'T PATTERN MYSELF AFTER ANYONE!
SO YOU'RE TRYING TO BE LIKE... NOBODY.
EXACTLY.
YOU'RE SUCCEEDING.
NAB!
I NEED TO WORK ON MY TRASH TALK.
CAN YOU GO DO IT ON THE BENCH?
Peirce

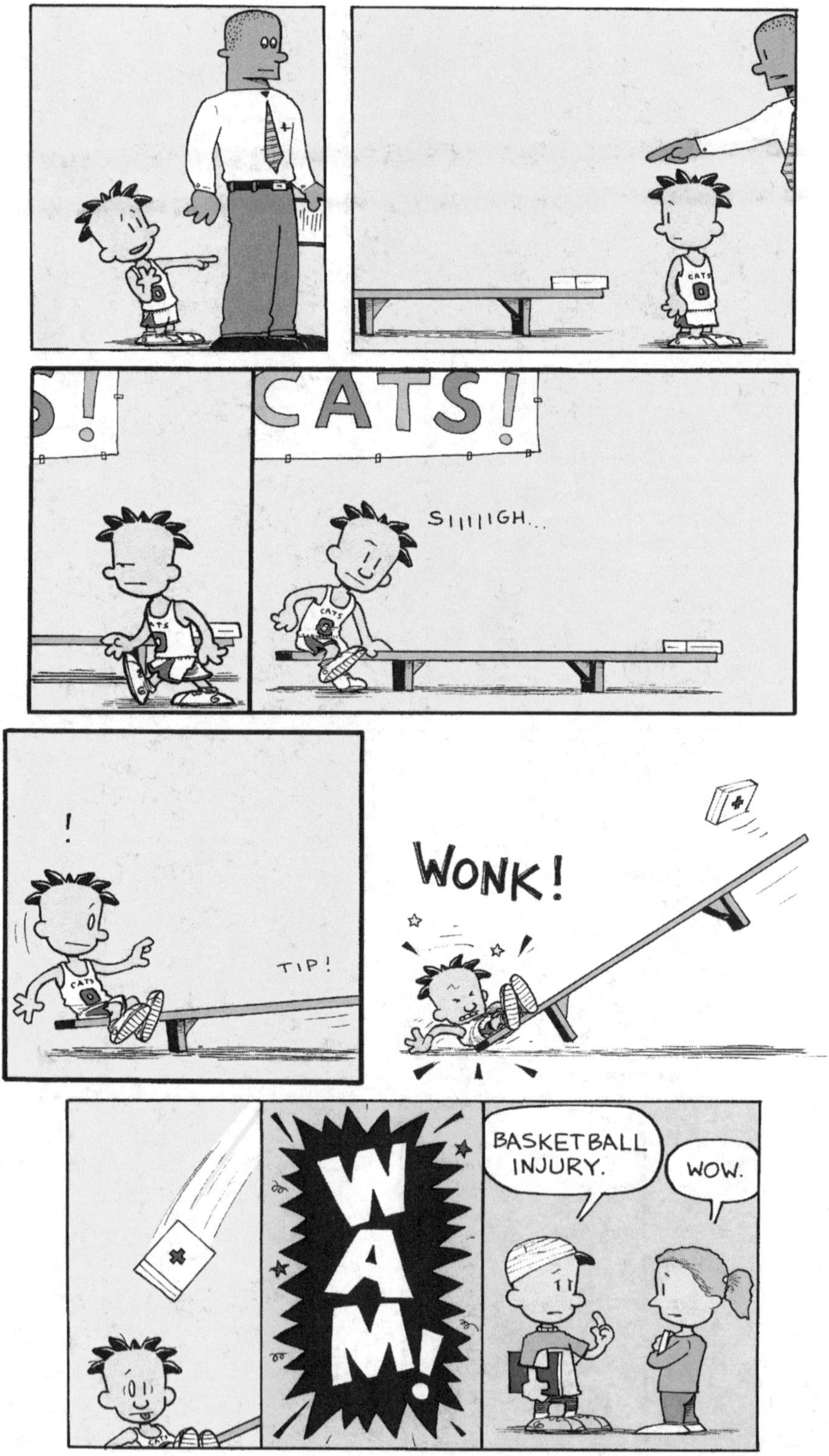
CATS!
SIIIIIGH...
!
TIP!
WONK!
WAM!
BASKETBALL INJURY.
WOW.

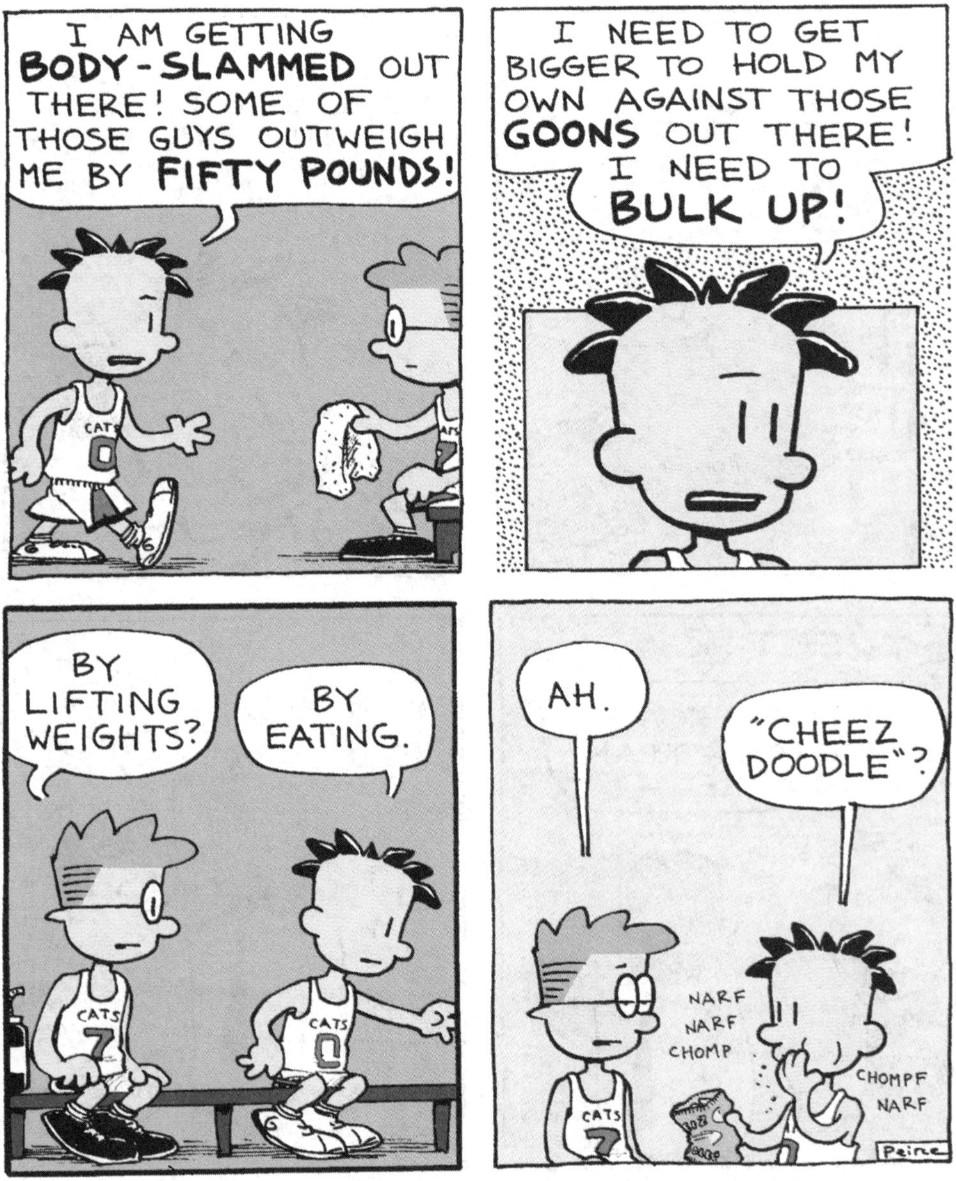
I AM GETTING BODY-SLAMMED OUT THERE! SOME OF THOSE GUYS OUTWEIGH ME BY FIFTY POUNDS!
CATS
I NEED TO GET BIGGER TO HOLD MY OWN AGAINST THOSE GOONS OUT THERE! I NEED TO BULK UP!
BY LIFTING WEIGHTS?
BY EATING.
CATS
CATS
AH.
"CHEEZ DOODLE"?
NARF
NARF
CHOMP
CHOMPF
NARF
CATS
Peirce

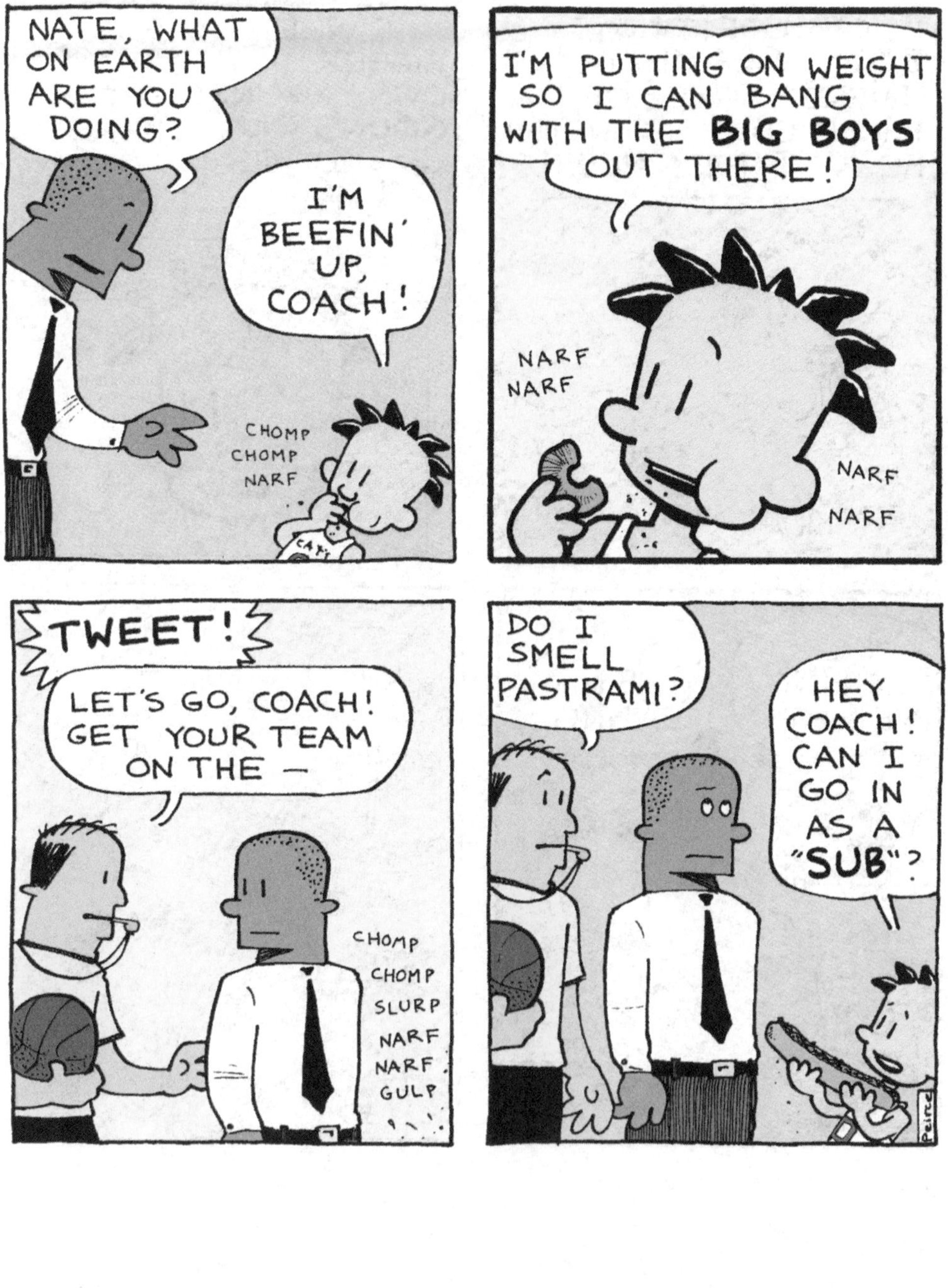
NATE, WHAT ON EARTH ARE YOU DOING?
I'M BEEFIN' UP, COACH!
CHOMP CHOMP NARF
I'M PUTTING ON WEIGHT SO I CAN BANG WITH THE **BIG BOYS** OUT THERE!
NARF NARF
NARF NARF
TWEET!
LET'S GO, COACH! GET YOUR TEAM ON THE –
CHOMP CHOMP SLURP NARF NARF GULP
DO I SMELL PASTRAMI?
HEY COACH! CAN I GO IN AS A "**SUB**"?
Peirce

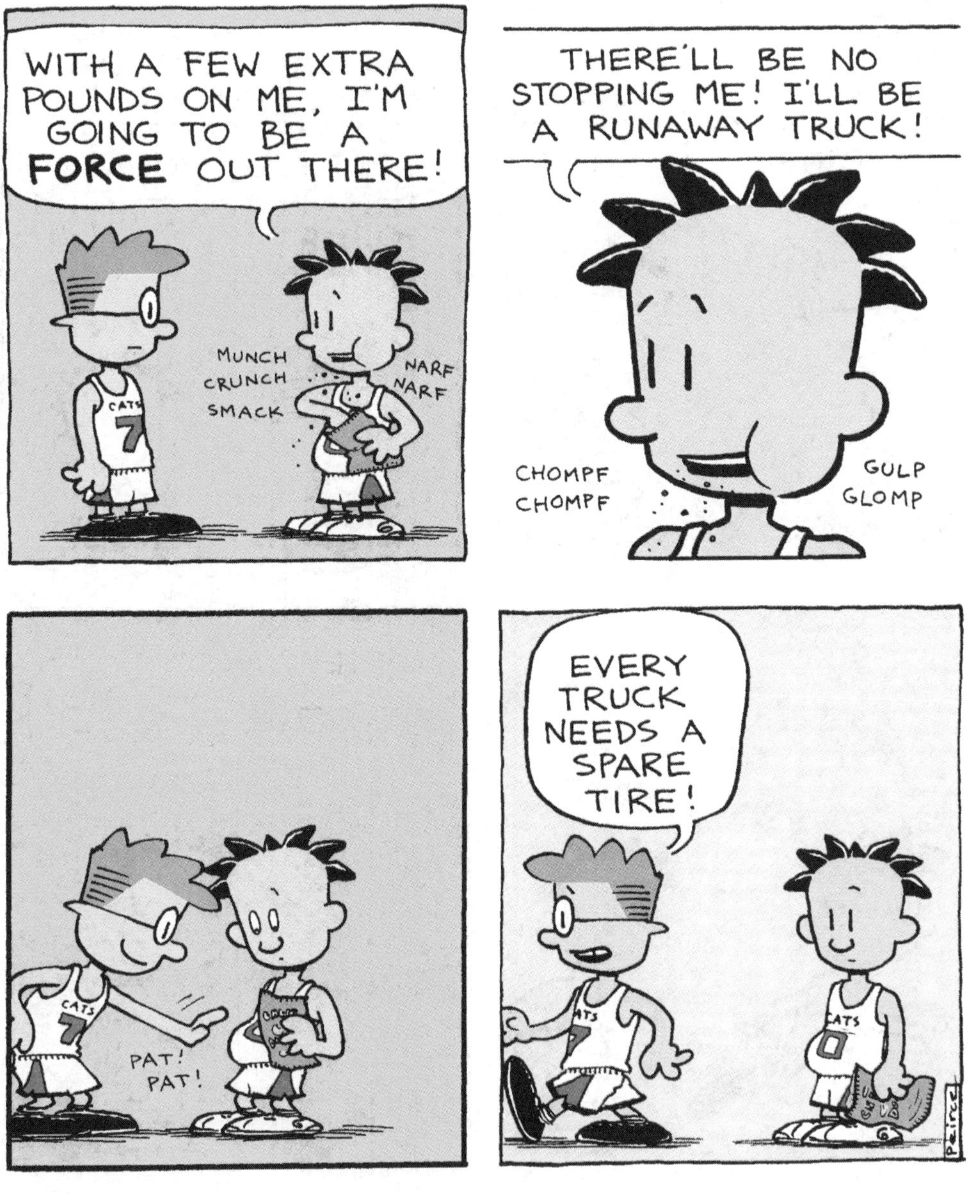
WITH A FEW EXTRA POUNDS ON ME, I'M GOING TO BE A **FORCE** OUT THERE!
MUNCH
CRUNCH
SMACK
NARF
NARF
CATS
7
THERE'LL BE NO STOPPING ME! I'LL BE A RUNAWAY TRUCK!
CHOMPF
CHOMPF
GULP
GLOMP
CATS
7
PAT!
PAT!
EVERY TRUCK NEEDS A SPARE TIRE!
CATS
0
PEIRCE

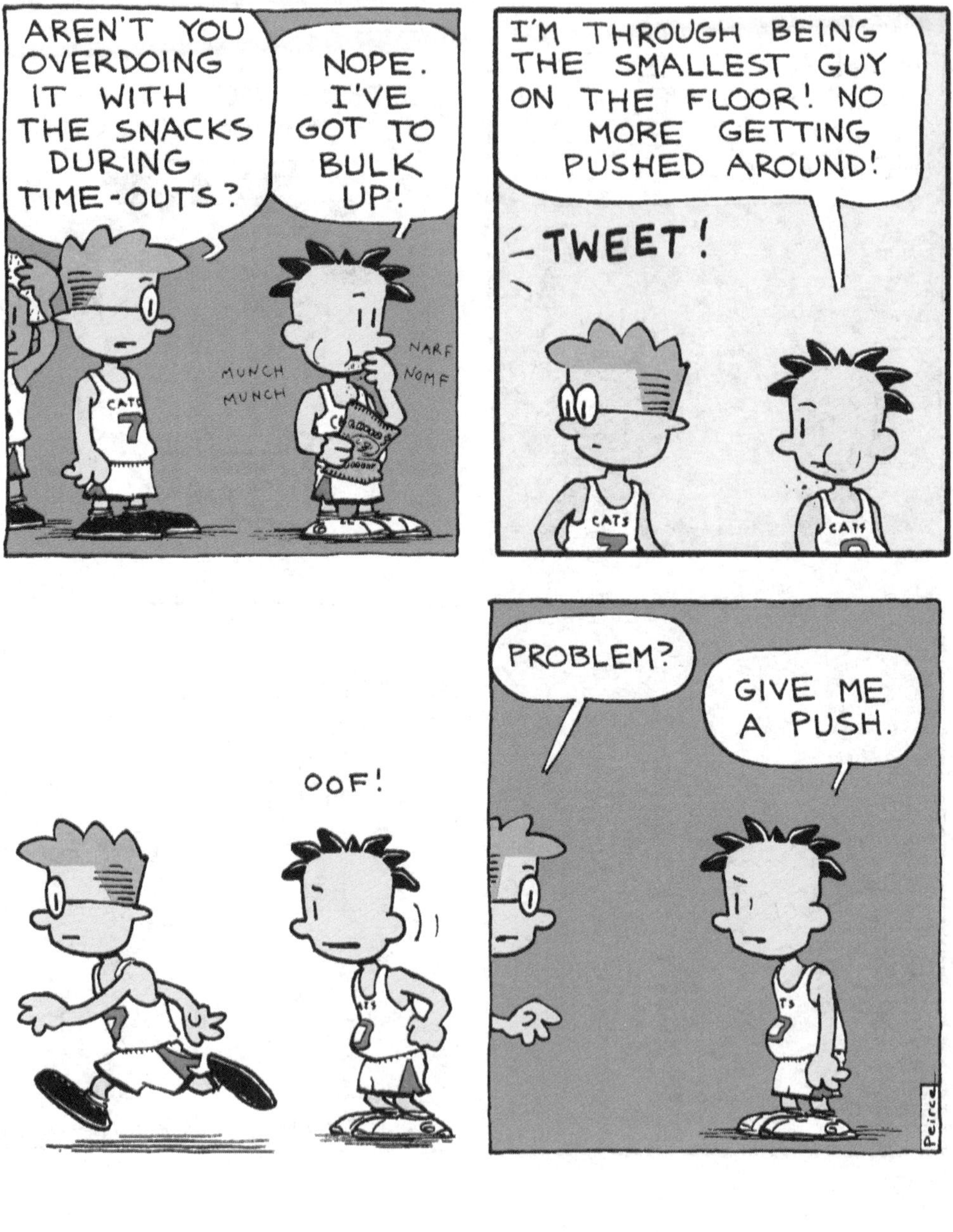
AREN'T YOU OVERDOING IT WITH THE SNACKS DURING TIME-OUTS?
NOPE. I'VE GOT TO BULK UP!
MUNCH MUNCH
NARF NOMF
I'M THROUGH BEING THE SMALLEST GUY ON THE FLOOR! NO MORE GETTING PUSHED AROUND!
TWEET!
OOF!
PROBLEM?
GIVE ME A PUSH.
Peirce

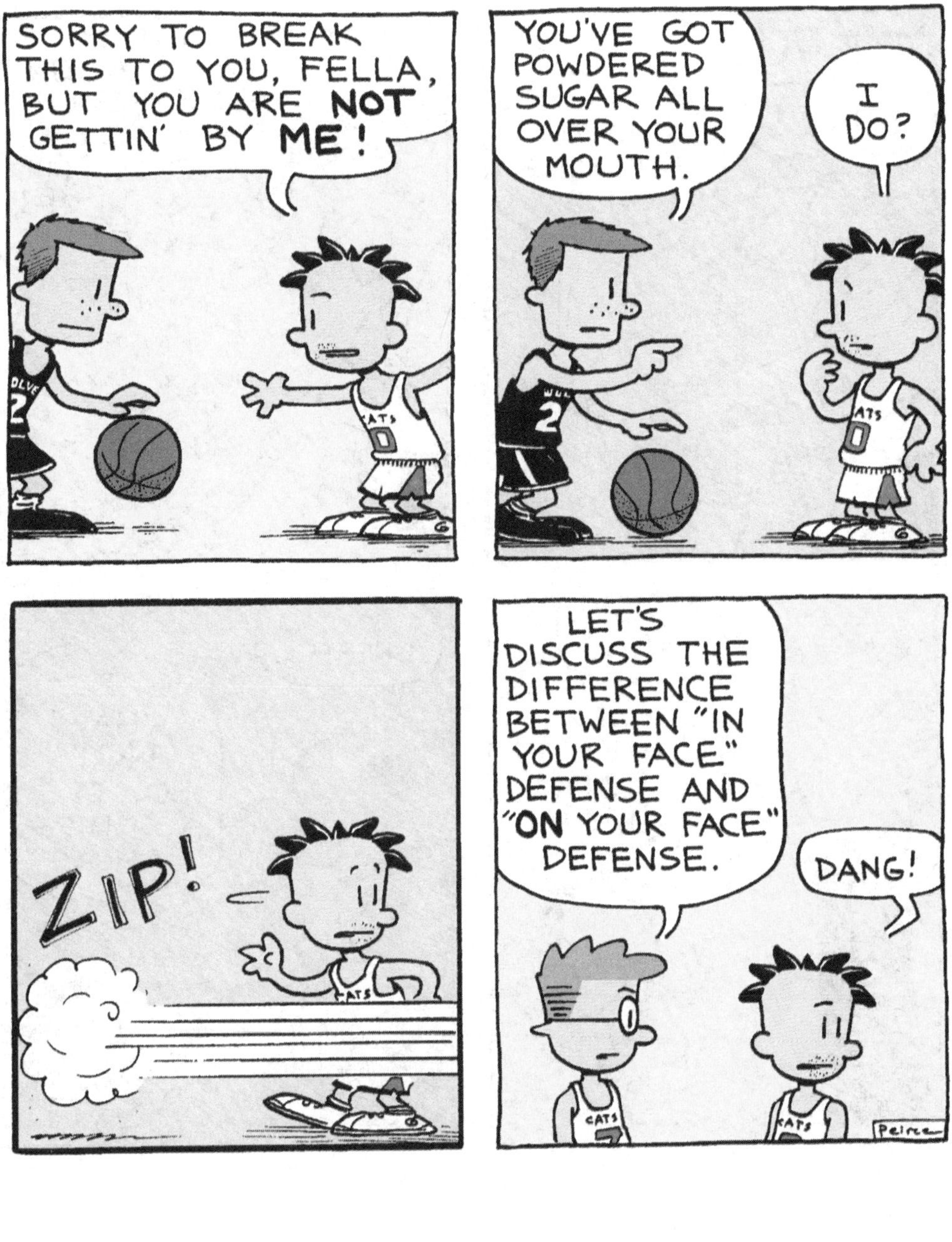
SORRY TO BREAK THIS TO YOU, FELLA, BUT YOU ARE **NOT** GETTIN' BY **ME**!
YOU'VE GOT POWDERED SUGAR ALL OVER YOUR MOUTH.
I DO?
ZIP!
LET'S DISCUSS THE DIFFERENCE BETWEEN "IN YOUR FACE" DEFENSE AND "**ON** YOUR FACE" DEFENSE.
DANG!
Peirce

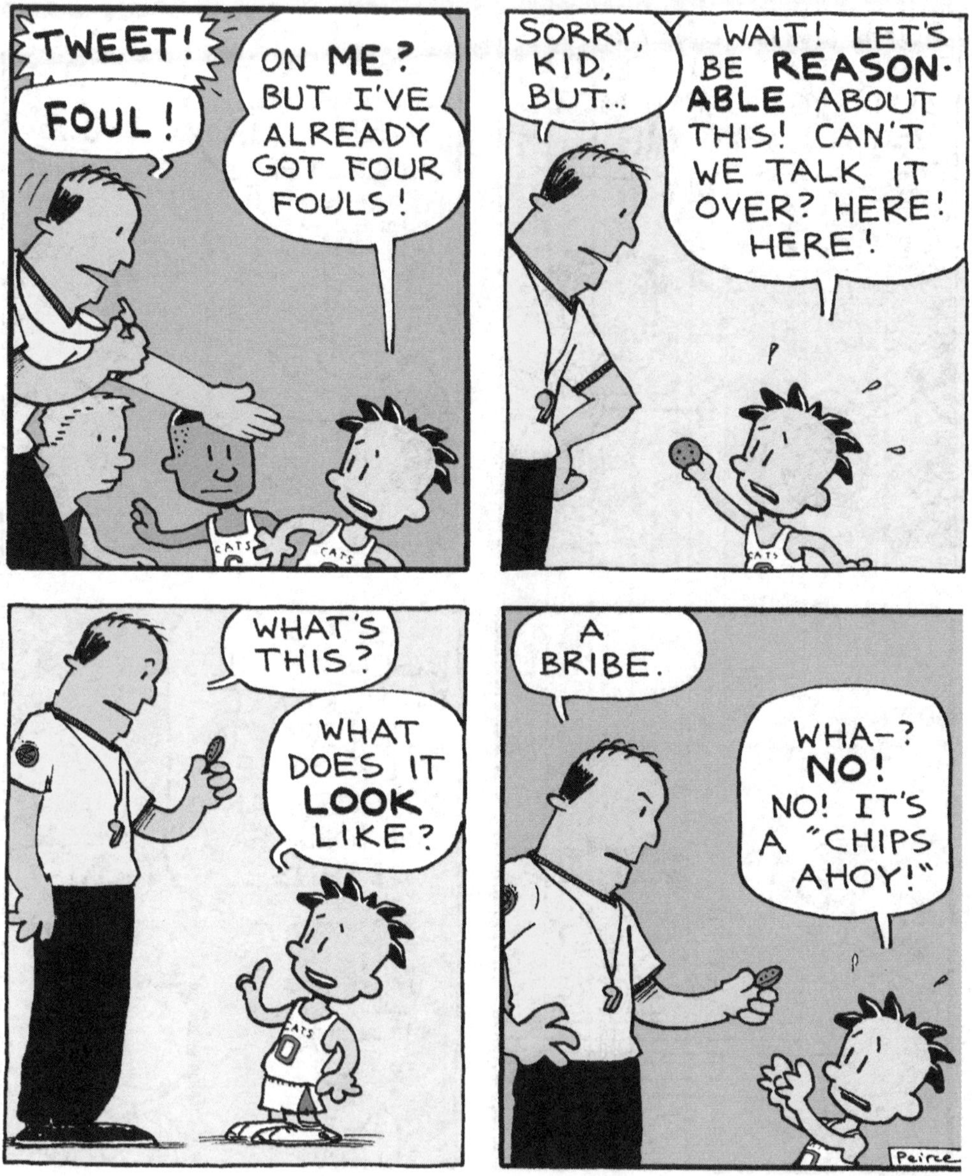
TWEET!
FOUL!
ON ME? BUT I'VE ALREADY GOT FOUR FOULS!
SORRY, KID, BUT...
WAIT! LET'S BE REASONABLE ABOUT THIS! CAN'T WE TALK IT OVER? HERE! HERE!
WHAT'S THIS?
WHAT DOES IT LOOK LIKE?
A BRIBE.
WHA-? NO! NO! IT'S A "CHIPS AHOY!"
Peirce

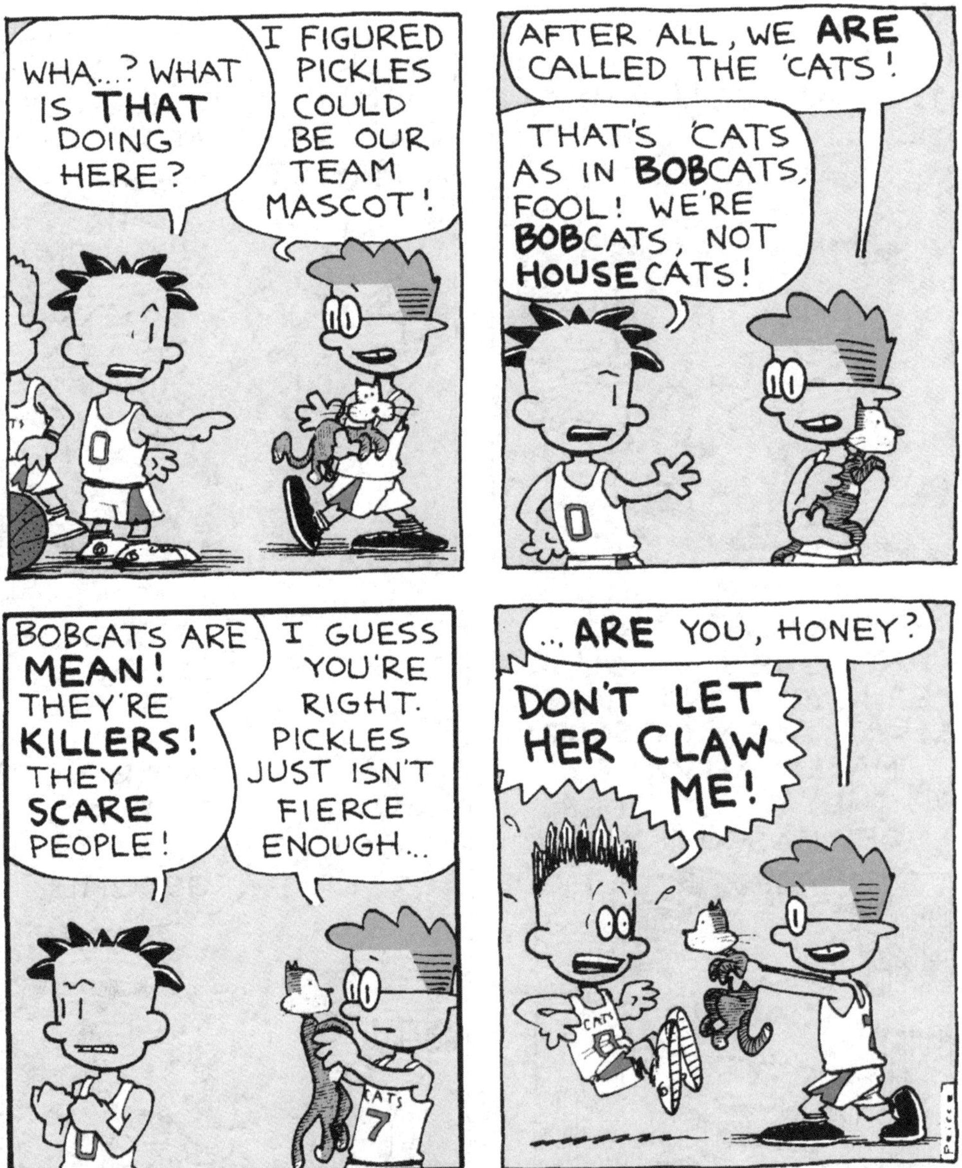
WHA...? WHAT IS THAT DOING HERE?
I FIGURED PICKLES COULD BE OUR TEAM MASCOT!
AFTER ALL, WE ARE CALLED THE 'CATS!
THAT'S 'CATS AS IN BOBCATS, FOOL! WE'RE BOBCATS, NOT HOUSECATS!
BOBCATS ARE MEAN! THEY'RE KILLERS! THEY SCARE PEOPLE!
I GUESS YOU'RE RIGHT. PICKLES JUST ISN'T FIERCE ENOUGH...
...ARE YOU, HONEY?
DON'T LET HER CLAW ME!

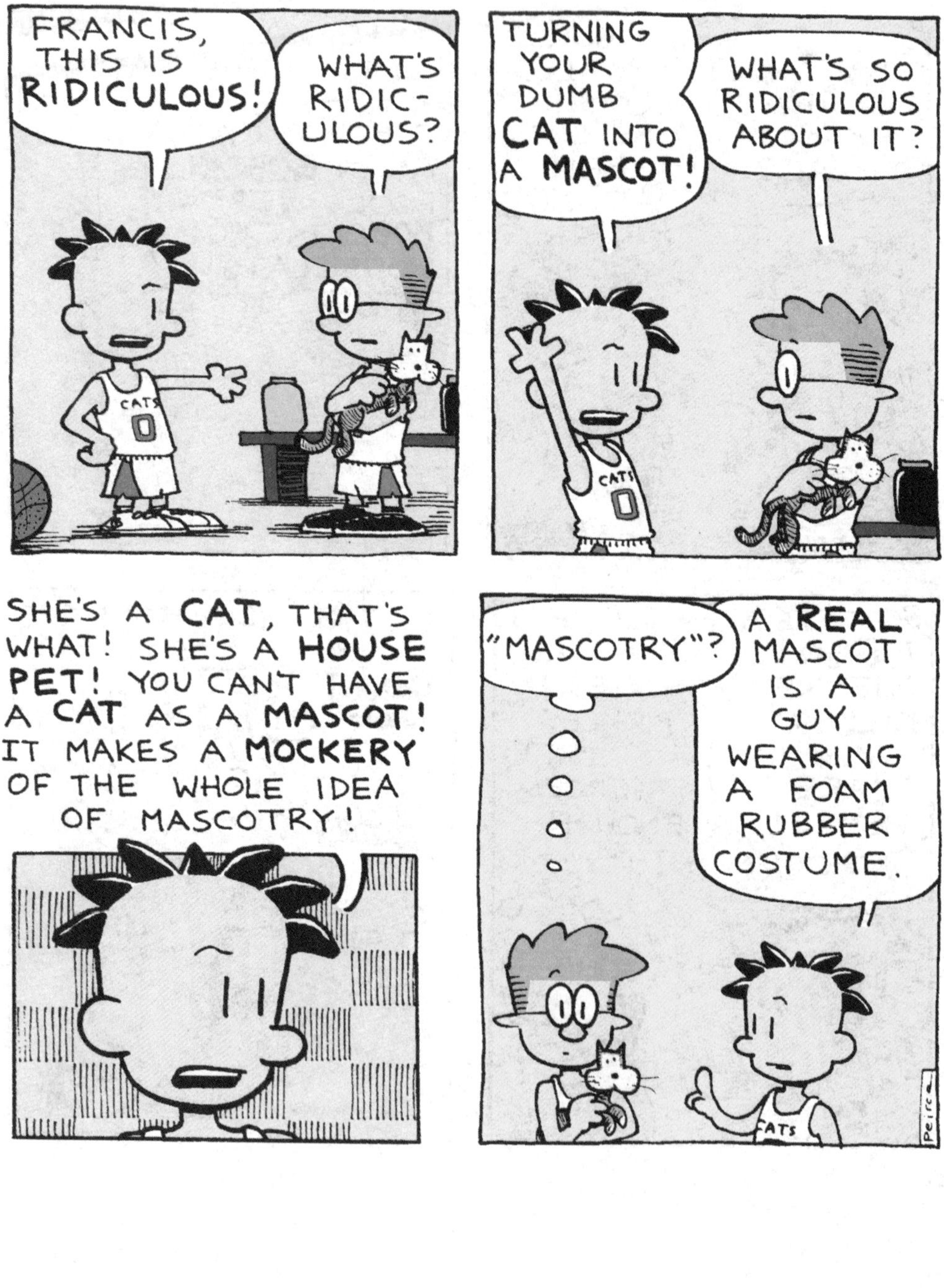
FRANCIS, THIS IS RIDICULOUS!
WHAT'S RIDIC-ULOUS?
TURNING YOUR DUMB CAT INTO A MASCOT!
WHAT'S SO RIDICULOUS ABOUT IT?
SHE'S A CAT, THAT'S WHAT! SHE'S A HOUSE PET! YOU CAN'T HAVE A CAT AS A MASCOT! IT MAKES A MOCKERY OF THE WHOLE IDEA OF MASCOTRY!
"MASCOTRY"?
A REAL MASCOT IS A GUY WEARING A FOAM RUBBER COSTUME.
Peirce

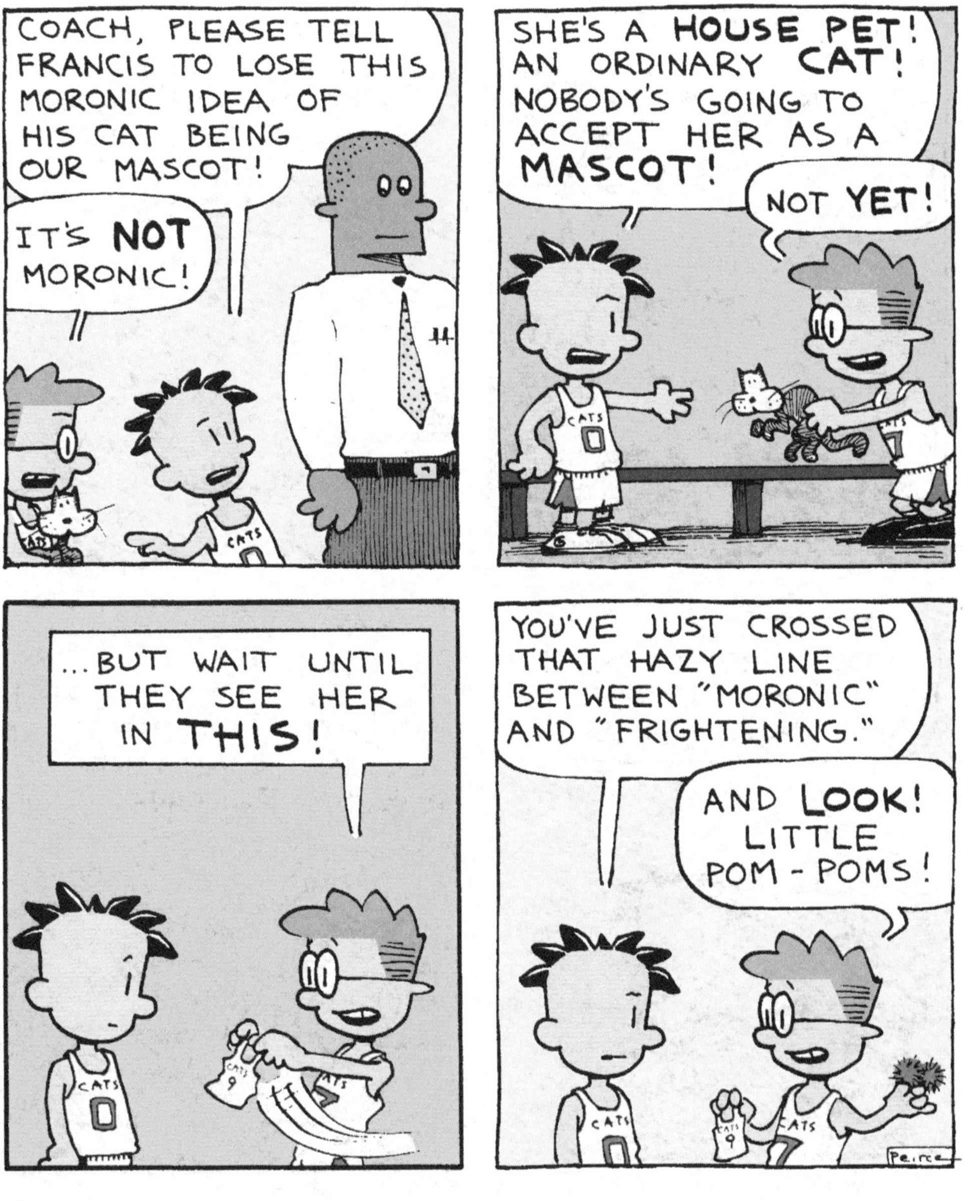
COACH, PLEASE TELL FRANCIS TO LOSE THIS MORONIC IDEA OF HIS CAT BEING OUR MASCOT!
IT'S NOT MORONIC!
SHE'S A HOUSE PET! AN ORDINARY CAT! NOBODY'S GOING TO ACCEPT HER AS A MASCOT!
NOT YET!
...BUT WAIT UNTIL THEY SEE HER IN THIS!
YOU'VE JUST CROSSED THAT HAZY LINE BETWEEN "MORONIC" AND "FRIGHTENING."
AND LOOK! LITTLE POM-POMS!
Peirce

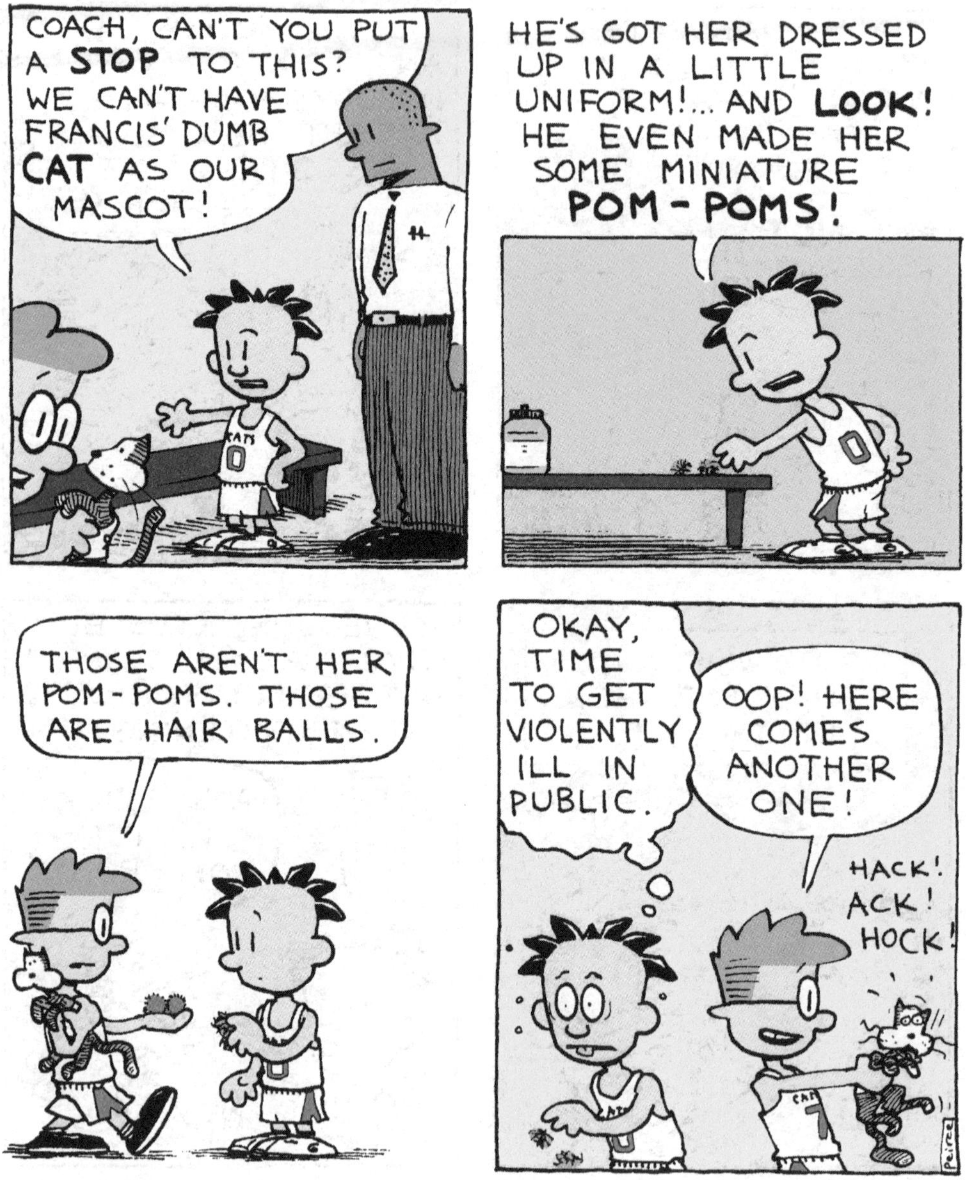
COACH, CAN'T YOU PUT A **STOP** TO THIS? WE CAN'T HAVE FRANCIS' DUMB **CAT** AS OUR MASCOT!
HE'S GOT HER DRESSED UP IN A LITTLE UNIFORM!... AND **LOOK**! HE EVEN MADE HER SOME MINIATURE **POM-POMS**!
THOSE AREN'T HER POM-POMS. THOSE ARE HAIR BALLS.
OKAY, TIME TO GET VIOLENTLY ILL IN PUBLIC.
OOP! HERE COMES ANOTHER ONE!
HACK! ACK! HOCK!
Peirce

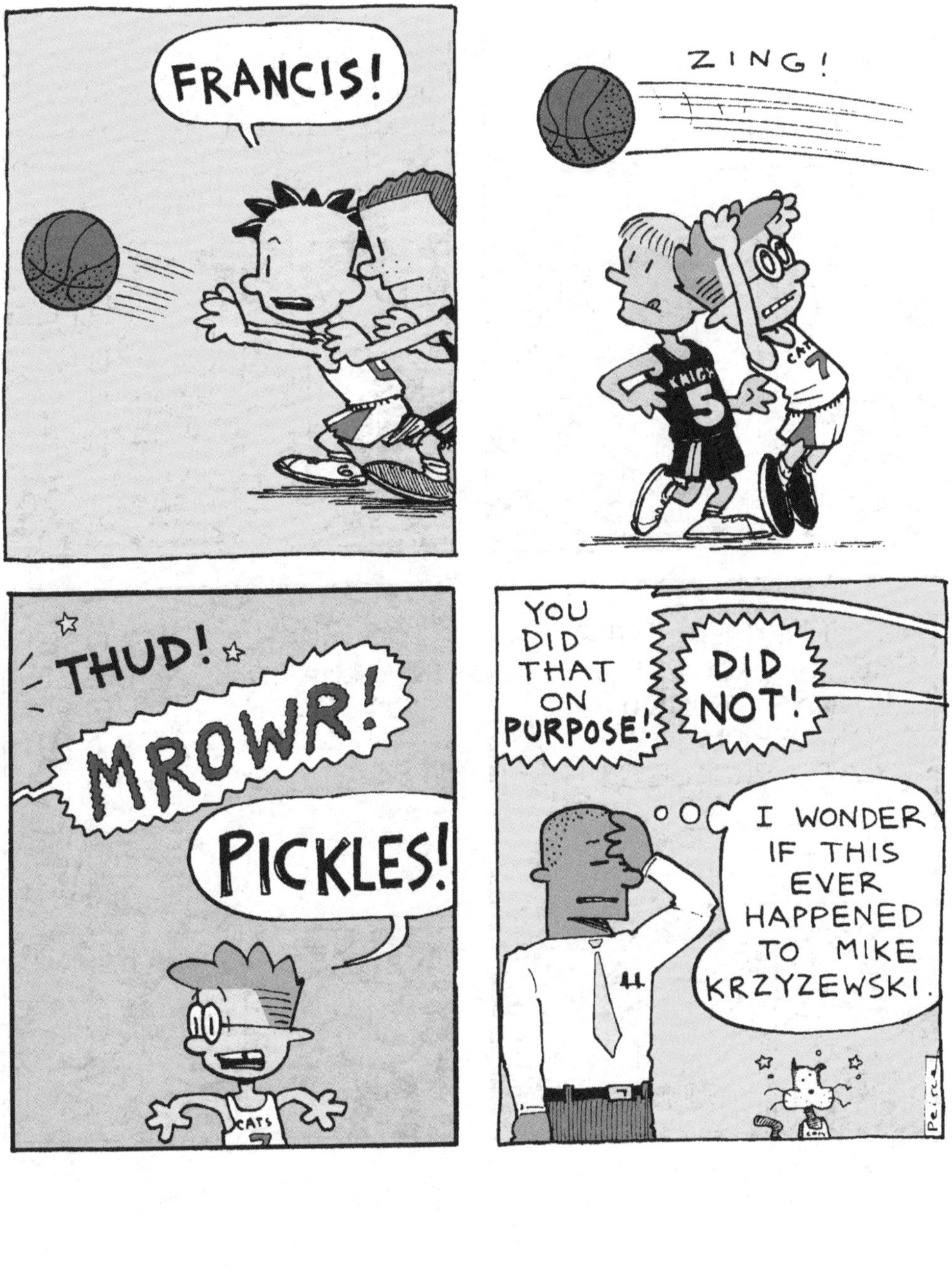
FRANCIS!
ZING!
THUD!
MROWR!
PICKLES!
YOU DID THAT ON PURPOSE!
DID NOT!
I WONDER IF THIS EVER HAPPENED TO MIKE KRZYZEWSKI.
Peirce

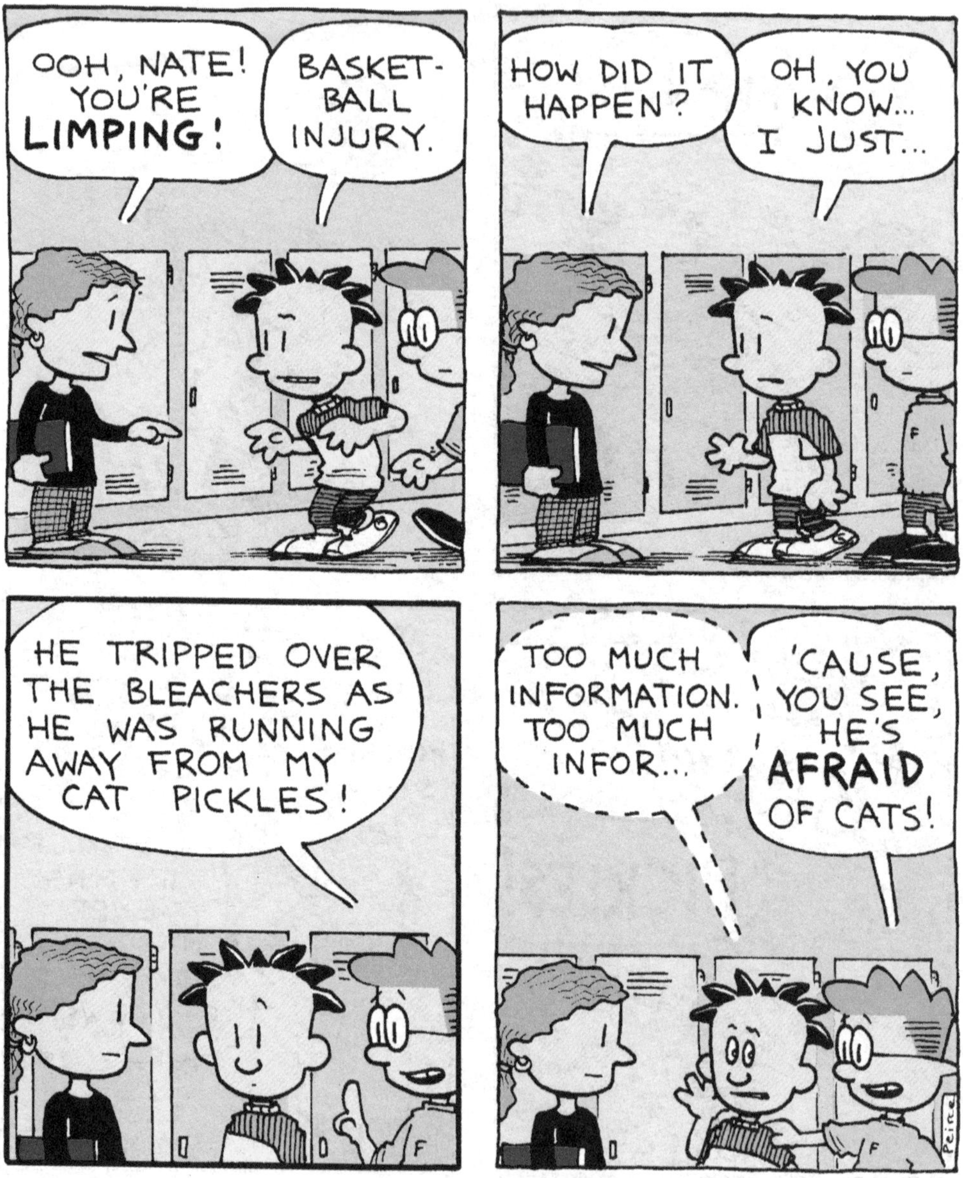
OOH, NATE! YOU'RE **LIMPING**!
BASKET-BALL INJURY.
HOW DID IT HAPPEN?
OH, YOU KNOW... I JUST...
HE TRIPPED OVER THE BLEACHERS AS HE WAS RUNNING AWAY FROM MY CAT PICKLES!
TOO MUCH INFORMATION. TOO MUCH INFOR...
'CAUSE, YOU SEE, HE'S **AFRAID** OF CATS!
Peirce

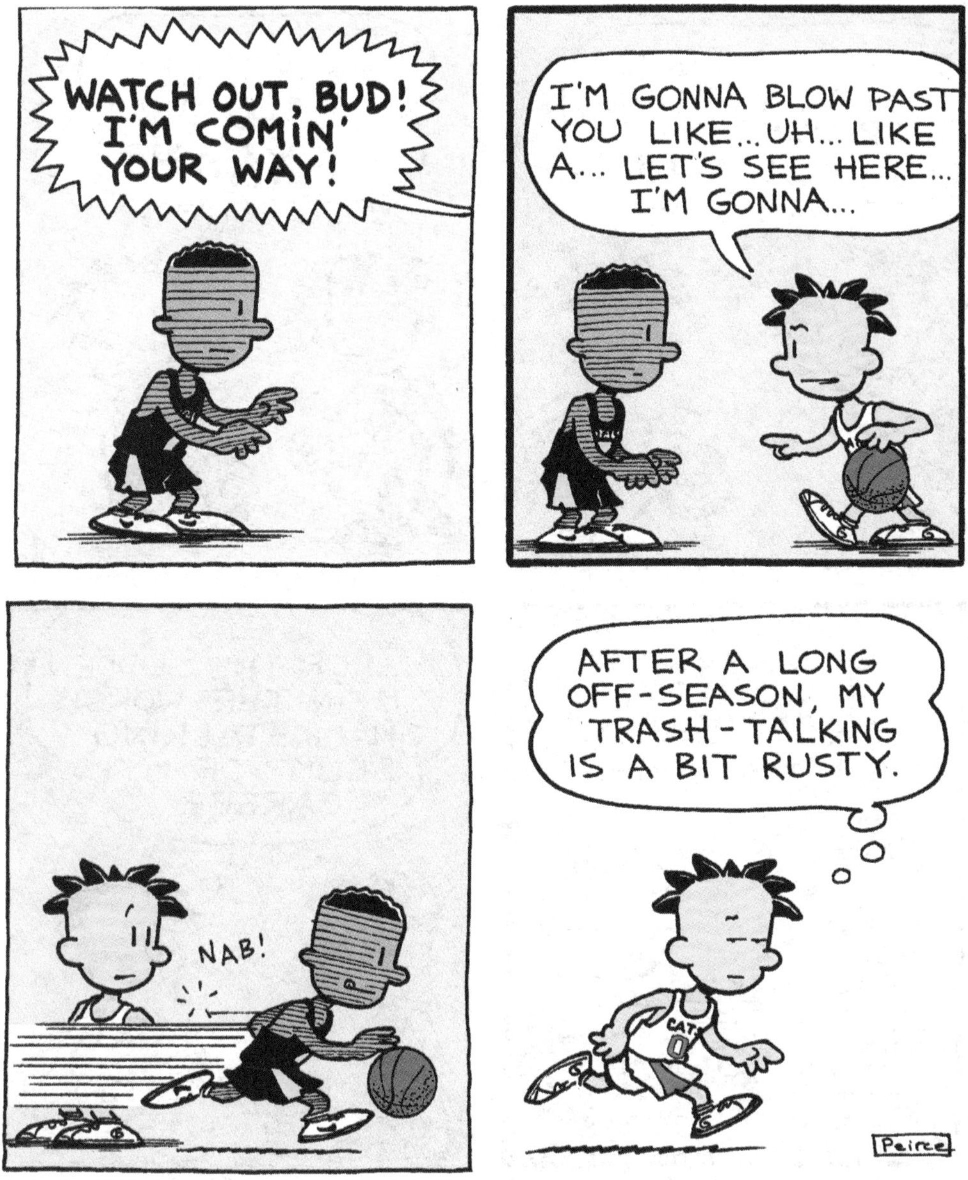
WATCH OUT, BUD! I'M COMIN' YOUR WAY!
I'M GONNA BLOW PAST YOU LIKE... UH... LIKE A... LET'S SEE HERE... I'M GONNA...
NAB!
AFTER A LONG OFF-SEASON, MY TRASH-TALKING IS A BIT RUSTY.
Peirce

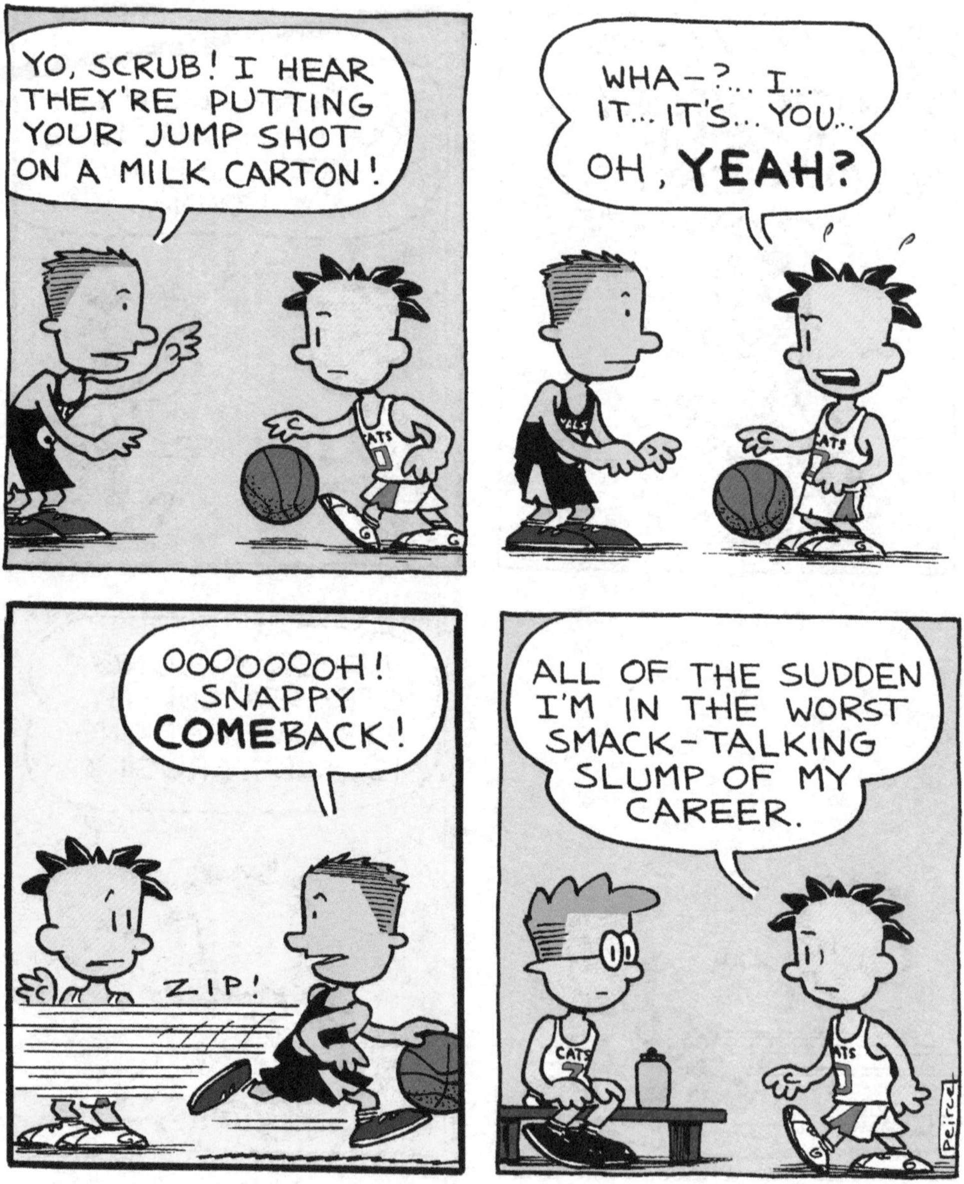

YO, SCRUB! I HEAR THEY'RE PUTTING YOUR JUMP SHOT ON A MILK CARTON!
WHA–?... I... IT... IT'S... YOU... OH, **YEAH?**
OOOOOOOH! SNAPPY **COME**BACK!
ZIP!
ALL OF THE SUDDEN I'M IN THE WORST SMACK-TALKING SLUMP OF MY CAREER.

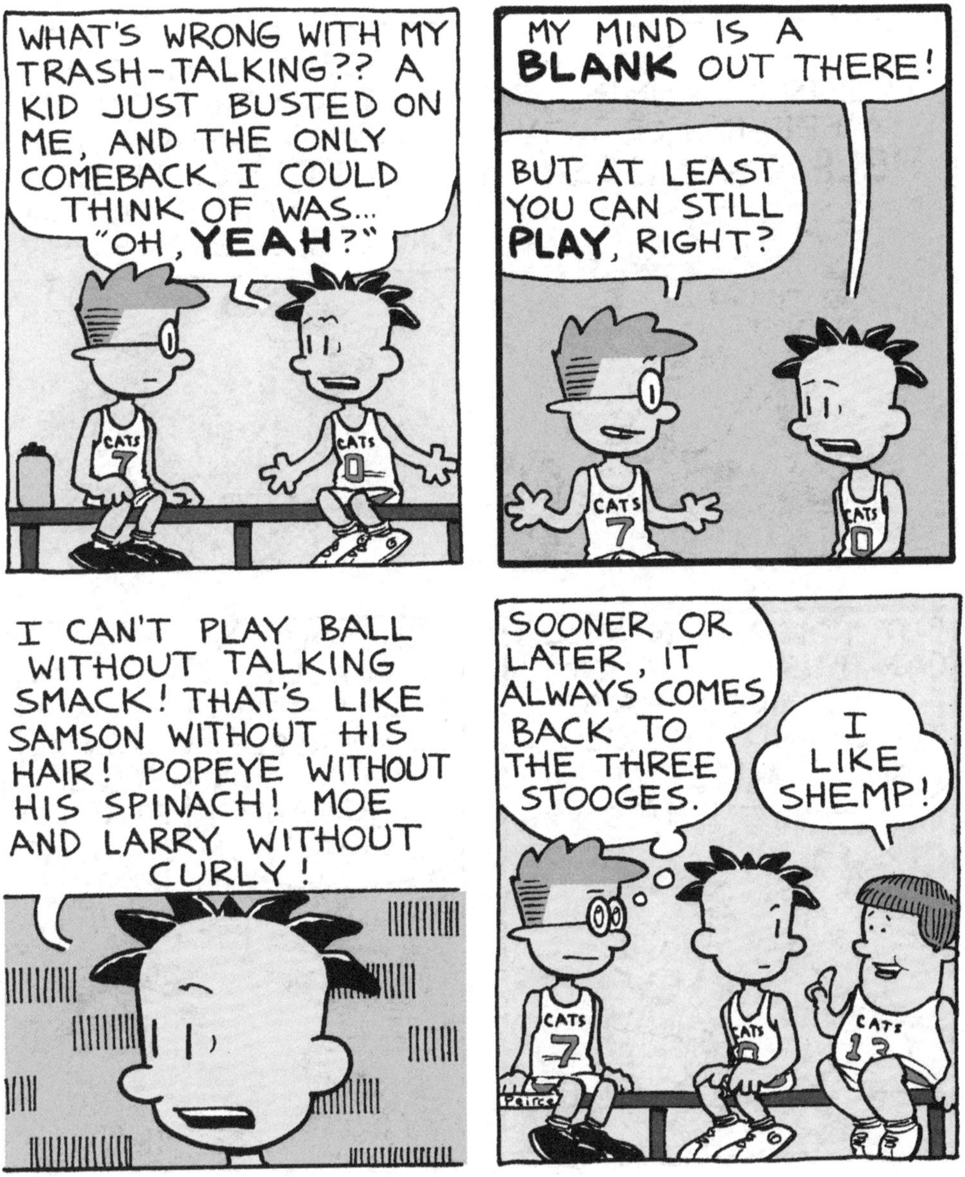
WHAT'S WRONG WITH MY TRASH-TALKING?? A KID JUST BUSTED ON ME, AND THE ONLY COMEBACK I COULD THINK OF WAS... "OH, YEAH?"
MY MIND IS A BLANK OUT THERE!
BUT AT LEAST YOU CAN STILL PLAY, RIGHT?
I CAN'T PLAY BALL WITHOUT TALKING SMACK! THAT'S LIKE SAMSON WITHOUT HIS HAIR! POPEYE WITHOUT HIS SPINACH! MOE AND LARRY WITHOUT CURLY!
SOONER OR LATER, IT ALWAYS COMES BACK TO THE THREE STOOGES.
I LIKE SHEMP!

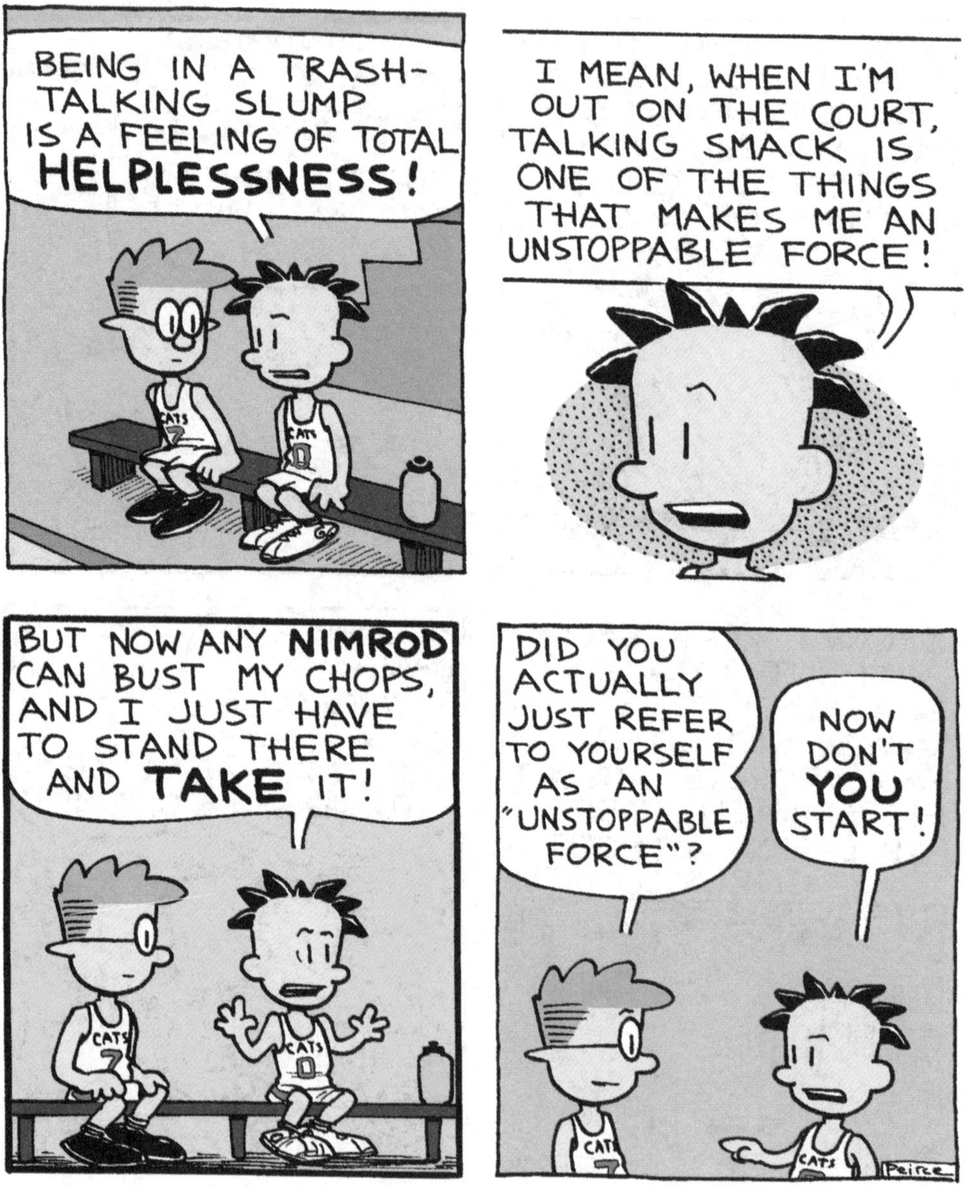
BEING IN A TRASH-TALKING SLUMP IS A FEELING OF TOTAL **HELPLESSNESS!**
CATS
7
CATS
0
I MEAN, WHEN I'M OUT ON THE COURT, TALKING SMACK IS ONE OF THE THINGS THAT MAKES ME AN UNSTOPPABLE FORCE!
BUT NOW ANY **NIMROD** CAN BUST MY CHOPS, AND I JUST HAVE TO STAND THERE AND **TAKE** IT!
CATS
7
CATS
0
DID YOU ACTUALLY JUST REFER TO YOURSELF AS AN "UNSTOPPABLE FORCE"?
NOW DON'T **YOU** START!
CATS
Peirce

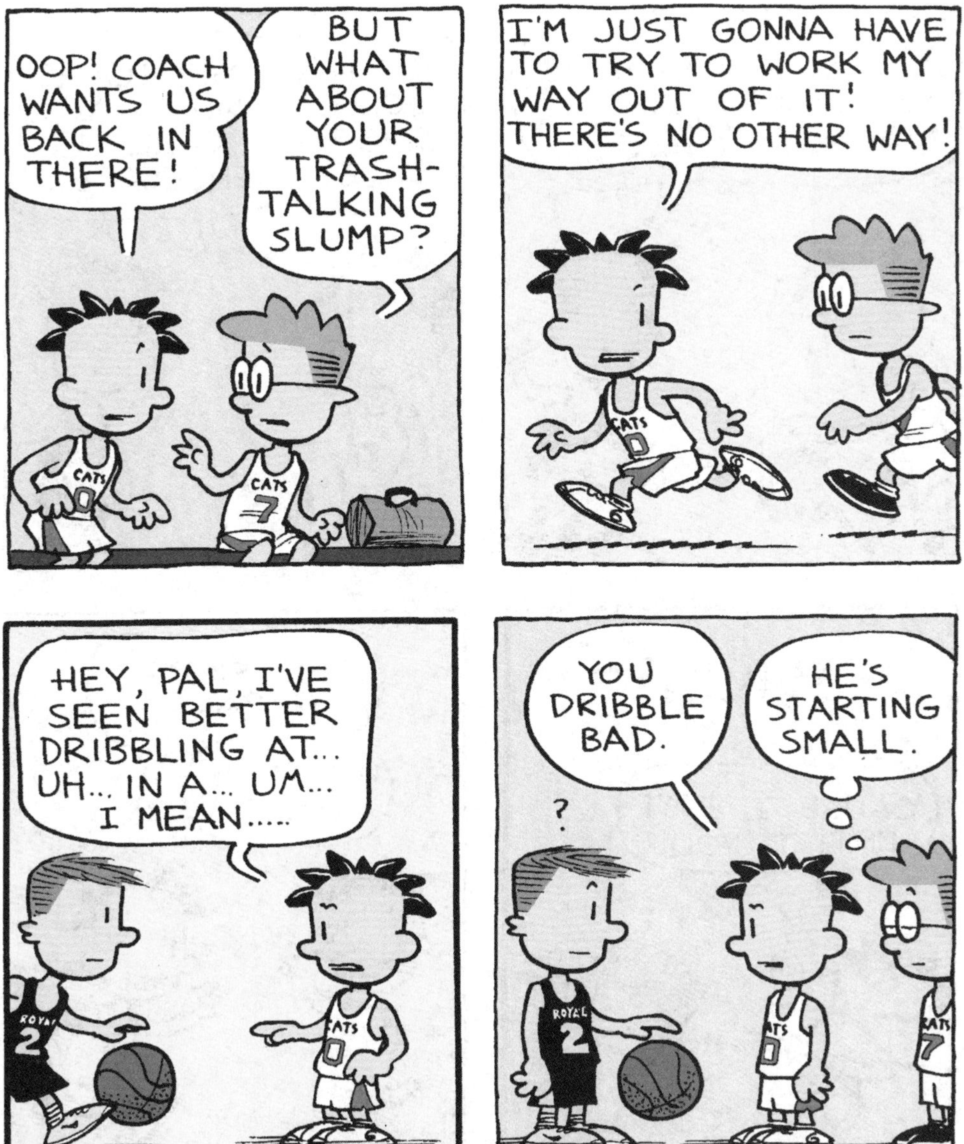
OOP! COACH WANTS US BACK IN THERE!
BUT WHAT ABOUT YOUR TRASH-TALKING SLUMP?
I'M JUST GONNA HAVE TO TRY TO WORK MY WAY OUT OF IT! THERE'S NO OTHER WAY!
HEY, PAL, I'VE SEEN BETTER DRIBBLING AT... UH... IN A... UM... I MEAN.....
?
YOU DRIBBLE BAD.
HE'S STARTING SMALL.
Peirce

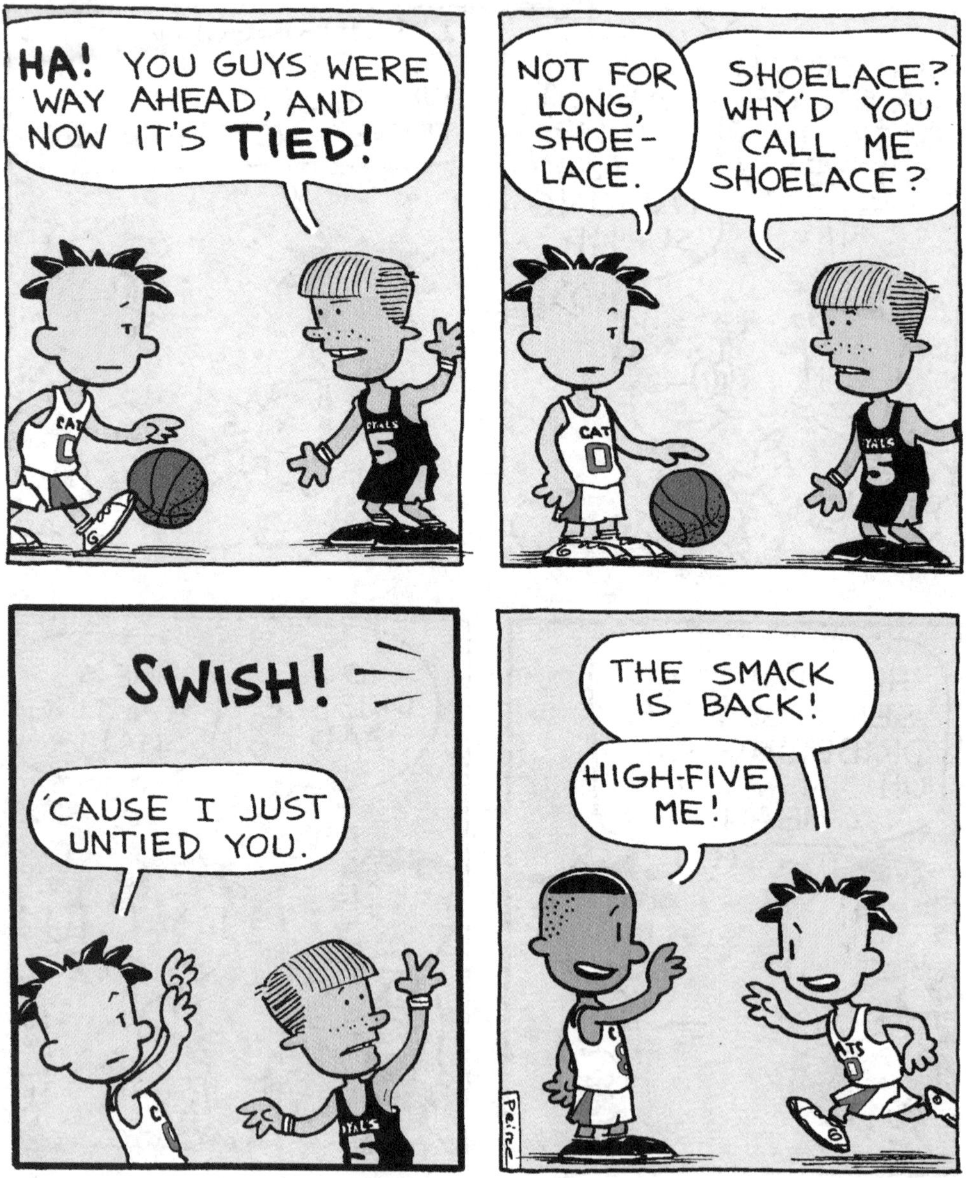
HA! YOU GUYS WERE WAY AHEAD, AND NOW IT'S TIED!
NOT FOR LONG, SHOE-LACE.
SHOELACE? WHY'D YOU CALL ME SHOELACE?
SWISH!
'CAUSE I JUST UNTIED YOU.
THE SMACK IS BACK!
HIGH-FIVE ME!

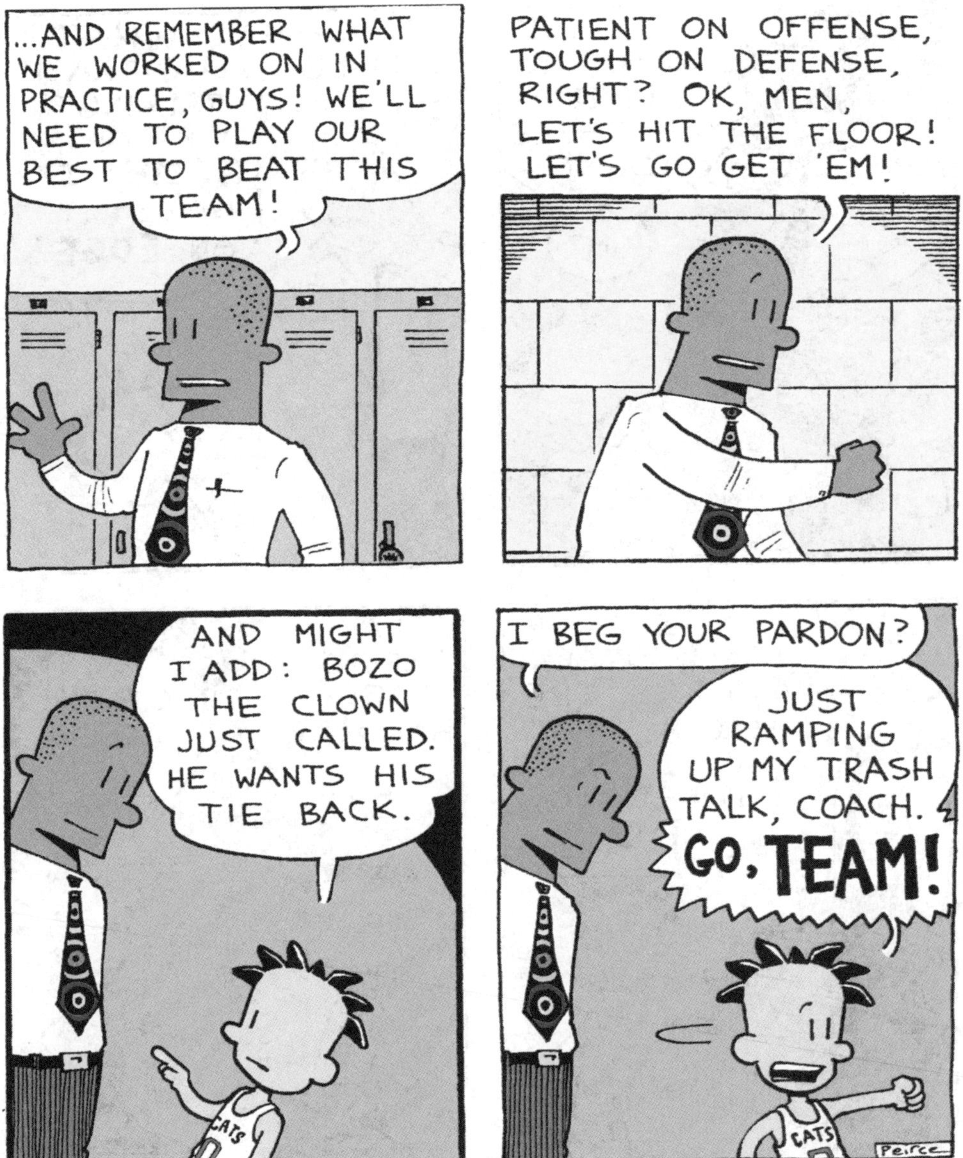
...AND REMEMBER WHAT WE WORKED ON IN PRACTICE, GUYS! WE'LL NEED TO PLAY OUR BEST TO BEAT THIS TEAM!
PATIENT ON OFFENSE, TOUGH ON DEFENSE, RIGHT? OK, MEN, LET'S HIT THE FLOOR! LET'S GO GET 'EM!
AND MIGHT I ADD: BOZO THE CLOWN JUST CALLED. HE WANTS HIS TIE BACK.
CATS
I BEG YOUR PARDON?
JUST RAMPING UP MY TRASH TALK, COACH.
GO, TEAM!
CATS
Peirce

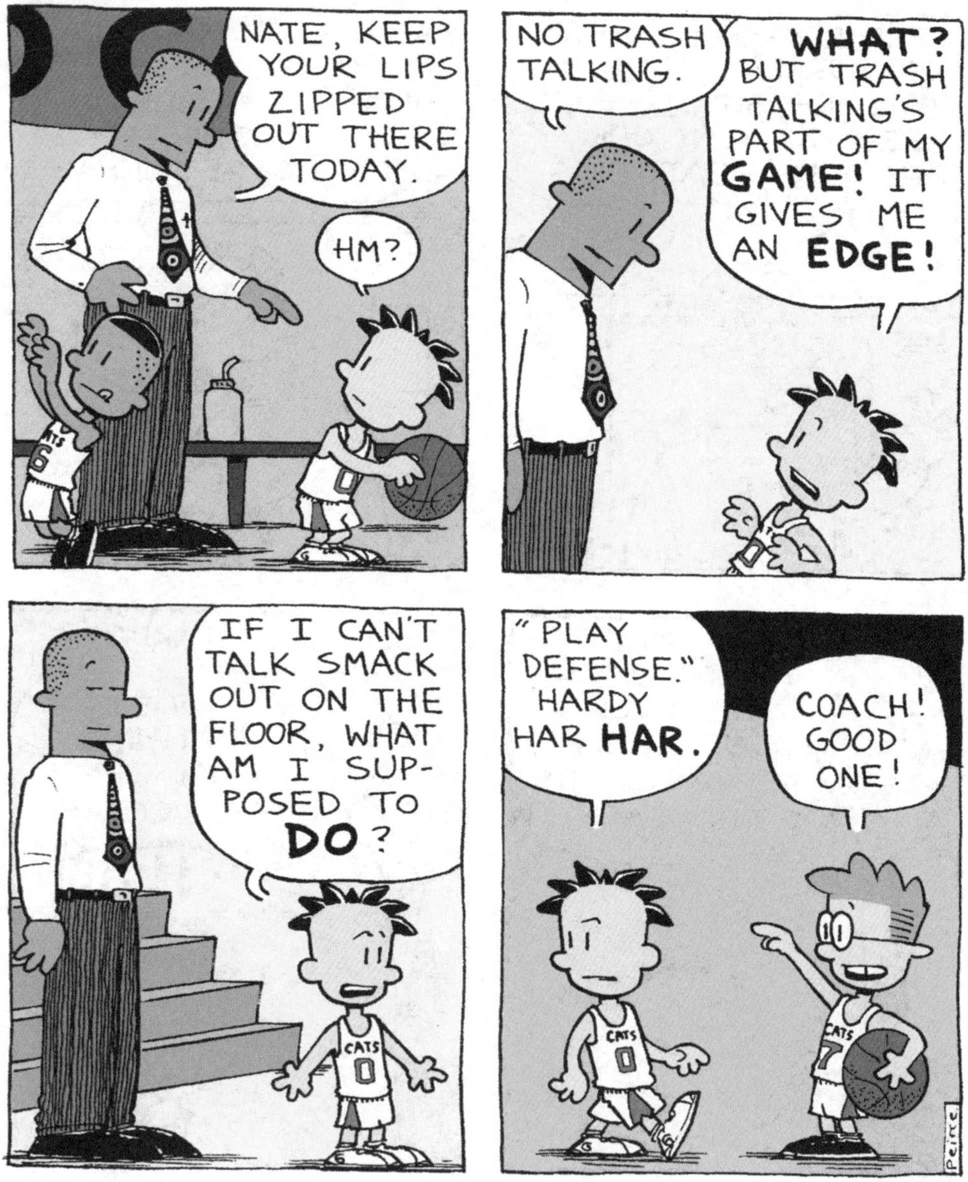
NATE, KEEP YOUR LIPS ZIPPED OUT THERE TODAY.
HM?
NO TRASH TALKING.
WHAT? BUT TRASH TALKING'S PART OF MY GAME! IT GIVES ME AN EDGE!
IF I CAN'T TALK SMACK OUT ON THE FLOOR, WHAT AM I SUPPOSED TO DO?
"PLAY DEFENSE." HARDY HAR HAR.
COACH! GOOD ONE!
Peirce

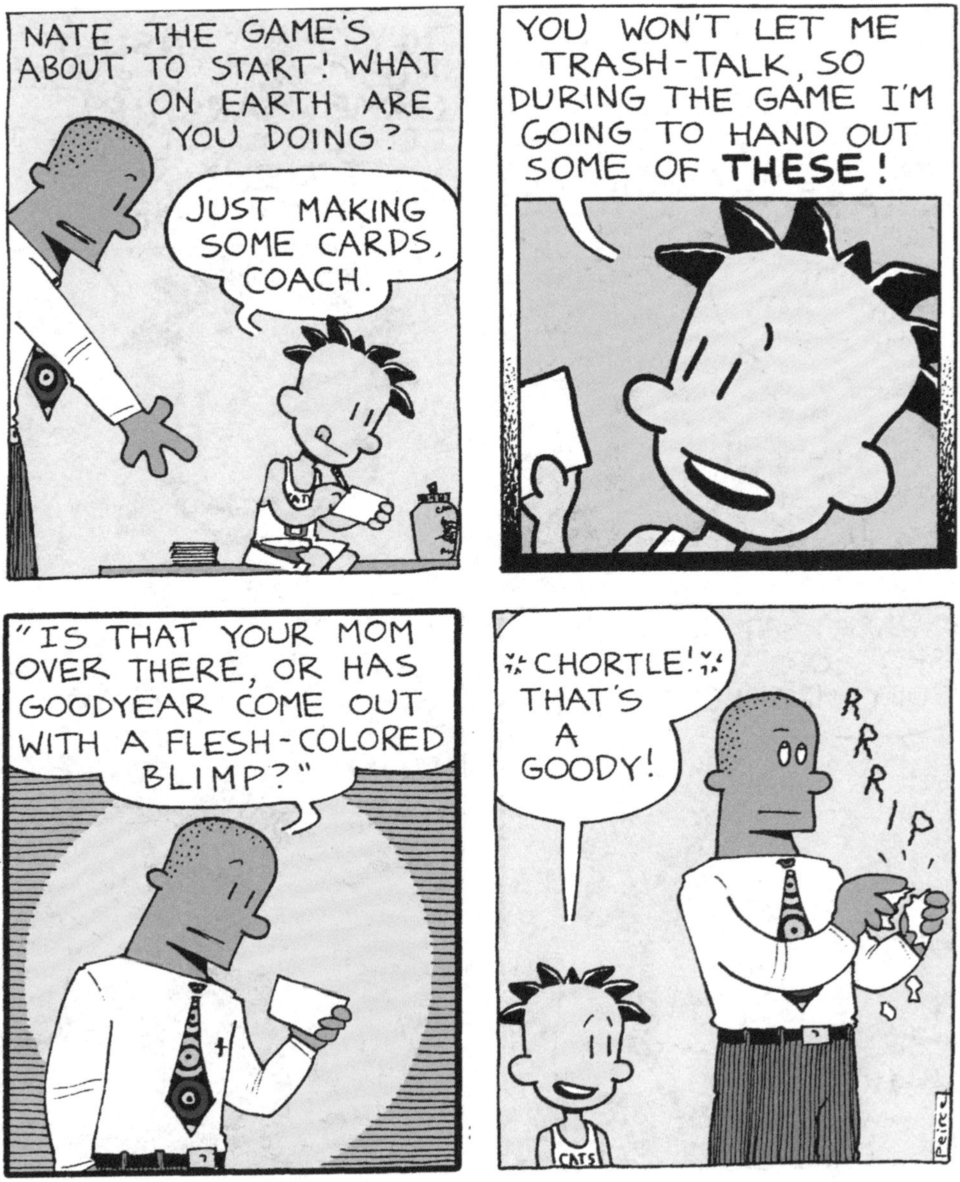

NATE, THE GAME'S ABOUT TO START! WHAT ON EARTH ARE YOU DOING?
JUST MAKING SOME CARDS, COACH.
YOU WON'T LET ME TRASH-TALK, SO DURING THE GAME I'M GOING TO HAND OUT SOME OF **THESE**!
"IS THAT YOUR MOM OVER THERE, OR HAS GOODYEAR COME OUT WITH A FLESH-COLORED BLIMP?"
CHORTLE! THAT'S A GOODY!
RRRIP
CATS

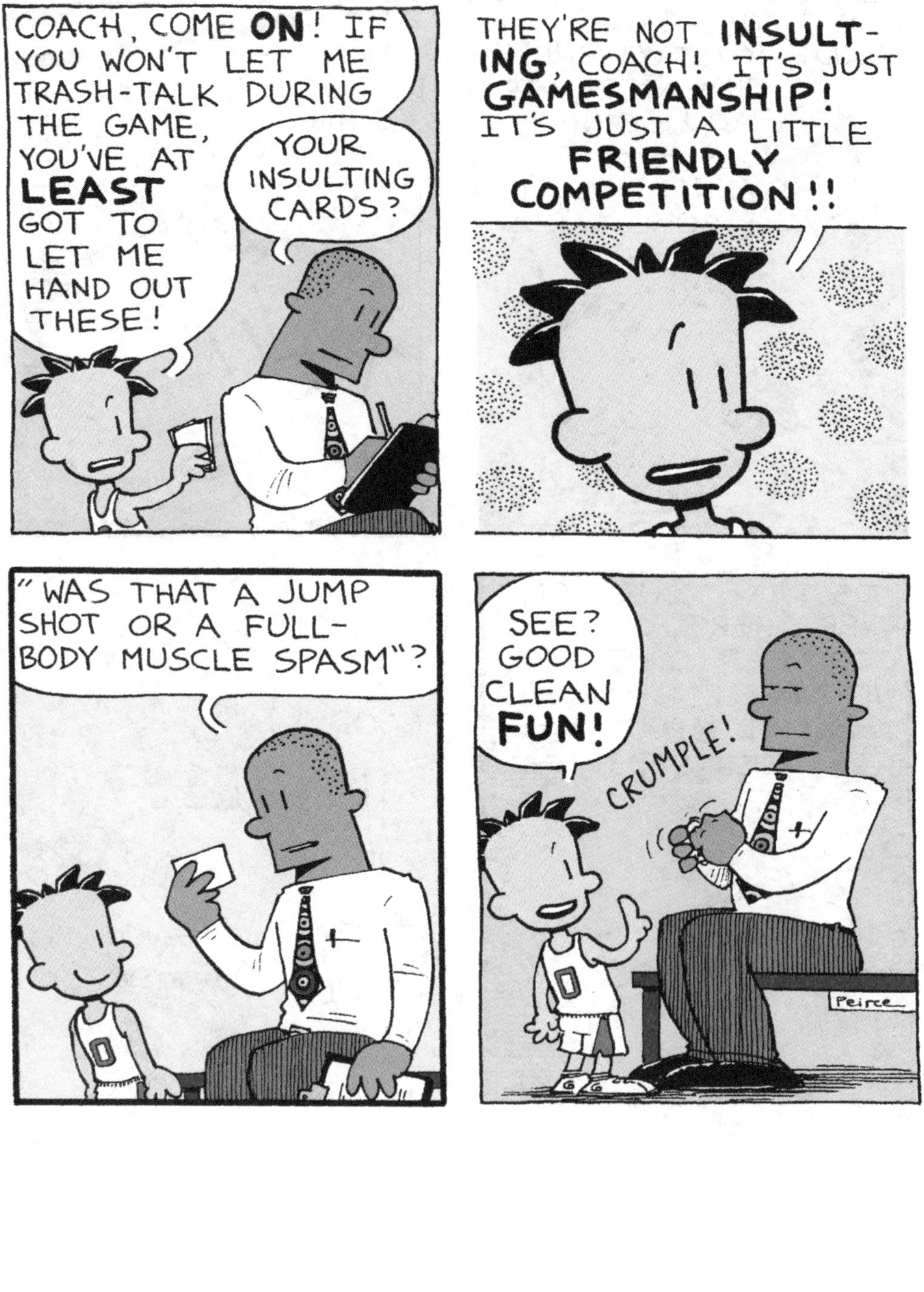
COACH, COME **ON**! IF YOU WON'T LET ME TRASH-TALK DURING THE GAME, YOU'VE AT **LEAST** GOT TO LET ME HAND OUT THESE!
YOUR INSULTING CARDS?
THEY'RE NOT **INSULTING**, COACH! IT'S JUST **GAMESMANSHIP!** IT'S JUST A LITTLE **FRIENDLY COMPETITION!!**
"WAS THAT A JUMP SHOT OR A FULL-BODY MUSCLE SPASM"?
SEE? GOOD CLEAN **FUN!**
CRUMPLE!
Peirce

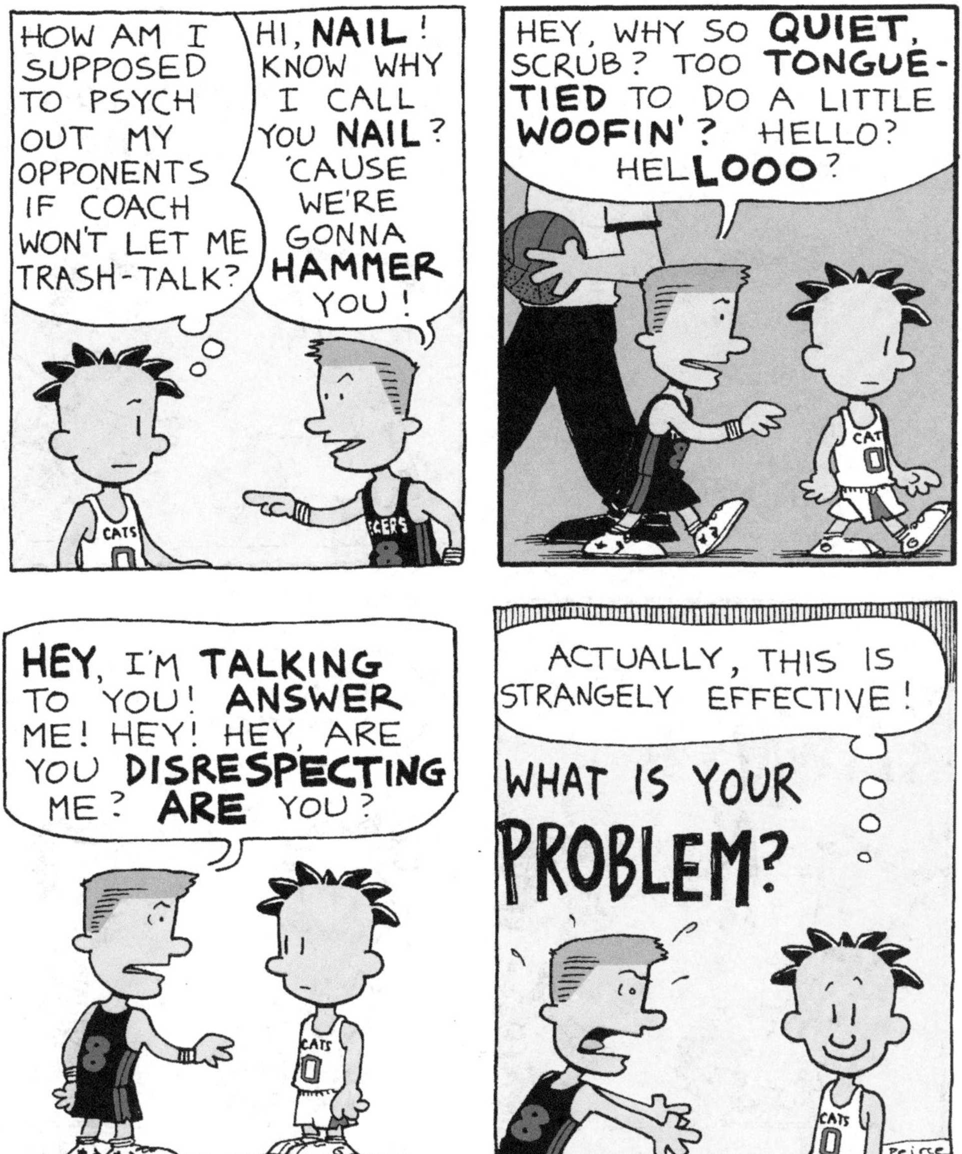
HOW AM I SUPPOSED TO PSYCH OUT MY OPPONENTS IF COACH WON'T LET ME TRASH-TALK?
HI, NAIL! KNOW WHY I CALL YOU NAIL? 'CAUSE WE'RE GONNA HAMMER YOU!
HEY, WHY SO QUIET, SCRUB? TOO TONGUE-TIED TO DO A LITTLE WOOFIN'? HELLO? HELLOOO?
HEY, I'M TALKING TO YOU! ANSWER ME! HEY! HEY, ARE YOU DISRESPECTING ME? ARE YOU?
ACTUALLY, THIS IS STRANGELY EFFECTIVE!
WHAT IS YOUR PROBLEM?
Peirce

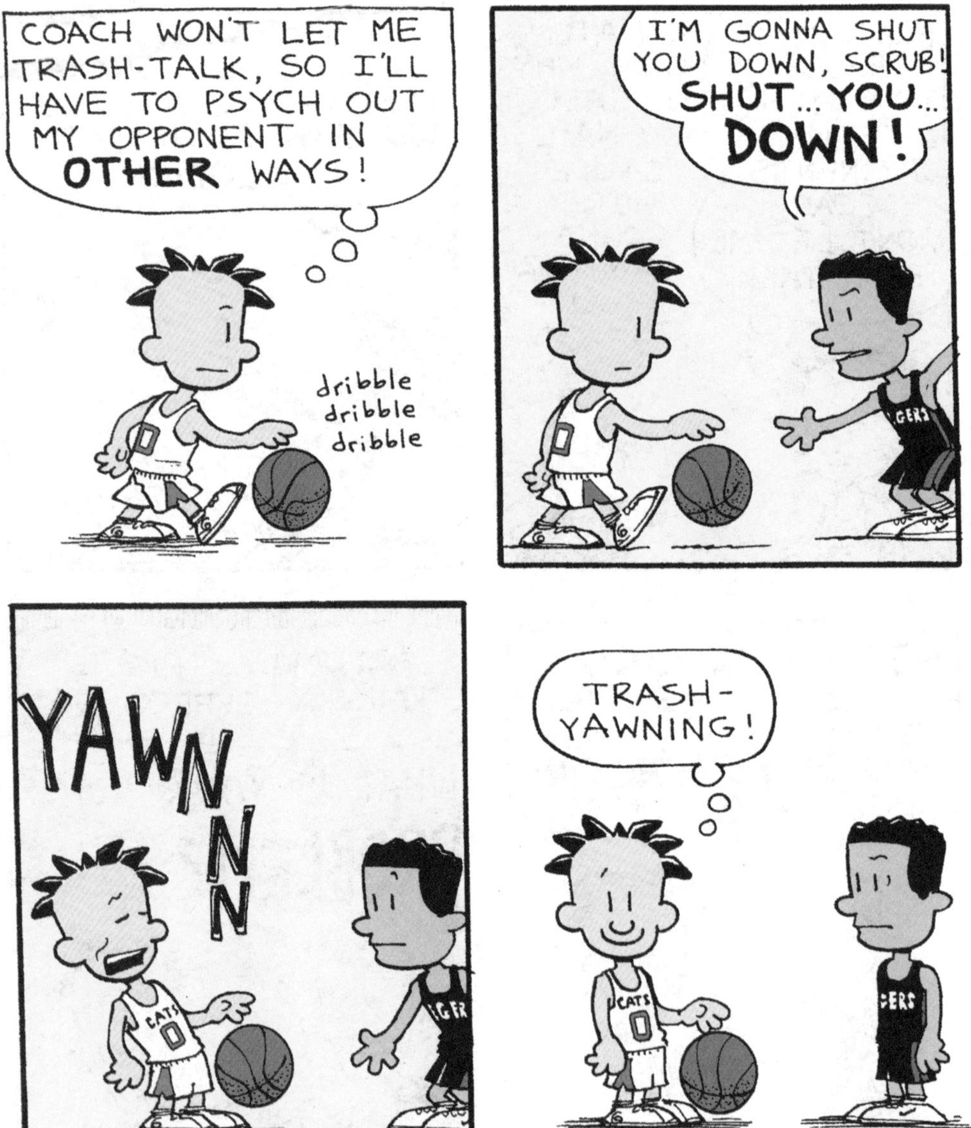
COACH WON'T LET ME TRASH-TALK, SO I'LL HAVE TO PSYCH OUT MY OPPONENT IN **OTHER** WAYS!
dribble dribble dribble
I'M GONNA SHUT YOU DOWN, SCRUB! **SHUT... YOU... DOWN!**
YAWNNNN
TRASH-YAWNING!
Peirce

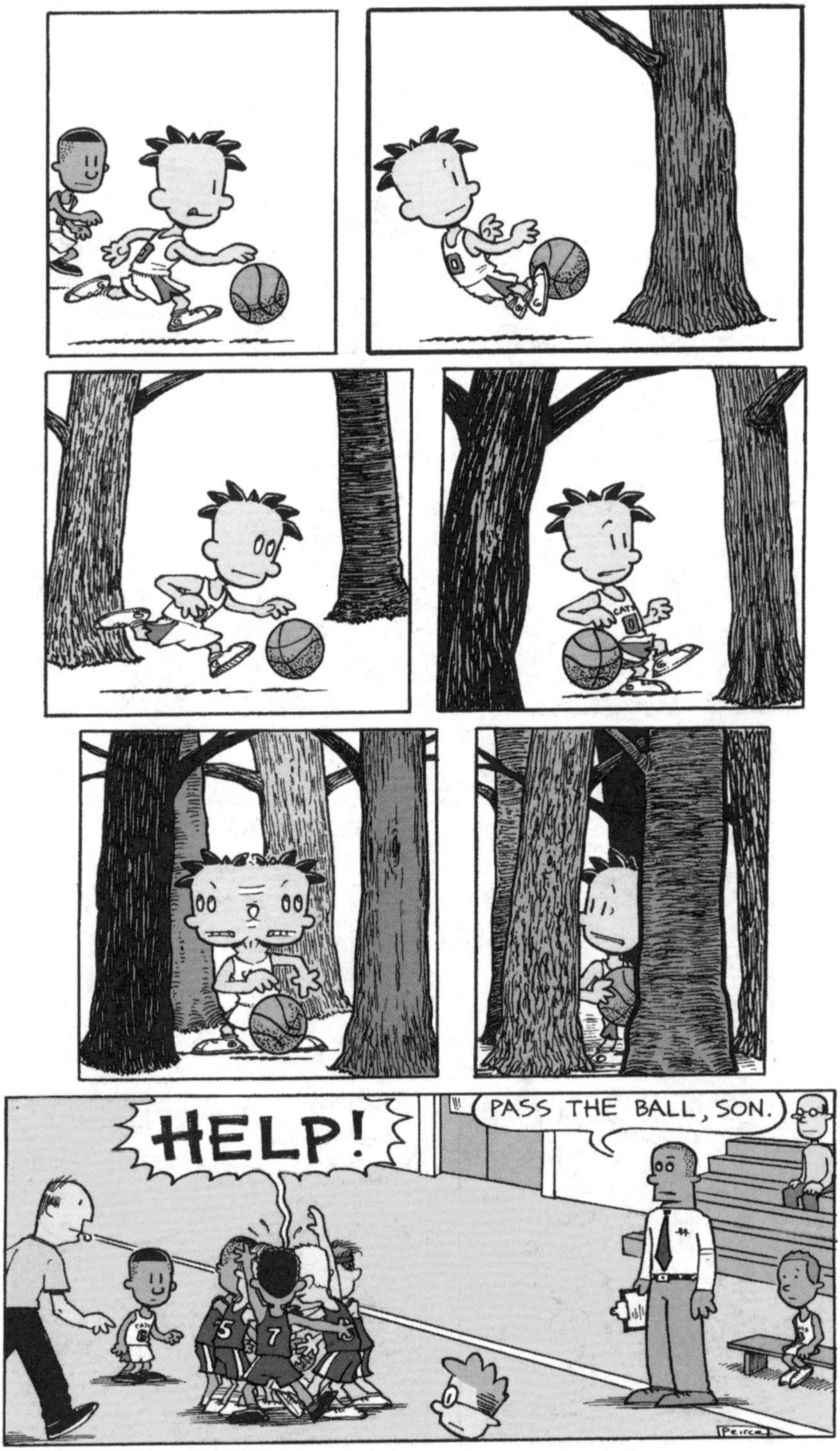
HELP!
PASS THE BALL, SON.

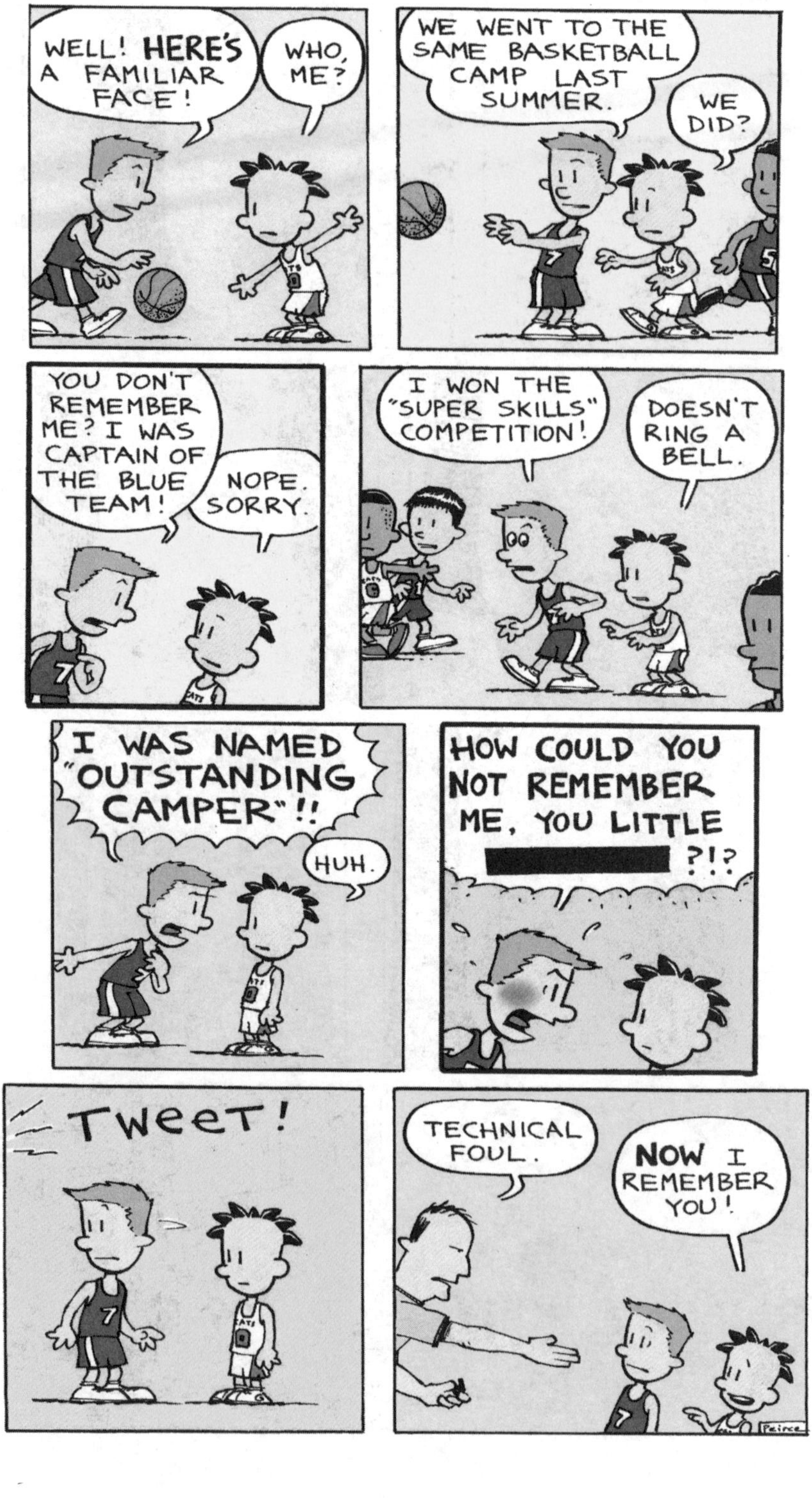

WELL! **HERE'S** A FAMILIAR FACE!
WHO, ME?
WE WENT TO THE SAME BASKETBALL CAMP LAST SUMMER.
WE DID?
YOU DON'T REMEMBER ME? I WAS CAPTAIN OF THE BLUE TEAM!
NOPE. SORRY.
I WON THE "SUPER SKILLS" COMPETITION!
DOESN'T RING A BELL.
I WAS NAMED "OUTSTANDING CAMPER"!!
HUH.
HOW COULD YOU NOT REMEMBER ME, YOU LITTLE [redacted] ?!?
TWEET!
TECHNICAL FOUL.
NOW I REMEMBER YOU!
Peirce

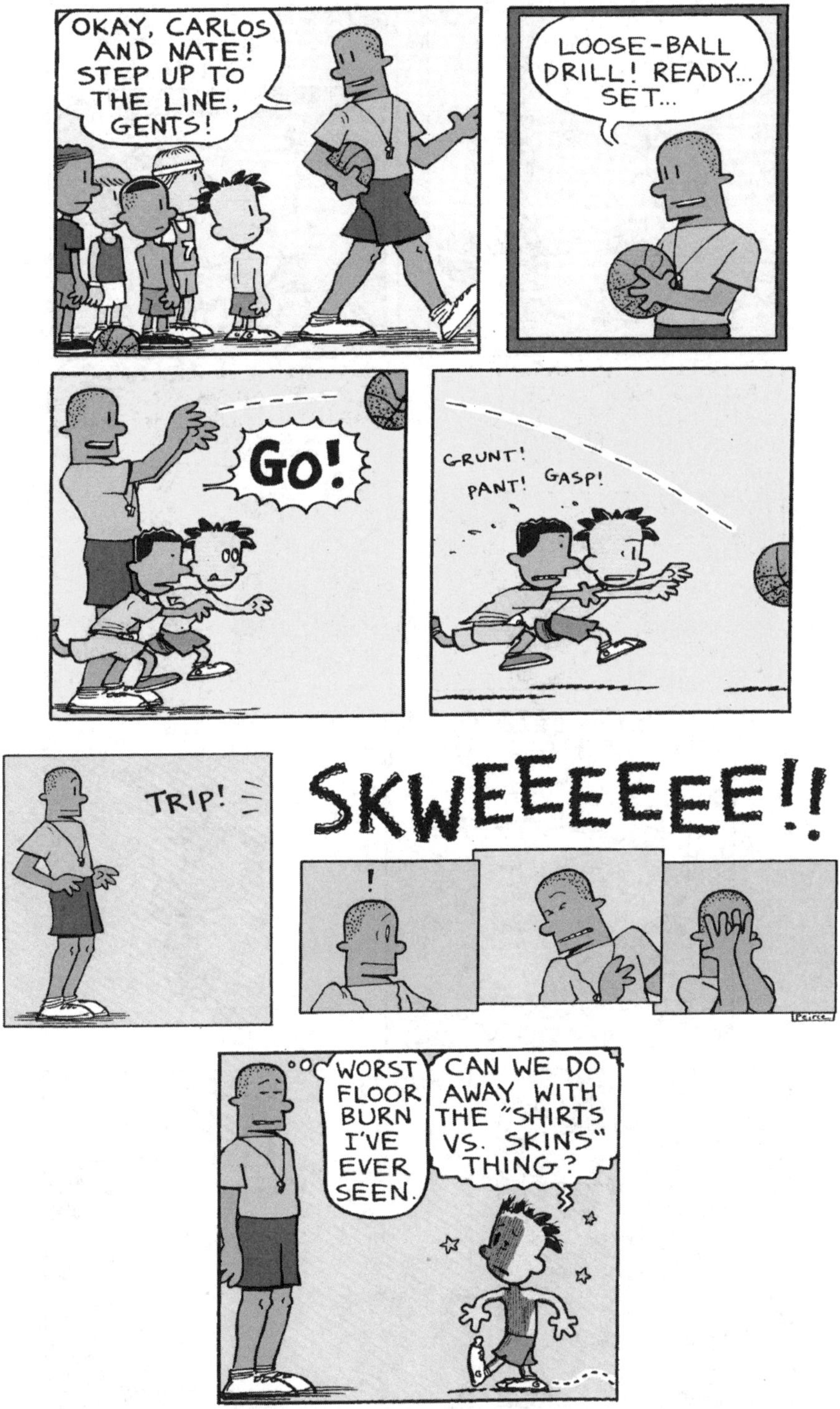
OKAY, CARLOS AND NATE! STEP UP TO THE LINE, GENTS!
LOOSE-BALL DRILL! READY... SET...
GO!
GRUNT!
PANT! GASP!
TRIP!
SKWEEEEEEE!!
WORST FLOOR BURN I'VE EVER SEEN.
CAN WE DO AWAY WITH THE "SHIRTS VS. SKINS" THING?

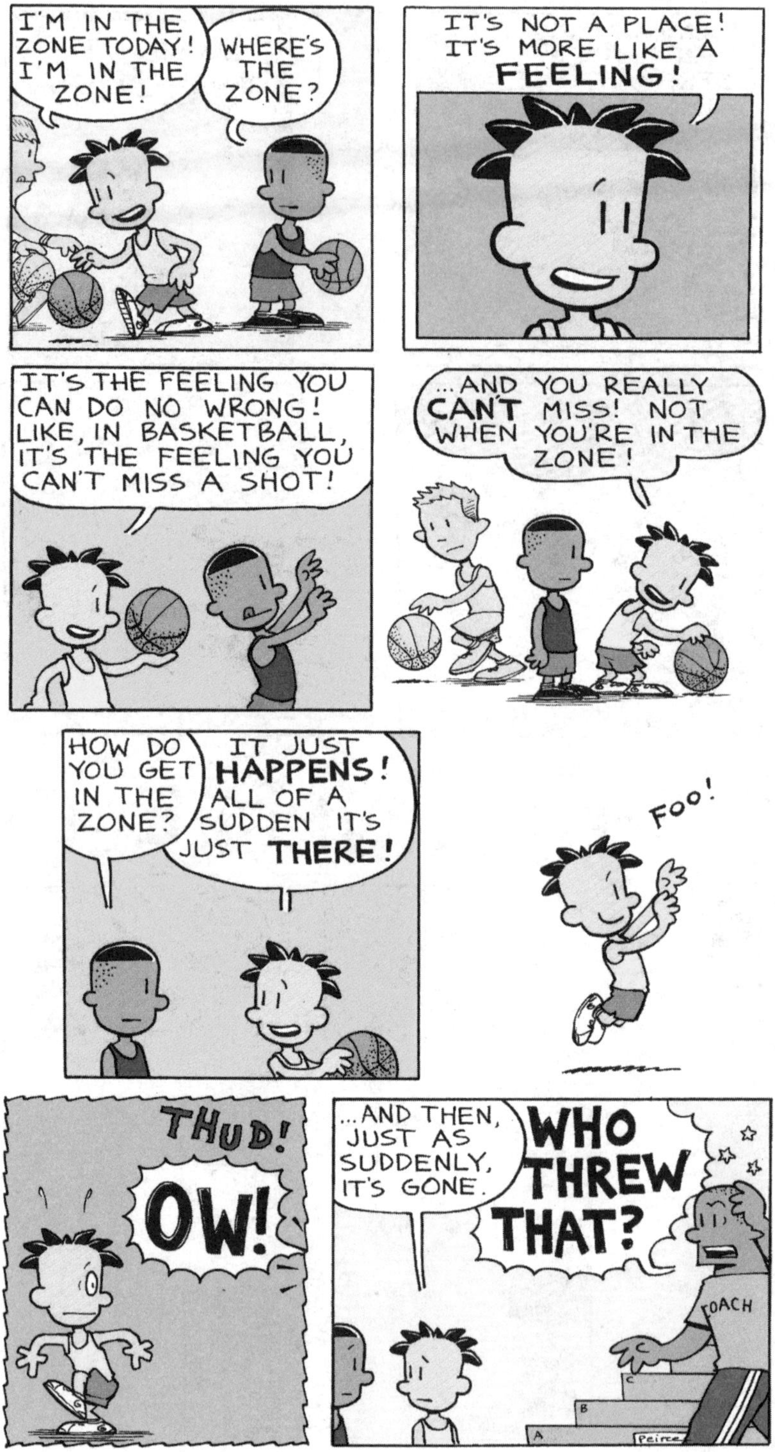
I'M IN THE ZONE TODAY! I'M IN THE ZONE!
WHERE'S THE ZONE?
IT'S NOT A PLACE! IT'S MORE LIKE A FEELING!
IT'S THE FEELING YOU CAN DO NO WRONG! LIKE, IN BASKETBALL, IT'S THE FEELING YOU CAN'T MISS A SHOT!
...AND YOU REALLY CAN'T MISS! NOT WHEN YOU'RE IN THE ZONE!
HOW DO YOU GET IN THE ZONE?
IT JUST HAPPENS! ALL OF A SUDDEN IT'S JUST THERE!
FOO!
THUD!
OW!
...AND THEN, JUST AS SUDDENLY, IT'S GONE.
WHO THREW THAT?
COACH
Peirce

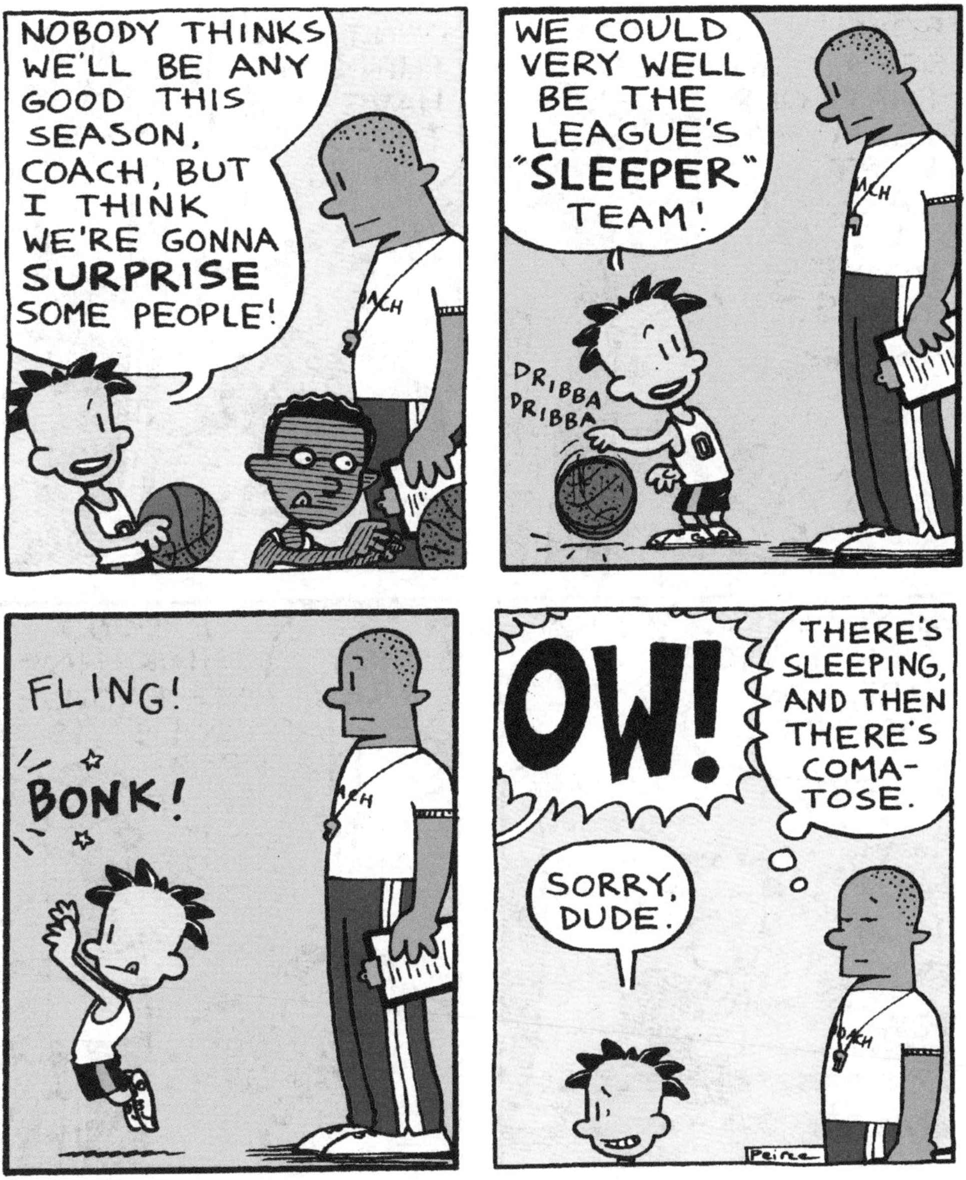
NOBODY THINKS WE'LL BE ANY GOOD THIS SEASON, COACH, BUT I THINK WE'RE GONNA SURPRISE SOME PEOPLE!
WE COULD VERY WELL BE THE LEAGUE'S "SLEEPER" TEAM!
DRIBBA DRIBBA
FLING!
BONK!
OW!
THERE'S SLEEPING, AND THEN THERE'S COMA-TOSE.
SORRY, DUDE.
Peirce

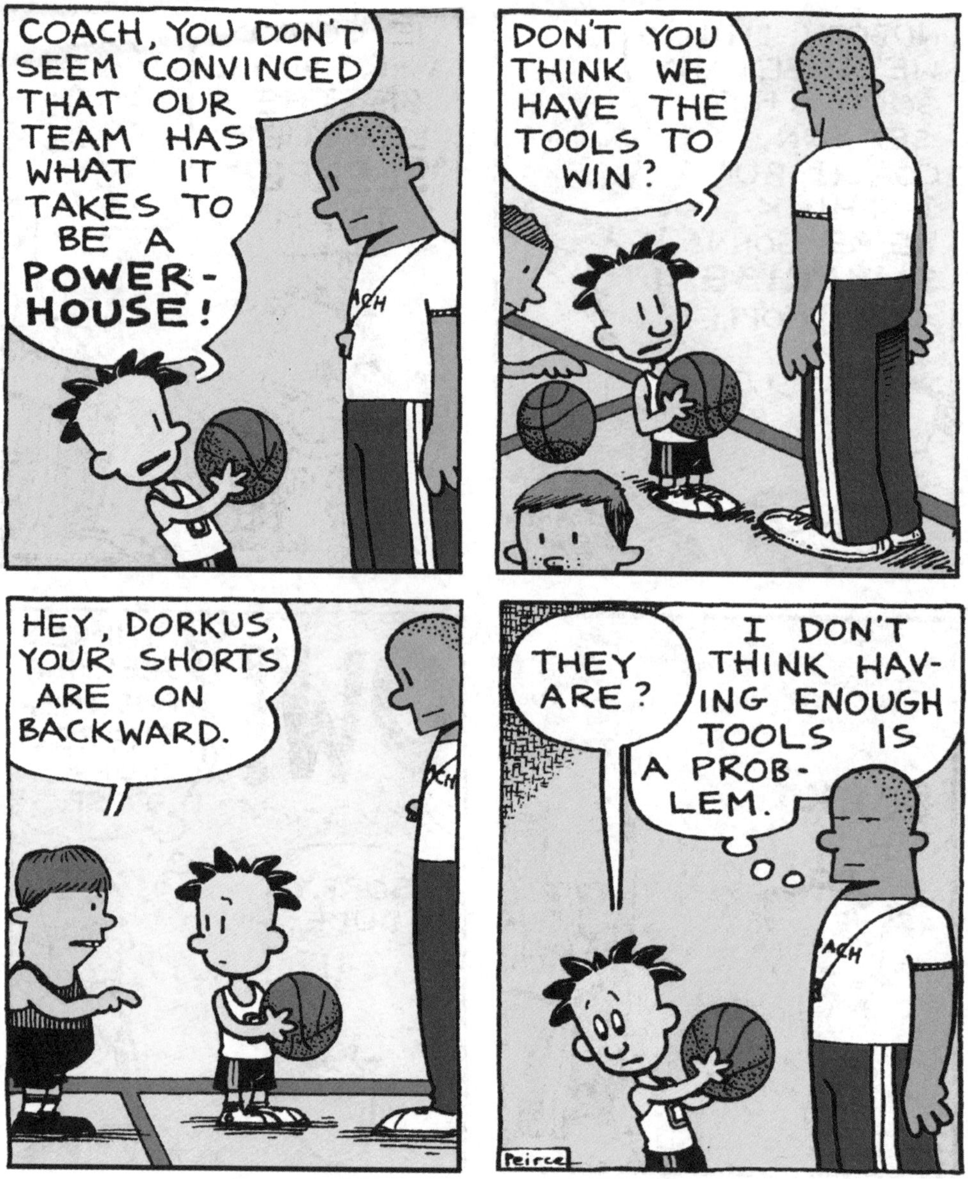
COACH, YOU DON'T SEEM CONVINCED THAT OUR TEAM HAS WHAT IT TAKES TO BE A **POWER-HOUSE!**
DON'T YOU THINK WE HAVE THE TOOLS TO WIN?
HEY, DORKUS, YOUR SHORTS ARE ON BACKWARD.
THEY ARE?
I DON'T THINK HAVING ENOUGH TOOLS IS A PROBLEM.
Peirce

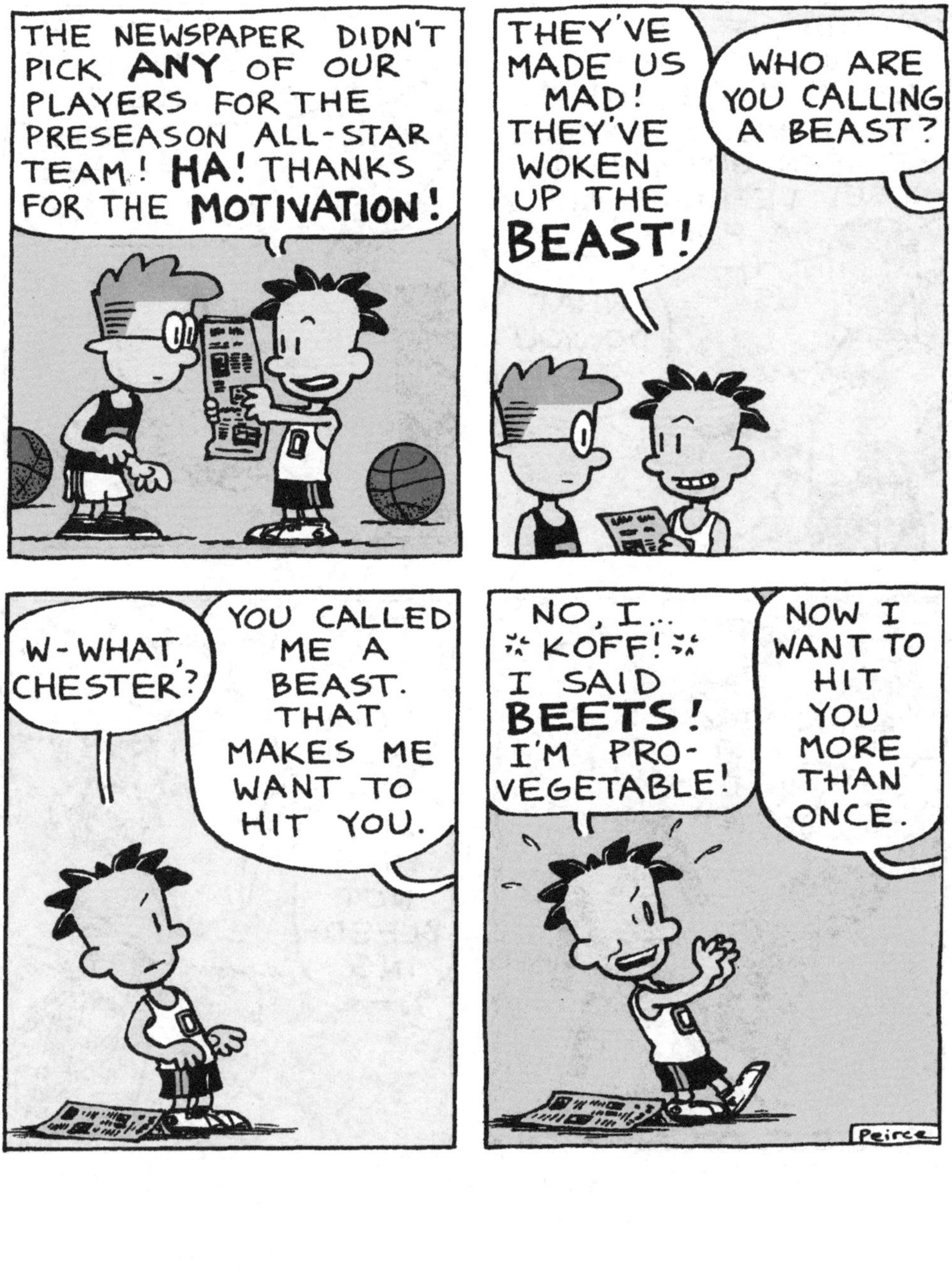
THE NEWSPAPER DIDN'T PICK **ANY** OF OUR PLAYERS FOR THE PRESEASON ALL-STAR TEAM! **HA!** THANKS FOR THE **MOTIVATION!**
THEY'VE MADE US MAD! THEY'VE WOKEN UP THE **BEAST!**
WHO ARE YOU CALLING A BEAST?
W-WHAT, CHESTER?
YOU CALLED ME A BEAST. THAT MAKES ME WANT TO HIT YOU.
NO, I... KOFF! I SAID **BEETS!** I'M PRO-VEGETABLE!
NOW I WANT TO HIT YOU MORE THAN ONCE.
Peirce

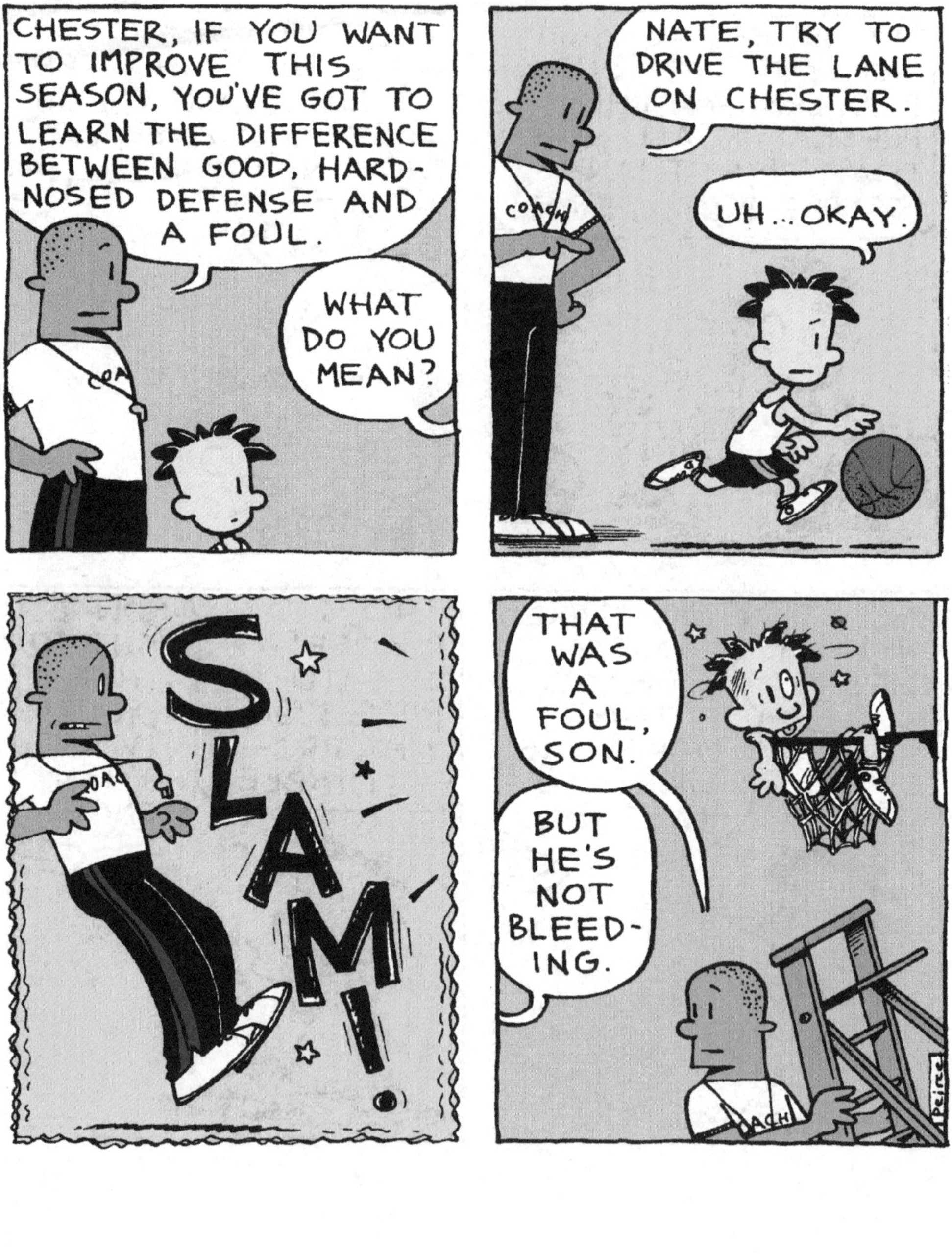
CHESTER, IF YOU WANT TO IMPROVE THIS SEASON, YOU'VE GOT TO LEARN THE DIFFERENCE BETWEEN GOOD, HARD-NOSED DEFENSE AND A FOUL.
WHAT DO YOU MEAN?
NATE, TRY TO DRIVE THE LANE ON CHESTER.
UH... OKAY.
COACH
SLAM!
THAT WAS A FOUL, SON.
BUT HE'S NOT BLEEDING.
Peirce

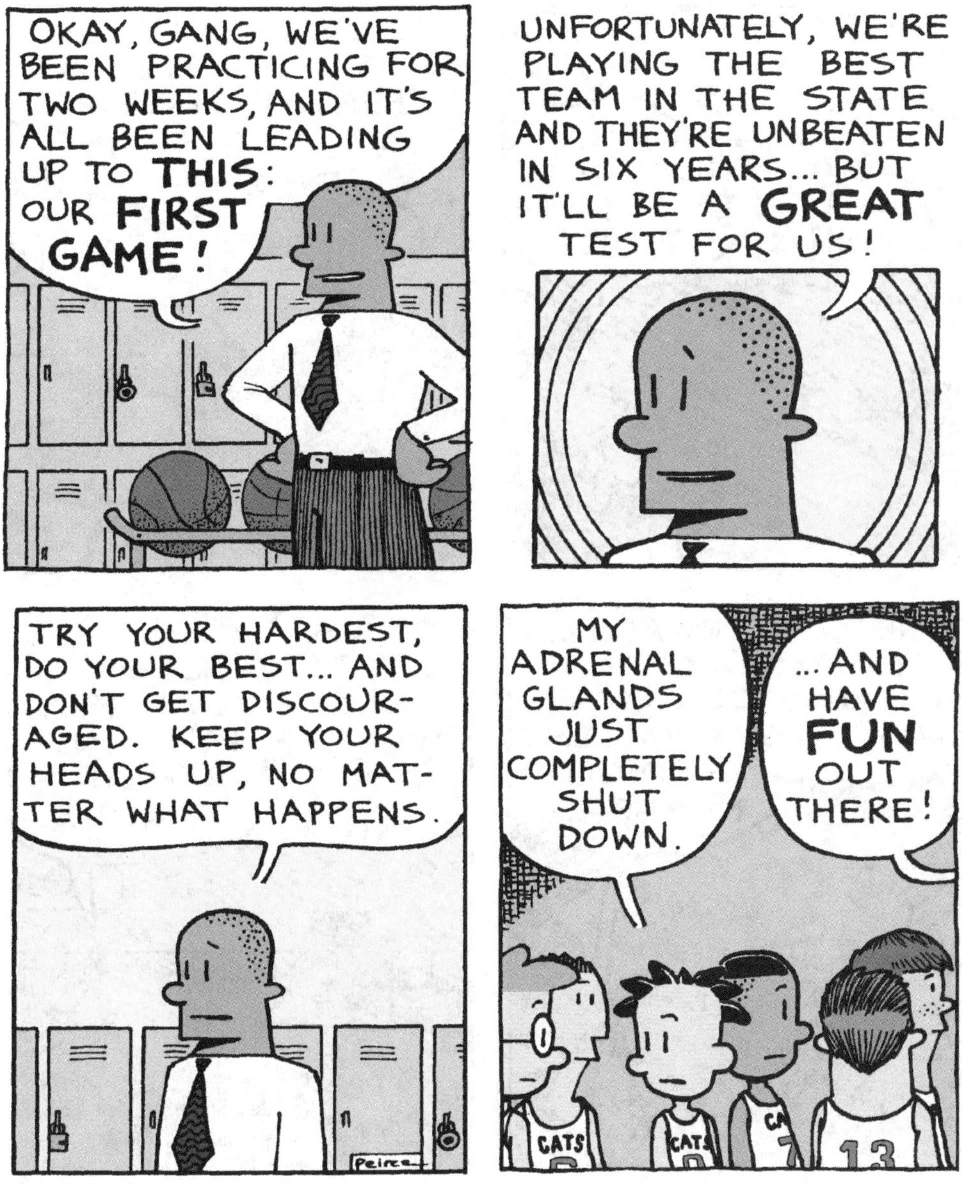
OKAY, GANG, WE'VE BEEN PRACTICING FOR TWO WEEKS, AND IT'S ALL BEEN LEADING UP TO **THIS**: OUR **FIRST GAME**!
UNFORTUNATELY, WE'RE PLAYING THE BEST TEAM IN THE STATE AND THEY'RE UNBEATEN IN SIX YEARS... BUT IT'LL BE A **GREAT** TEST FOR US!
TRY YOUR HARDEST, DO YOUR BEST... AND DON'T GET DISCOURAGED. KEEP YOUR HEADS UP, NO MATTER WHAT HAPPENS.
Peirce
MY ADRENAL GLANDS JUST COMPLETELY SHUT DOWN.
...AND HAVE **FUN** OUT THERE!
CATS
CATS
13

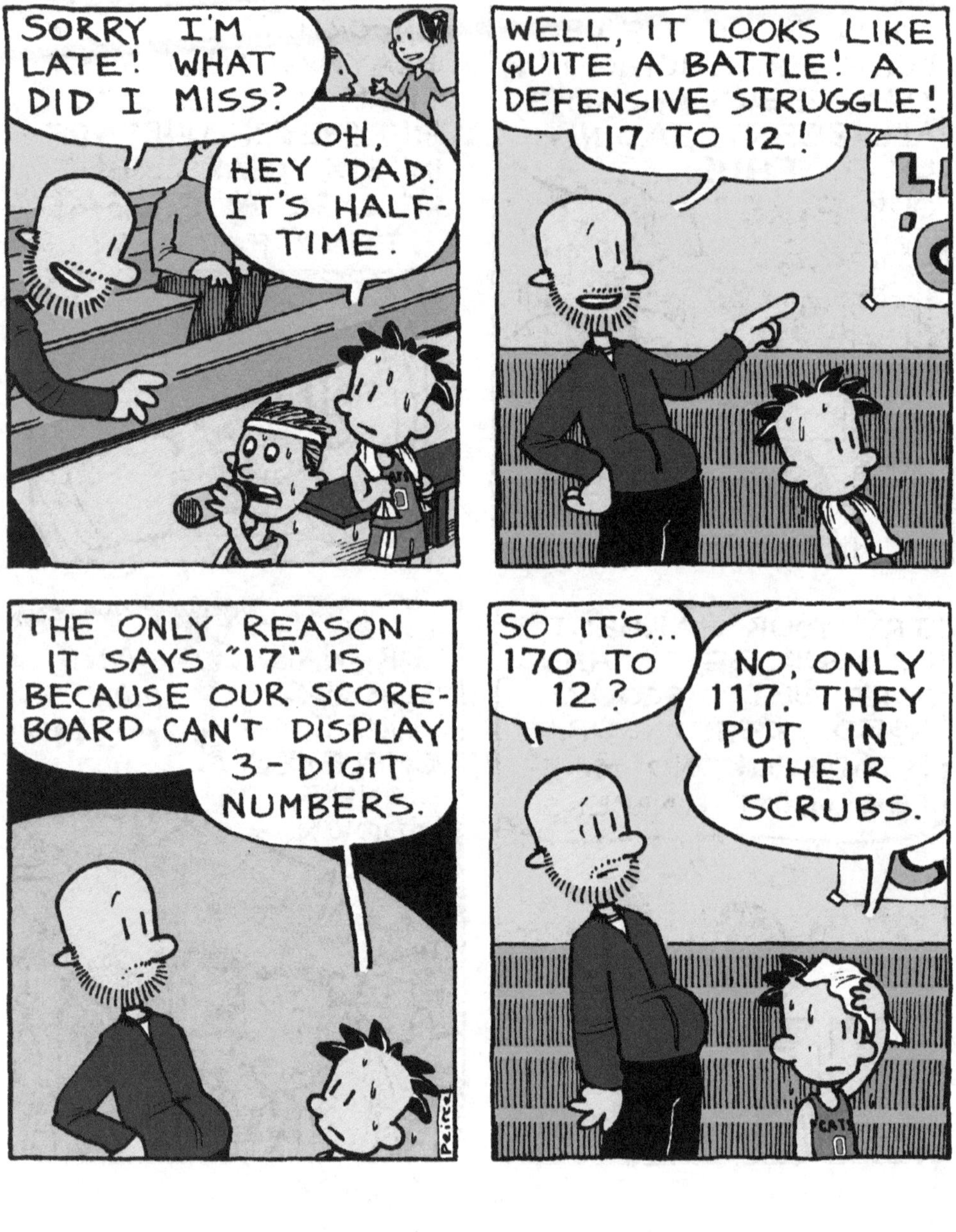
SORRY I'M LATE! WHAT DID I MISS?
OH, HEY DAD. IT'S HALF-TIME.
WELL, IT LOOKS LIKE QUITE A BATTLE! A DEFENSIVE STRUGGLE! 17 TO 12!
THE ONLY REASON IT SAYS "17" IS BECAUSE OUR SCORE-BOARD CAN'T DISPLAY 3-DIGIT NUMBERS.
SO IT'S... 170 TO 12?
NO, ONLY 117. THEY PUT IN THEIR SCRUBS.

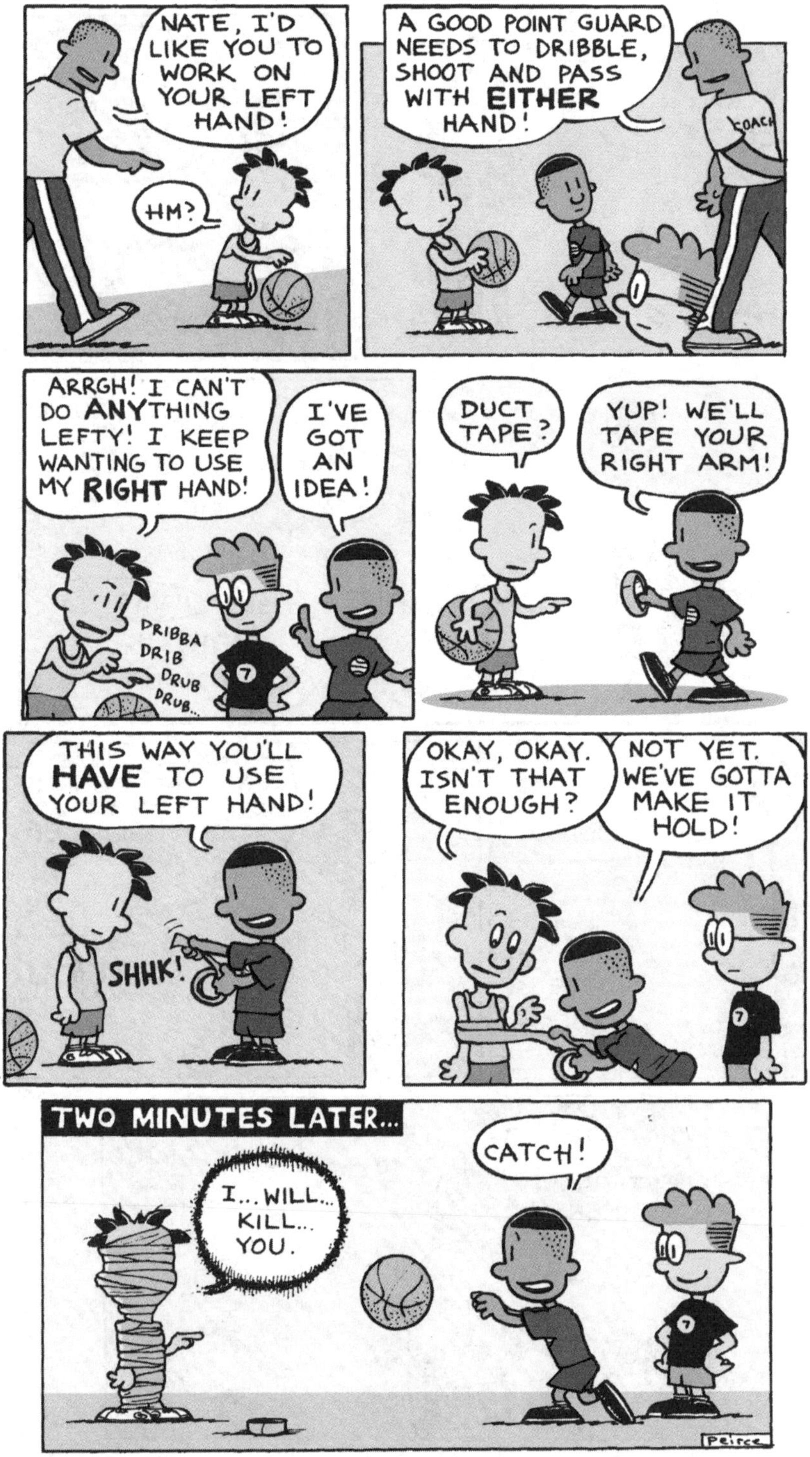
NATE, I'D LIKE YOU TO WORK ON YOUR LEFT HAND!
HM?
A GOOD POINT GUARD NEEDS TO DRIBBLE, SHOOT AND PASS WITH **EITHER** HAND!
COACH
ARRGH! I CAN'T DO **ANY**THING LEFTY! I KEEP WANTING TO USE MY **RIGHT** HAND!
I'VE GOT AN IDEA!
DRIBBA DRIB DRUB DRUB...
DUCT TAPE?
YUP! WE'LL TAPE YOUR RIGHT ARM!
THIS WAY YOU'LL **HAVE** TO USE YOUR LEFT HAND!
SHHK!
OKAY, OKAY. ISN'T THAT ENOUGH?
NOT YET. WE'VE GOTTA MAKE IT HOLD!
TWO MINUTES LATER...
I... WILL... KILL... YOU.
CATCH!
Peirce

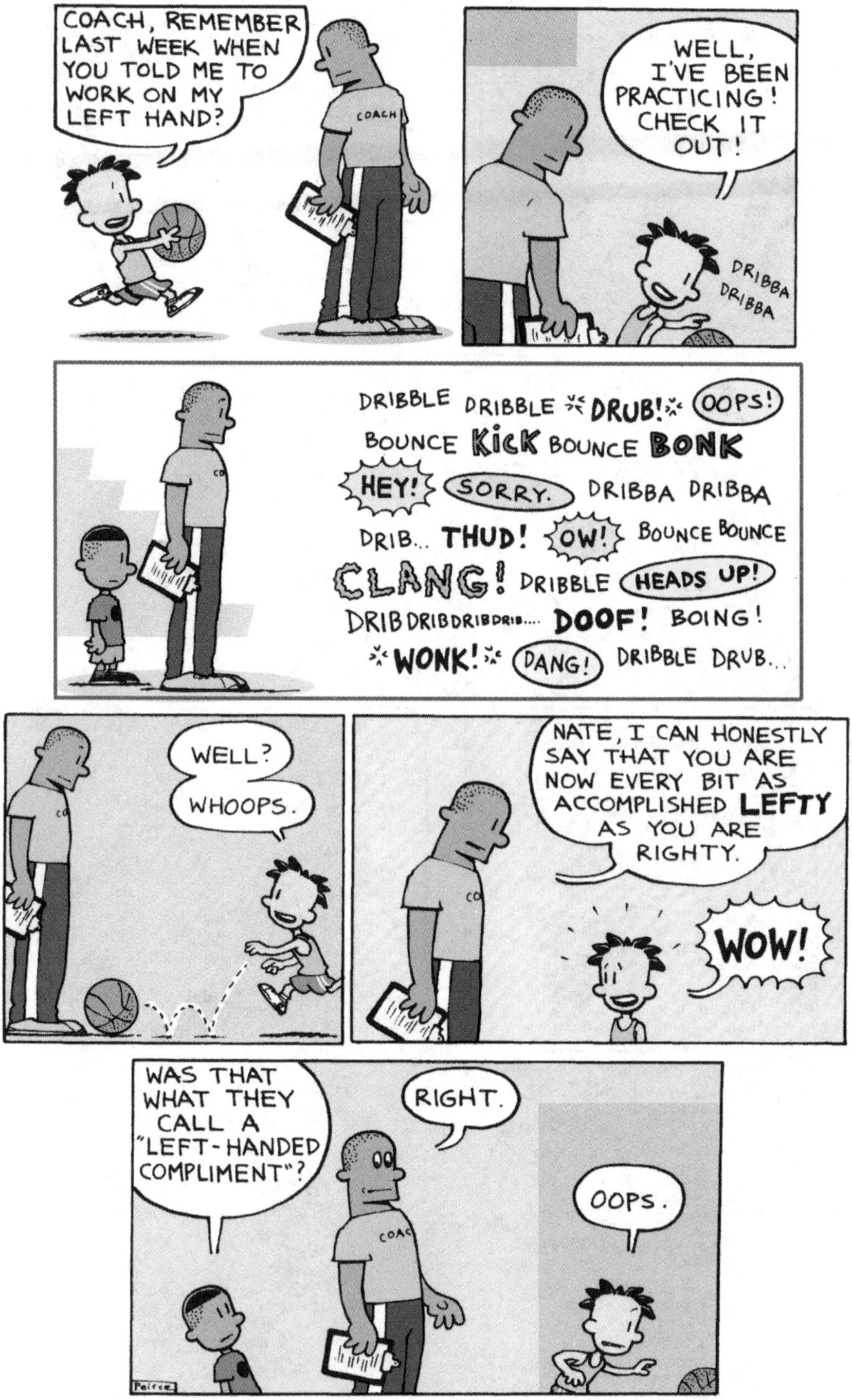
COACH, REMEMBER LAST WEEK WHEN YOU TOLD ME TO WORK ON MY LEFT HAND?
COACH
WELL, I'VE BEEN PRACTICING! CHECK IT OUT!
DRIBBA DRIBBA
DRIBBLE DRIBBLE DRUB! OOPS!
BOUNCE KICK BOUNCE BONK
HEY! SORRY. DRIBBA DRIBBA
DRIB... THUD! OW! BOUNCE BOUNCE
CLANG! DRIBBLE HEADS UP!
DRIB DRIBDRIBDRIB.... DOOF! BOING!
WONK! DANG! DRIBBLE DRUB...
WELL?
WHOOPS.
NATE, I CAN HONESTLY SAY THAT YOU ARE NOW EVERY BIT AS ACCOMPLISHED LEFTY AS YOU ARE RIGHTY.
WOW!
WAS THAT WHAT THEY CALL A "LEFT-HANDED COMPLIMENT"?
RIGHT.
OOPS.
Peirce

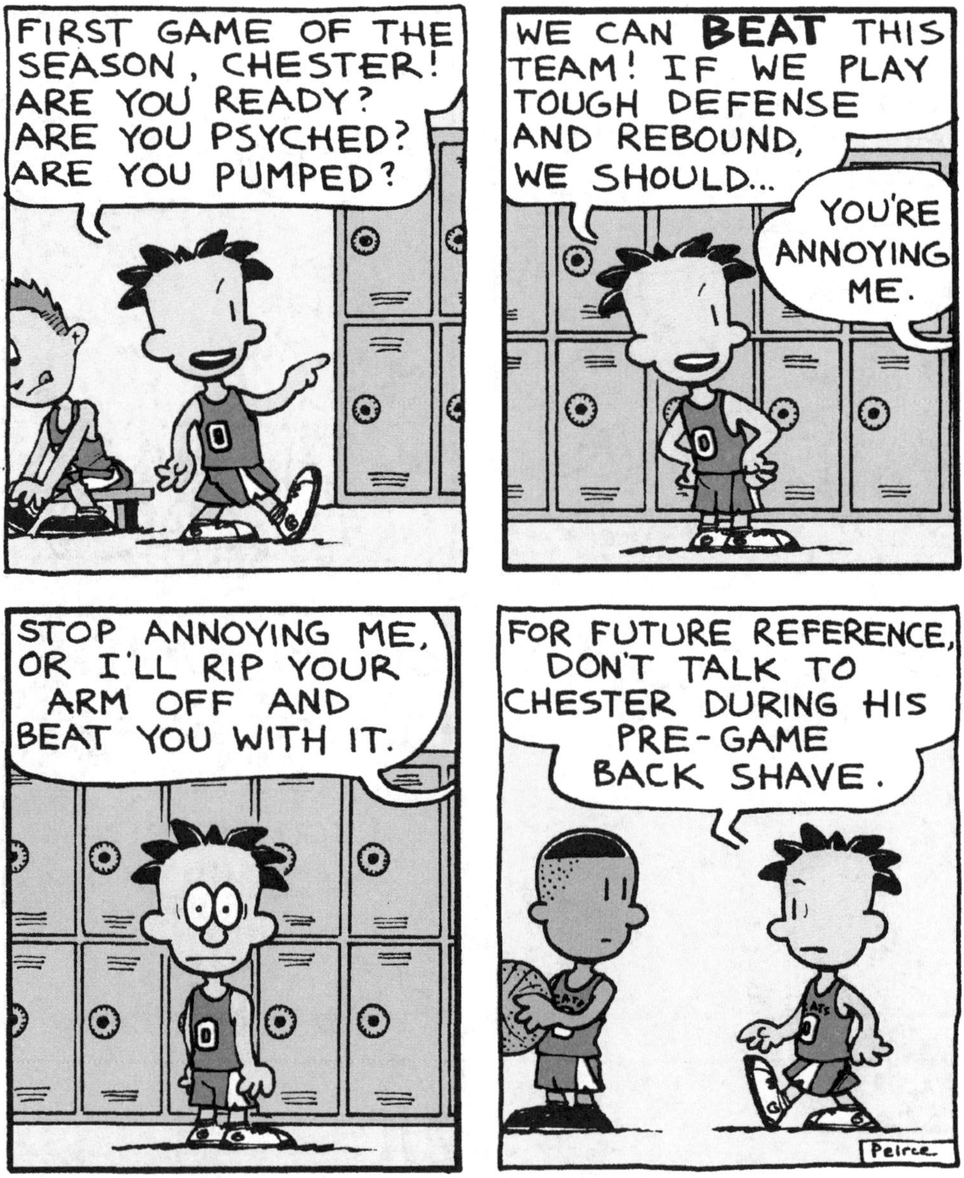
FIRST GAME OF THE SEASON, CHESTER! ARE YOU READY? ARE YOU PSYCHED? ARE YOU PUMPED?
WE CAN BEAT THIS TEAM! IF WE PLAY TOUGH DEFENSE AND REBOUND, WE SHOULD...
YOU'RE ANNOYING ME.
STOP ANNOYING ME, OR I'LL RIP YOUR ARM OFF AND BEAT YOU WITH IT.
FOR FUTURE REFERENCE, DON'T TALK TO CHESTER DURING HIS PRE-GAME BACK SHAVE.
Peirce

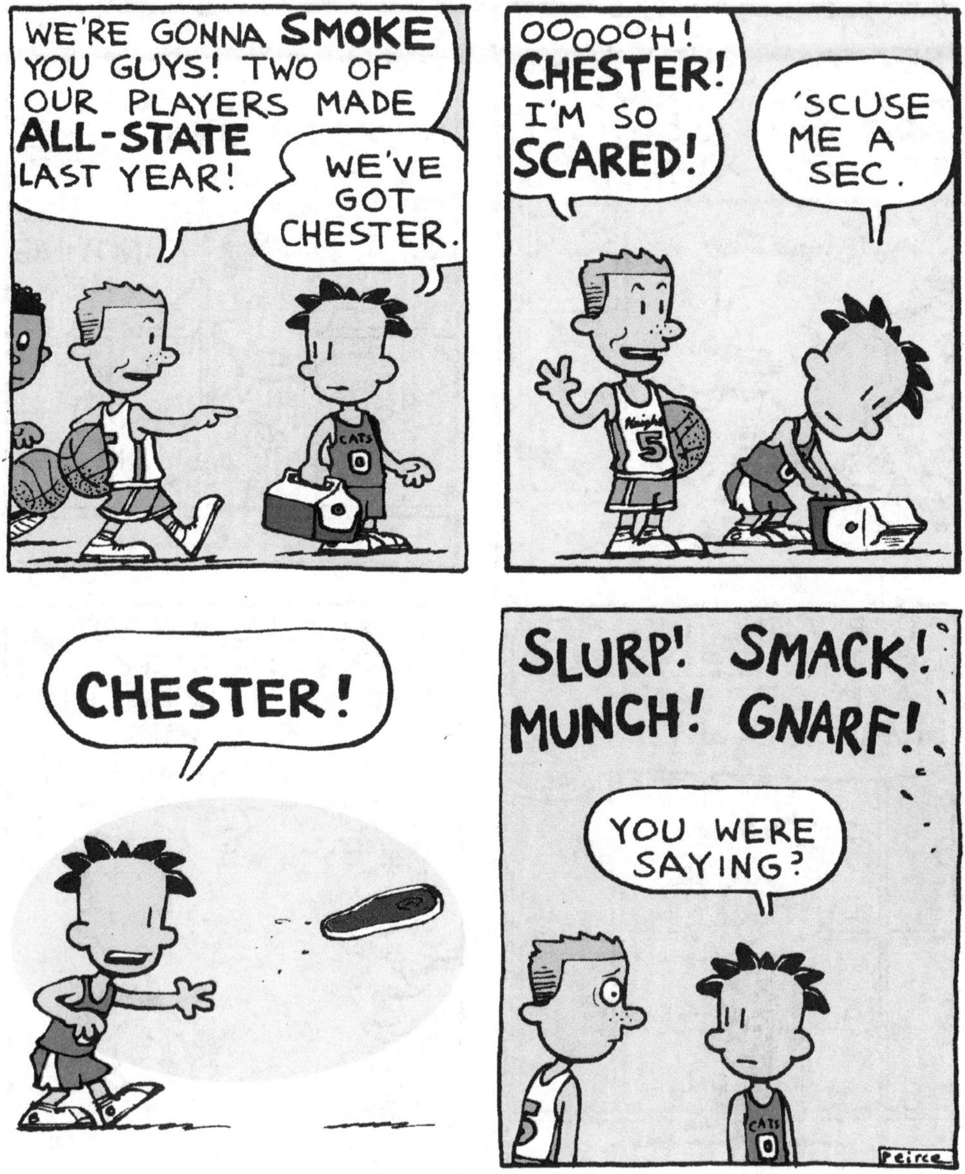
WE'RE GONNA SMOKE YOU GUYS! TWO OF OUR PLAYERS MADE ALL-STATE LAST YEAR!
WE'VE GOT CHESTER.
CATS 0
OOOOOH! CHESTER! I'M SO SCARED!
'SCUSE ME A SEC.
5
CHESTER!
SLURP! SMACK! MUNCH! GNARF!
YOU WERE SAYING?
CATS 0
Peirce

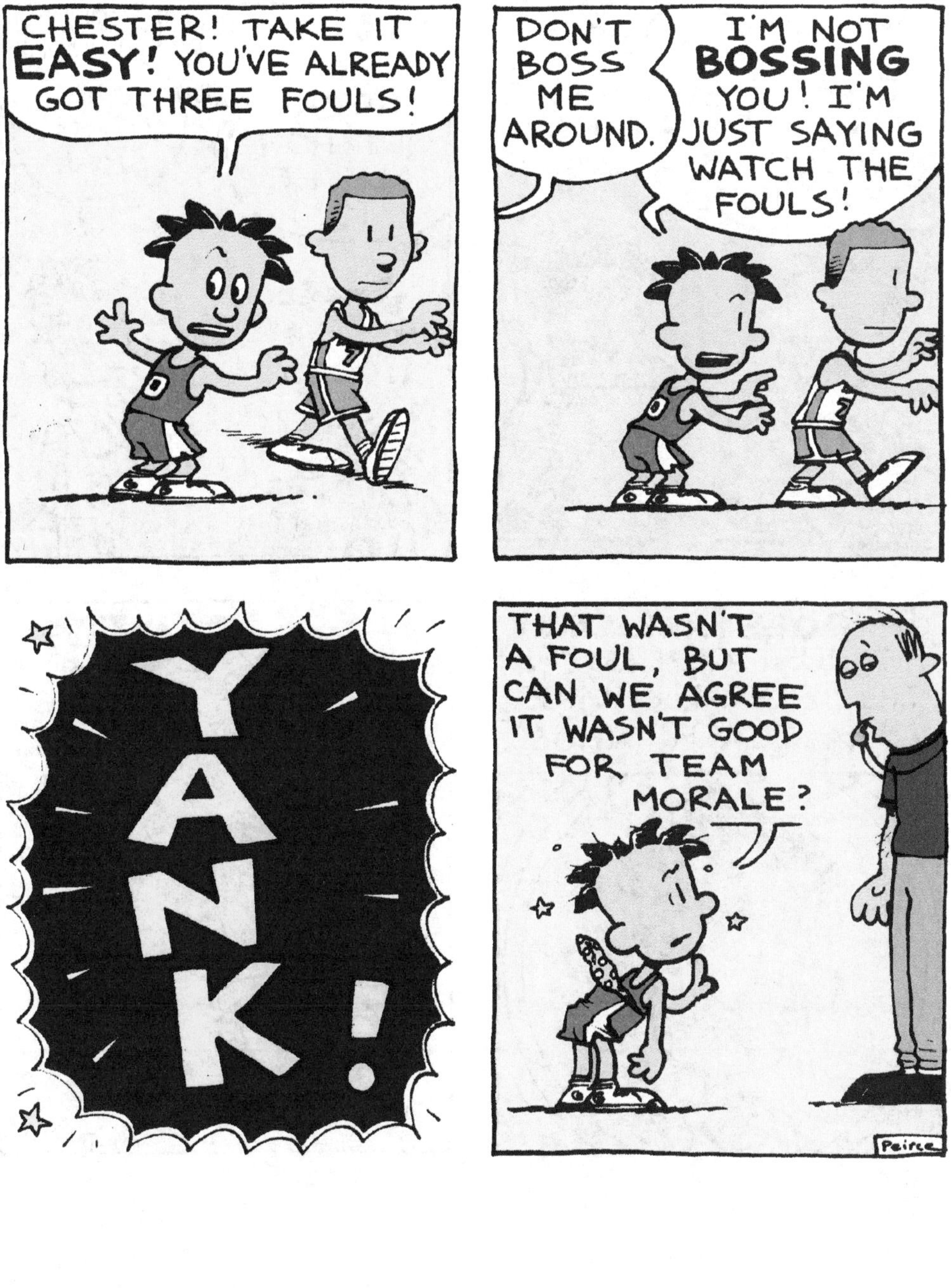
CHESTER! TAKE IT EASY! YOU'VE ALREADY GOT THREE FOULS!
DON'T BOSS ME AROUND.
I'M NOT BOSSING YOU! I'M JUST SAYING WATCH THE FOULS!
YANK!
THAT WASN'T A FOUL, BUT CAN WE AGREE IT WASN'T GOOD FOR TEAM MORALE?
Peirce

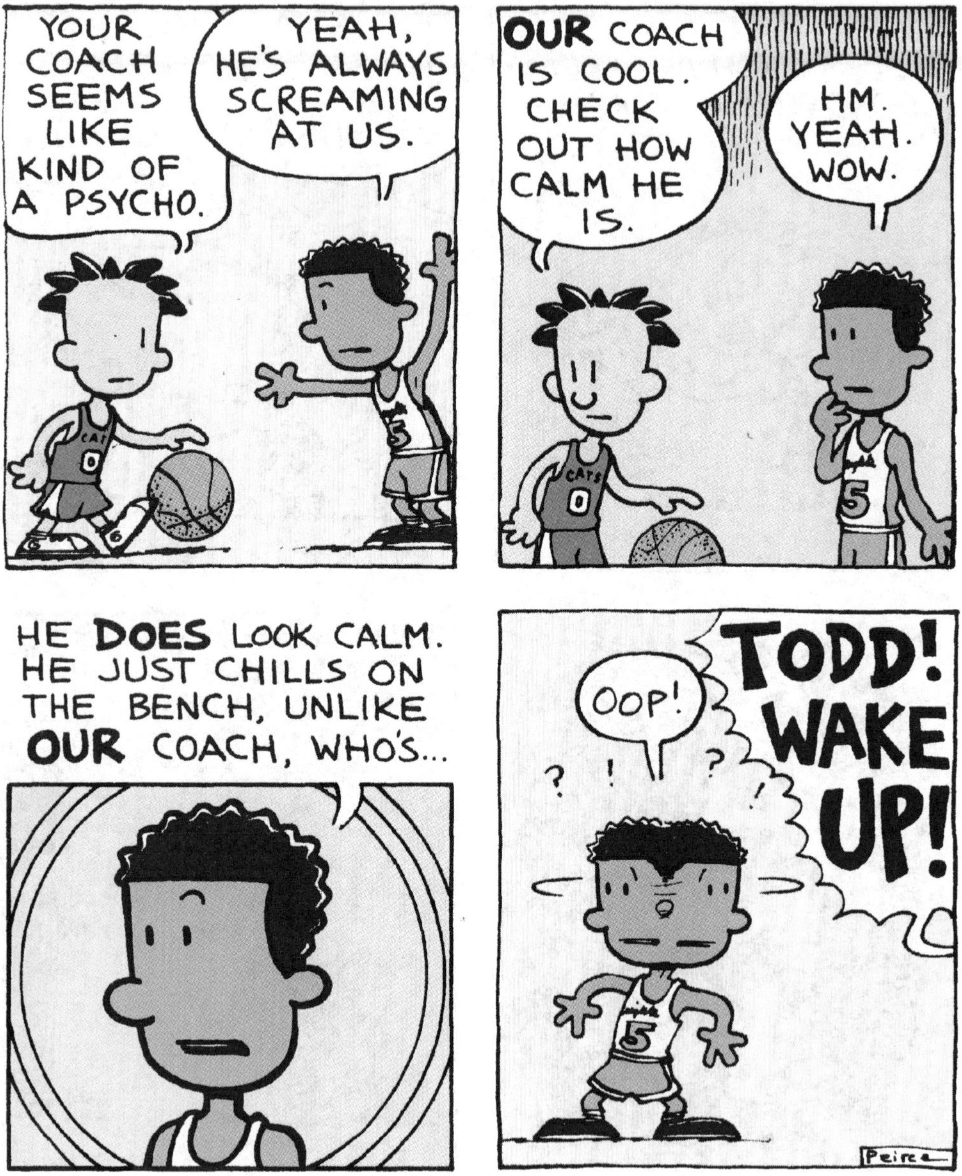
YOUR COACH SEEMS LIKE KIND OF A PSYCHO.
YEAH, HE'S ALWAYS SCREAMING AT US.
OUR COACH IS COOL. CHECK OUT HOW CALM HE IS.
HM. YEAH. WOW.
HE DOES LOOK CALM. HE JUST CHILLS ON THE BENCH, UNLIKE OUR COACH, WHO'S...
TODD! WAKE UP!
OOP!
Peirce

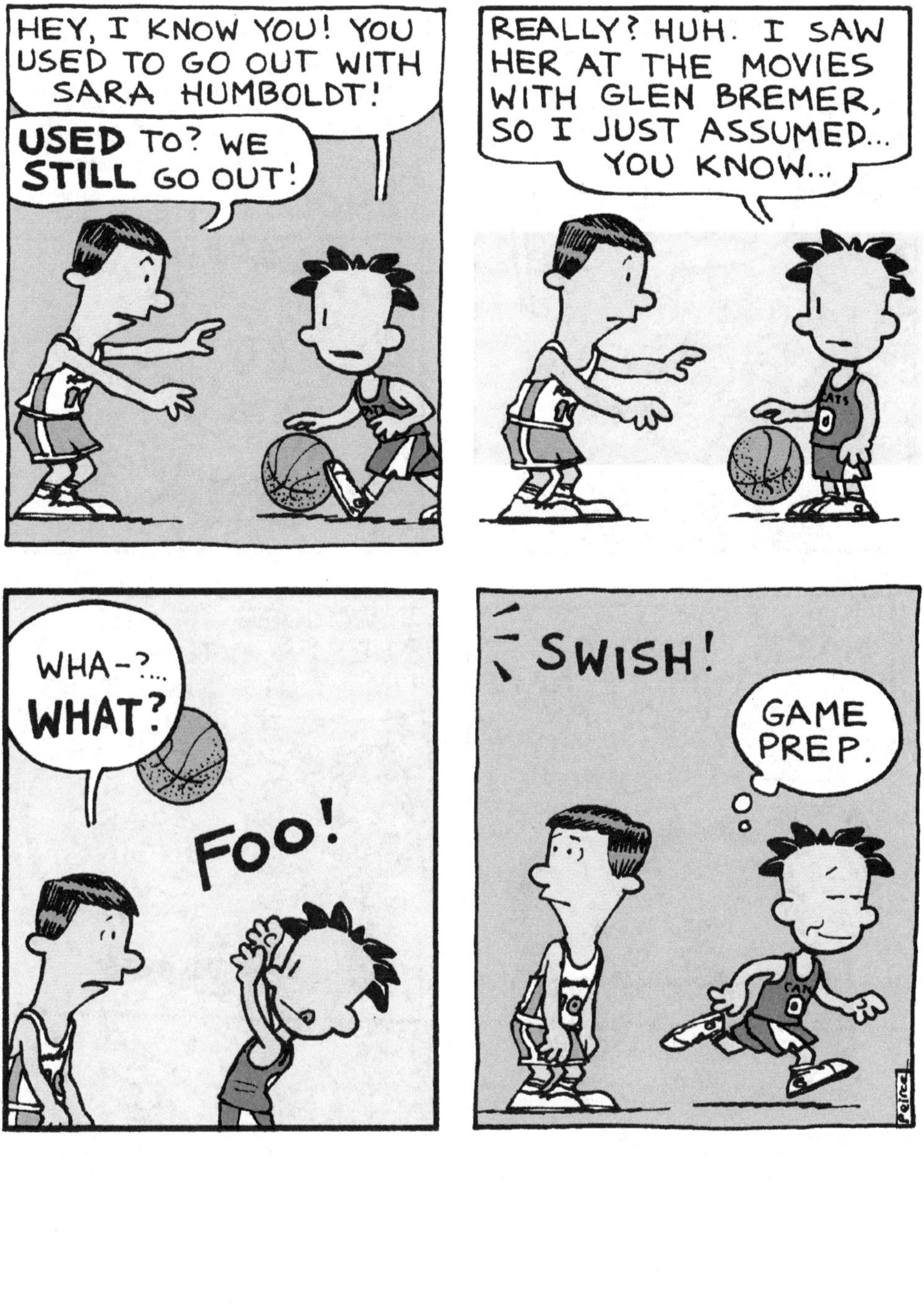
HEY, I KNOW YOU! YOU USED TO GO OUT WITH SARA HUMBOLDT!
USED TO? WE STILL GO OUT!
REALLY? HUH. I SAW HER AT THE MOVIES WITH GLEN BREMER, SO I JUST ASSUMED... YOU KNOW...
WHA-?... WHAT?
FOO!
SWISH!
GAME PREP.

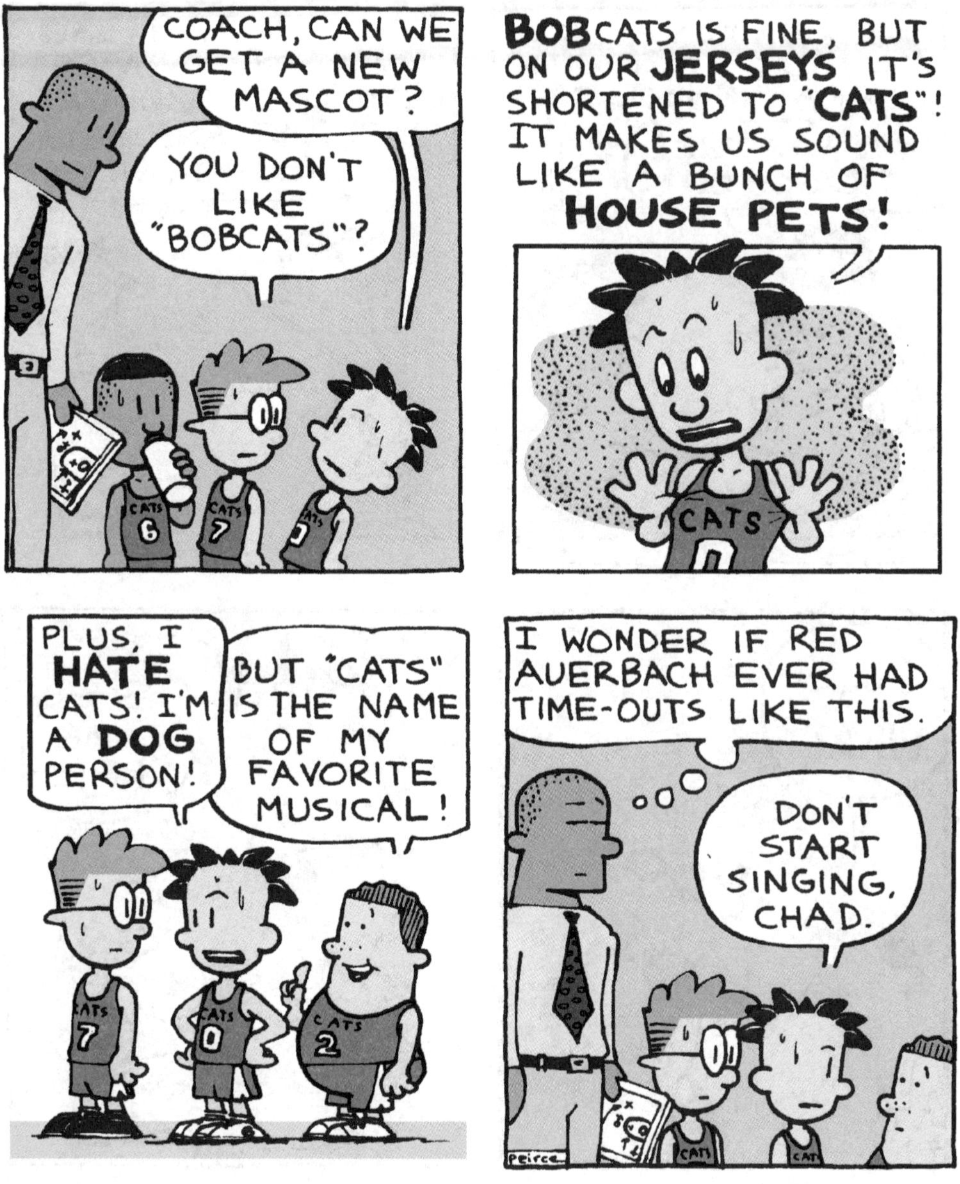
COACH, CAN WE GET A NEW MASCOT?
YOU DON'T LIKE "BOBCATS"?
CATS 6
CATS 7
BOBCATS IS FINE, BUT ON OUR JERSEYS IT'S SHORTENED TO "CATS"! IT MAKES US SOUND LIKE A BUNCH OF HOUSE PETS!
CATS
PLUS, I HATE CATS! I'M A DOG PERSON!
BUT "CATS" IS THE NAME OF MY FAVORITE MUSICAL!
CATS 7
CATS 0
CATS 2
I WONDER IF RED AUERBACH EVER HAD TIME-OUTS LIKE THIS.
DON'T START SINGING, CHAD.
peirce

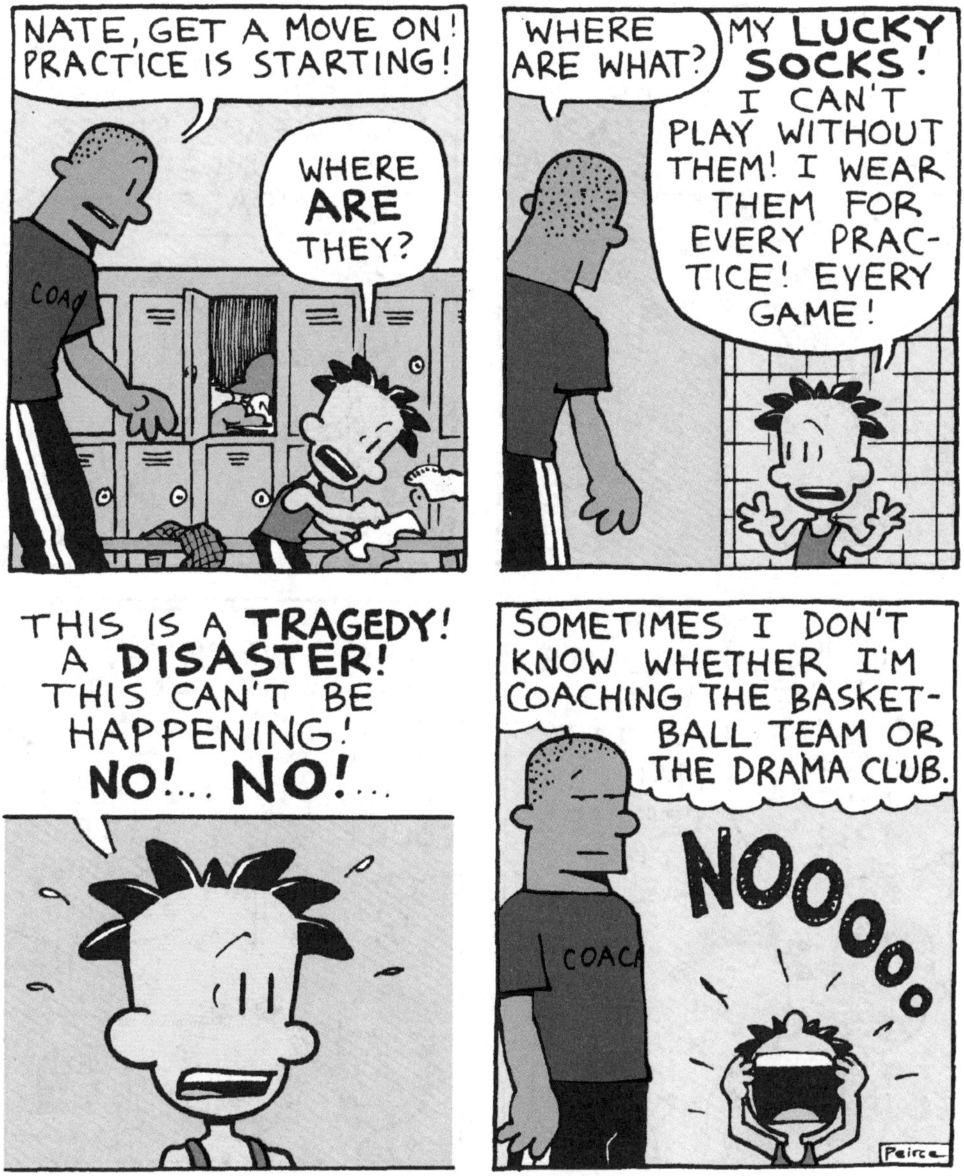

NATE, GET A MOVE ON! PRACTICE IS STARTING!
WHERE **ARE** THEY?
WHERE ARE WHAT?
MY **LUCKY SOCKS**! I CAN'T PLAY WITHOUT THEM! I WEAR THEM FOR EVERY PRAC-TICE! EVERY GAME!
THIS IS A **TRAGEDY**! A **DISASTER**! THIS CAN'T BE HAPPENING! **NO!... NO!**...
SOMETIMES I DON'T KNOW WHETHER I'M COACHING THE BASKET-BALL TEAM OR THE DRAMA CLUB.
NOOOOOO
Peirce

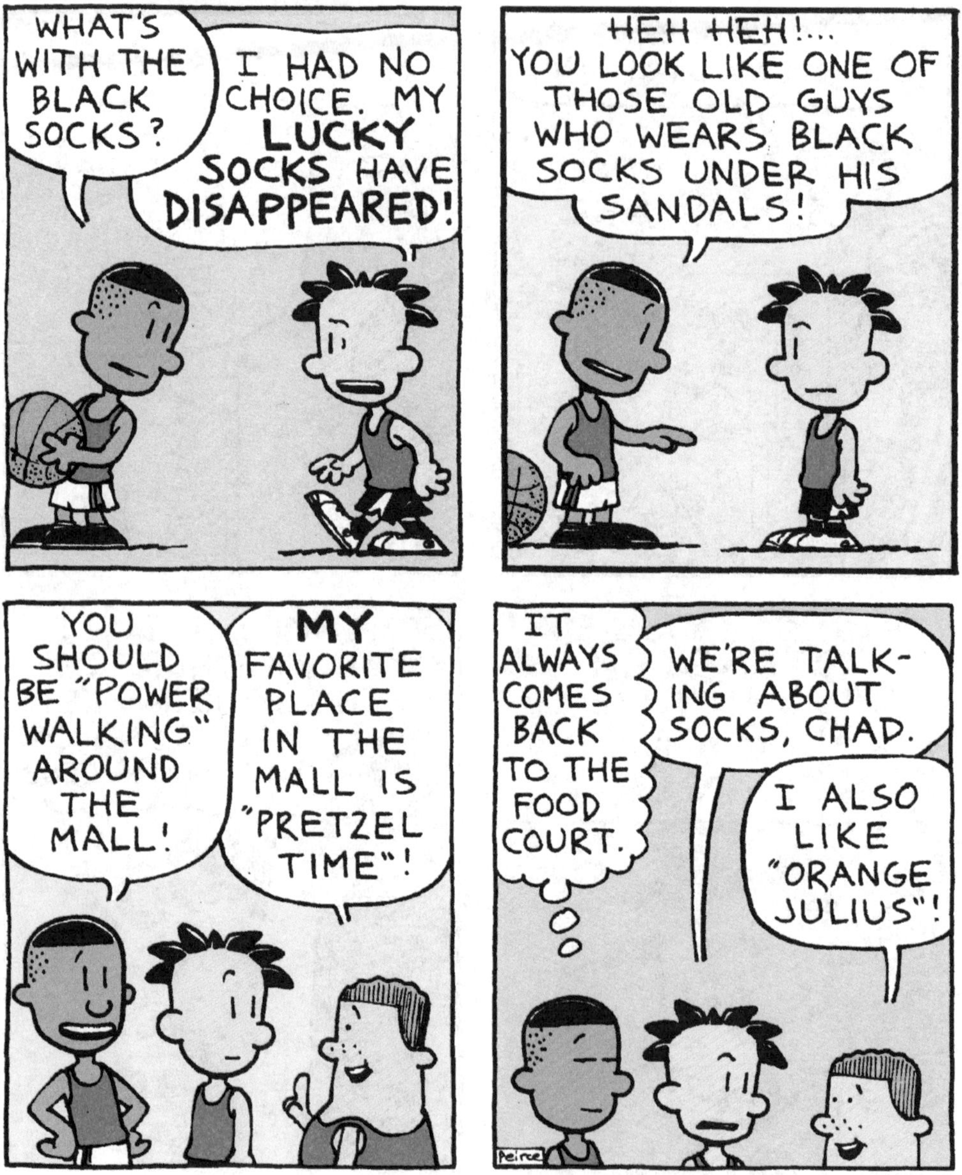
WHAT'S WITH THE BLACK SOCKS?
I HAD NO CHOICE. MY LUCKY SOCKS HAVE DISAPPEARED!
HEH HEH!... YOU LOOK LIKE ONE OF THOSE OLD GUYS WHO WEARS BLACK SOCKS UNDER HIS SANDALS!
YOU SHOULD BE "POWER WALKING" AROUND THE MALL!
MY FAVORITE PLACE IN THE MALL IS "PRETZEL TIME"!
IT ALWAYS COMES BACK TO THE FOOD COURT.
WE'RE TALKING ABOUT SOCKS, CHAD.
I ALSO LIKE "ORANGE JULIUS"!
Peirce

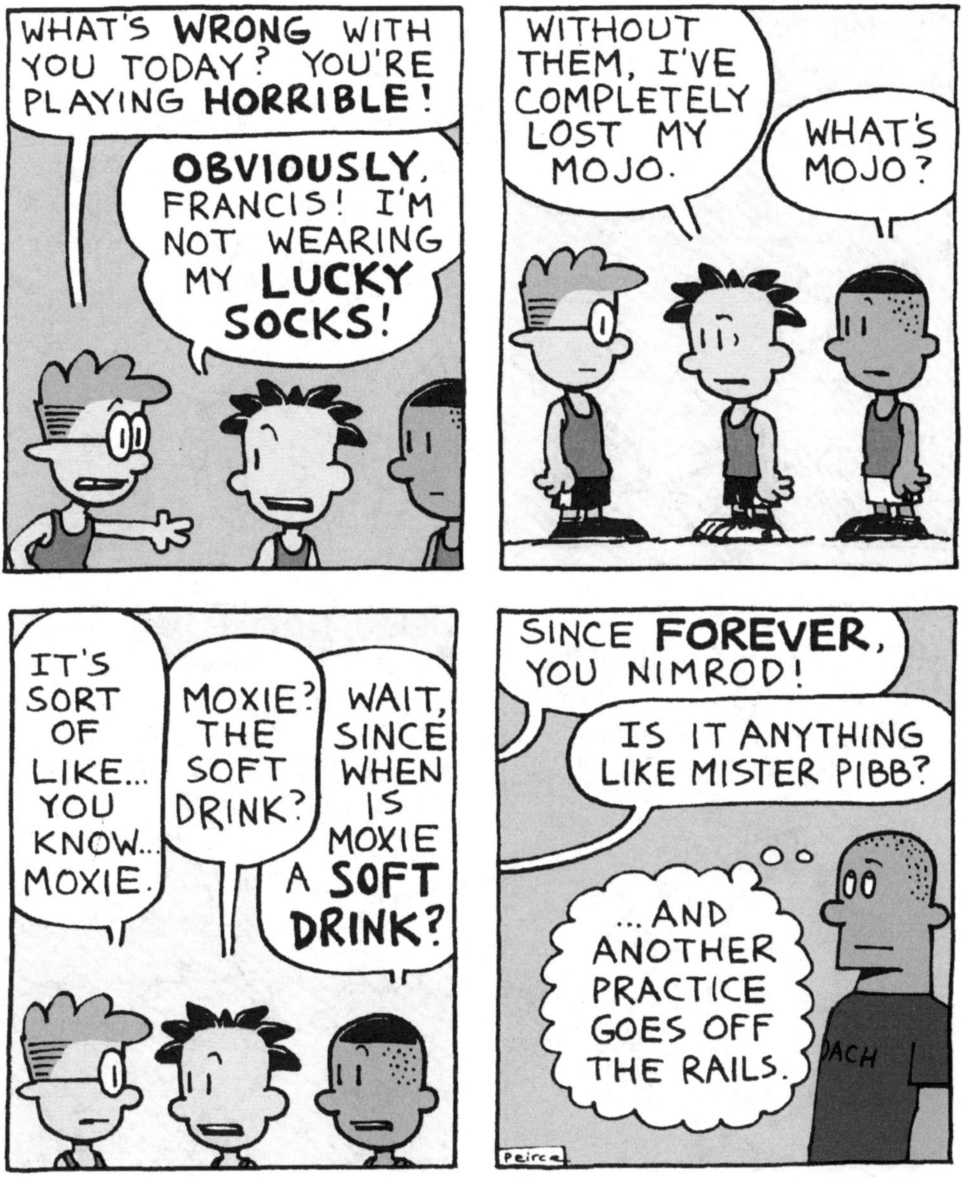
WHAT'S WRONG WITH YOU TODAY? YOU'RE PLAYING HORRIBLE!
OBVIOUSLY, FRANCIS! I'M NOT WEARING MY LUCKY SOCKS!
WITHOUT THEM, I'VE COMPLETELY LOST MY MOJO.
WHAT'S MOJO?
IT'S SORT OF LIKE... YOU KNOW... MOXIE.
MOXIE? THE SOFT DRINK?
WAIT, SINCE WHEN IS MOXIE A SOFT DRINK?
SINCE FOREVER, YOU NIMROD!
IS IT ANYTHING LIKE MISTER PIBB?
...AND ANOTHER PRACTICE GOES OFF THE RAILS.
Peirce

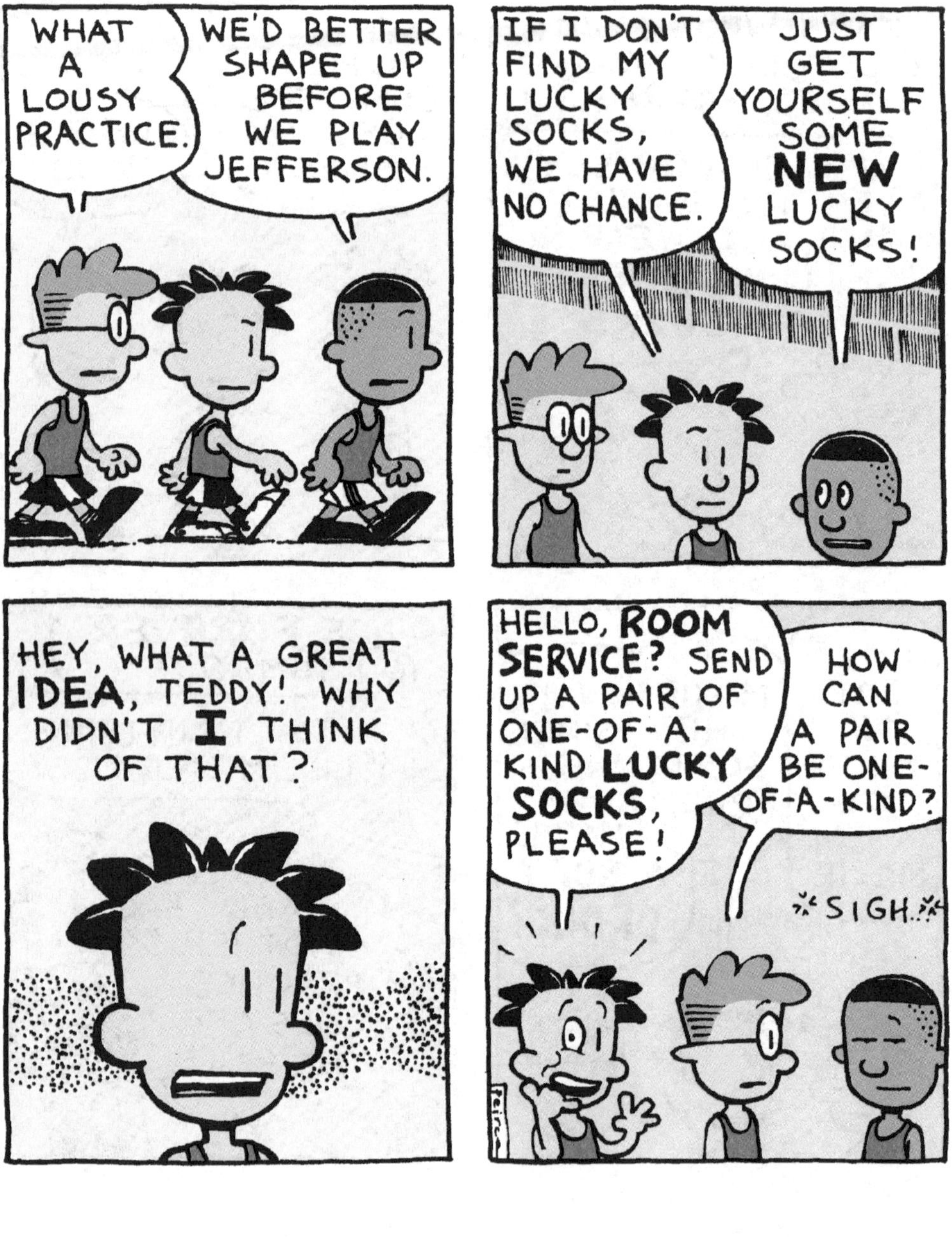
WHAT A LOUSY PRACTICE.
WE'D BETTER SHAPE UP BEFORE WE PLAY JEFFERSON.
IF I DON'T FIND MY LUCKY SOCKS, WE HAVE NO CHANCE.
JUST GET YOURSELF SOME NEW LUCKY SOCKS!
HEY, WHAT A GREAT IDEA, TEDDY! WHY DIDN'T I THINK OF THAT?
HELLO, ROOM SERVICE? SEND UP A PAIR OF ONE-OF-A-KIND LUCKY SOCKS, PLEASE!
HOW CAN A PAIR BE ONE-OF-A-KIND?
SIGH

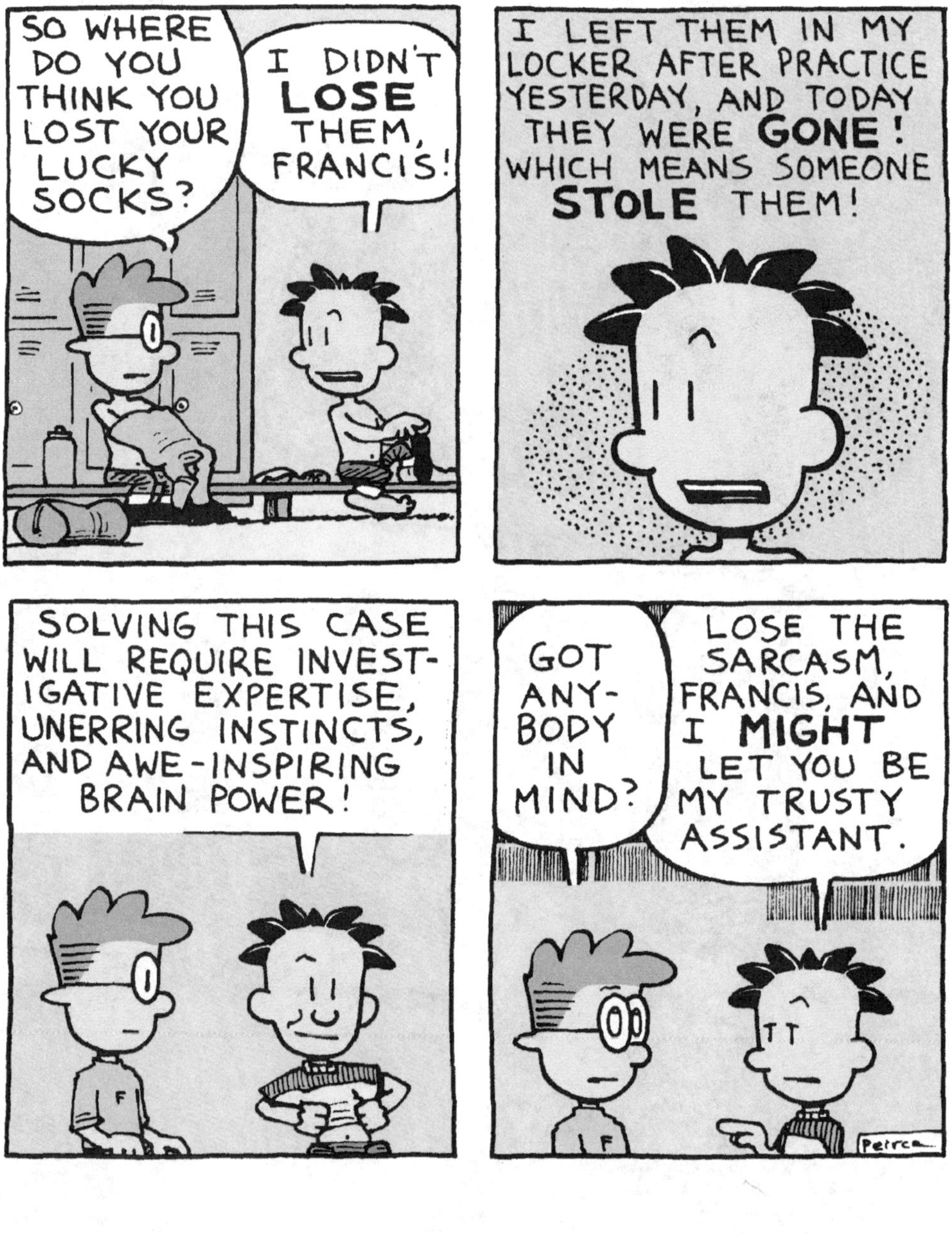
SO WHERE DO YOU THINK YOU LOST YOUR LUCKY SOCKS?
I DIDN'T **LOSE** THEM, FRANCIS!
I LEFT THEM IN MY LOCKER AFTER PRACTICE YESTERDAY, AND TODAY THEY WERE **GONE**! WHICH MEANS SOMEONE **STOLE** THEM!
SOLVING THIS CASE WILL REQUIRE INVESTIGATIVE EXPERTISE, UNERRING INSTINCTS, AND AWE-INSPIRING BRAIN POWER!
GOT ANYBODY IN MIND?
LOSE THE SARCASM, FRANCIS, AND I **MIGHT** LET YOU BE MY TRUSTY ASSISTANT.
Peirce

PLAY BALL!

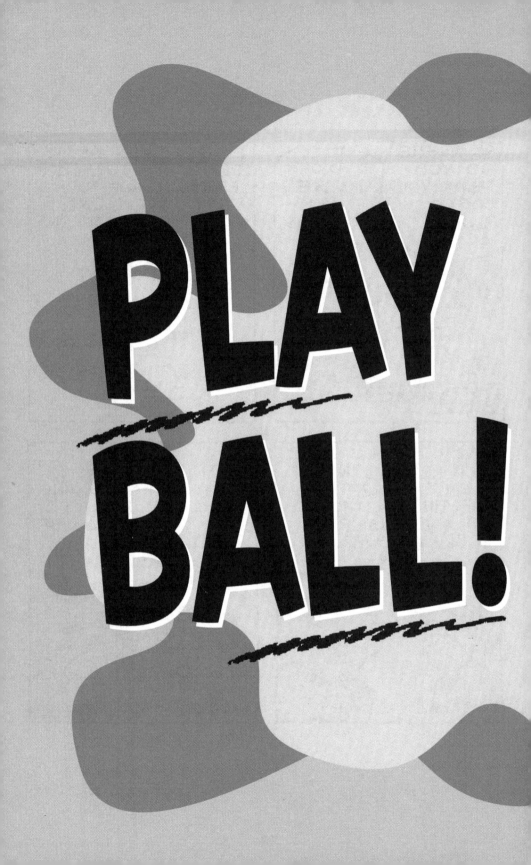

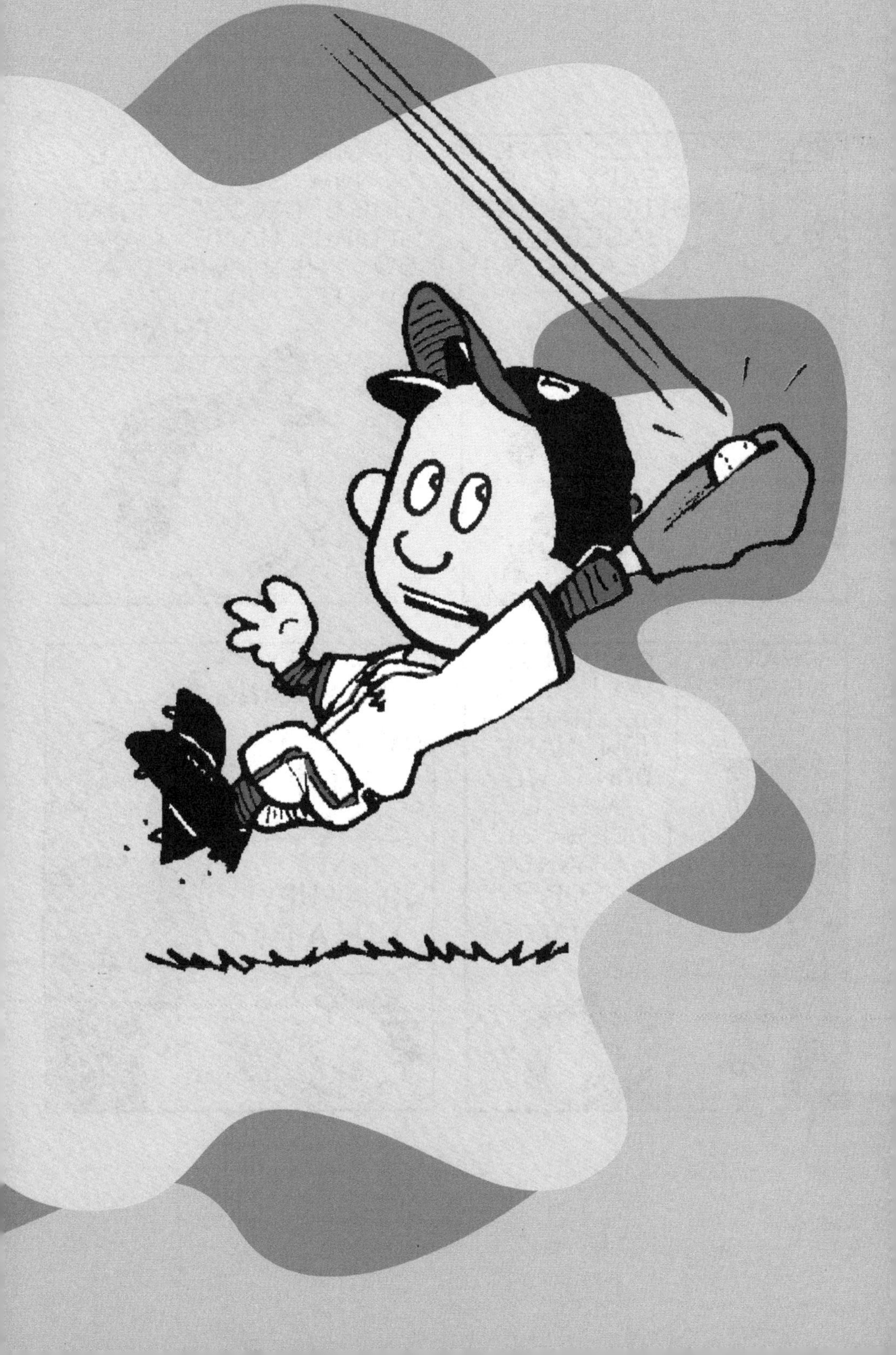

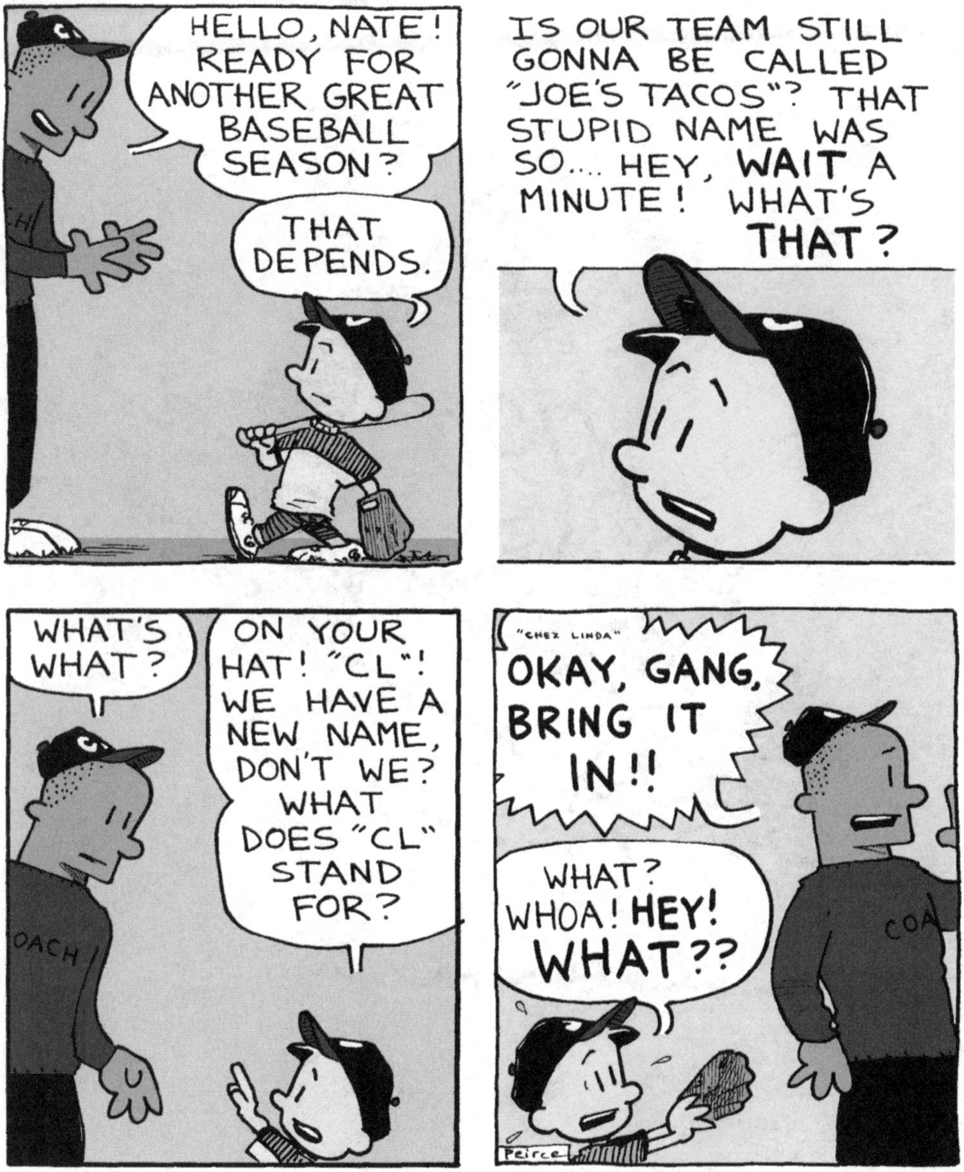
HELLO, NATE! READY FOR ANOTHER GREAT BASEBALL SEASON?
THAT DEPENDS.
IS OUR TEAM STILL GONNA BE CALLED "JOE'S TACOS"? THAT STUPID NAME WAS SO.... HEY, WAIT A MINUTE! WHAT'S THAT?
WHAT'S WHAT?
ON YOUR HAT! "CL"! WE HAVE A NEW NAME, DON'T WE? WHAT DOES "CL" STAND FOR?
"CHEZ LINDA"
OKAY, GANG, BRING IT IN!!
WHAT? WHOA! HEY! WHAT??
Peirce

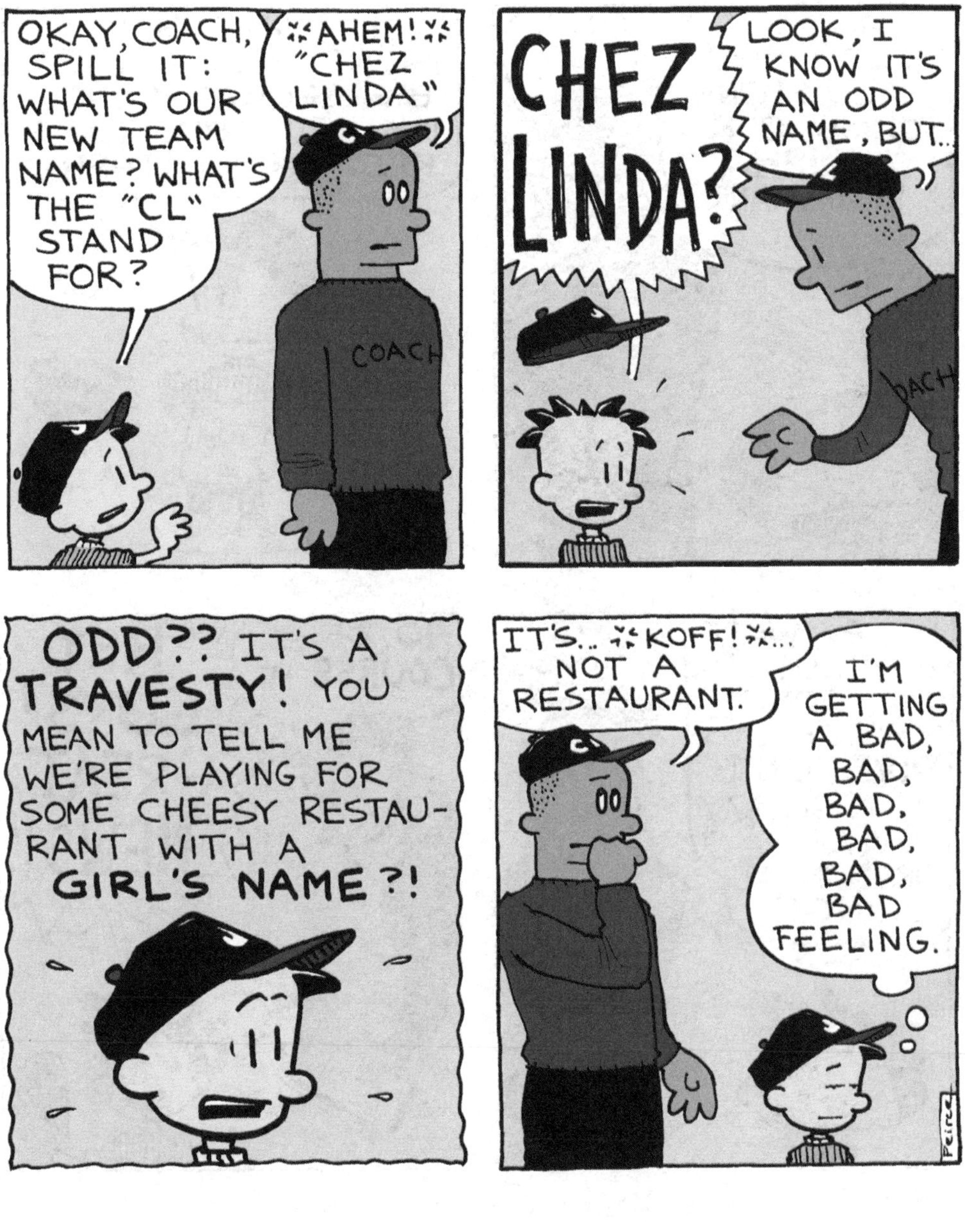
OKAY, COACH, SPILL IT: WHAT'S OUR NEW TEAM NAME? WHAT'S THE "CL" STAND FOR?
AHEM! "CHEZ LINDA"
COACH
CHEZ LINDA?
LOOK, I KNOW IT'S AN ODD NAME, BUT...
ODD?? IT'S A TRAVESTY! YOU MEAN TO TELL ME WE'RE PLAYING FOR SOME CHEESY RESTAU-RANT WITH A GIRL'S NAME?!
IT'S... *KOFF!*... NOT A RESTAURANT.
I'M GETTING A BAD, BAD, BAD, BAD, BAD, BAD FEELING.
Peirce

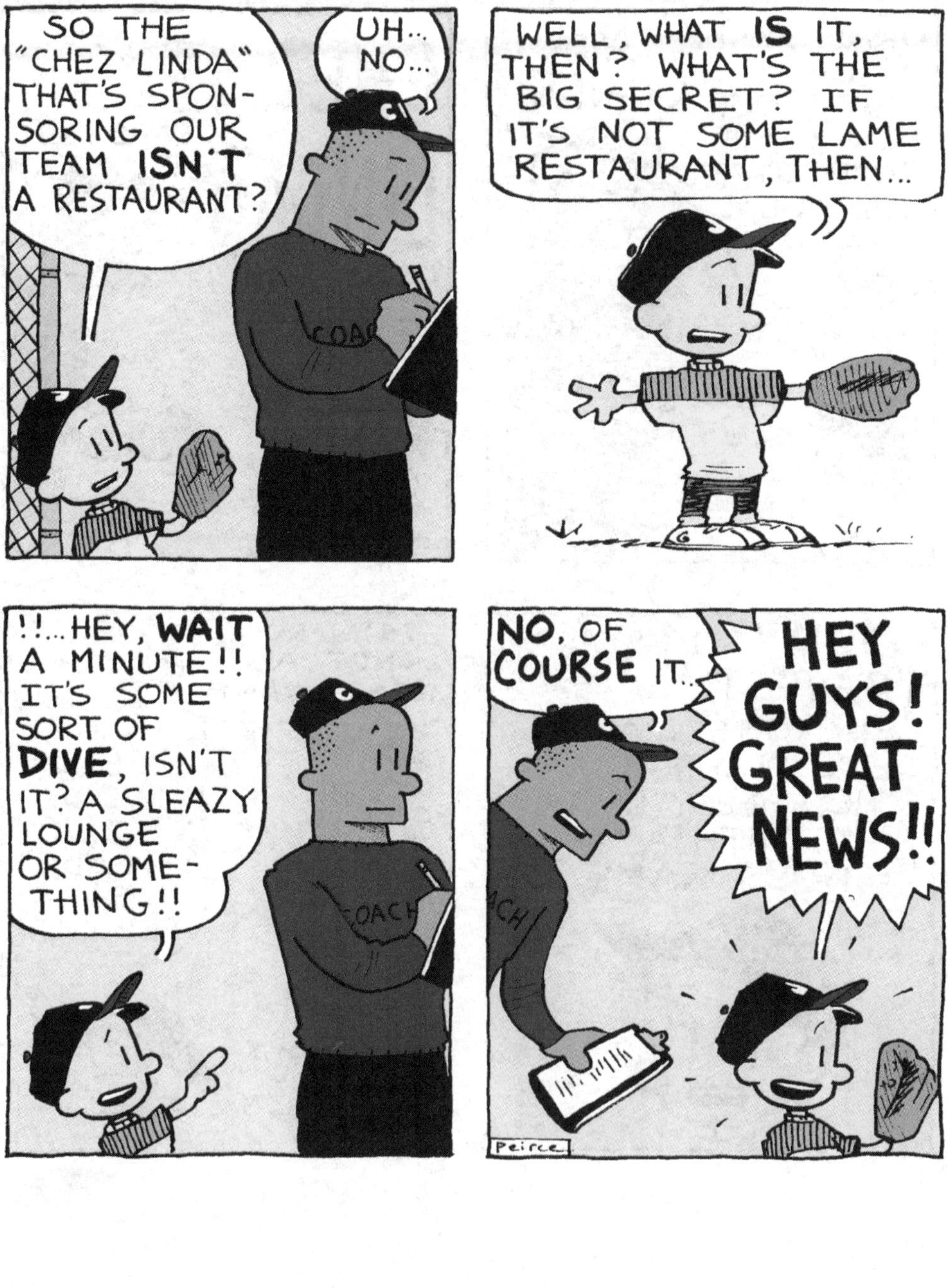
SO THE "CHEZ LINDA" THAT'S SPON-SORING OUR TEAM ISN'T A RESTAURANT?
UH... NO...
WELL, WHAT IS IT, THEN? WHAT'S THE BIG SECRET? IF IT'S NOT SOME LAME RESTAURANT, THEN...
!!...HEY, WAIT A MINUTE!! IT'S SOME SORT OF DIVE, ISN'T IT? A SLEAZY LOUNGE OR SOME-THING!!
NO, OF COURSE IT...
HEY GUYS! GREAT NEWS!!
Peirce

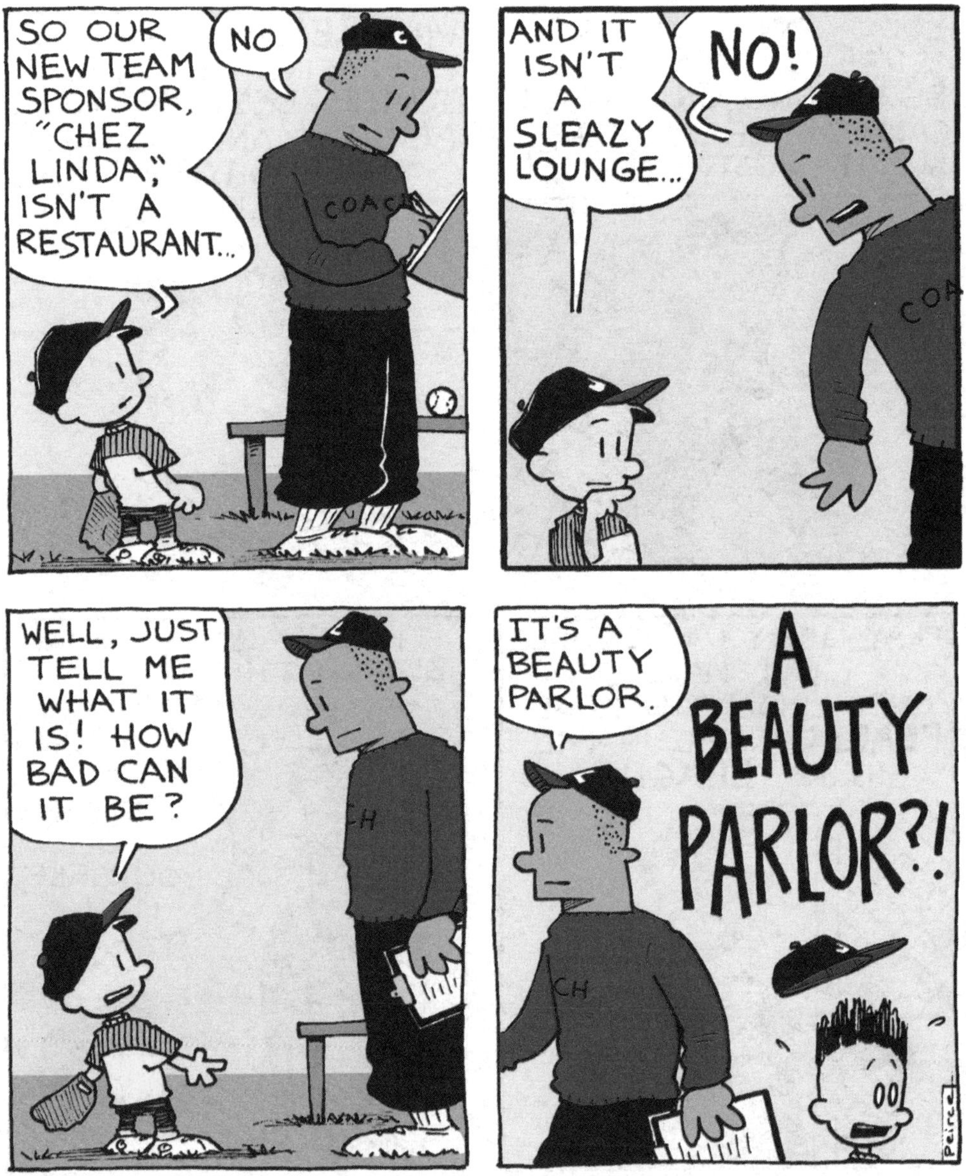
SO OUR NEW TEAM SPONSOR, "CHEZ LINDA," ISN'T A RESTAURANT...
NO
AND IT ISN'T A SLEAZY LOUNGE...
NO!
WELL, JUST TELL ME WHAT IT IS! HOW BAD CAN IT BE?
IT'S A BEAUTY PARLOR.
A BEAUTY PARLOR?!
Peirce

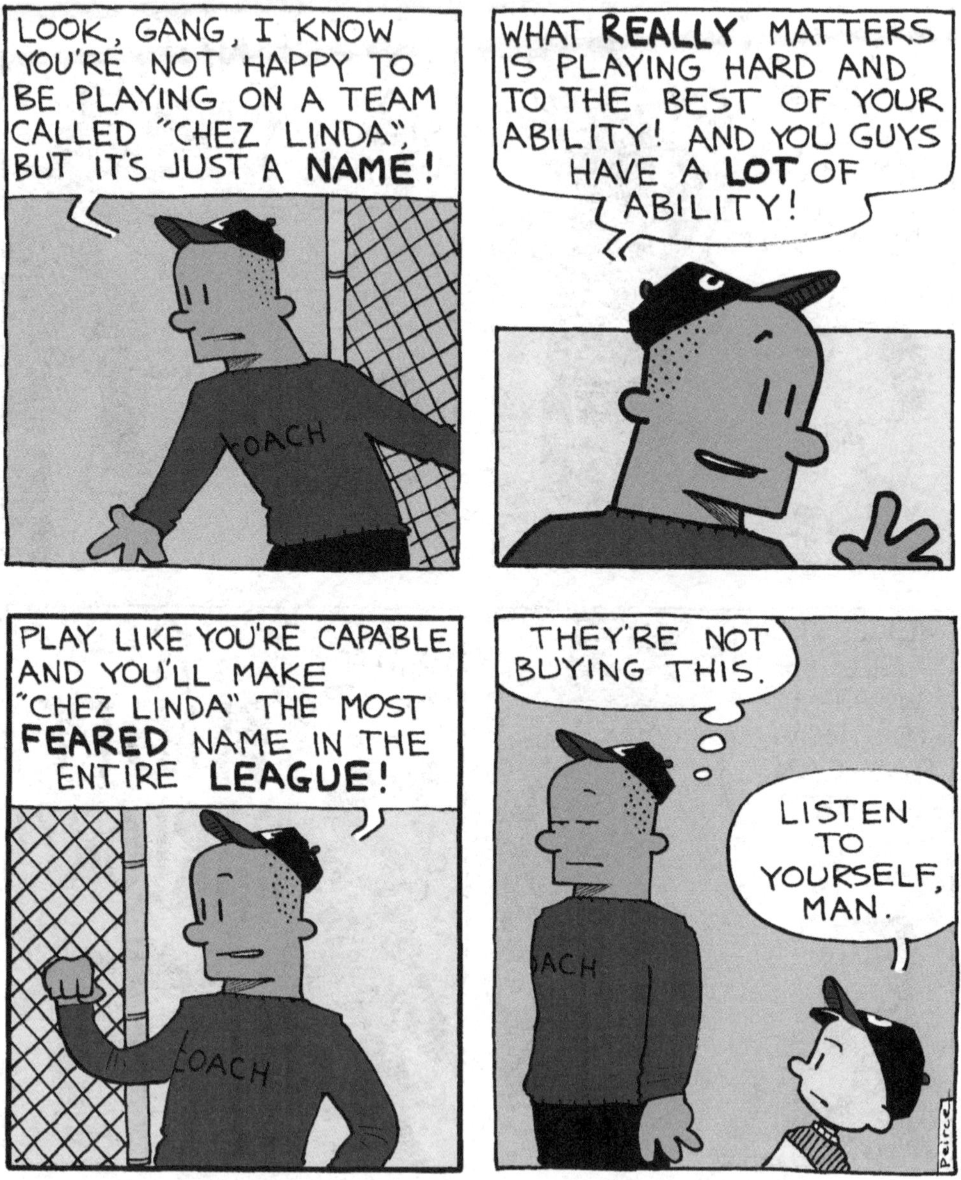
LOOK, GANG, I KNOW YOU'RE NOT HAPPY TO BE PLAYING ON A TEAM CALLED "CHEZ LINDA", BUT IT'S JUST A NAME!
COACH
WHAT REALLY MATTERS IS PLAYING HARD AND TO THE BEST OF YOUR ABILITY! AND YOU GUYS HAVE A LOT OF ABILITY!
PLAY LIKE YOU'RE CAPABLE AND YOU'LL MAKE "CHEZ LINDA" THE MOST FEARED NAME IN THE ENTIRE LEAGUE!
OACH
THEY'RE NOT BUYING THIS.
LISTEN TO YOURSELF, MAN.
ACH
Peirce

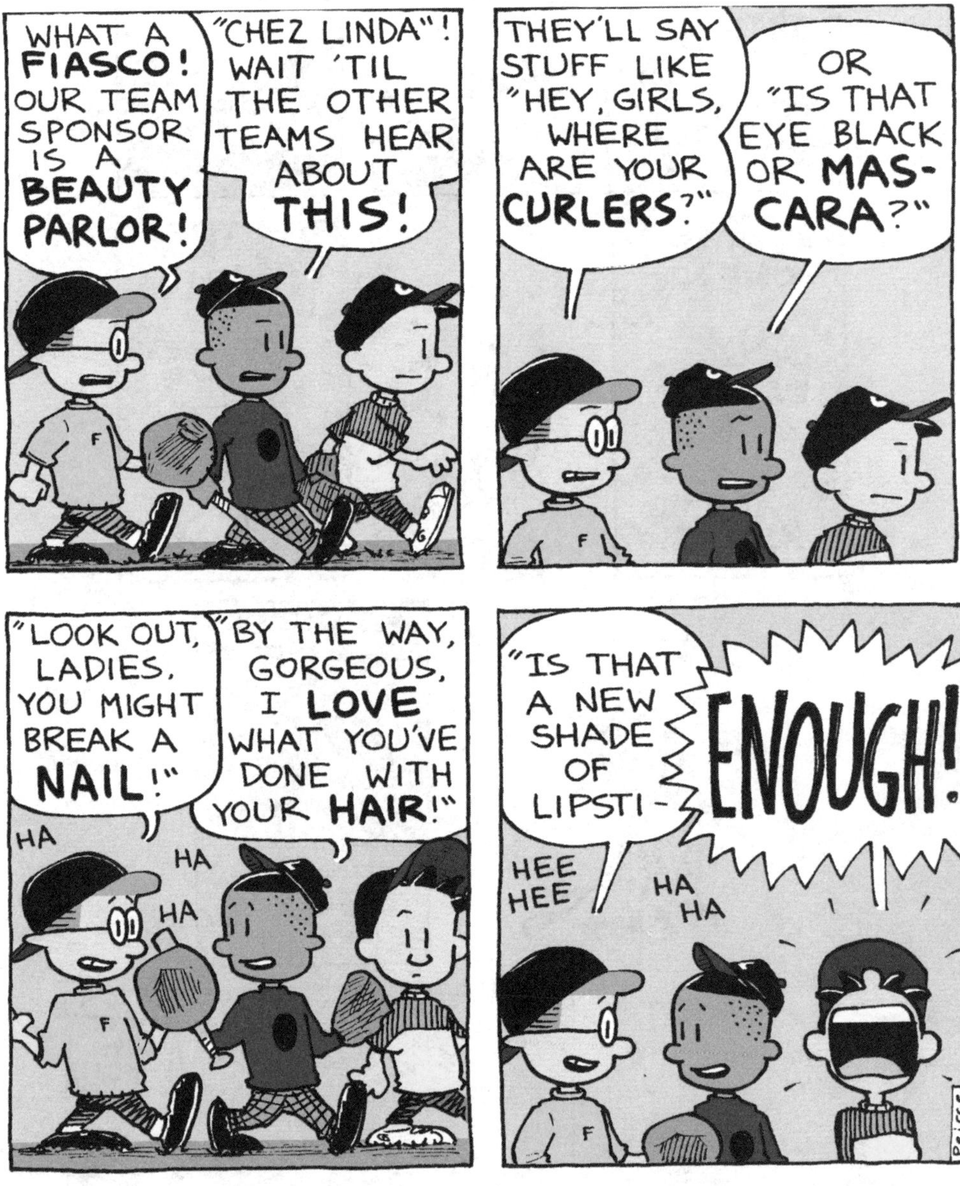
WHAT A FIASCO! OUR TEAM SPONSOR IS A BEAUTY PARLOR!
"CHEZ LINDA"! WAIT 'TIL THE OTHER TEAMS HEAR ABOUT THIS!
THEY'LL SAY STUFF LIKE "HEY, GIRLS, WHERE ARE YOUR CURLERS?"
OR "IS THAT EYE BLACK OR MAS-CARA?"
"LOOK OUT, LADIES. YOU MIGHT BREAK A NAIL!"
"BY THE WAY, GORGEOUS, I LOVE WHAT YOU'VE DONE WITH YOUR HAIR!"
HA
HA
HA
"IS THAT A NEW SHADE OF LIPSTI-
ENOUGH!
HEE HEE
HA HA
Peirce

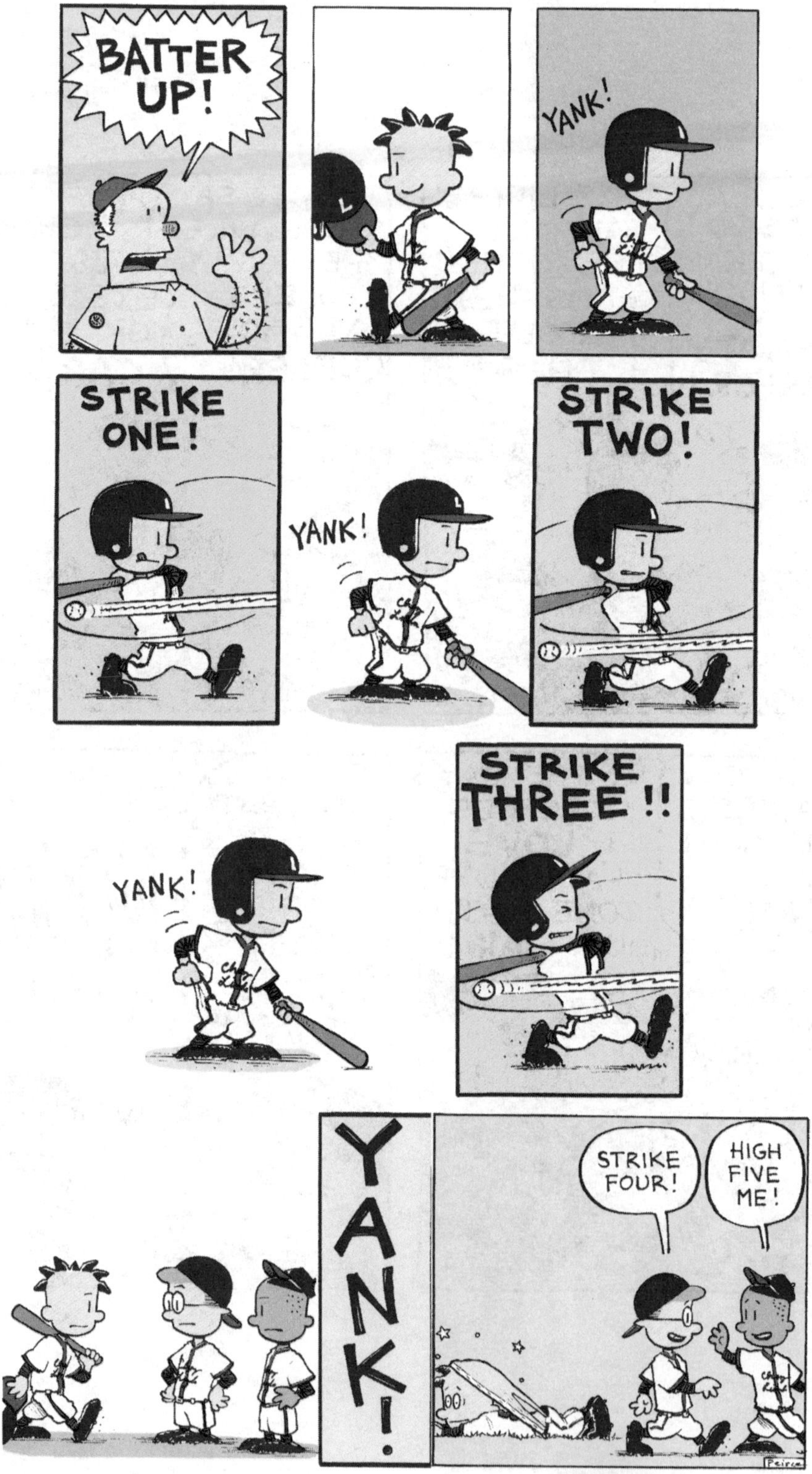
BATTER UP!
YANK!
STRIKE ONE!
YANK!
STRIKE TWO!
YANK!
STRIKE THREE!!
YANK!
STRIKE FOUR!
HIGH FIVE ME!
Peirce

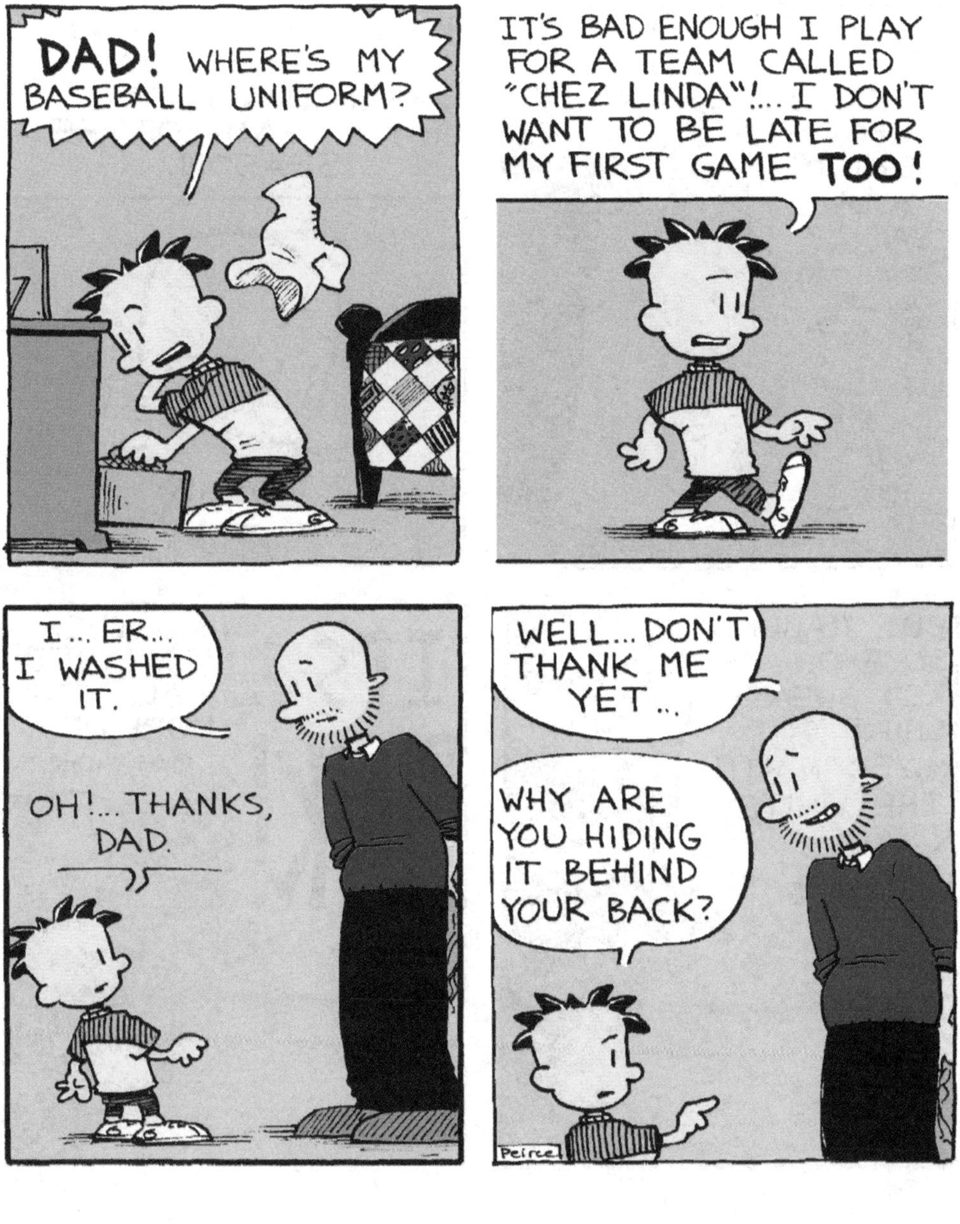
DAD! WHERE'S MY BASEBALL UNIFORM?
IT'S BAD ENOUGH I PLAY FOR A TEAM CALLED "CHEZ LINDA"!... I DON'T WANT TO BE LATE FOR MY FIRST GAME TOO!
I... ER... I WASHED IT.
OH!... THANKS, DAD.
WELL... DON'T THANK ME YET...
WHY ARE YOU HIDING IT BEHIND YOUR BACK?
Peirce

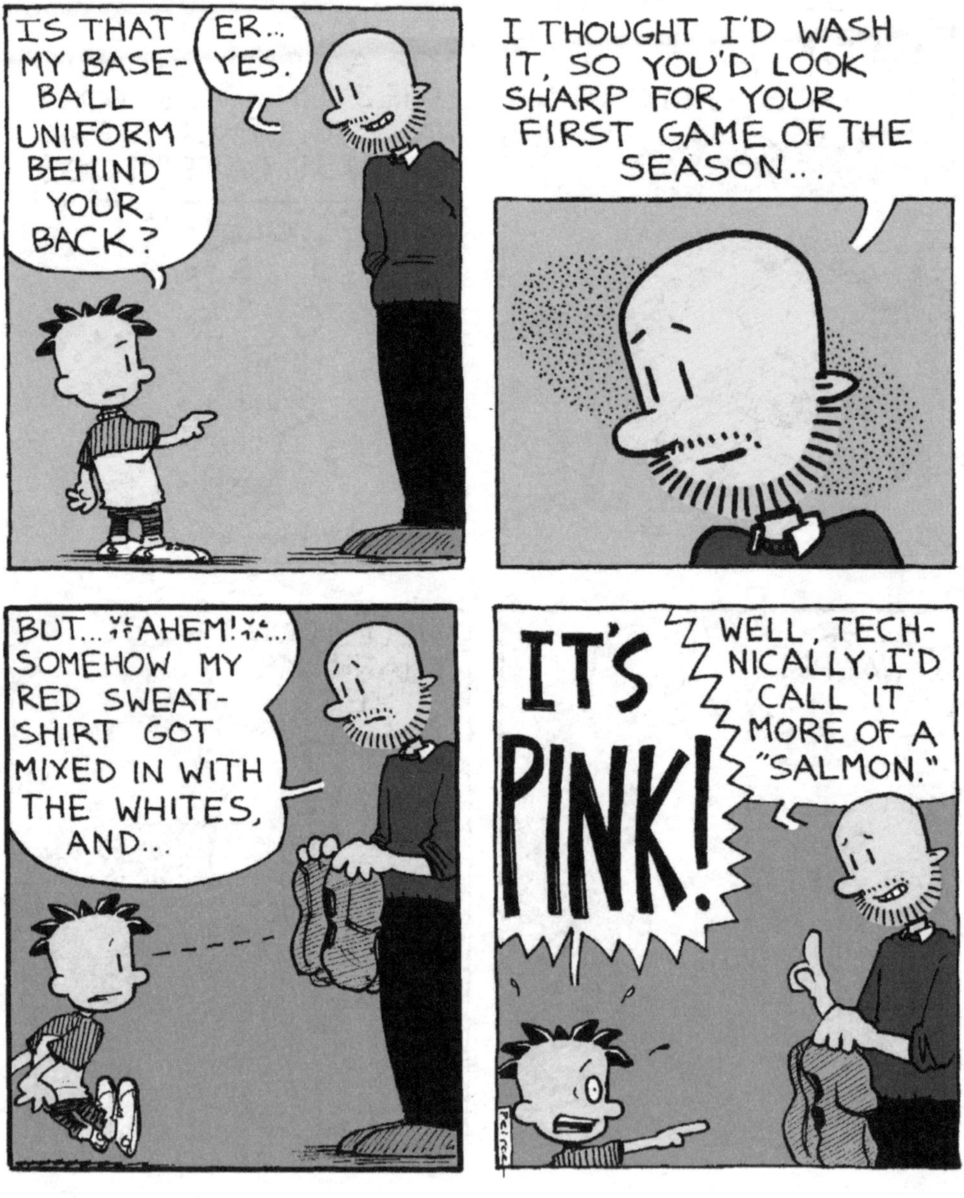
IS THAT MY BASE-BALL UNIFORM BEHIND YOUR BACK?
ER... YES.
I THOUGHT I'D WASH IT, SO YOU'D LOOK SHARP FOR YOUR FIRST GAME OF THE SEASON...
BUT... AHEM!... SOMEHOW MY RED SWEAT-SHIRT GOT MIXED IN WITH THE WHITES, AND...
IT'S PINK!
WELL, TECH-NICALLY, I'D CALL IT MORE OF A "SALMON."

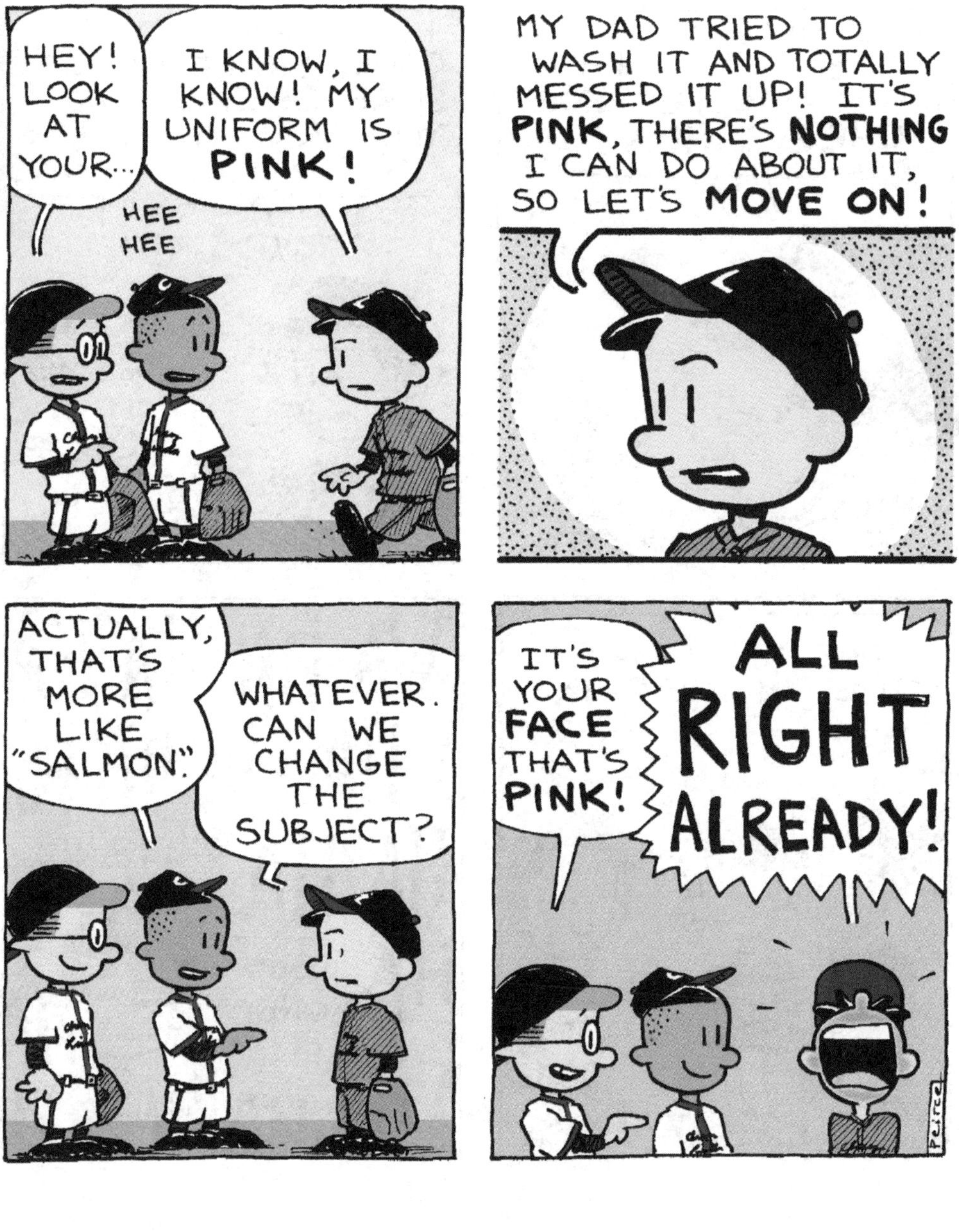
HEY! LOOK AT YOUR...
I KNOW, I KNOW! MY UNIFORM IS PINK!
HEE HEE
MY DAD TRIED TO WASH IT AND TOTALLY MESSED IT UP! IT'S PINK, THERE'S NOTHING I CAN DO ABOUT IT, SO LET'S MOVE ON!
ACTUALLY, THAT'S MORE LIKE "SALMON."
WHATEVER. CAN WE CHANGE THE SUBJECT?
IT'S YOUR FACE THAT'S PINK!
ALL RIGHT ALREADY!
Peirce

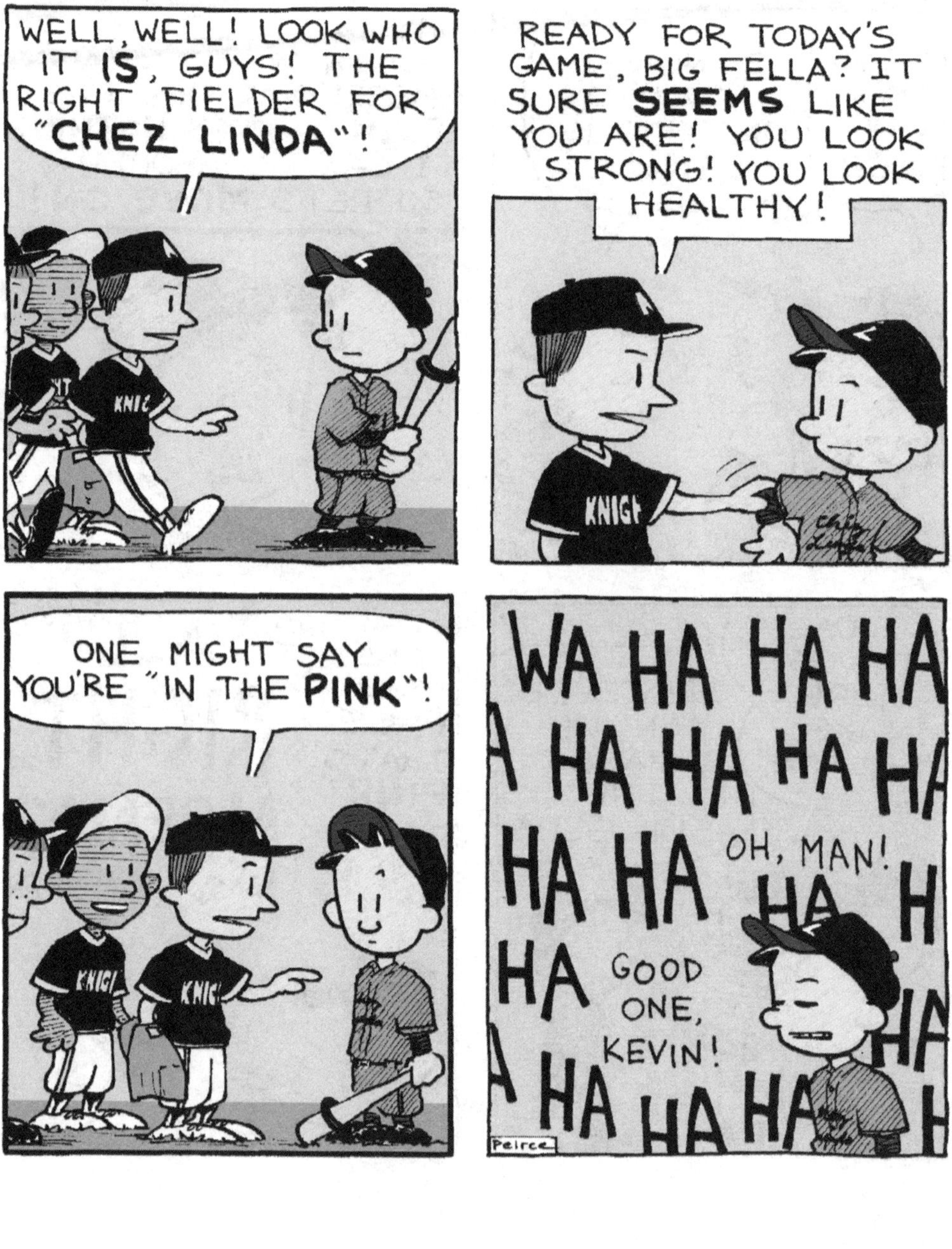
WELL, WELL! LOOK WHO IT IS, GUYS! THE RIGHT FIELDER FOR "CHEZ LINDA"!
READY FOR TODAY'S GAME, BIG FELLA? IT SURE SEEMS LIKE YOU ARE! YOU LOOK STRONG! YOU LOOK HEALTHY!
ONE MIGHT SAY YOU'RE "IN THE PINK"!
WA HA HA HA HA HA HA HA HA HA HA HA HA HA HA HA HA HA HA
OH, MAN!
GOOD ONE, KEVIN!
Peirce

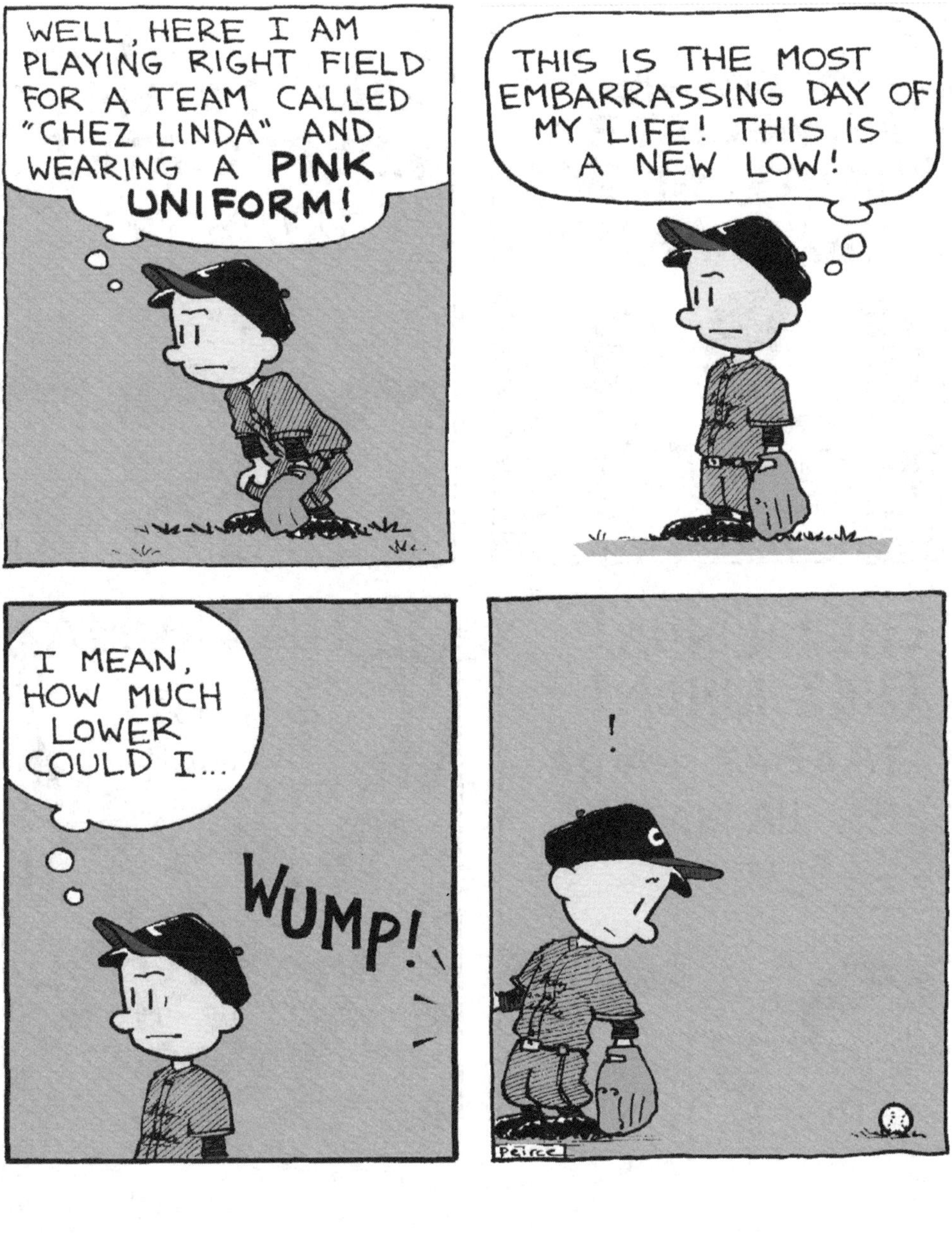
WELL, HERE I AM PLAYING RIGHT FIELD FOR A TEAM CALLED "CHEZ LINDA" AND WEARING A **PINK UNIFORM!**
THIS IS THE MOST EMBARRASSING DAY OF MY LIFE! THIS IS A NEW LOW!
I MEAN, HOW MUCH LOWER COULD I...
WUMP!
!
PEIRCE

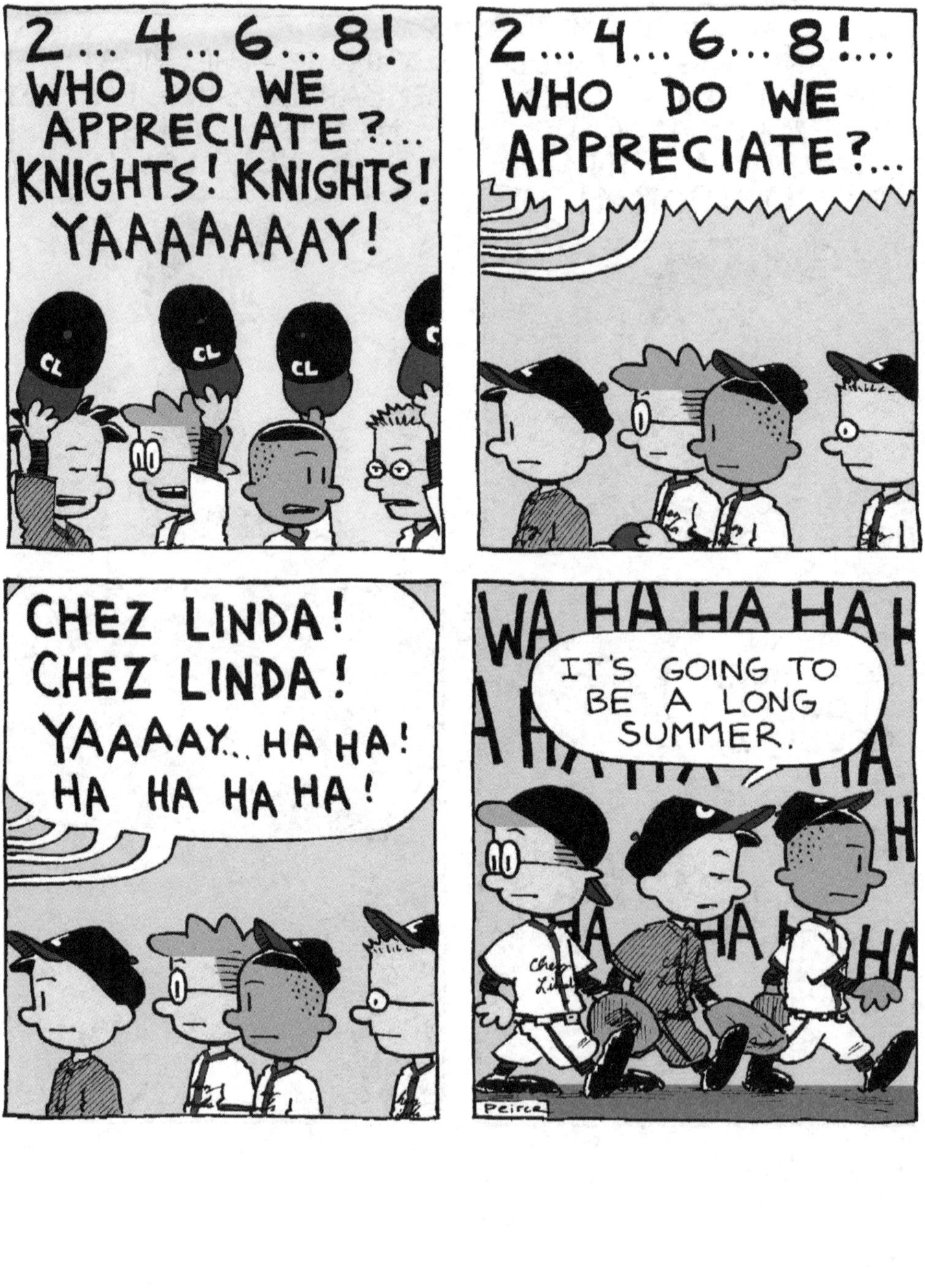
2... 4... 6... 8!
WHO DO WE APPRECIATE?...
KNIGHTS! KNIGHTS!
YAAAAAAAY!
2... 4... 6... 8!...
WHO DO WE APPRECIATE?...
CHEZ LINDA! CHEZ LINDA! YAAAAY... HA HA! HA HA HA HA!
WA HA HA HA HA
IT'S GOING TO BE A LONG SUMMER.
Peirce

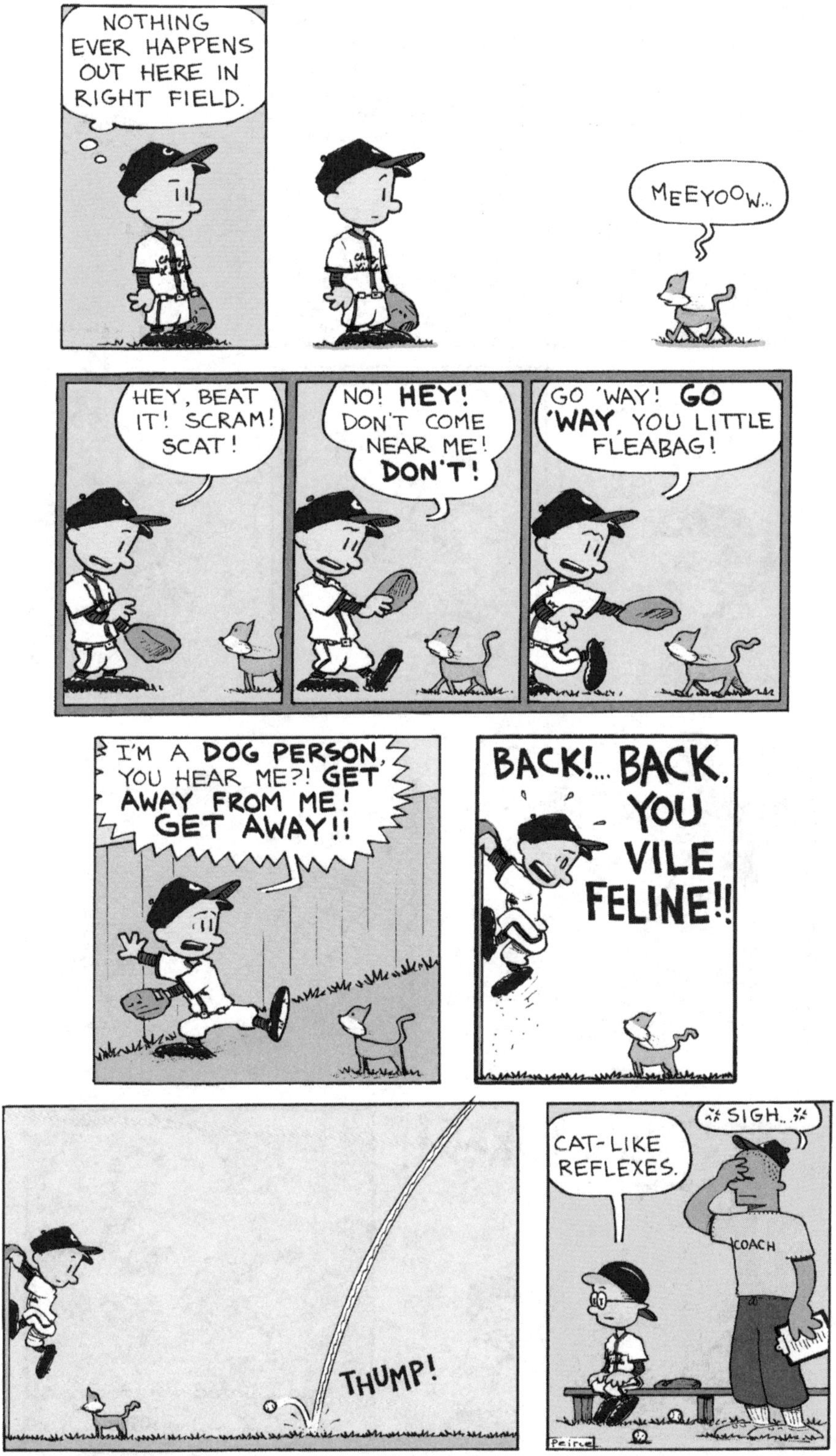
NOTHING EVER HAPPENS OUT HERE IN RIGHT FIELD.
MEEYOOW...
HEY, BEAT IT! SCRAM! SCAT!
NO! HEY! DON'T COME NEAR ME! DON'T!
GO 'WAY! GO 'WAY, YOU LITTLE FLEABAG!
I'M A DOG PERSON, YOU HEAR ME?! GET AWAY FROM ME! GET AWAY!!
BACK!... BACK, YOU VILE FELINE!!
THUMP!
SIGH...
CAT-LIKE REFLEXES.
COACH
Peirce

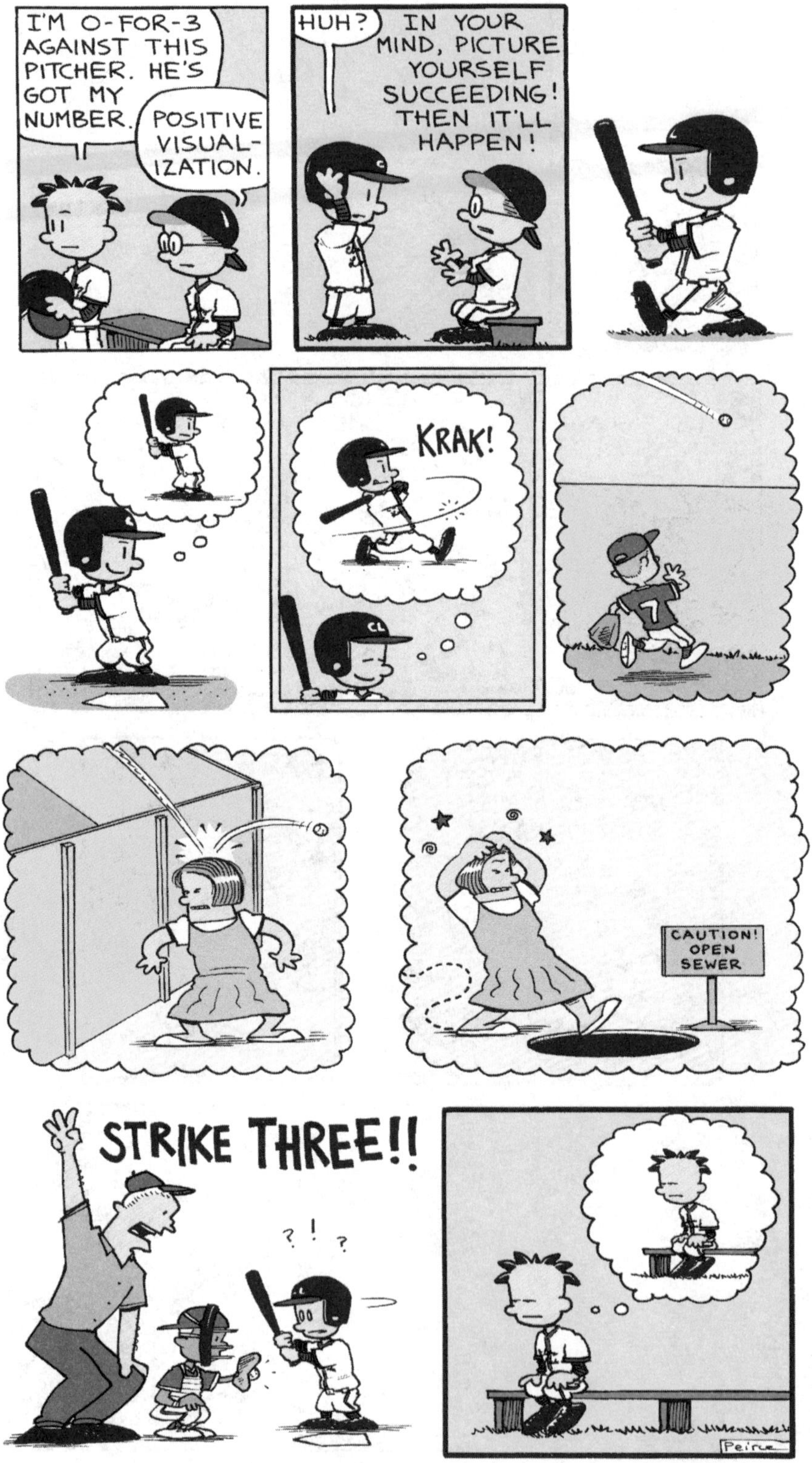
I'M O-FOR-3 AGAINST THIS PITCHER. HE'S GOT MY NUMBER.
POSITIVE VISUALIZATION.
HUH?
IN YOUR MIND, PICTURE YOURSELF SUCCEEDING! THEN IT'LL HAPPEN!
KRAK!
7
CAUTION! OPEN SEWER
STRIKE THREE!!
? ! ?
Peirce

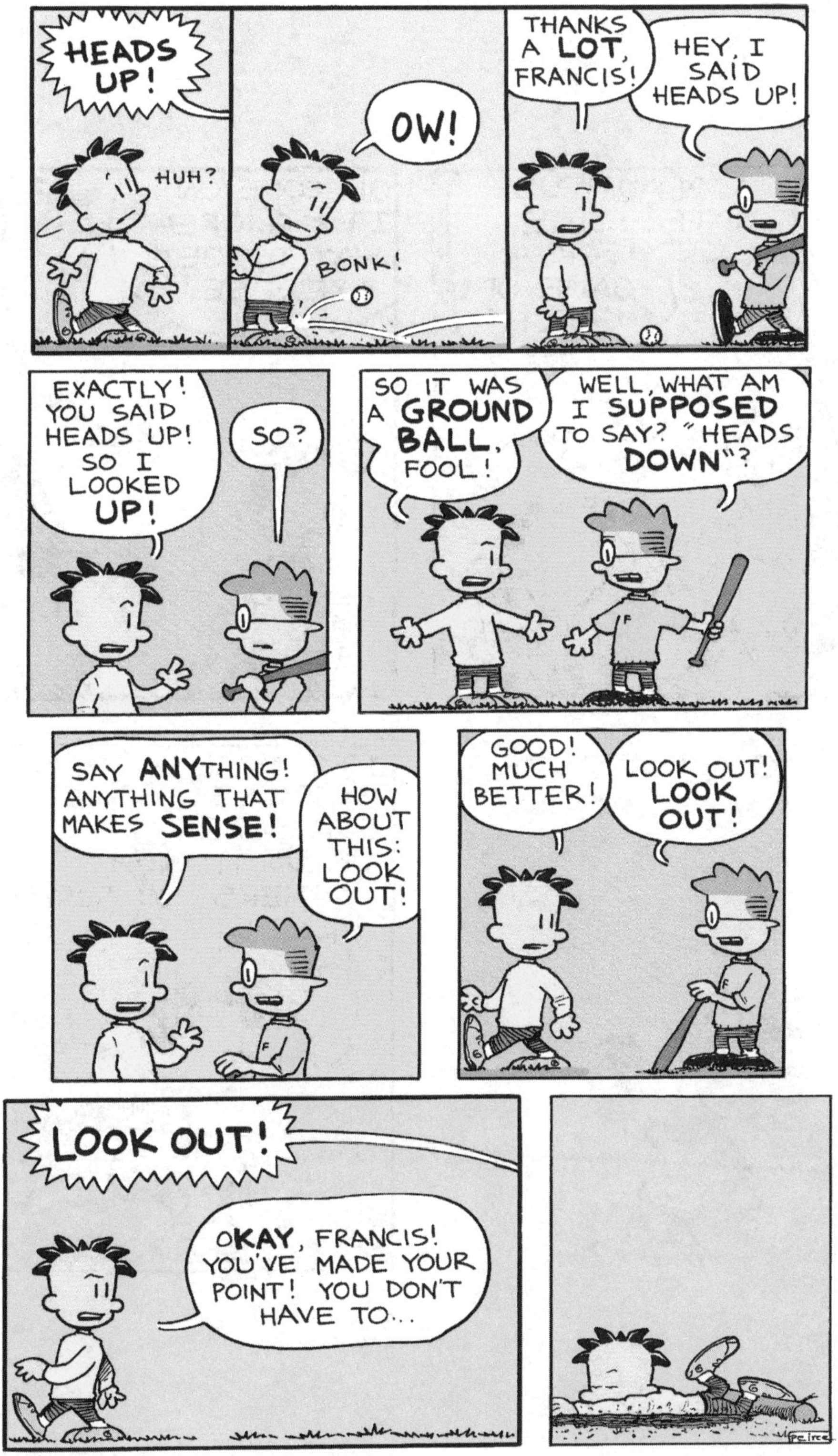
HEADS UP!
HUH?
OW!
BONK!
THANKS A LOT, FRANCIS!
HEY, I SAID HEADS UP!
EXACTLY! YOU SAID HEADS UP! SO I LOOKED UP!
SO?
SO IT WAS A GROUND BALL, FOOL!
WELL, WHAT AM I SUPPOSED TO SAY? "HEADS DOWN"?
SAY ANYTHING! ANYTHING THAT MAKES SENSE!
HOW ABOUT THIS: LOOK OUT!
GOOD! MUCH BETTER!
LOOK OUT! LOOK OUT!
LOOK OUT!
OKAY, FRANCIS! YOU'VE MADE YOUR POINT! YOU DON'T HAVE TO...

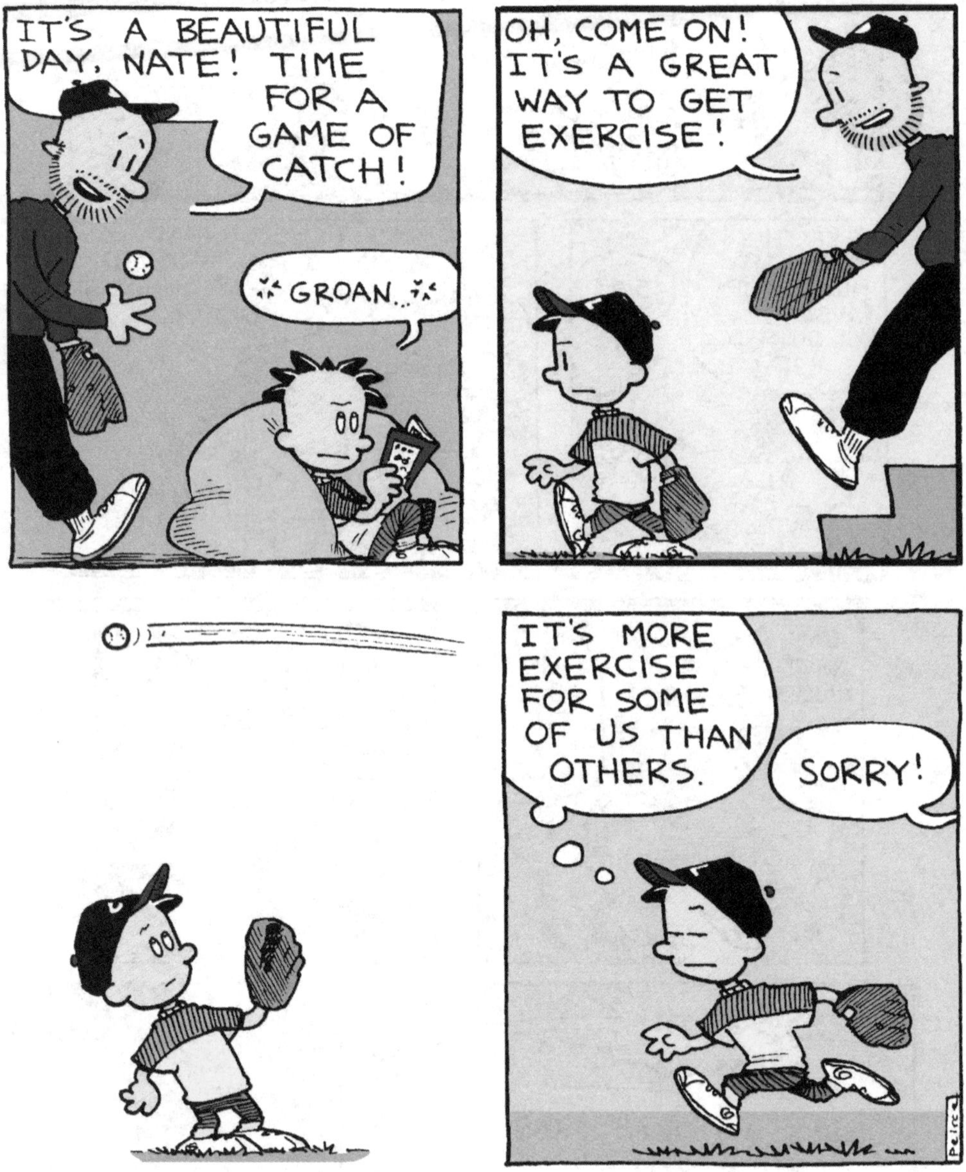
IT'S A BEAUTIFUL DAY, NATE! TIME FOR A GAME OF CATCH!
GROAN...
OH, COME ON! IT'S A GREAT WAY TO GET EXERCISE!
IT'S MORE EXERCISE FOR SOME OF US THAN OTHERS.
SORRY!
Peirce

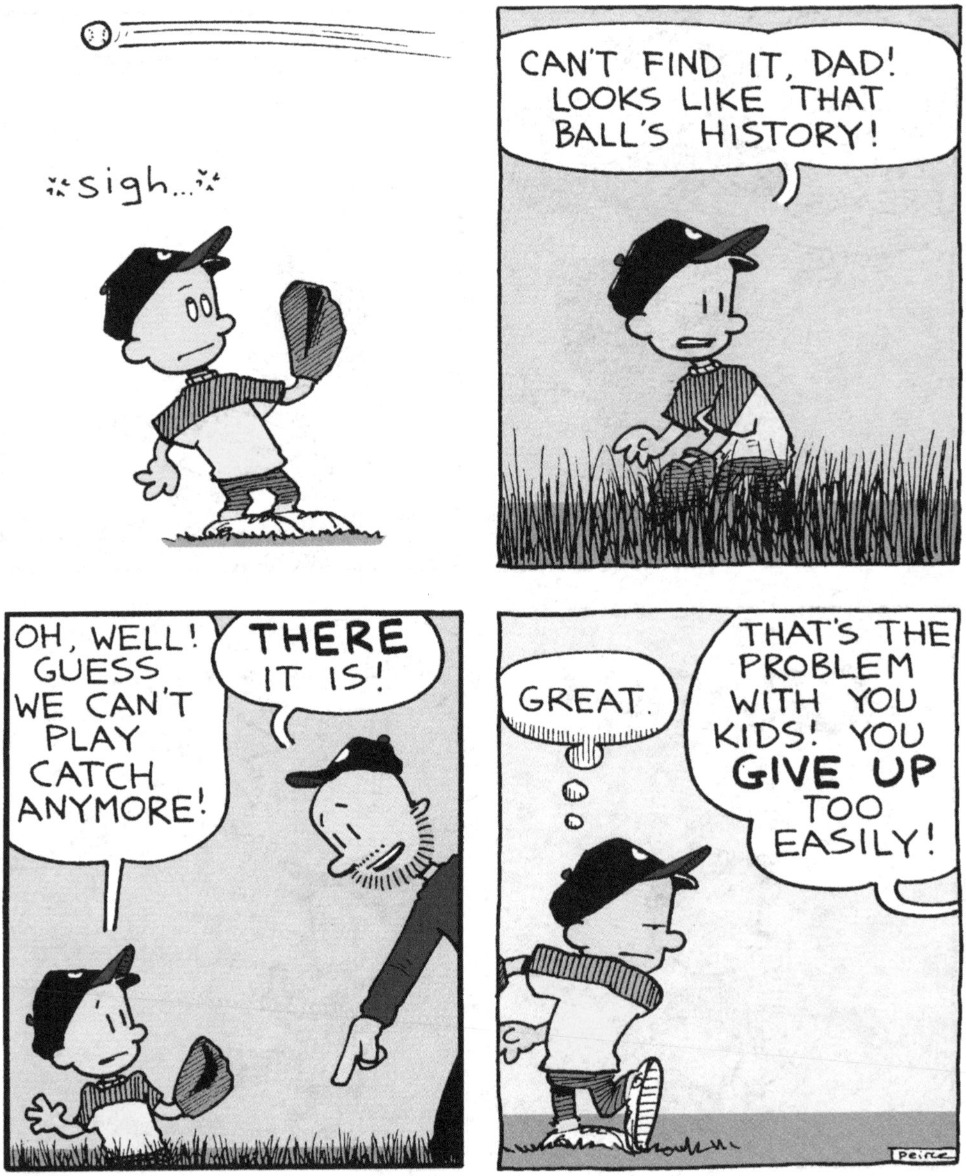

sigh...
CAN'T FIND IT, DAD! LOOKS LIKE THAT BALL'S HISTORY!
OH, WELL! GUESS WE CAN'T PLAY CATCH ANYMORE!
THERE IT IS!
GREAT.
THAT'S THE PROBLEM WITH YOU KIDS! YOU GIVE UP TOO EASILY!
peirce

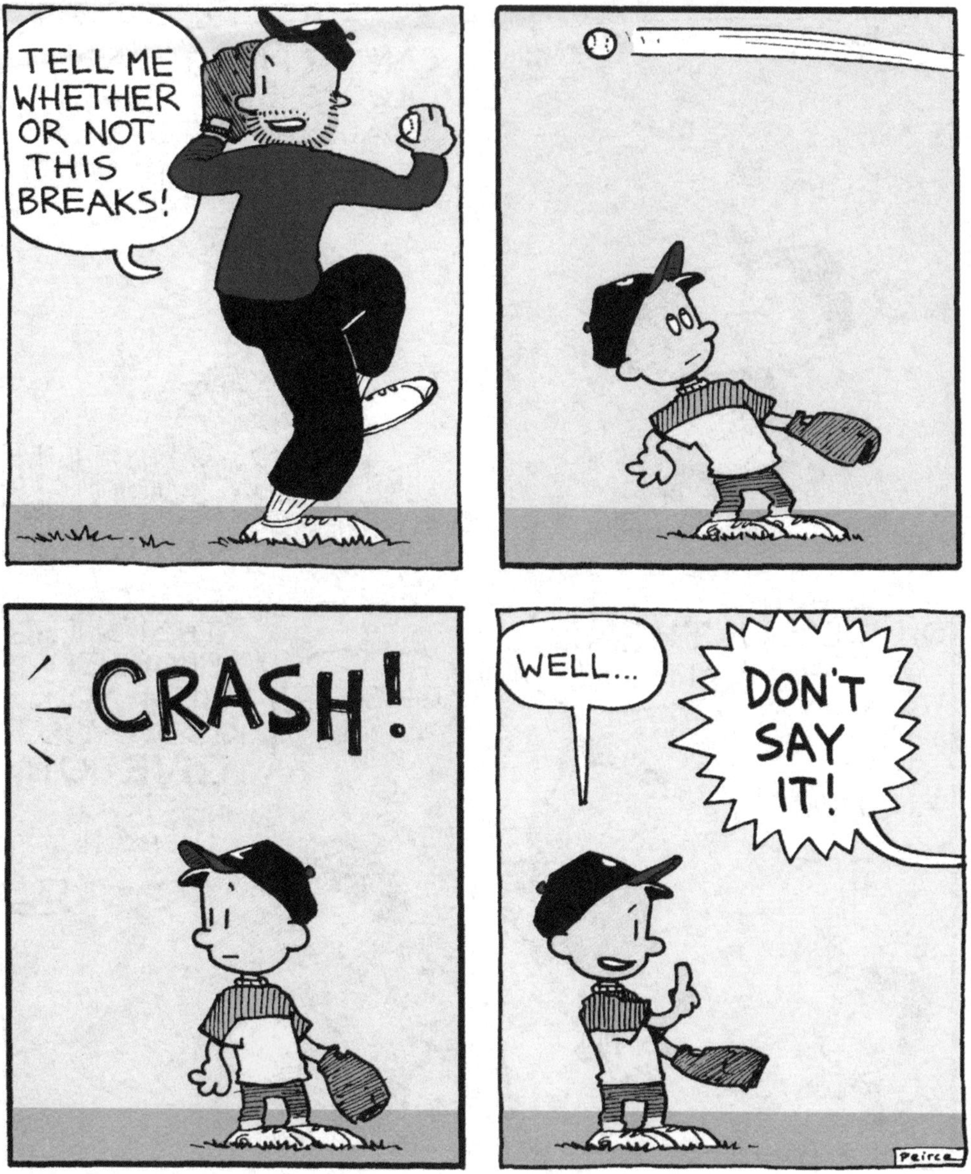
TELL ME WHETHER OR NOT THIS BREAKS!
CRASH!
WELL...
DON'T SAY IT!
Peirce

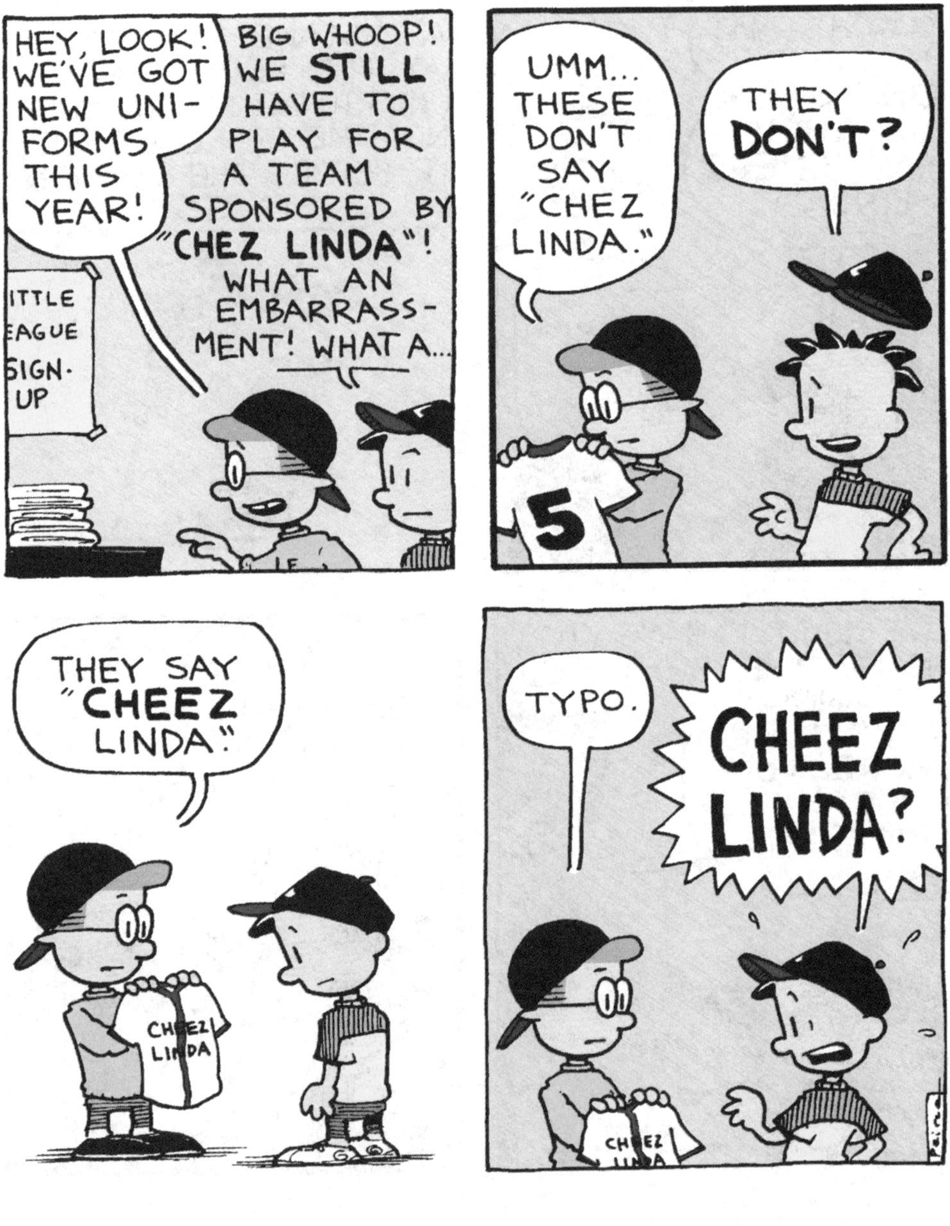
HEY, LOOK! WE'VE GOT NEW UNIFORMS THIS YEAR!
BIG WHOOP! WE STILL HAVE TO PLAY FOR A TEAM SPONSORED BY "CHEZ LINDA"! WHAT AN EMBARRASSMENT! WHAT A...
ITTLE EAGUE SIGN-UP
UMM... THESE DON'T SAY "CHEZ LINDA."
THEY DON'T?
5
THEY SAY "CHEEZ LINDA."
CHEEZ LINDA
TYPO.
CHEEZ LINDA?

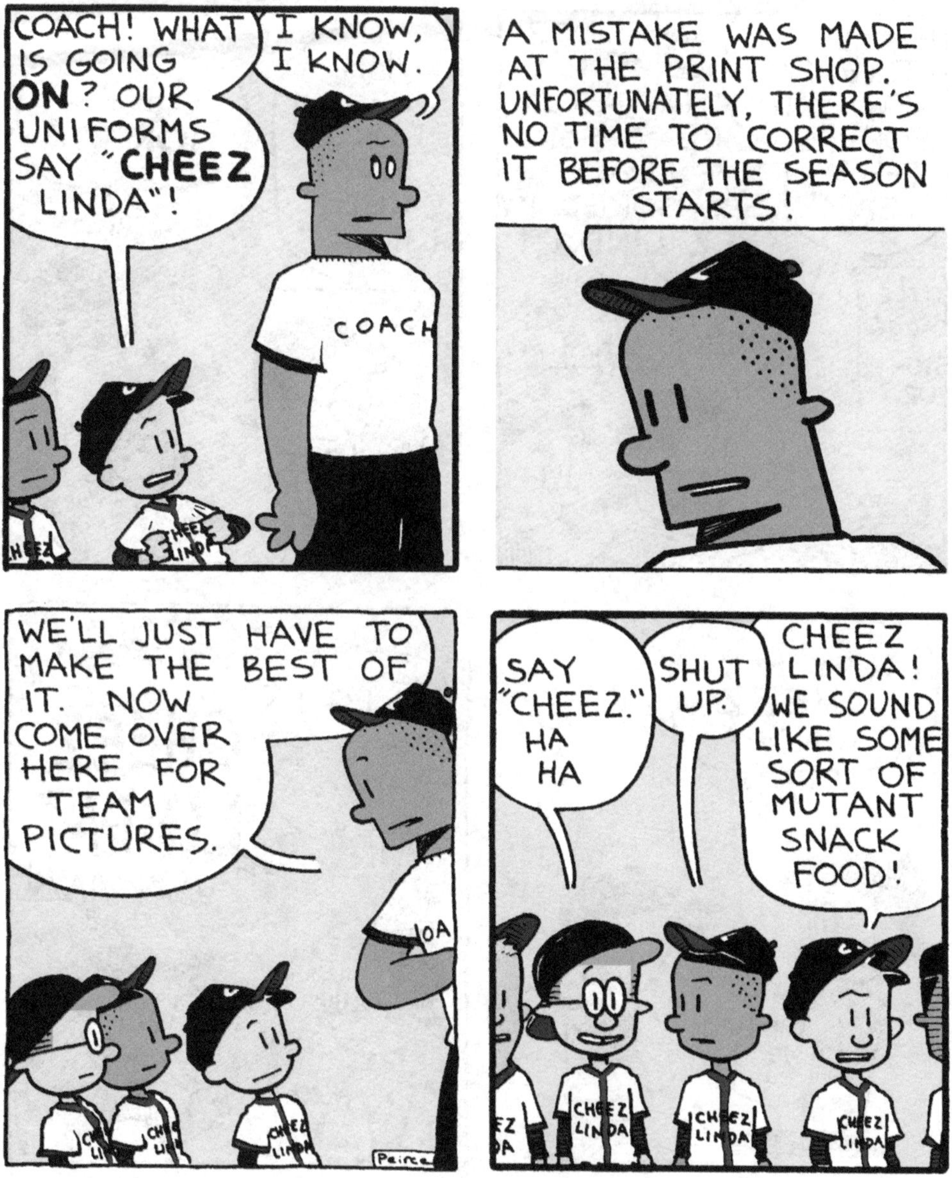
COACH! WHAT IS GOING **ON**? OUR UNIFORMS SAY "**CHEEZ** LINDA"!
I KNOW, I KNOW.
COACH
A MISTAKE WAS MADE AT THE PRINT SHOP. UNFORTUNATELY, THERE'S NO TIME TO CORRECT IT BEFORE THE SEASON STARTS!
WE'LL JUST HAVE TO MAKE THE BEST OF IT. NOW COME OVER HERE FOR TEAM PICTURES.
SAY "CHEEZ." HA HA
SHUT UP.
CHEEZ LINDA! WE SOUND LIKE SOME SORT OF MUTANT SNACK FOOD!
CHEEZ LINDA
CHEEZ LINDA
CHEEZ LINDA
Peirce

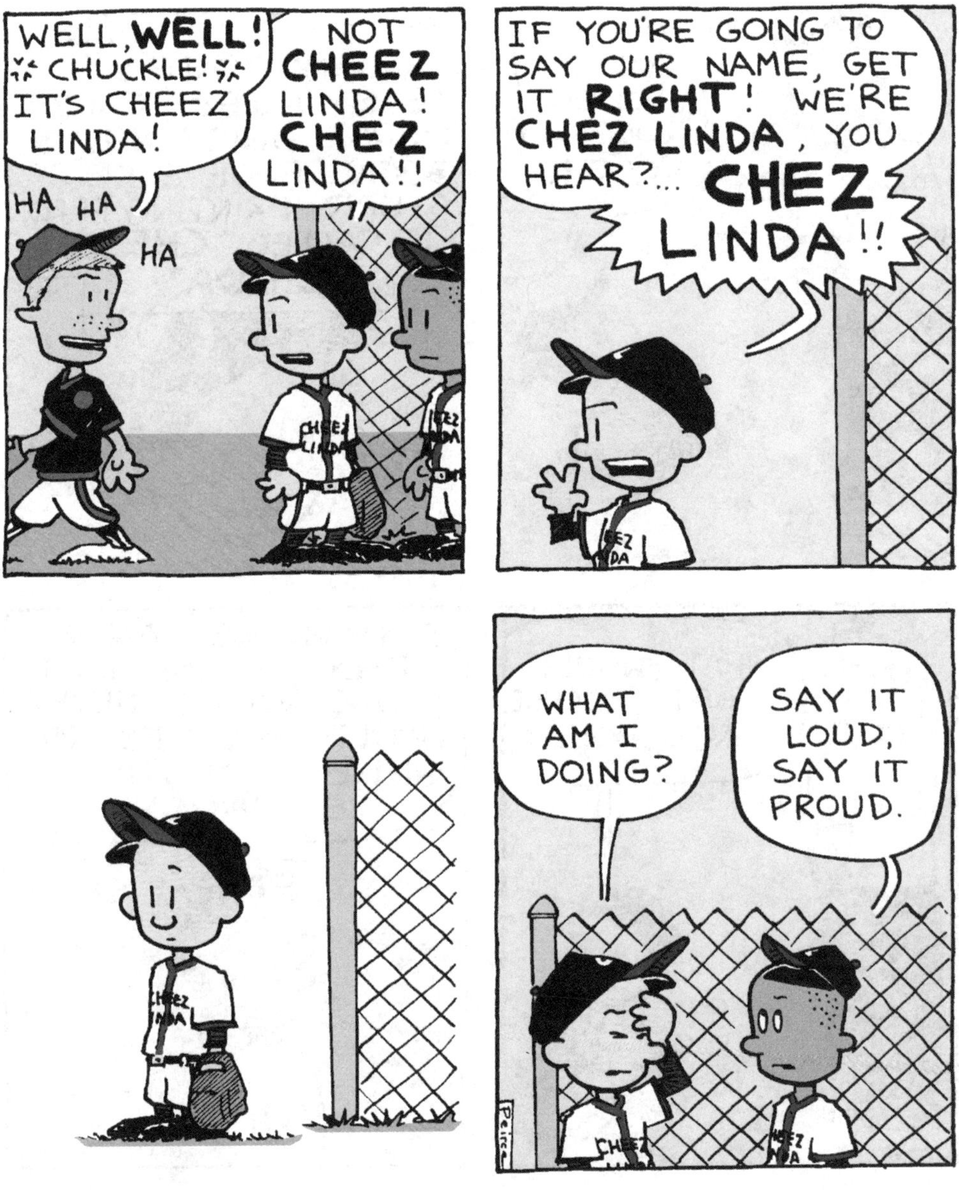
WELL, WELL! *CHUCKLE!* IT'S CHEEZ LINDA!
HA HA HA
NOT CHEEZ LINDA! CHEZ LINDA!!
IF YOU'RE GOING TO SAY OUR NAME, GET IT RIGHT! WE'RE CHEZ LINDA, YOU HEAR?... CHEZ LINDA!!
WHAT AM I DOING?
SAY IT LOUD, SAY IT PROUD.

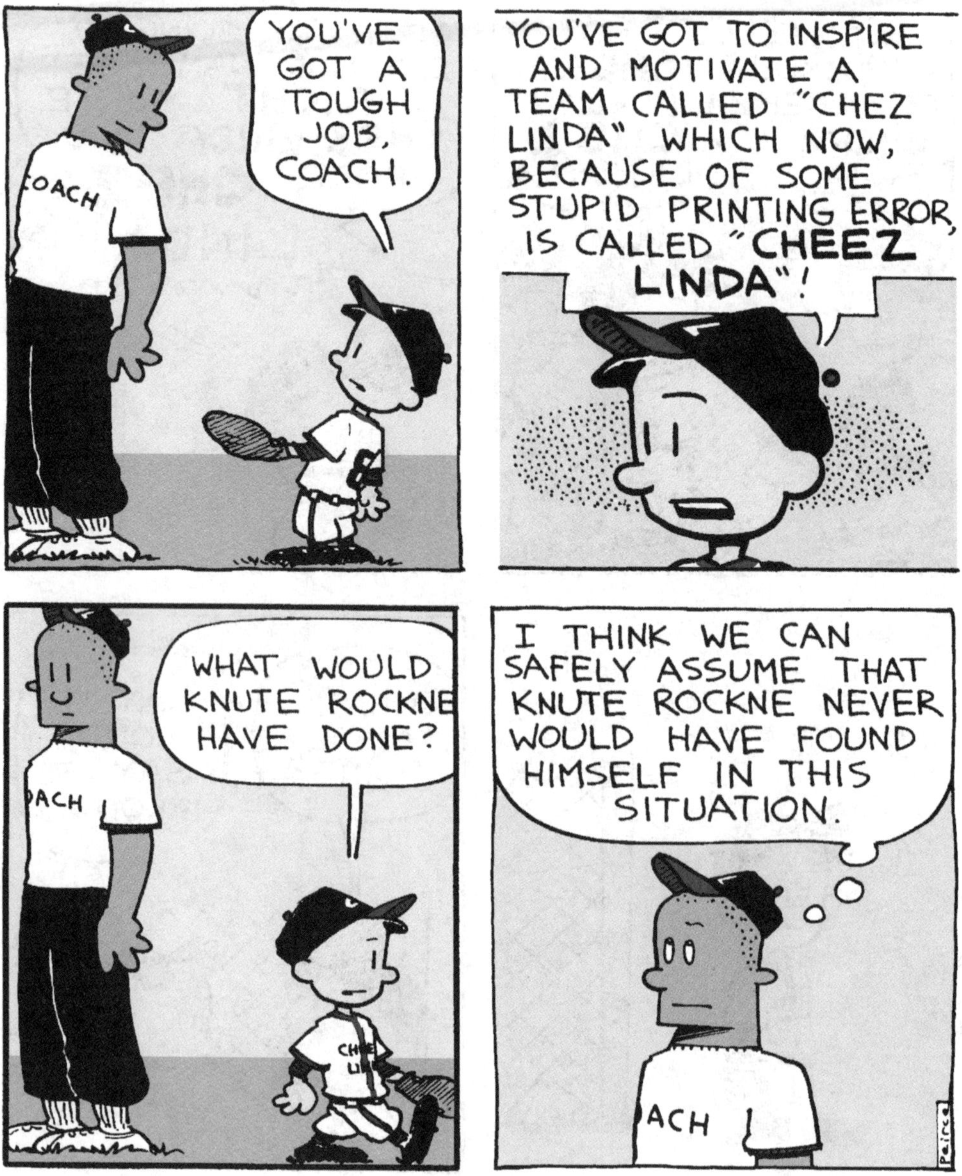
COACH
YOU'VE GOT A TOUGH JOB, COACH.
YOU'VE GOT TO INSPIRE AND MOTIVATE A TEAM CALLED "CHEZ LINDA" WHICH NOW, BECAUSE OF SOME STUPID PRINTING ERROR, IS CALLED "CHEEZ LINDA"!
ACH
WHAT WOULD KNUTE ROCKNE HAVE DONE?
I THINK WE CAN SAFELY ASSUME THAT KNUTE ROCKNE NEVER WOULD HAVE FOUND HIMSELF IN THIS SITUATION.
ACH
Peirce

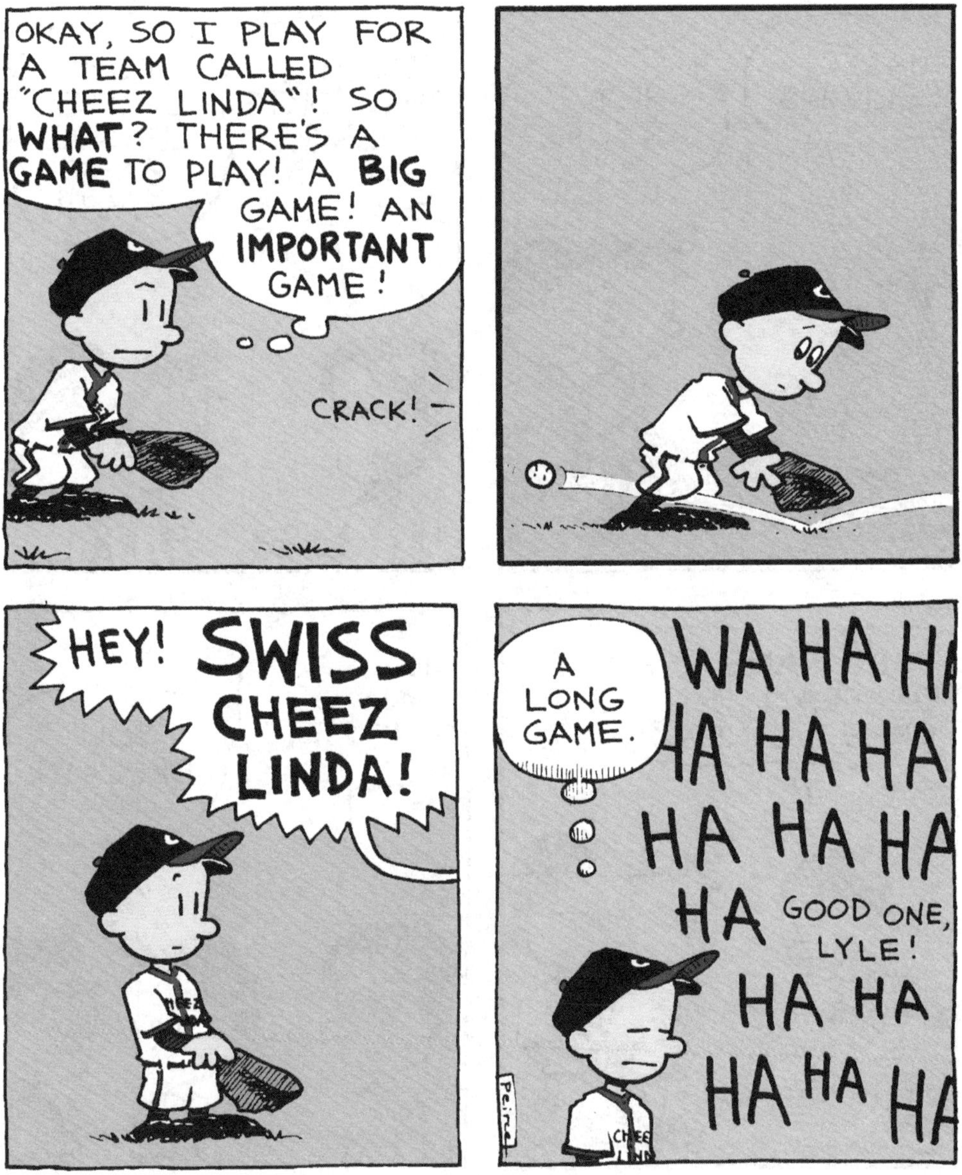
OKAY, SO I PLAY FOR A TEAM CALLED "CHEEZ LINDA"! SO WHAT? THERE'S A GAME TO PLAY! A BIG GAME! AN IMPORTANT GAME!
CRACK!
HEY! SWISS CHEEZ LINDA!
A LONG GAME.
WA HA HA HA HA HA HA HA HA HA HA
GOOD ONE, LYLE!
HA HA HA HA HA
Peirce

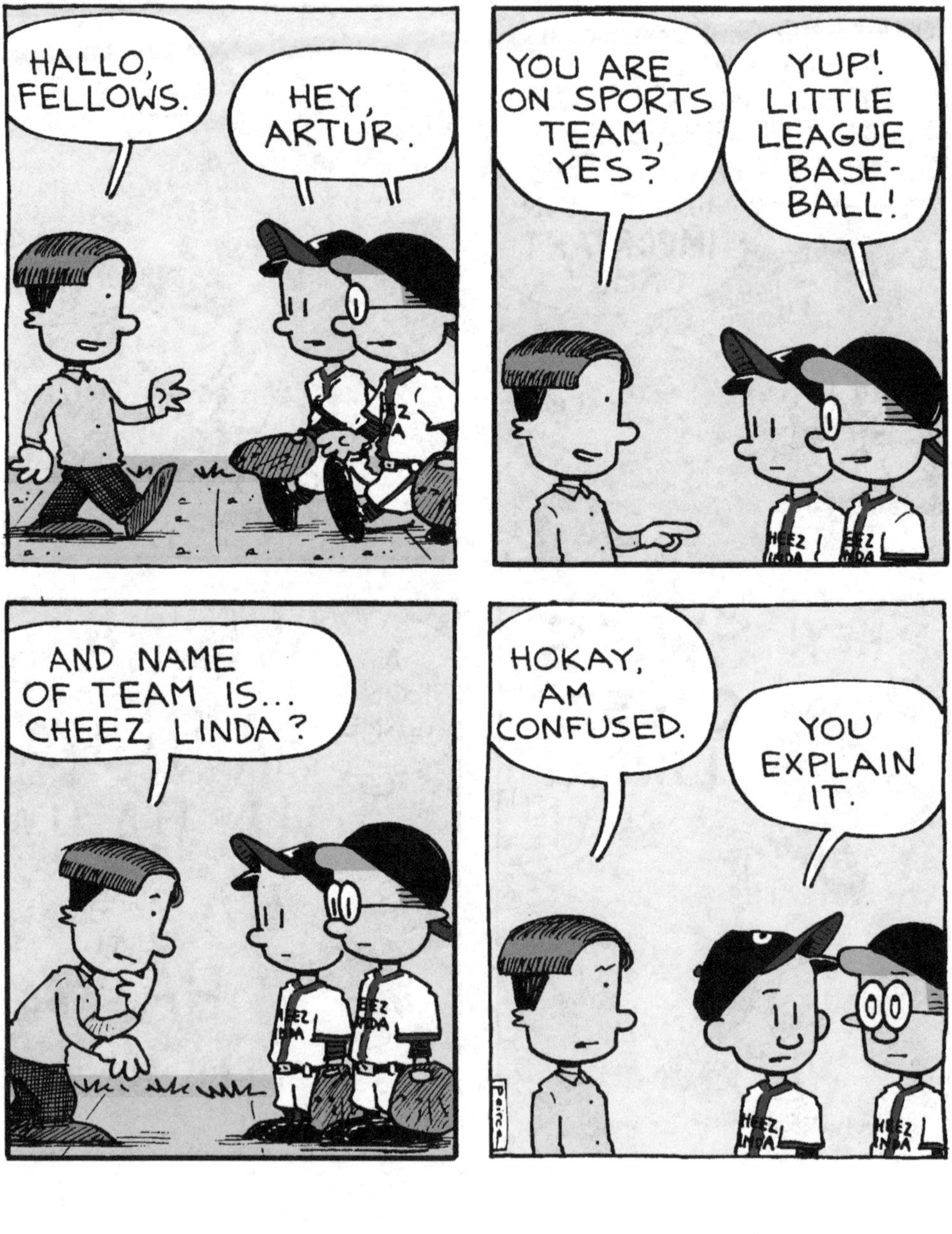
HALLO, FELLOWS.
HEY, ARTUR.
YOU ARE ON SPORTS TEAM, YES?
YUP! LITTLE LEAGUE BASE-BALL!
AND NAME OF TEAM IS... CHEEZ LINDA?
HOKAY, AM CONFUSED.
YOU EXPLAIN IT.

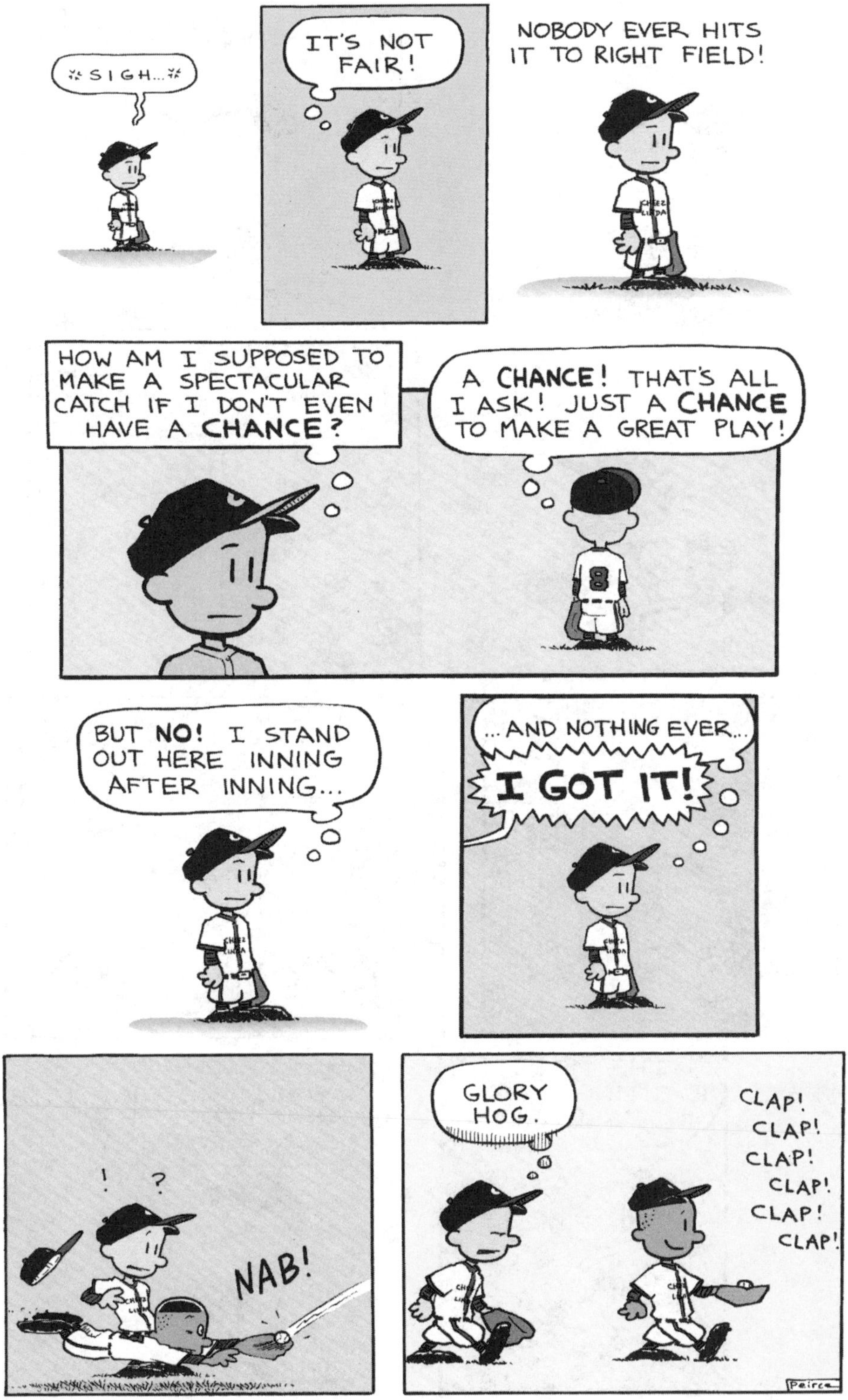
SIGH...
IT'S NOT FAIR!
NOBODY EVER HITS IT TO RIGHT FIELD!
HOW AM I SUPPOSED TO MAKE A SPECTACULAR CATCH IF I DON'T EVEN HAVE A CHANCE?
A CHANCE! THAT'S ALL I ASK! JUST A CHANCE TO MAKE A GREAT PLAY!
BUT NO! I STAND OUT HERE INNING AFTER INNING...
...AND NOTHING EVER...
I GOT IT!
! ?
NAB!
GLORY HOG.
CLAP!
CLAP!
CLAP!
CLAP!
CLAP!
CLAP!
Peirce

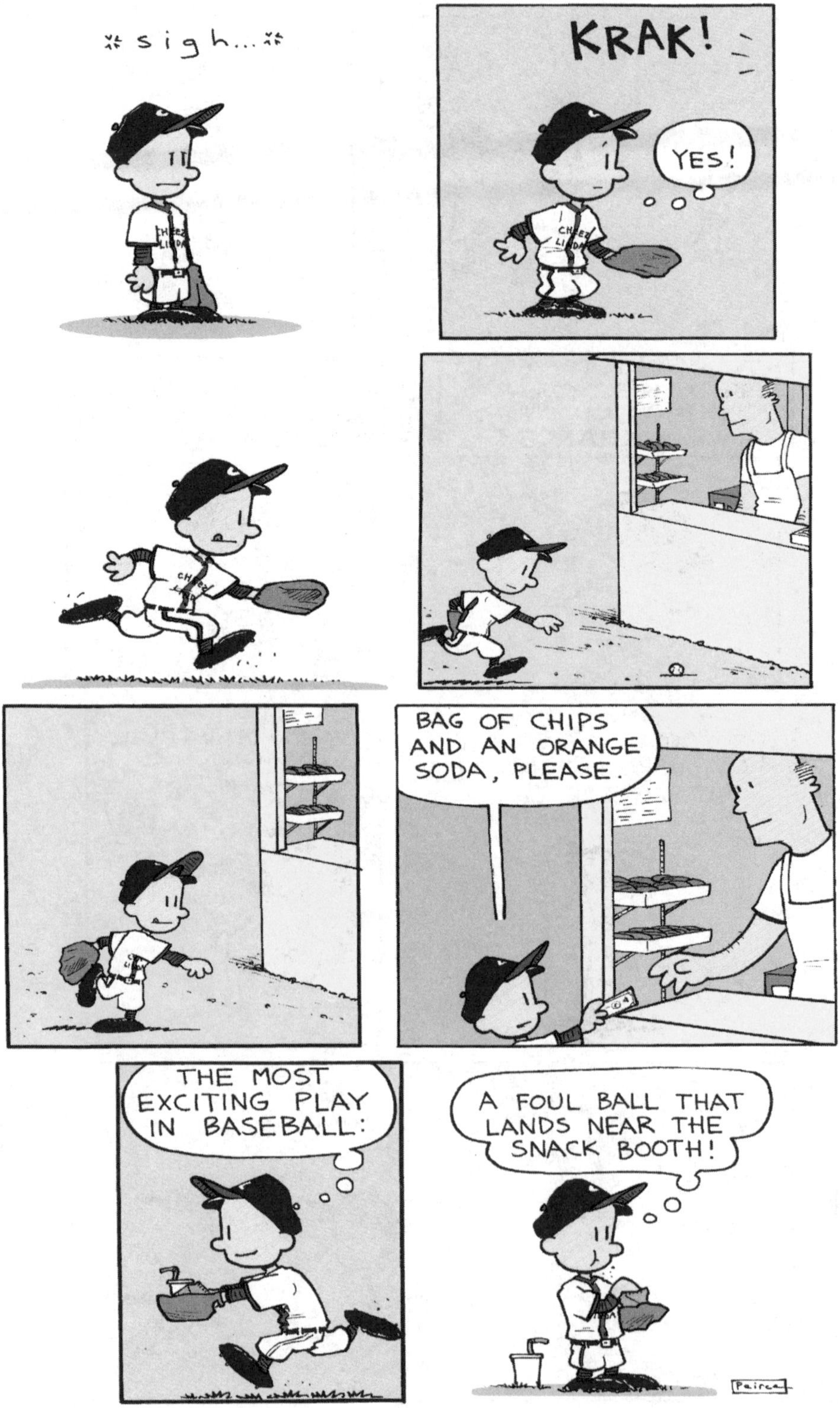
sigh...
KRAK!
YES!
BAG OF CHIPS AND AN ORANGE SODA, PLEASE.
THE MOST EXCITING PLAY IN BASEBALL:
A FOUL BALL THAT LANDS NEAR THE SNACK BOOTH!
Peirce

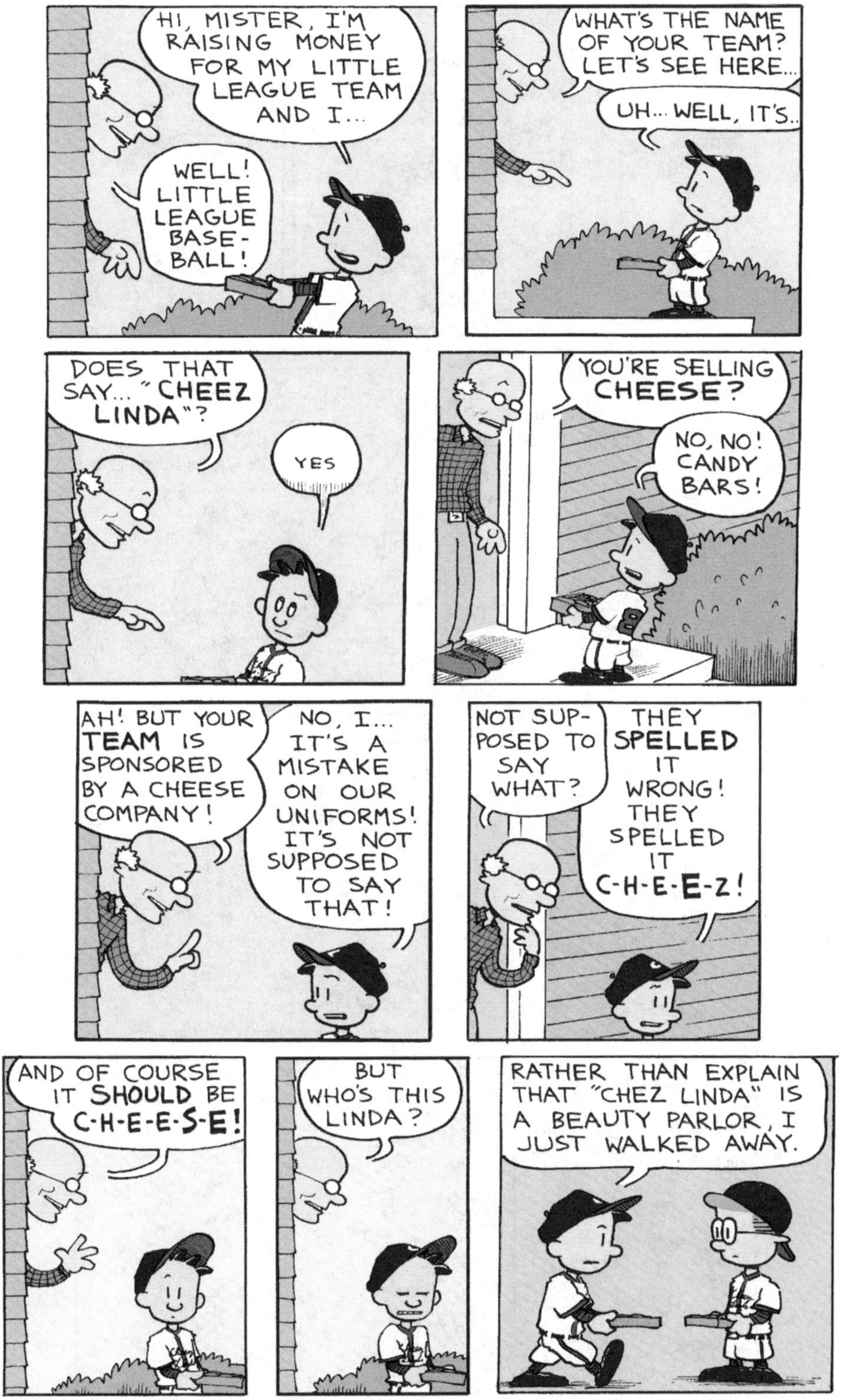
HI, MISTER, I'M RAISING MONEY FOR MY LITTLE LEAGUE TEAM AND I...
WELL! LITTLE LEAGUE BASE-BALL!
WHAT'S THE NAME OF YOUR TEAM? LET'S SEE HERE...
UH... WELL, IT'S...
DOES THAT SAY... "CHEEZ LINDA"?
YES
YOU'RE SELLING CHEESE?
NO, NO! CANDY BARS!
AH! BUT YOUR TEAM IS SPONSORED BY A CHEESE COMPANY!
NO, I... IT'S A MISTAKE ON OUR UNIFORMS! IT'S NOT SUPPOSED TO SAY THAT!
NOT SUP-POSED TO SAY WHAT?
THEY SPELLED IT WRONG! THEY SPELLED IT C-H-E-E-Z!
AND OF COURSE IT SHOULD BE C-H-E-E-S-E!
BUT WHO'S THIS LINDA?
RATHER THAN EXPLAIN THAT "CHEZ LINDA" IS A BEAUTY PARLOR, I JUST WALKED AWAY.

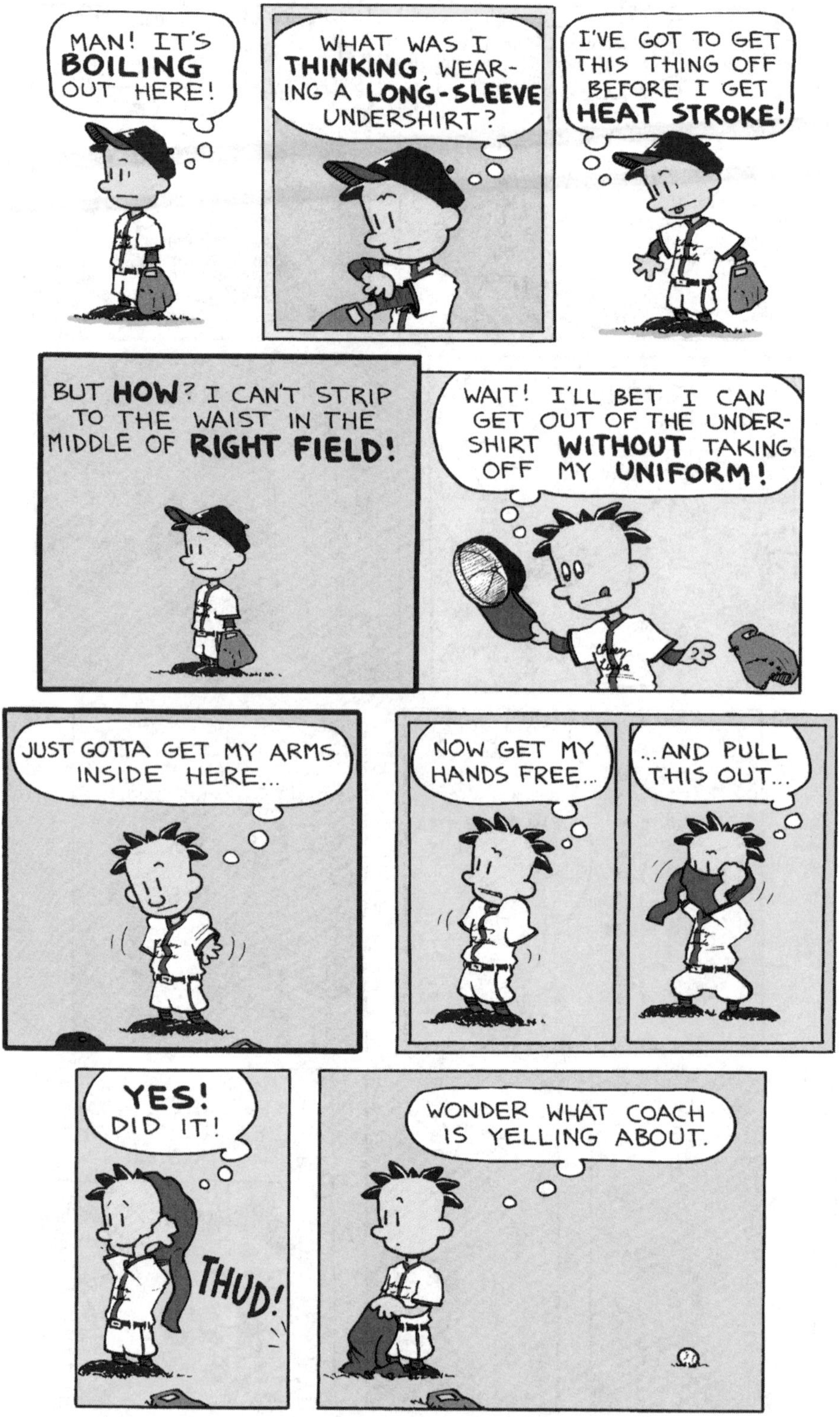
MAN! IT'S **BOILING** OUT HERE!
WHAT WAS I **THINKING**, WEARING A **LONG-SLEEVE** UNDERSHIRT?
I'VE GOT TO GET THIS THING OFF BEFORE I GET **HEAT STROKE!**
BUT **HOW**? I CAN'T STRIP TO THE WAIST IN THE MIDDLE OF **RIGHT FIELD!**
WAIT! I'LL BET I CAN GET OUT OF THE UNDERSHIRT **WITHOUT** TAKING OFF MY **UNIFORM!**
JUST GOTTA GET MY ARMS INSIDE HERE...
NOW GET MY HANDS FREE...
...AND PULL THIS OUT...
YES! DID IT!
THUD!
WONDER WHAT COACH IS YELLING ABOUT.

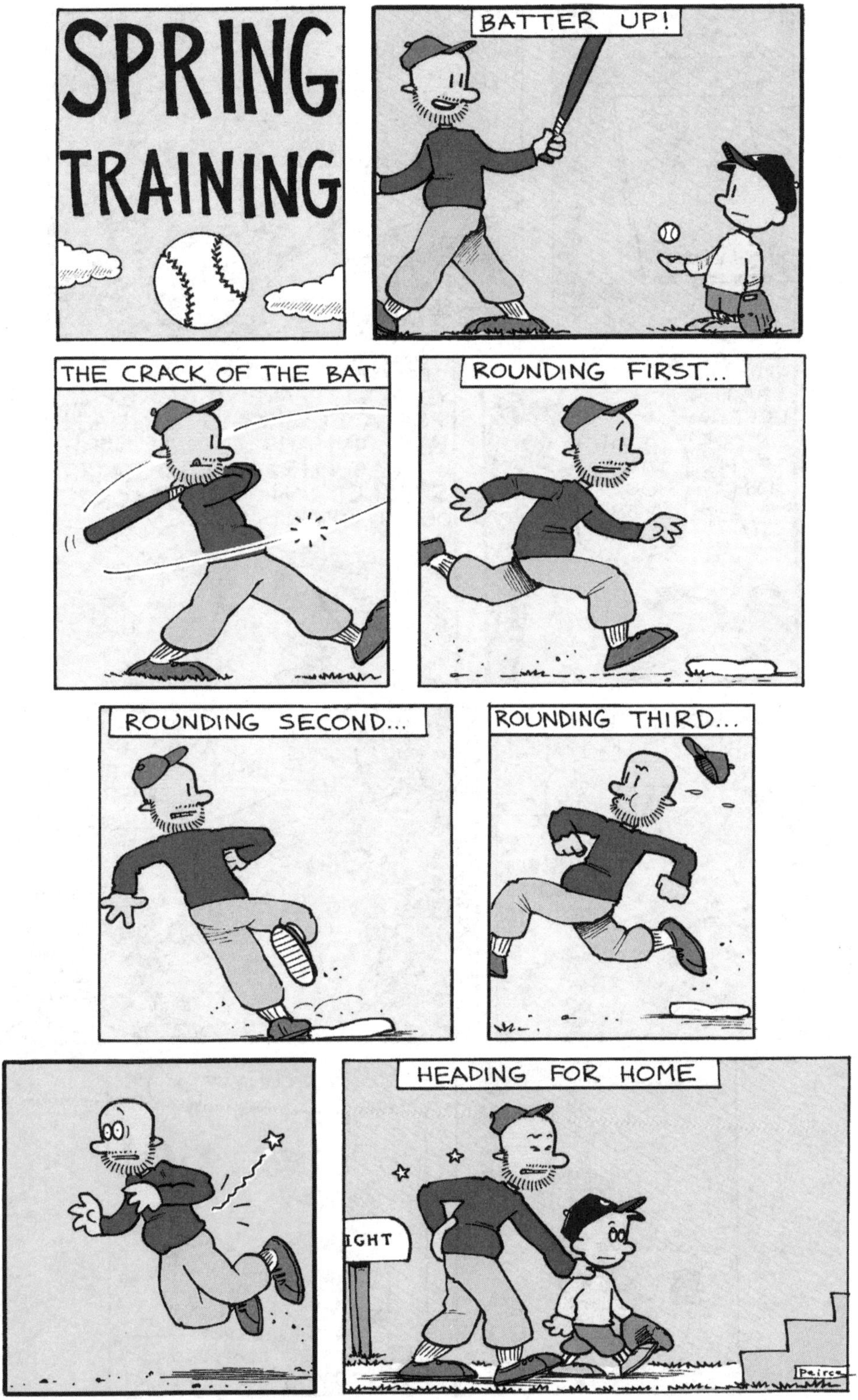
SPRING TRAINING
BATTER UP!
THE CRACK OF THE BAT
ROUNDING FIRST...
ROUNDING SECOND...
ROUNDING THIRD...
HEADING FOR HOME
IGHT
Peirce

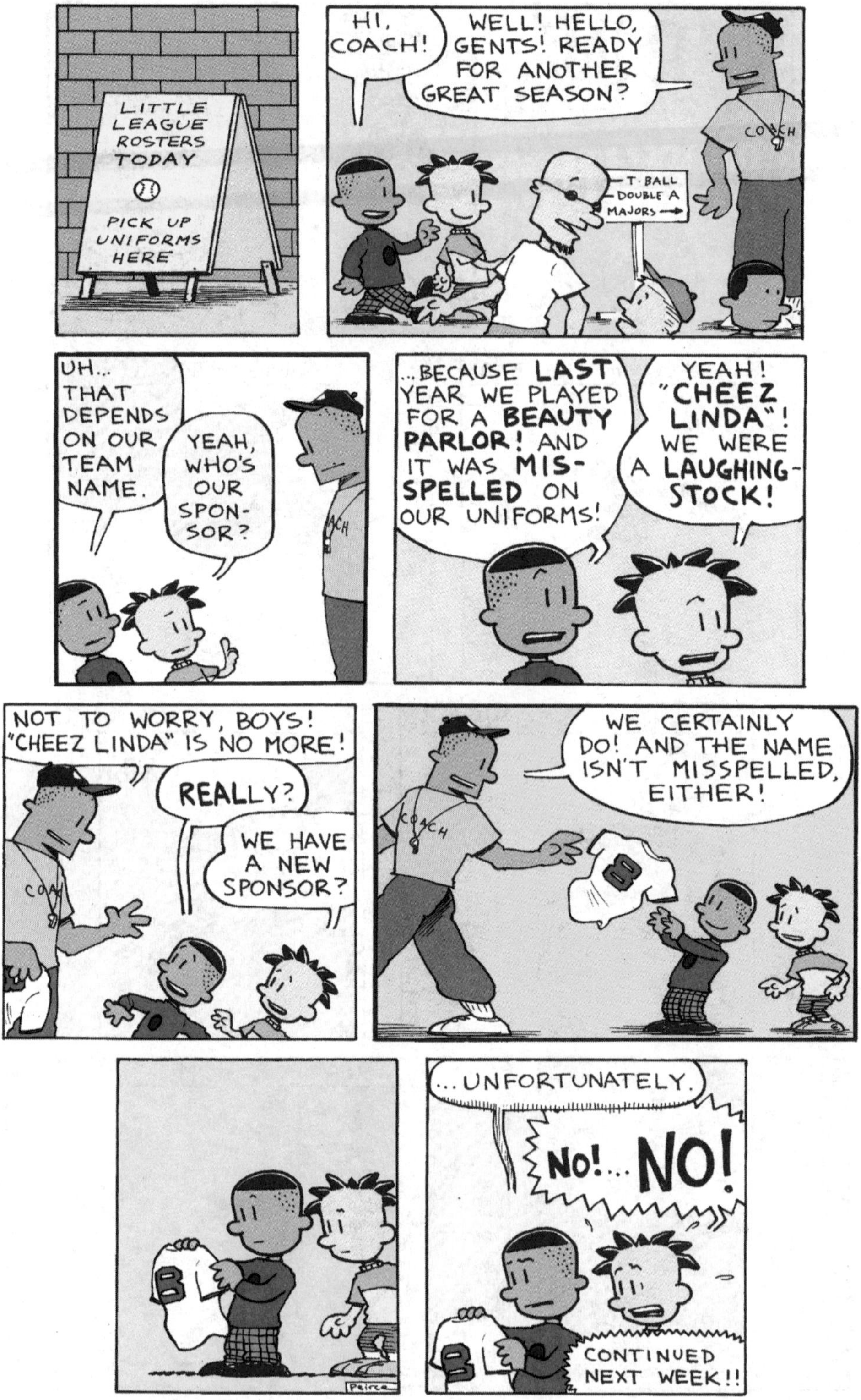
LITTLE LEAGUE ROSTERS TODAY
PICK UP UNIFORMS HERE
HI, COACH!
WELL! HELLO, GENTS! READY FOR ANOTHER GREAT SEASON?
COACH
T-BALL
DOUBLE A
MAJORS
UH... THAT DEPENDS ON OUR TEAM NAME.
YEAH, WHO'S OUR SPONSOR?
...BECAUSE **LAST** YEAR WE PLAYED FOR A **BEAUTY PARLOR!** AND IT WAS **MIS-SPELLED** ON OUR UNIFORMS!
YEAH! "**CHEEZ LINDA**"! WE WERE A **LAUGHING-STOCK!**
NOT TO WORRY, BOYS! "CHEEZ LINDA" IS NO MORE!
REALLY?
WE HAVE A NEW SPONSOR?
WE CERTAINLY DO! AND THE NAME ISN'T MISSPELLED, EITHER!
Peirce
...UNFORTUNATELY.
NO!... NO!
CONTINUED NEXT WEEK!!

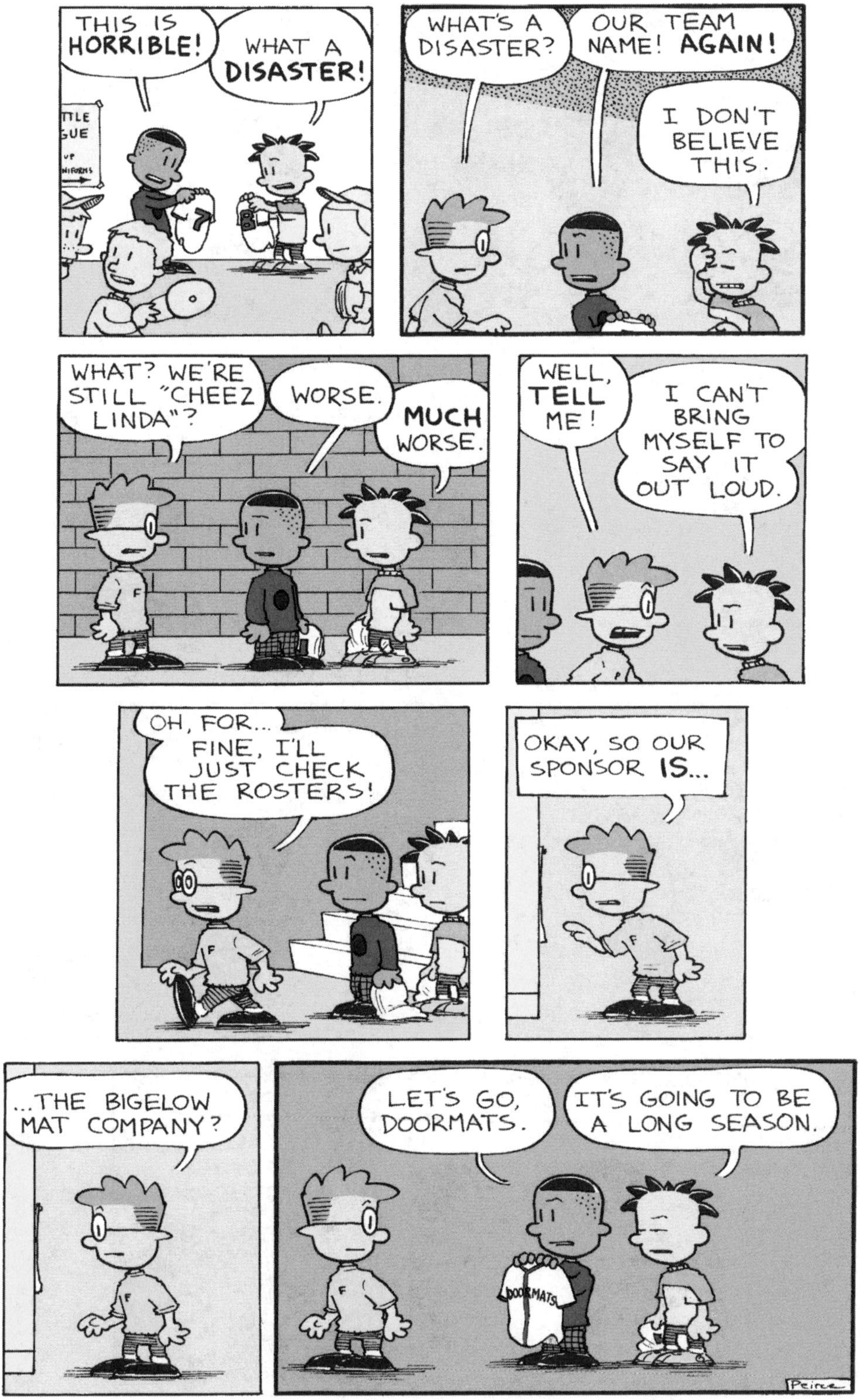

THIS IS HORRIBLE!
WHAT A DISASTER!
TTLE GUE UP NIFORMS
WHAT'S A DISASTER?
OUR TEAM NAME! AGAIN!
I DON'T BELIEVE THIS.
WHAT? WE'RE STILL "CHEEZ LINDA"?
WORSE.
MUCH WORSE.
WELL, TELL ME!
I CAN'T BRING MYSELF TO SAY IT OUT LOUD.
OH, FOR...
FINE, I'LL JUST CHECK THE ROSTERS!
OKAY, SO OUR SPONSOR IS...
...THE BIGELOW MAT COMPANY?
LET'S GO, DOORMATS.
IT'S GOING TO BE A LONG SEASON.
DOORMATS
Peirce

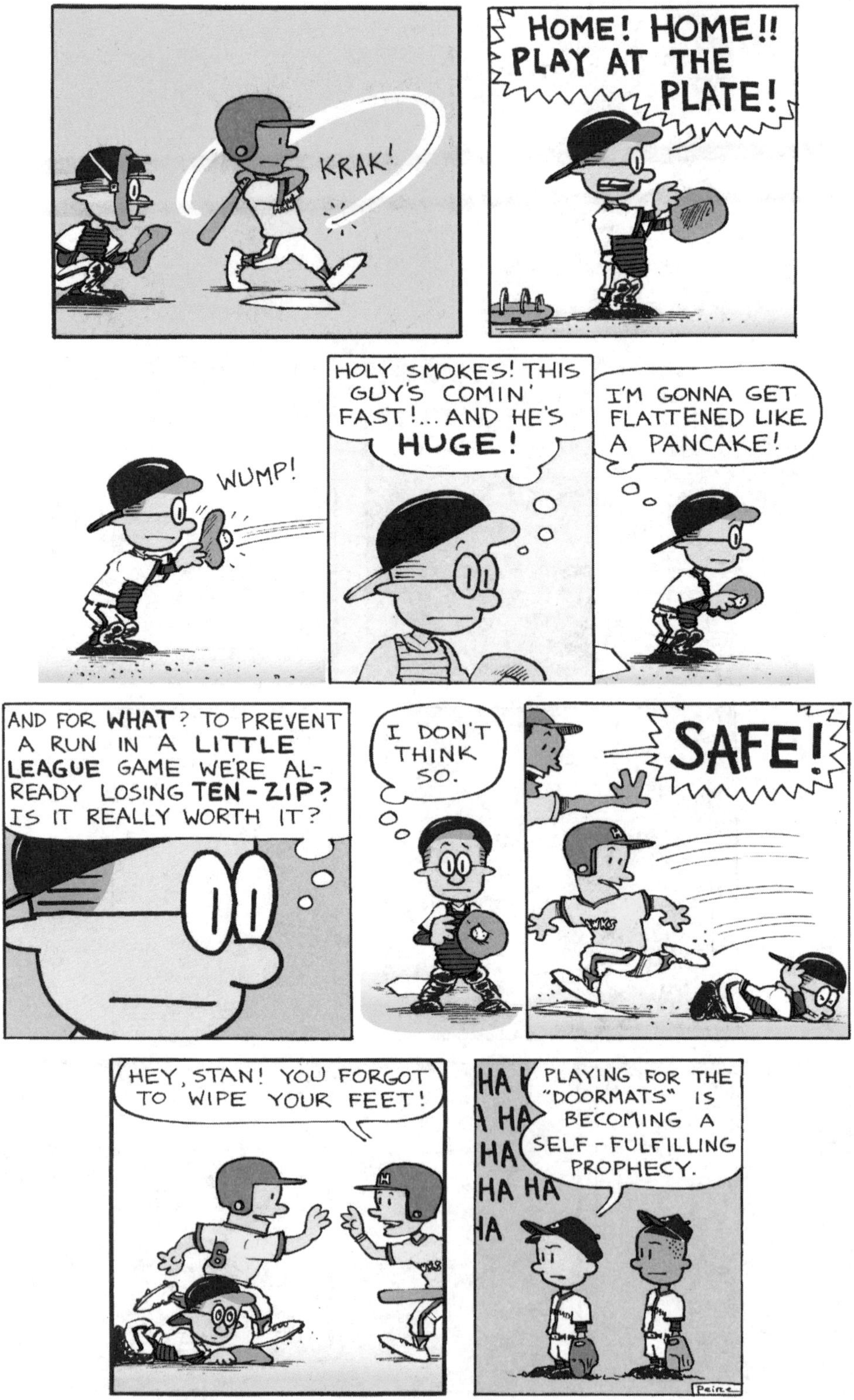
KRAK!
HOME! HOME!! PLAY AT THE PLATE!
WUMP!
HOLY SMOKES! THIS GUY'S COMIN' FAST!... AND HE'S HUGE!
I'M GONNA GET FLATTENED LIKE A PANCAKE!
AND FOR WHAT? TO PREVENT A RUN IN A LITTLE LEAGUE GAME WE'RE AL-READY LOSING TEN-ZIP? IS IT REALLY WORTH IT?
I DON'T THINK SO.
SAFE!
HEY, STAN! YOU FORGOT TO WIPE YOUR FEET!
HA HA HA HA HA HA HA HA
PLAYING FOR THE "DOORMATS" IS BECOMING A SELF-FULFILLING PROPHECY.
Peirce

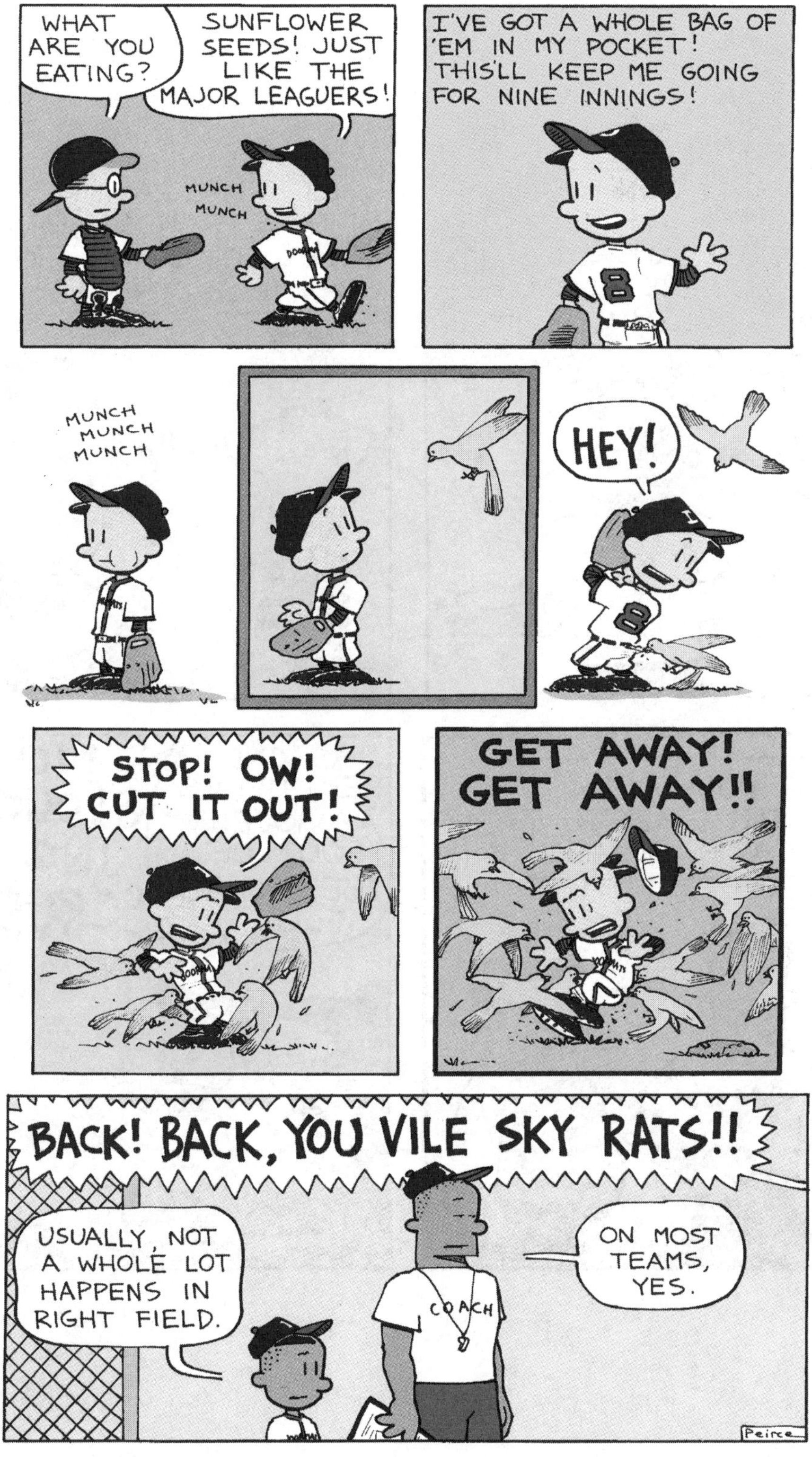
WHAT ARE YOU EATING?
SUNFLOWER SEEDS! JUST LIKE THE MAJOR LEAGUERS!
MUNCH MUNCH
I'VE GOT A WHOLE BAG OF 'EM IN MY POCKET! THIS'LL KEEP ME GOING FOR NINE INNINGS!
MUNCH MUNCH MUNCH
HEY!
STOP! OW! CUT IT OUT!
GET AWAY! GET AWAY!!
BACK! BACK, YOU VILE SKY RATS!!
USUALLY, NOT A WHOLE LOT HAPPENS IN RIGHT FIELD.
ON MOST TEAMS, YES.
COACH
Peirce

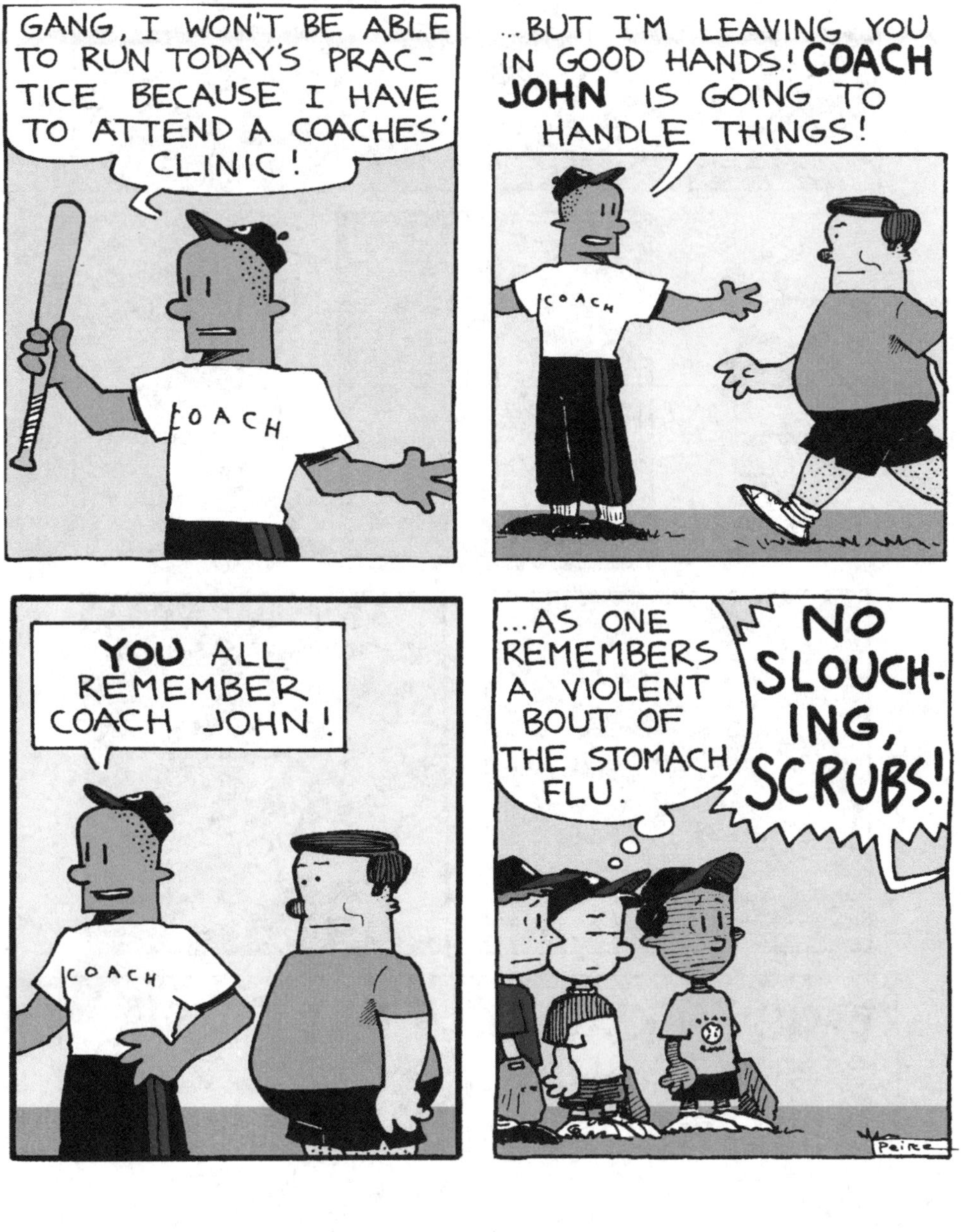
GANG, I WON'T BE ABLE TO RUN TODAY'S PRAC- TICE BECAUSE I HAVE TO ATTEND A COACHES' CLINIC!
COACH
...BUT I'M LEAVING YOU IN GOOD HANDS! COACH JOHN IS GOING TO HANDLE THINGS!
COACH
YOU ALL REMEMBER COACH JOHN!
COACH
...AS ONE REMEMBERS A VIOLENT BOUT OF THE STOMACH FLU.
NO SLOUCH- ING, SCRUBS!
Peirce

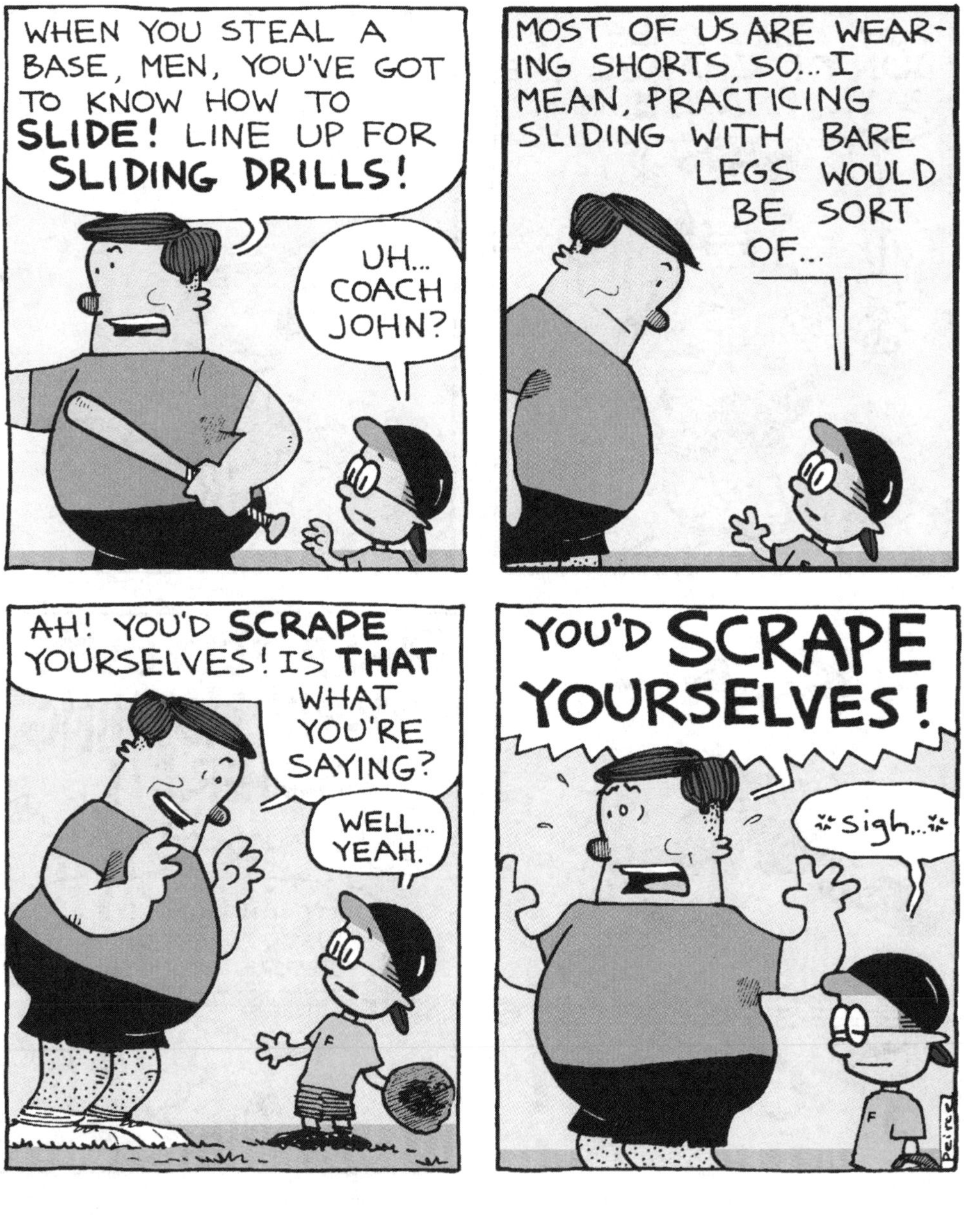
WHEN YOU STEAL A BASE, MEN, YOU'VE GOT TO KNOW HOW TO SLIDE! LINE UP FOR SLIDING DRILLS!
UH... COACH JOHN?
MOST OF US ARE WEARING SHORTS, SO... I MEAN, PRACTICING SLIDING WITH BARE LEGS WOULD BE SORT OF...
AH! YOU'D SCRAPE YOURSELVES! IS THAT WHAT YOU'RE SAYING?
WELL... YEAH.
YOU'D SCRAPE YOURSELVES!
sigh...
F
Peirce

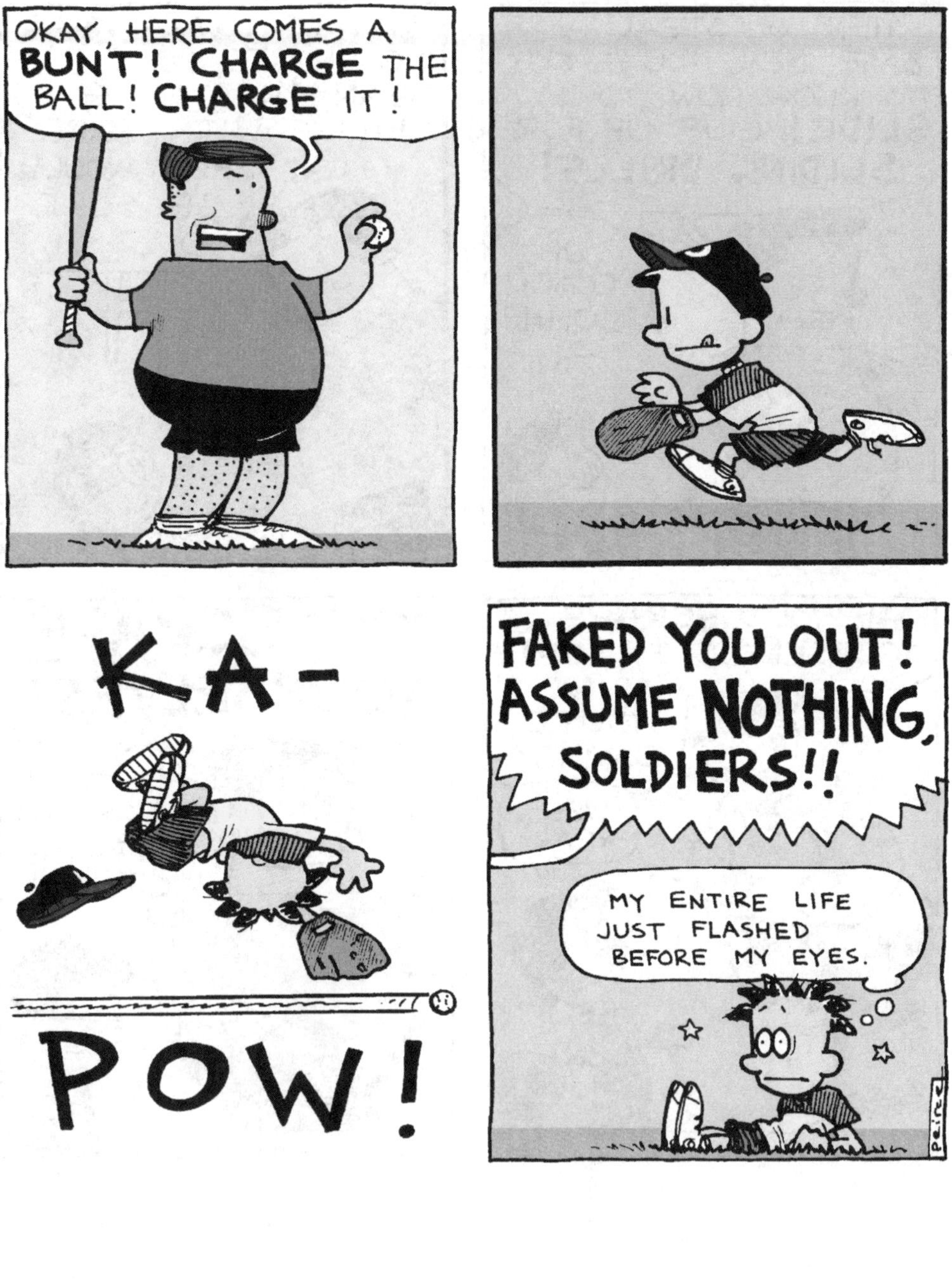
OKAY, HERE COMES A BUNT! CHARGE THE BALL! CHARGE IT!
KA-
POW!
FAKED YOU OUT! ASSUME NOTHING, SOLDIERS!!
MY ENTIRE LIFE JUST FLASHED BEFORE MY EYES.
PEIRCE

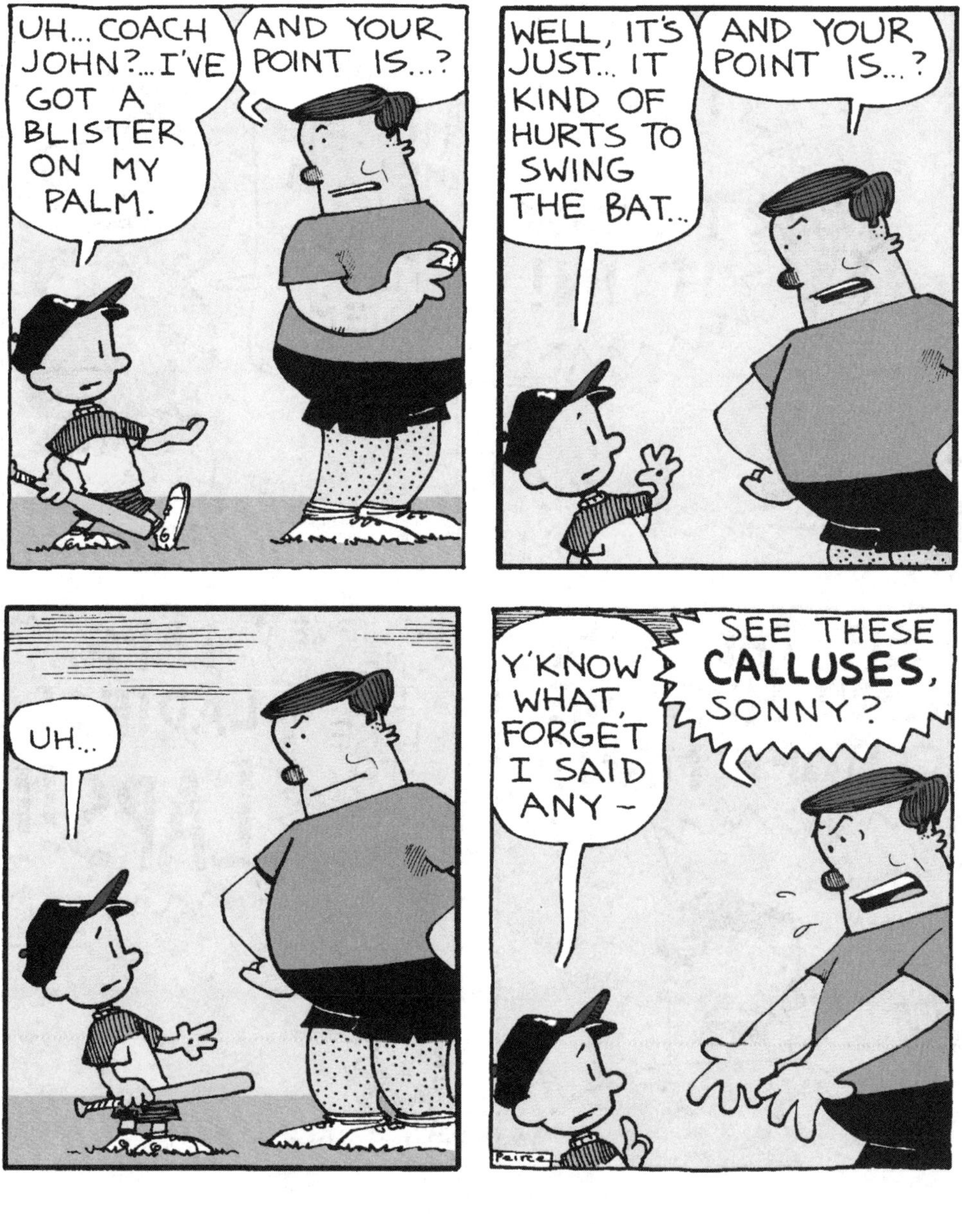
UH... COACH JOHN?... I'VE GOT A BLISTER ON MY PALM.
AND YOUR POINT IS...?
WELL, IT'S JUST... IT KIND OF HURTS TO SWING THE BAT...
AND YOUR POINT IS...?
UH...
Y'KNOW WHAT, FORGET I SAID ANY-
SEE THESE **CALLUSES**, SONNY?
Peirce

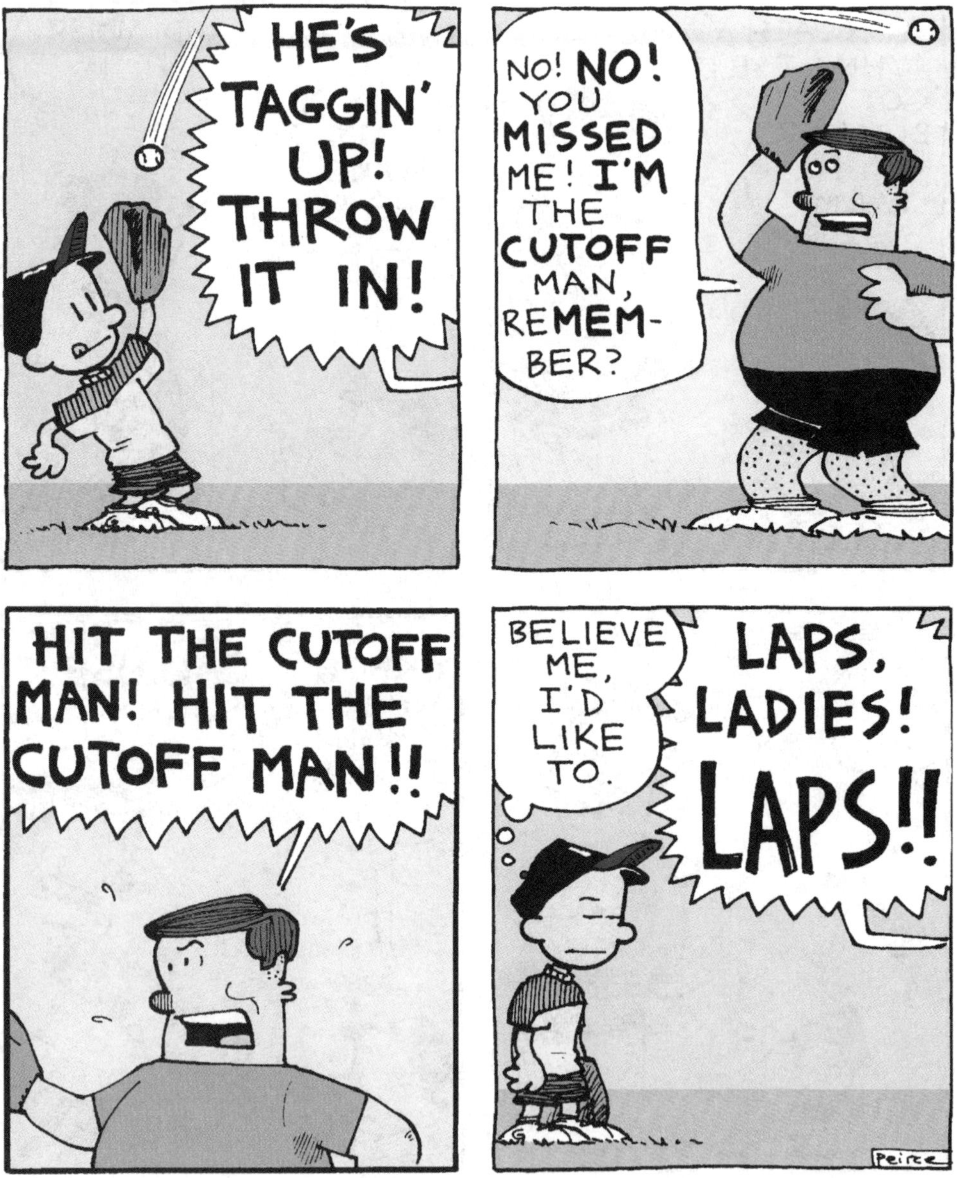
HE'S TAGGIN' UP! THROW IT IN!
NO! NO! YOU MISSED ME! I'M THE CUTOFF MAN, REMEMBER?
HIT THE CUTOFF MAN! HIT THE CUTOFF MAN!!
BELIEVE ME, I'D LIKE TO.
LAPS, LADIES! LAPS!!
Peirce

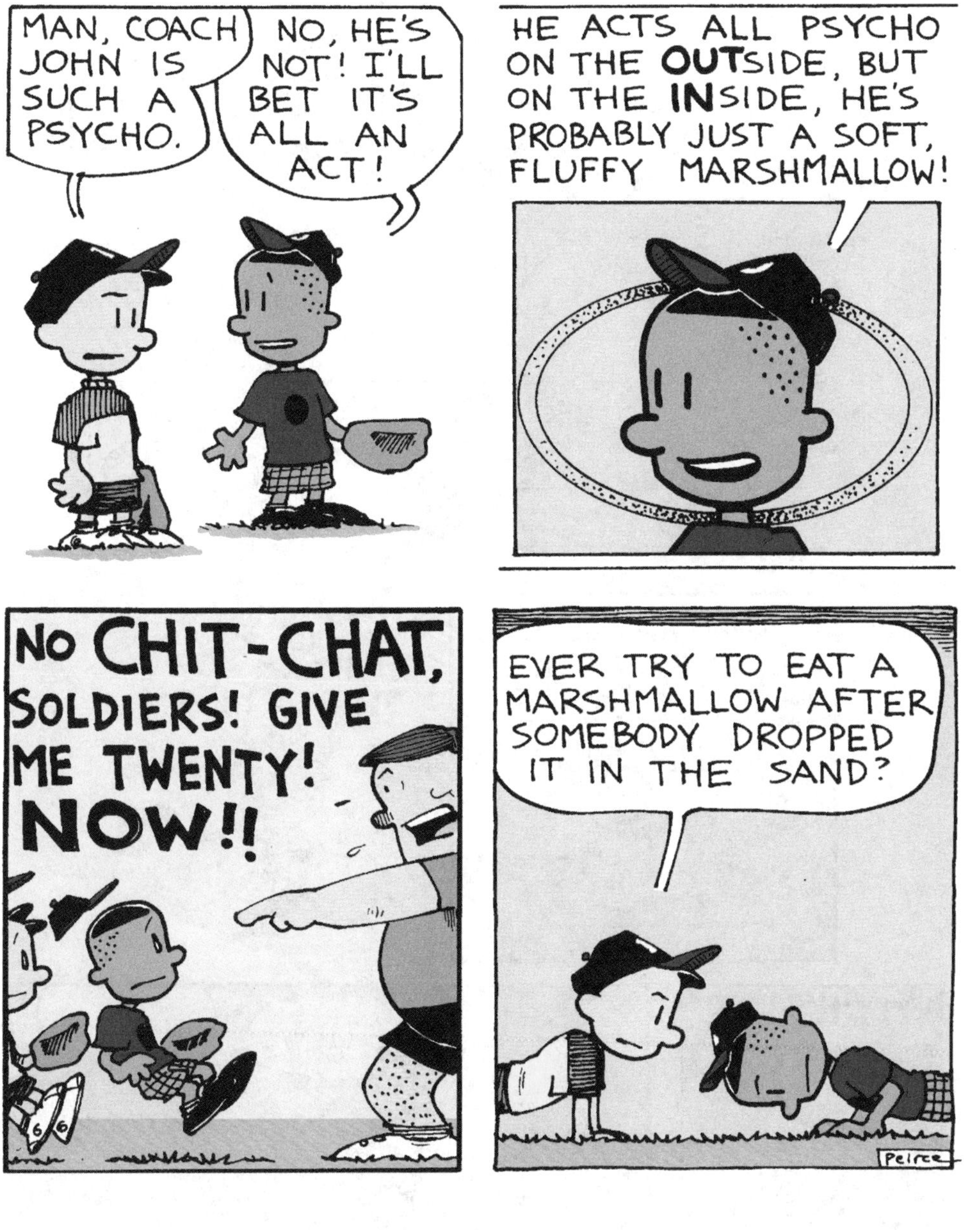
MAN, COACH JOHN IS SUCH A PSYCHO.
NO, HE'S NOT! I'LL BET IT'S ALL AN ACT!
HE ACTS ALL PSYCHO ON THE OUTSIDE, BUT ON THE INSIDE, HE'S PROBABLY JUST A SOFT, FLUFFY MARSHMALLOW!
NO CHIT-CHAT, SOLDIERS! GIVE ME TWENTY! NOW!!
EVER TRY TO EAT A MARSHMALLOW AFTER SOMEBODY DROPPED IT IN THE SAND?
Peirce

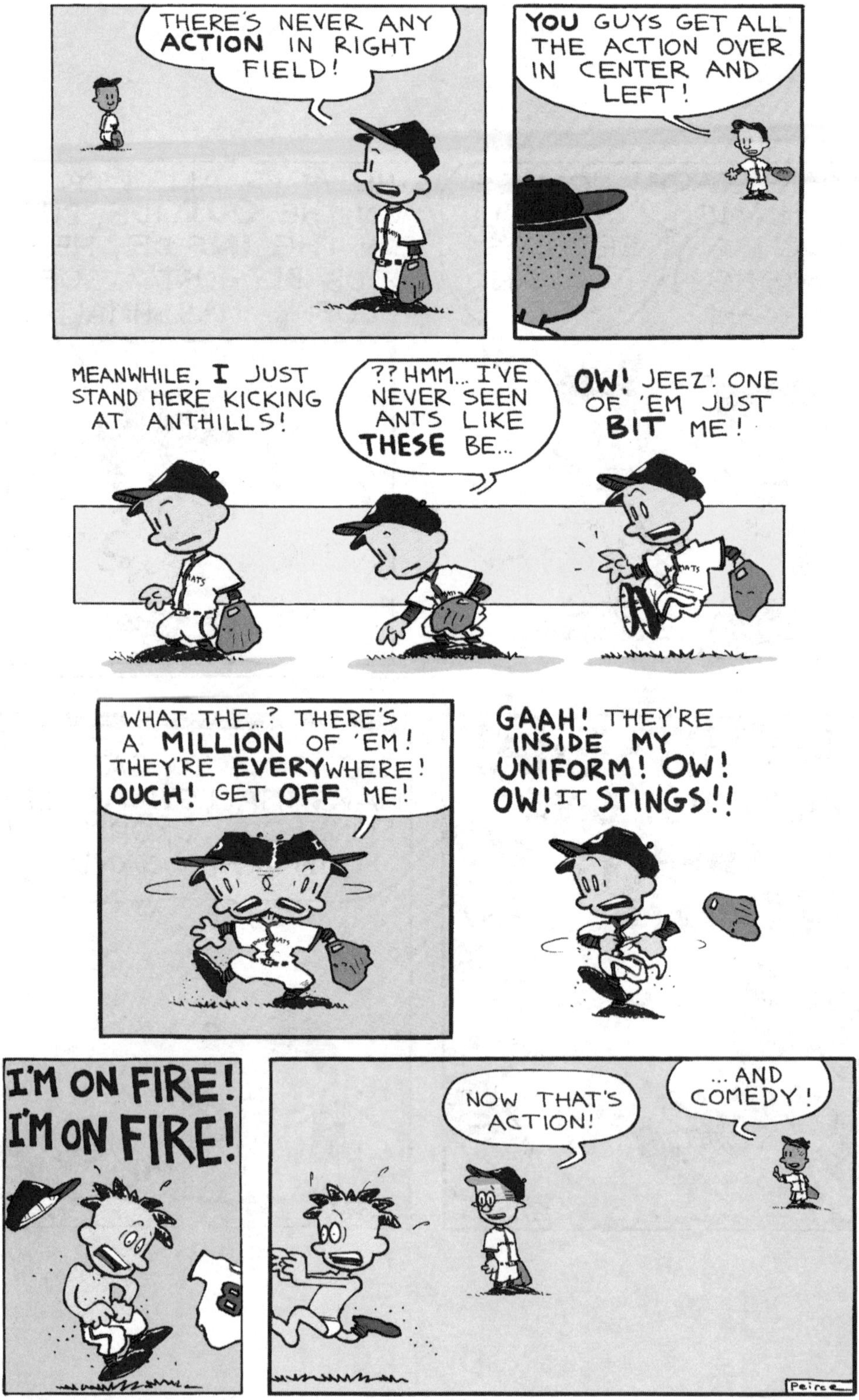
THERE'S NEVER ANY ACTION IN RIGHT FIELD!
YOU GUYS GET ALL THE ACTION OVER IN CENTER AND LEFT!
MEANWHILE, I JUST STAND HERE KICKING AT ANTHILLS!
?? HMM... I'VE NEVER SEEN ANTS LIKE THESE BE...
OW! JEEZ! ONE OF 'EM JUST BIT ME!
WHAT THE...? THERE'S A MILLION OF 'EM! THEY'RE EVERYWHERE! OUCH! GET OFF ME!
GAAH! THEY'RE INSIDE MY UNIFORM! OW! OW! IT STINGS!!
I'M ON FIRE! I'M ON FIRE!
NOW THAT'S ACTION!
...AND COMEDY!
Peirce

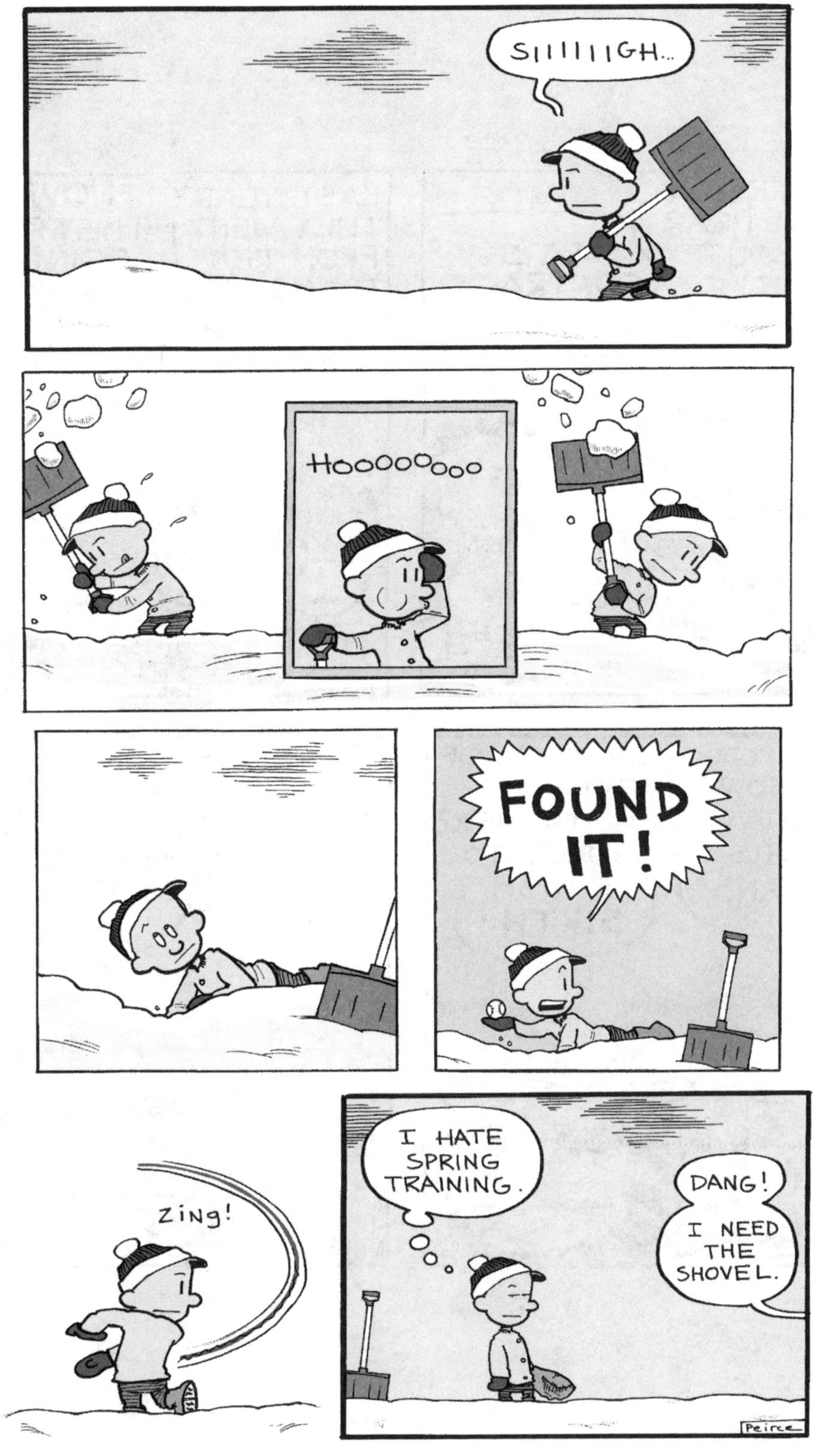
SIIIIIIGH...
HOOOOOOOO
FOUND IT!
ZING!
I HATE SPRING TRAINING.
DANG!
I NEED THE SHOVEL.
Peirce

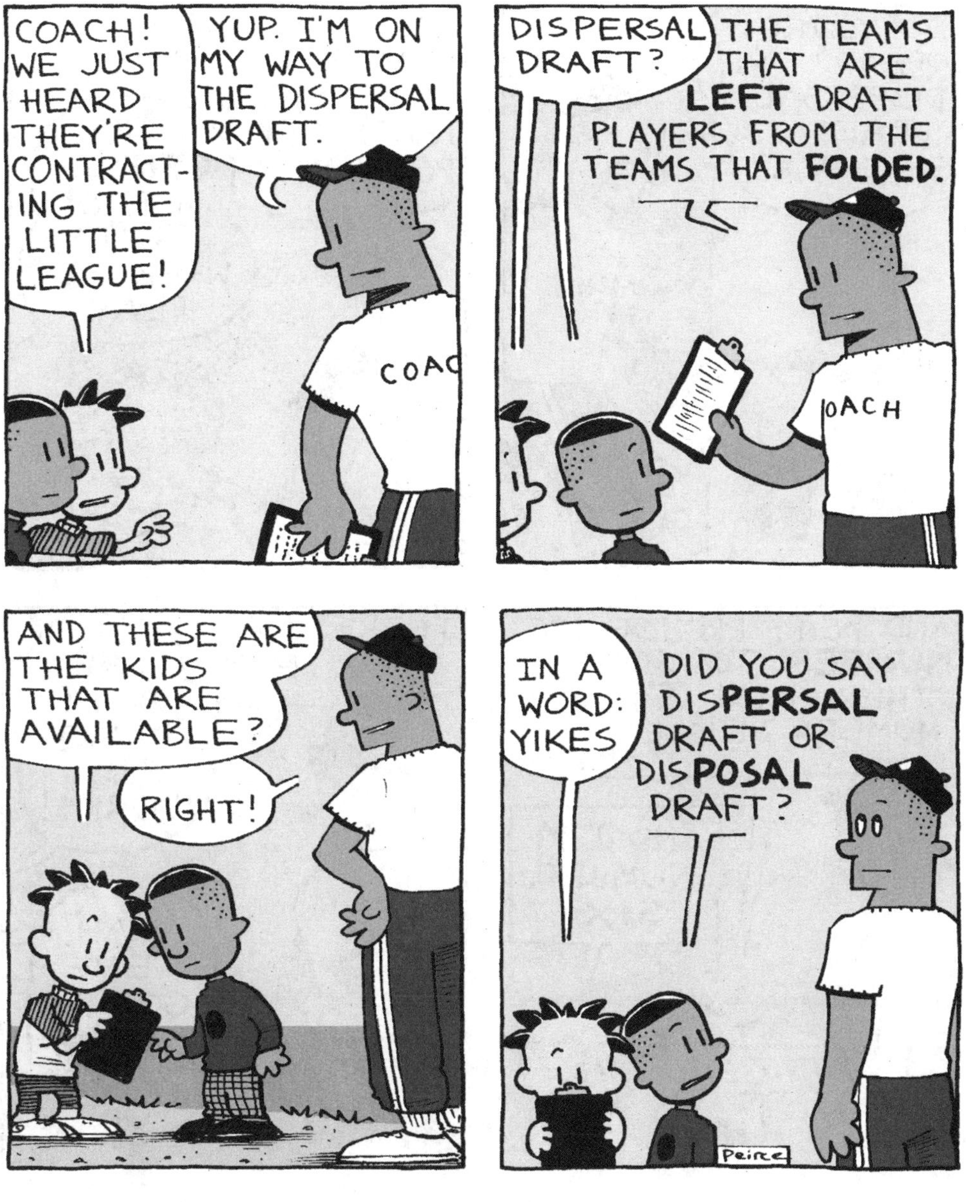
COACH! WE JUST HEARD THEY'RE CONTRACTING THE LITTLE LEAGUE!
YUP. I'M ON MY WAY TO THE DISPERSAL DRAFT.
COACH
DISPERSAL DRAFT?
THE TEAMS THAT ARE **LEFT** DRAFT PLAYERS FROM THE TEAMS THAT **FOLDED.**
OACH
AND THESE ARE THE KIDS THAT ARE AVAILABLE?
RIGHT!
IN A WORD: YIKES
DID YOU SAY DIS**PERSAL** DRAFT OR DIS**POSAL** DRAFT?
Peirce

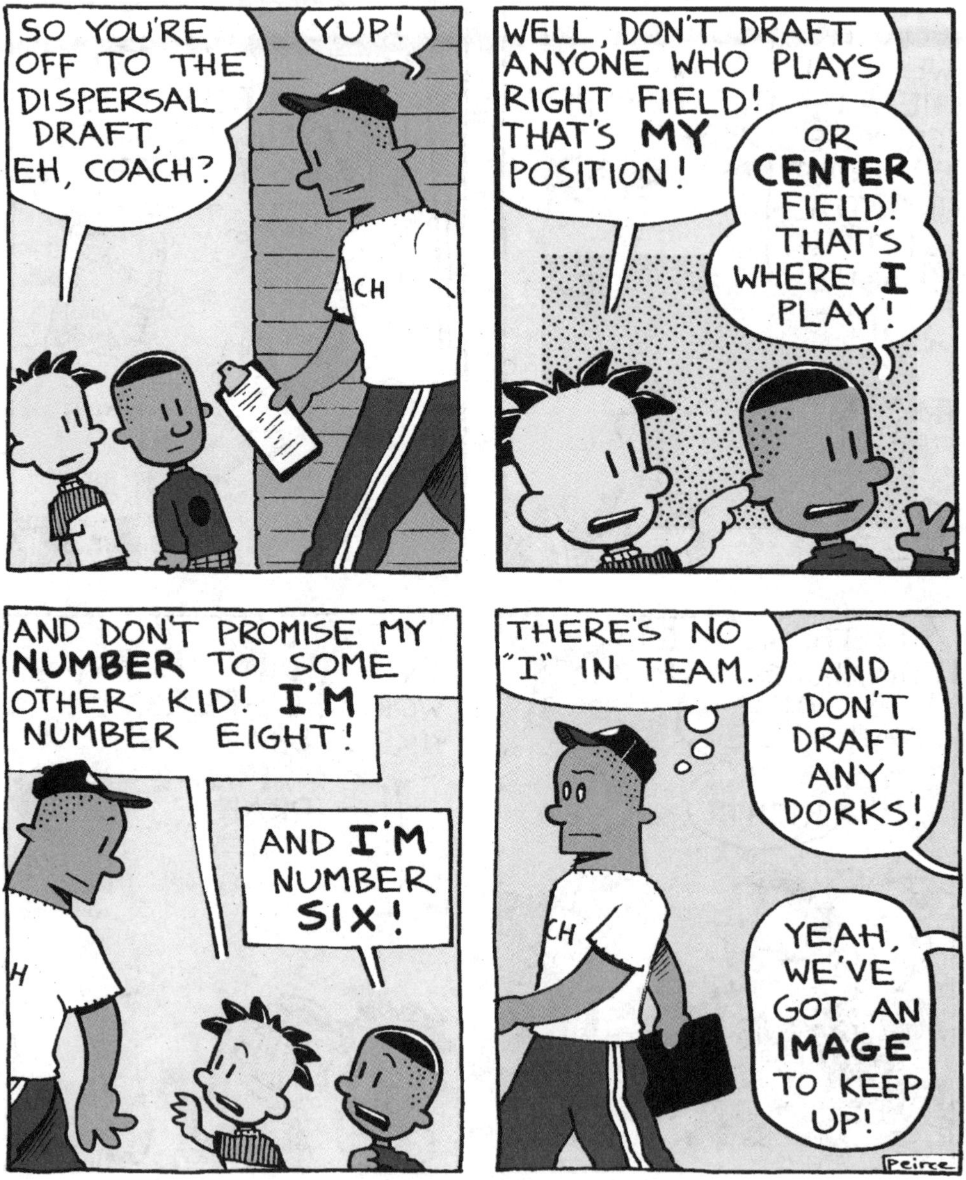
SO YOU'RE OFF TO THE DISPERSAL DRAFT, EH, COACH?
YUP!
WELL, DON'T DRAFT ANYONE WHO PLAYS RIGHT FIELD! THAT'S **MY** POSITION!
OR **CENTER** FIELD! THAT'S WHERE **I** PLAY!
AND DON'T PROMISE MY **NUMBER** TO SOME OTHER KID! **I'M** NUMBER EIGHT!
AND **I'M** NUMBER **SIX**!
THERE'S NO "I" IN TEAM.
AND DON'T DRAFT ANY DORKS!
YEAH, WE'VE GOT AN **IMAGE** TO KEEP UP!
Peirce

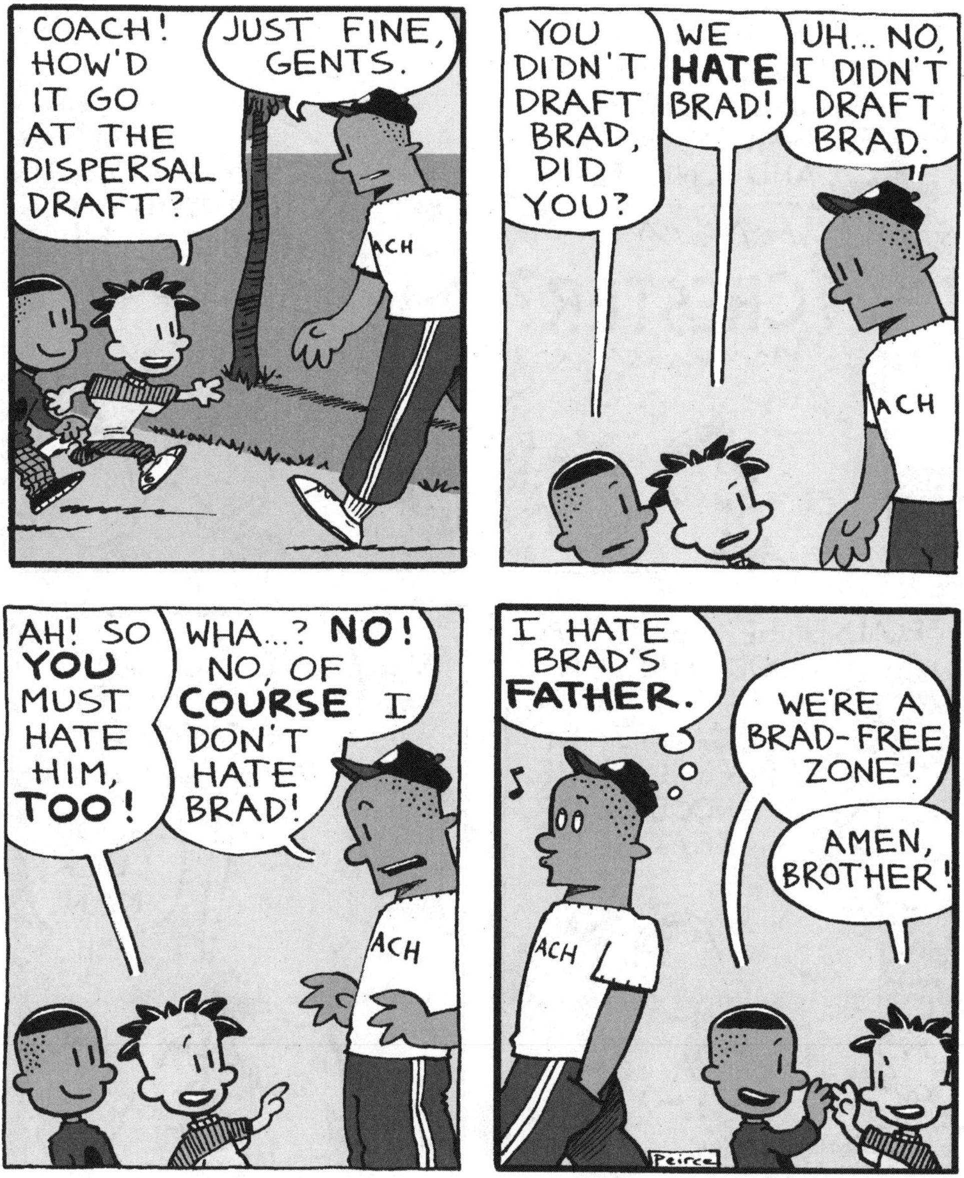
COACH! HOW'D IT GO AT THE DISPERSAL DRAFT?
JUST FINE, GENTS.
ACH
YOU DIDN'T DRAFT BRAD, DID YOU?
WE **HATE** BRAD!
UH... NO, I DIDN'T DRAFT BRAD.
ACH
AH! SO **YOU** MUST HATE HIM, **TOO**!
WHA...? **NO!** NO, OF **COURSE** I DON'T HATE BRAD!
ACH
I HATE BRAD'S **FATHER**.
WE'RE A BRAD-FREE ZONE!
AMEN, BROTHER!
ACH
Peirce

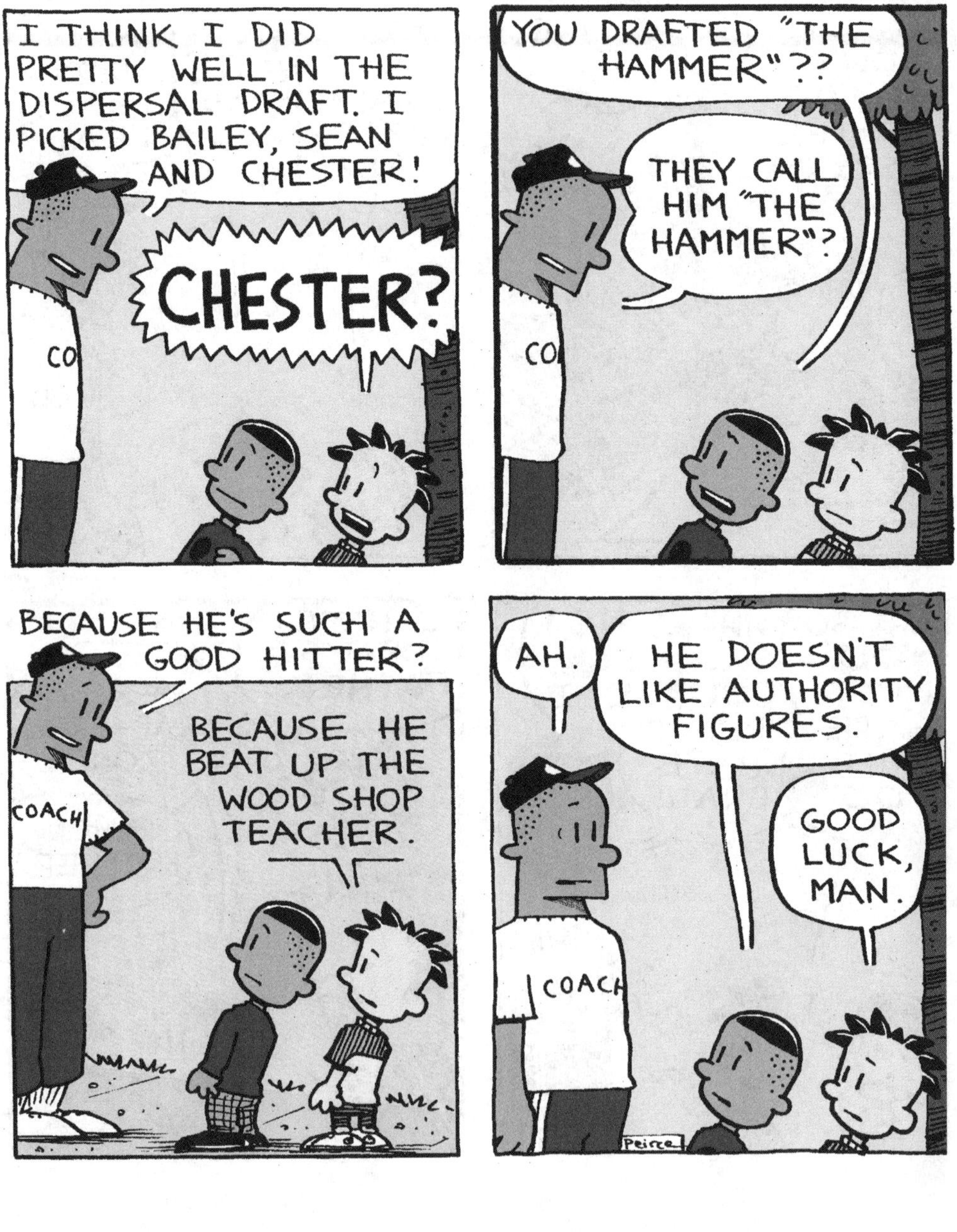
I THINK I DID PRETTY WELL IN THE DISPERSAL DRAFT. I PICKED BAILEY, SEAN AND CHESTER!
CHESTER?
COACH
YOU DRAFTED "THE HAMMER"??
THEY CALL HIM "THE HAMMER"?
BECAUSE HE'S SUCH A GOOD HITTER?
BECAUSE HE BEAT UP THE WOOD SHOP TEACHER.
AH.
HE DOESN'T LIKE AUTHORITY FIGURES.
GOOD LUCK, MAN.
Peirce

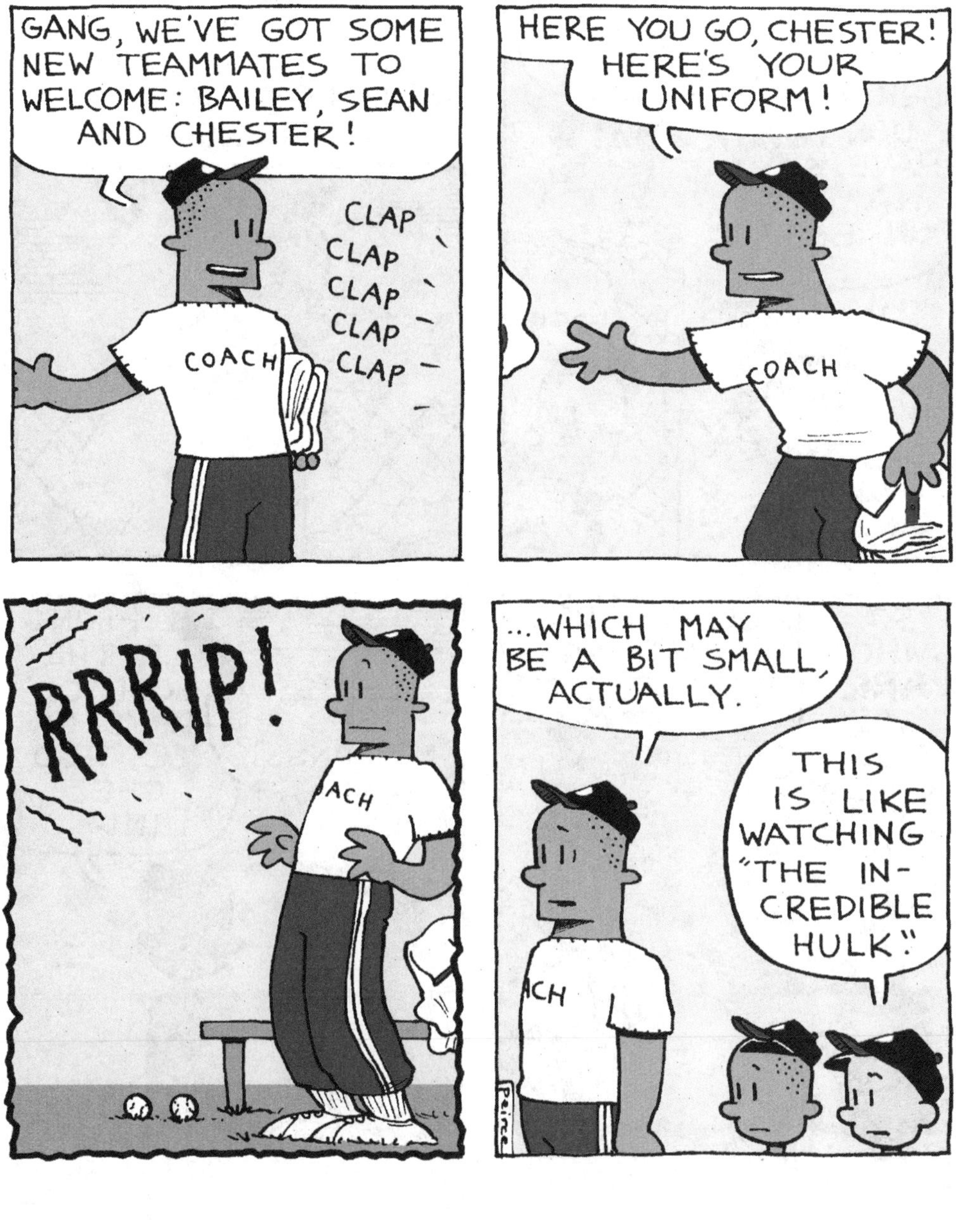
GANG, WE'VE GOT SOME NEW TEAMMATES TO WELCOME: BAILEY, SEAN AND CHESTER!
CLAP CLAP CLAP CLAP CLAP
COACH
HERE YOU GO, CHESTER! HERE'S YOUR UNIFORM!
COACH
RRRIP!
...WHICH MAY BE A BIT SMALL, ACTUALLY.
THIS IS LIKE WATCHING "THE INCREDIBLE HULK."

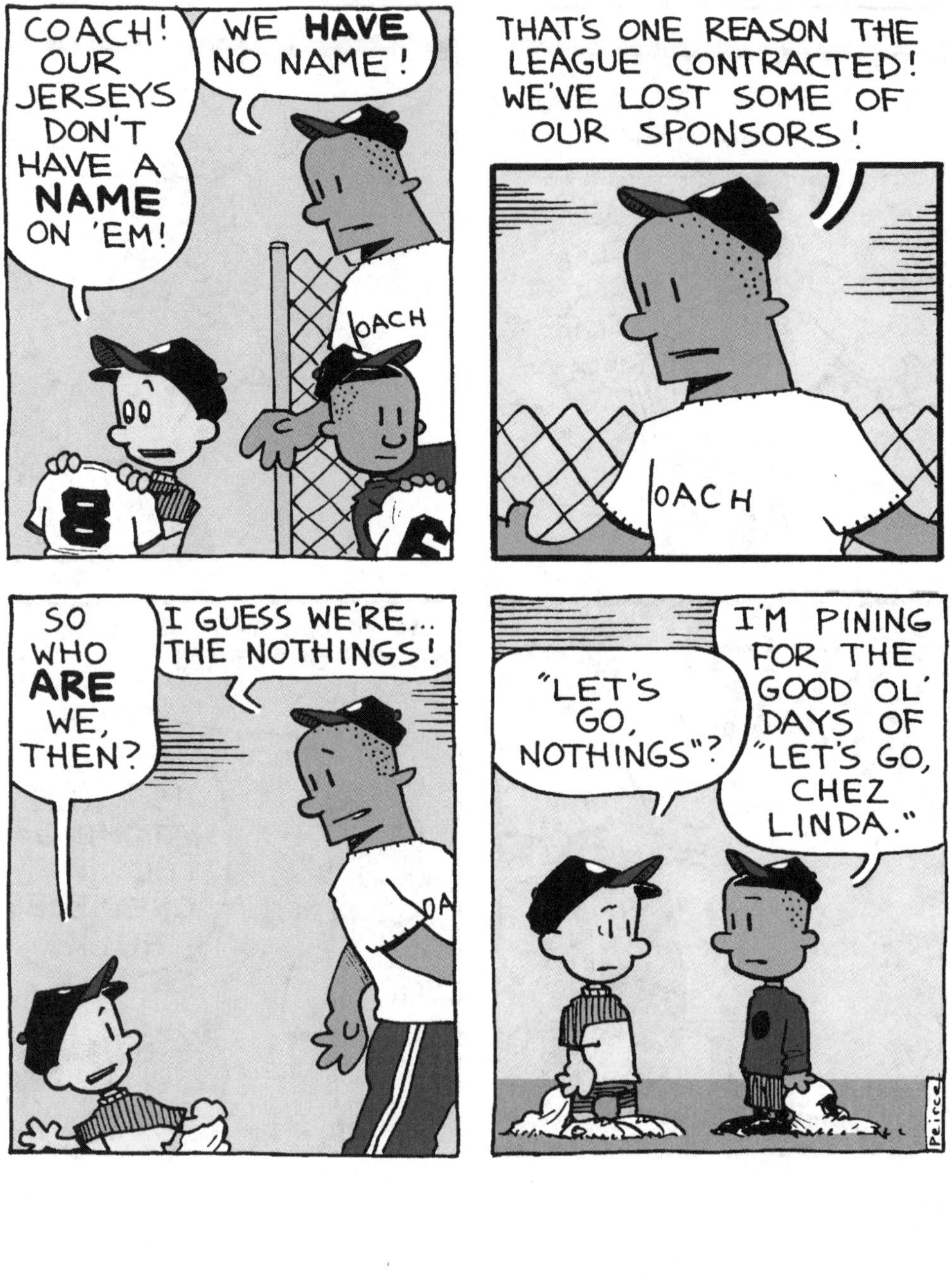

COACH! OUR JERSEYS DON'T HAVE A **NAME** ON 'EM!
WE **HAVE** NO NAME!
OACH
THAT'S ONE REASON THE LEAGUE CONTRACTED! WE'VE LOST SOME OF OUR SPONSORS!
OACH
SO WHO **ARE** WE, THEN?
I GUESS WE'RE... THE NOTHINGS!
"LET'S GO, NOTHINGS"?
I'M PINING FOR THE GOOD OL' DAYS OF "LET'S GO, CHEZ LINDA."
Peirce

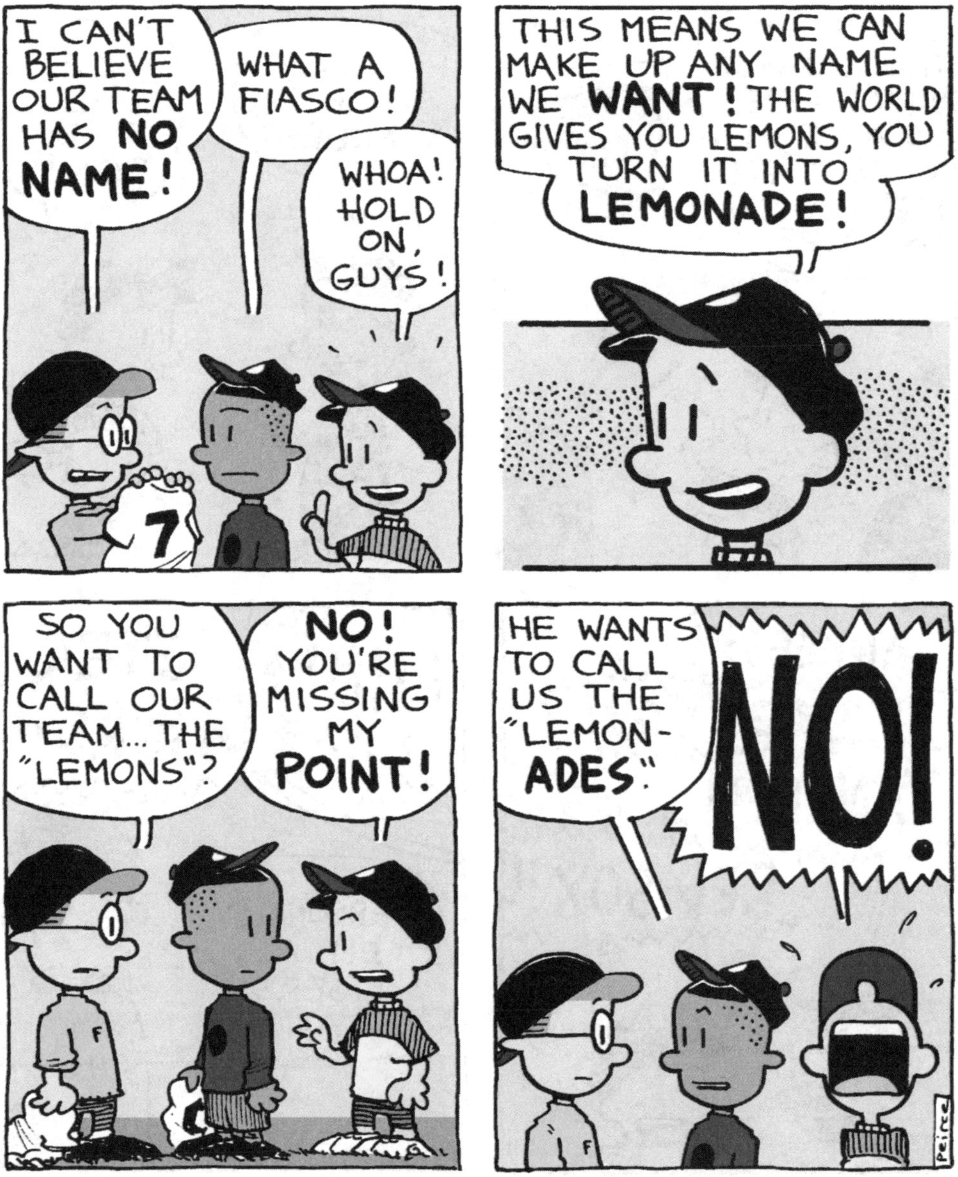
I CAN'T BELIEVE OUR TEAM HAS **NO NAME**!
WHAT A FIASCO!
WHOA! HOLD ON, GUYS!
THIS MEANS WE CAN MAKE UP ANY NAME WE **WANT**! THE WORLD GIVES YOU LEMONS, YOU TURN IT INTO **LEMONADE**!
SO YOU WANT TO CALL OUR TEAM... THE "LEMONS"?
NO! YOU'RE MISSING MY **POINT**!
HE WANTS TO CALL US THE "LEMON-**ADES**."
NO!

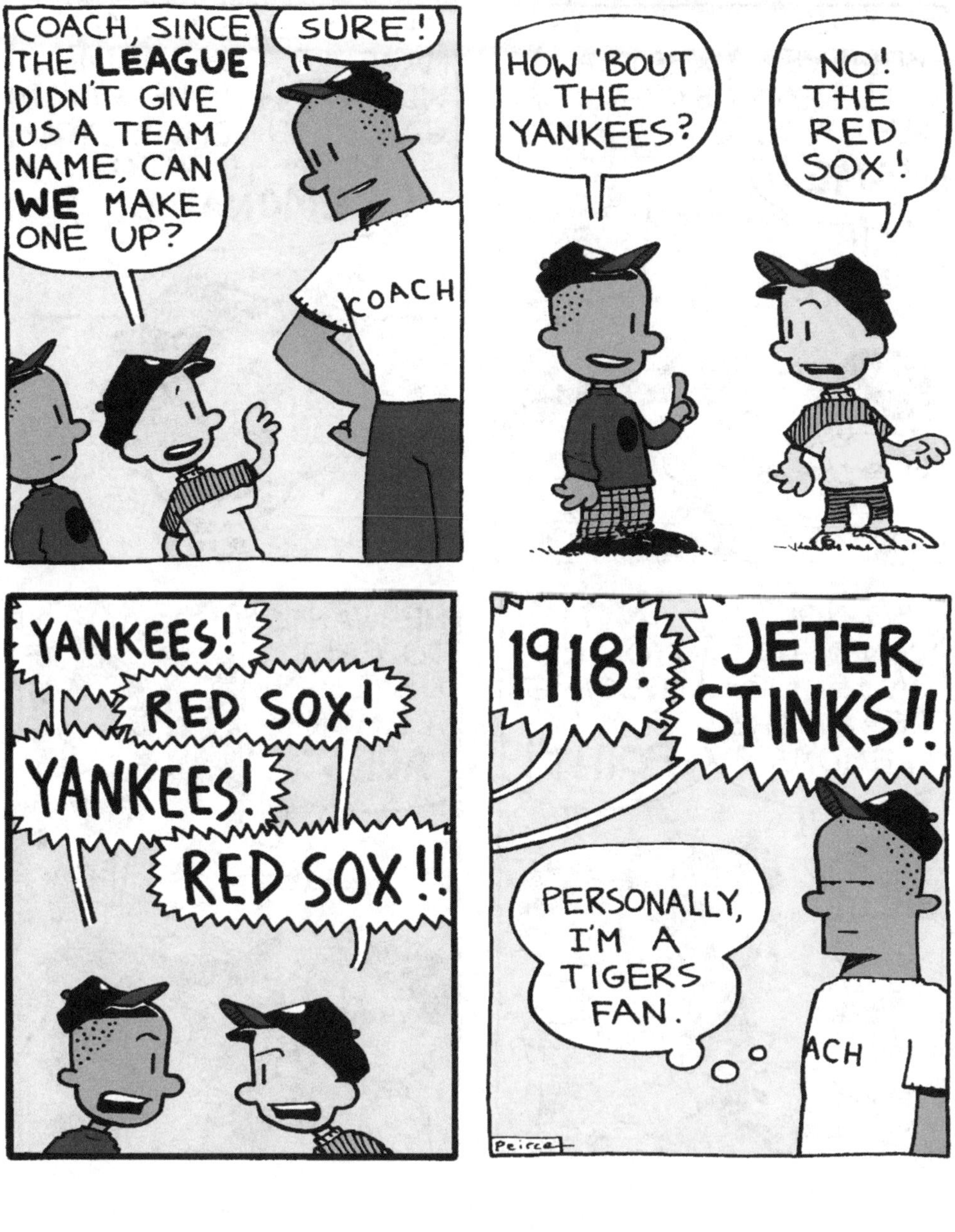
COACH, SINCE THE **LEAGUE** DIDN'T GIVE US A TEAM NAME, CAN **WE** MAKE ONE UP?
SURE!
COACH
HOW 'BOUT THE YANKEES?
NO! THE RED SOX!
YANKEES!
RED SOX!
YANKEES!
RED SOX!!
1918!
JETER STINKS!!
PERSONALLY, I'M A TIGERS FAN.
ACH
Peirce

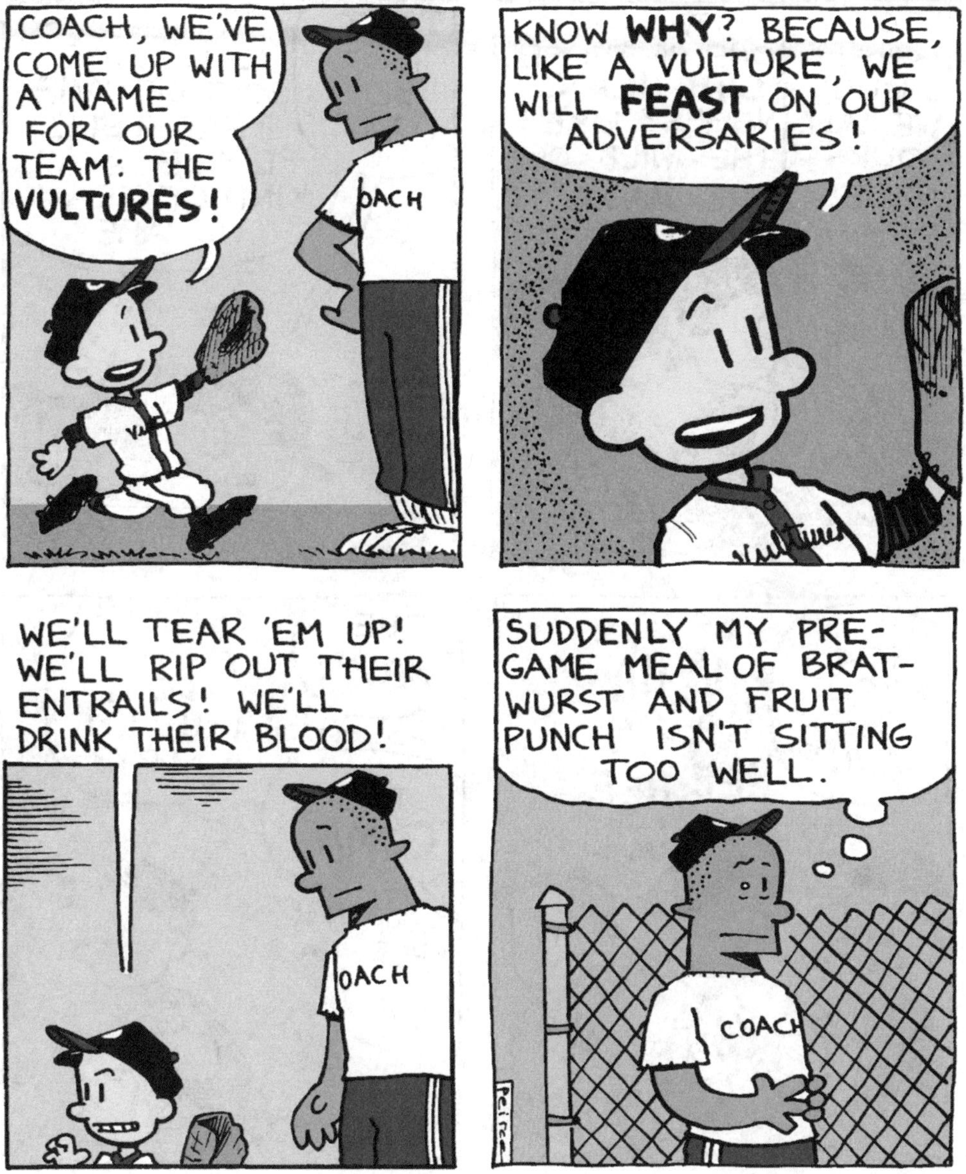
COACH, WE'VE COME UP WITH A NAME FOR OUR TEAM: THE **VULTURES**!
OACH
KNOW **WHY**? BECAUSE, LIKE A VULTURE, WE WILL **FEAST** ON OUR ADVERSARIES!
WE'LL TEAR 'EM UP! WE'LL RIP OUT THEIR ENTRAILS! WE'LL DRINK THEIR BLOOD!
OACH
SUDDENLY MY PRE-GAME MEAL OF BRAT-WURST AND FRUIT PUNCH ISN'T SITTING TOO WELL.
COACH
Peirce

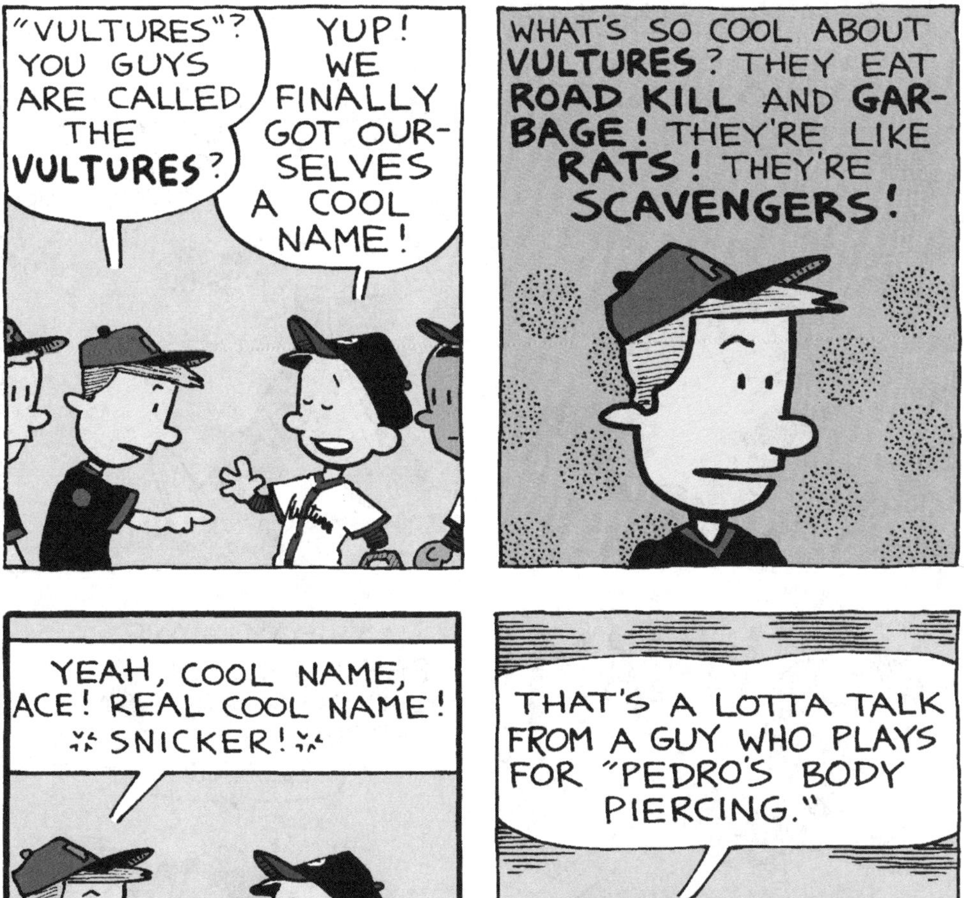
"VULTURES"? YOU GUYS ARE CALLED THE VULTURES?
YUP! WE FINALLY GOT OURSELVES A COOL NAME!
WHAT'S SO COOL ABOUT VULTURES? THEY EAT ROAD KILL AND GARBAGE! THEY'RE LIKE RATS! THEY'RE SCAVENGERS!
YEAH, COOL NAME, ACE! REAL COOL NAME! *SNICKER!*
THAT'S A LOTTA TALK FROM A GUY WHO PLAYS FOR "PEDRO'S BODY PIERCING."
Peirce

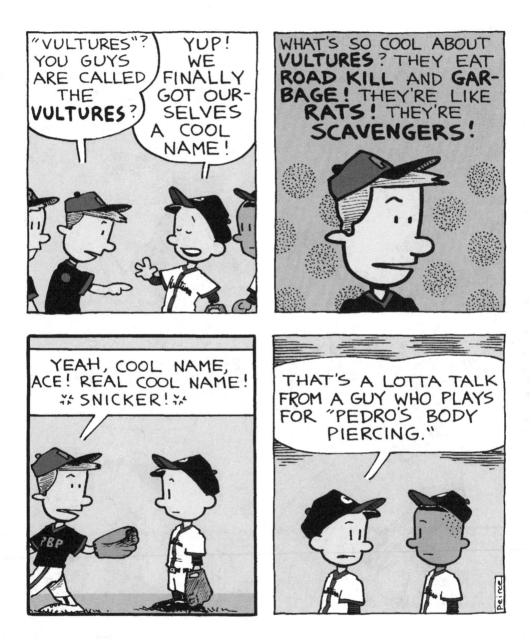

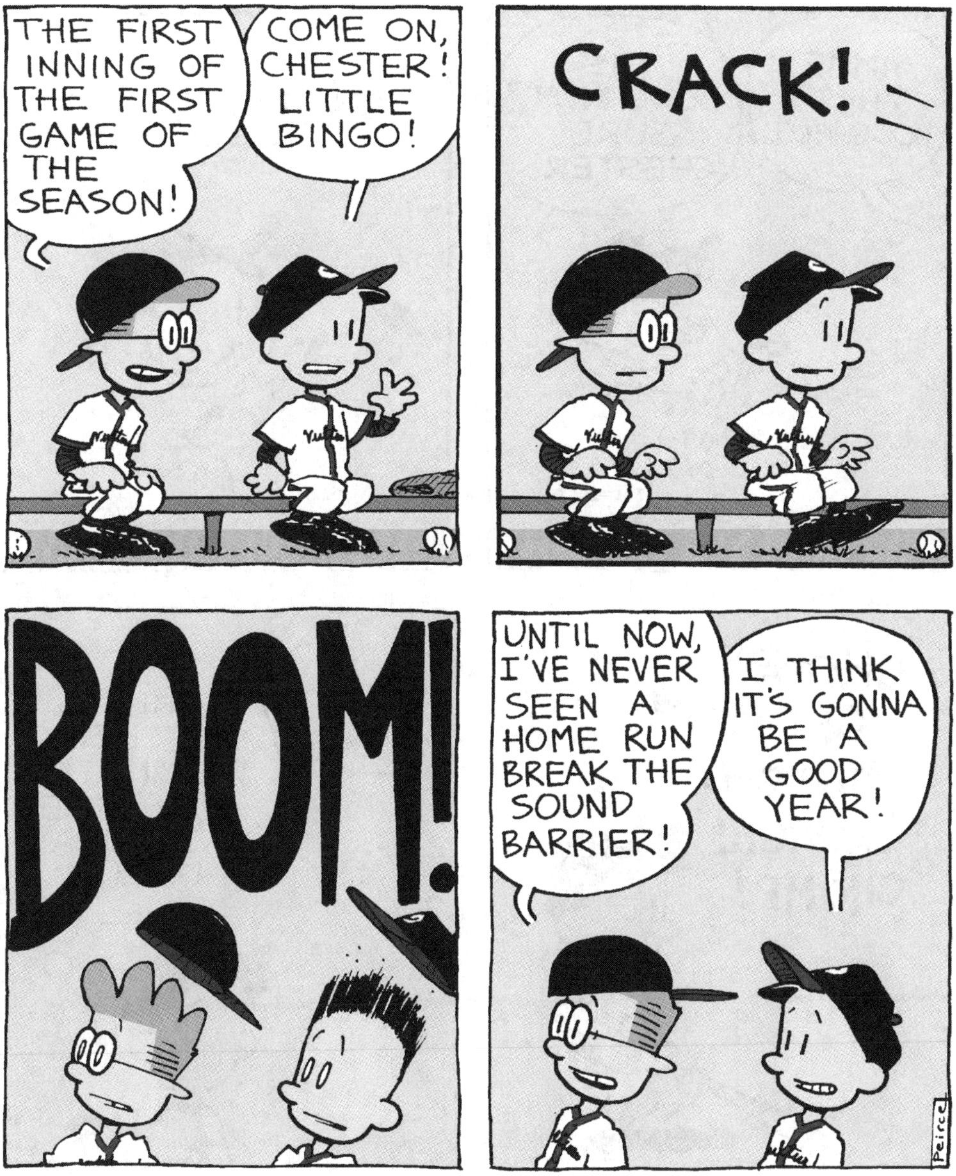
THE FIRST INNING OF THE FIRST GAME OF THE SEASON!
COME ON, CHESTER! LITTLE BINGO!
CRACK!
BOOM!
UNTIL NOW, I'VE NEVER SEEN A HOME RUN BREAK THE SOUND BARRIER!
I THINK IT'S GONNA BE A GOOD YEAR!
Peirce

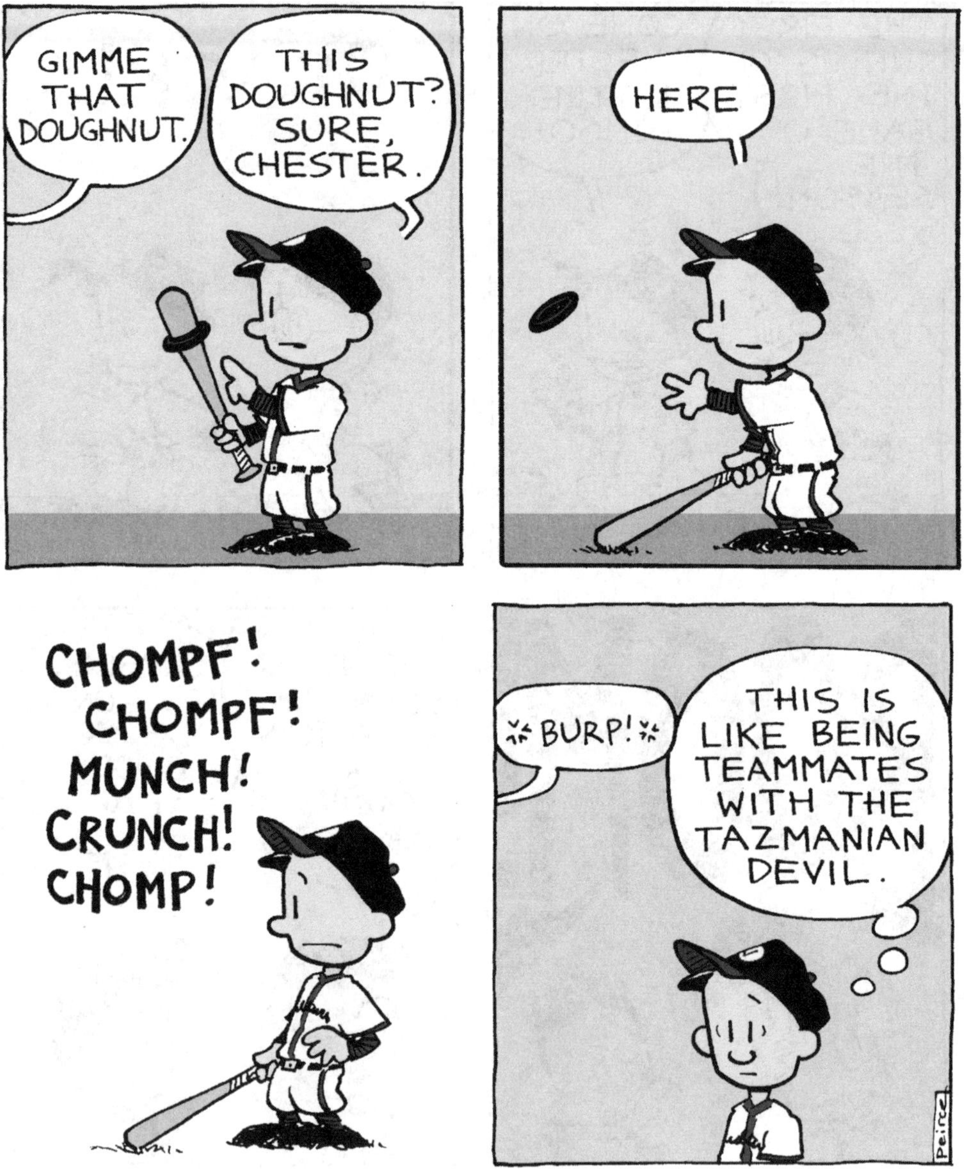
GIMME THAT DOUGHNUT.
THIS DOUGHNUT? SURE, CHESTER.
HERE
CHOMPF! CHOMPF! MUNCH! CRUNCH! CHOMP!
BURP!
THIS IS LIKE BEING TEAMMATES WITH THE TAZMANIAN DEVIL.
Peirce

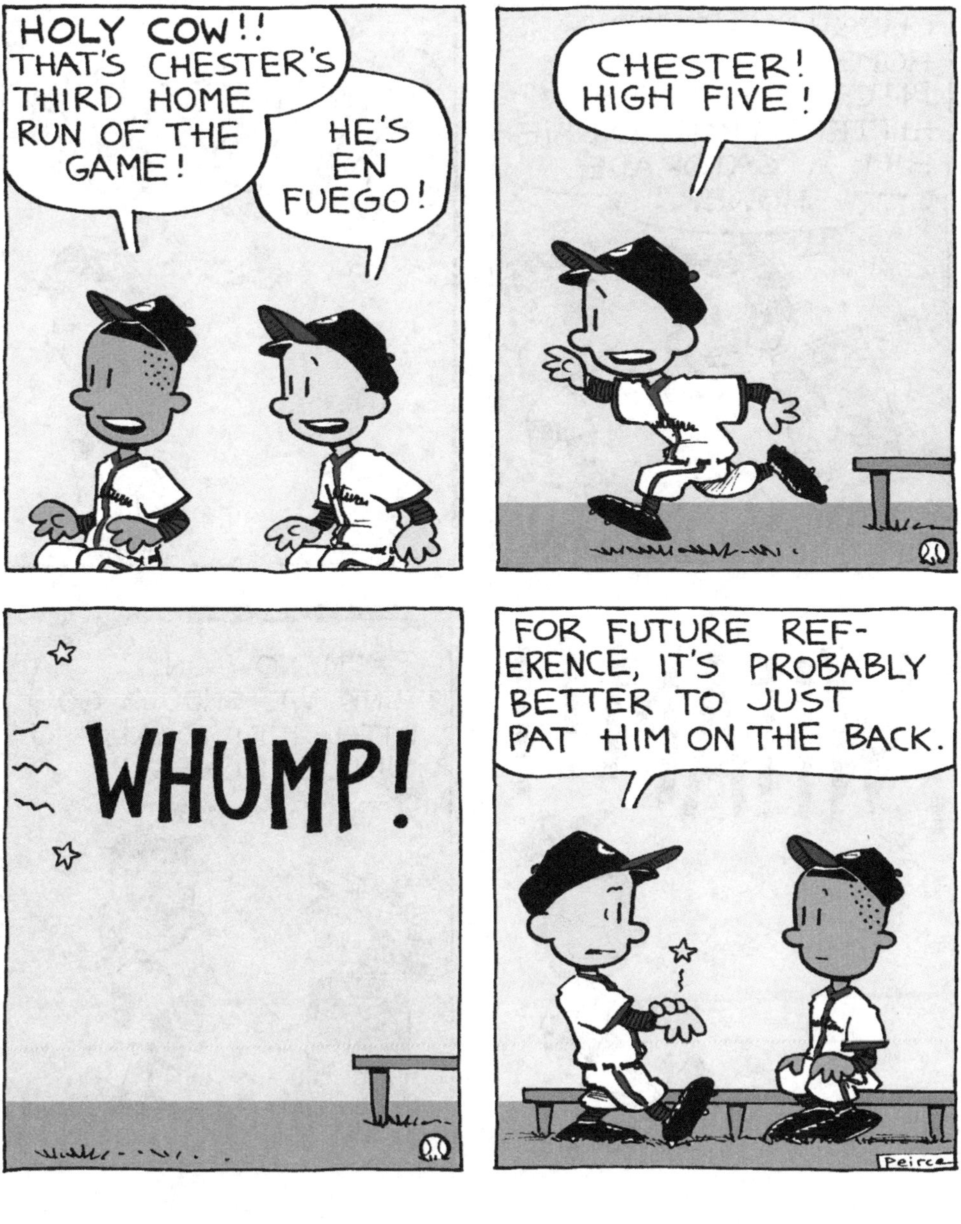
HOLY COW!! THAT'S CHESTER'S THIRD HOME RUN OF THE GAME!
HE'S EN FUEGO!
CHESTER! HIGH FIVE!
WHUMP!
FOR FUTURE REF- ERENCE, IT'S PROBABLY BETTER TO JUST PAT HIM ON THE BACK.
Peirce

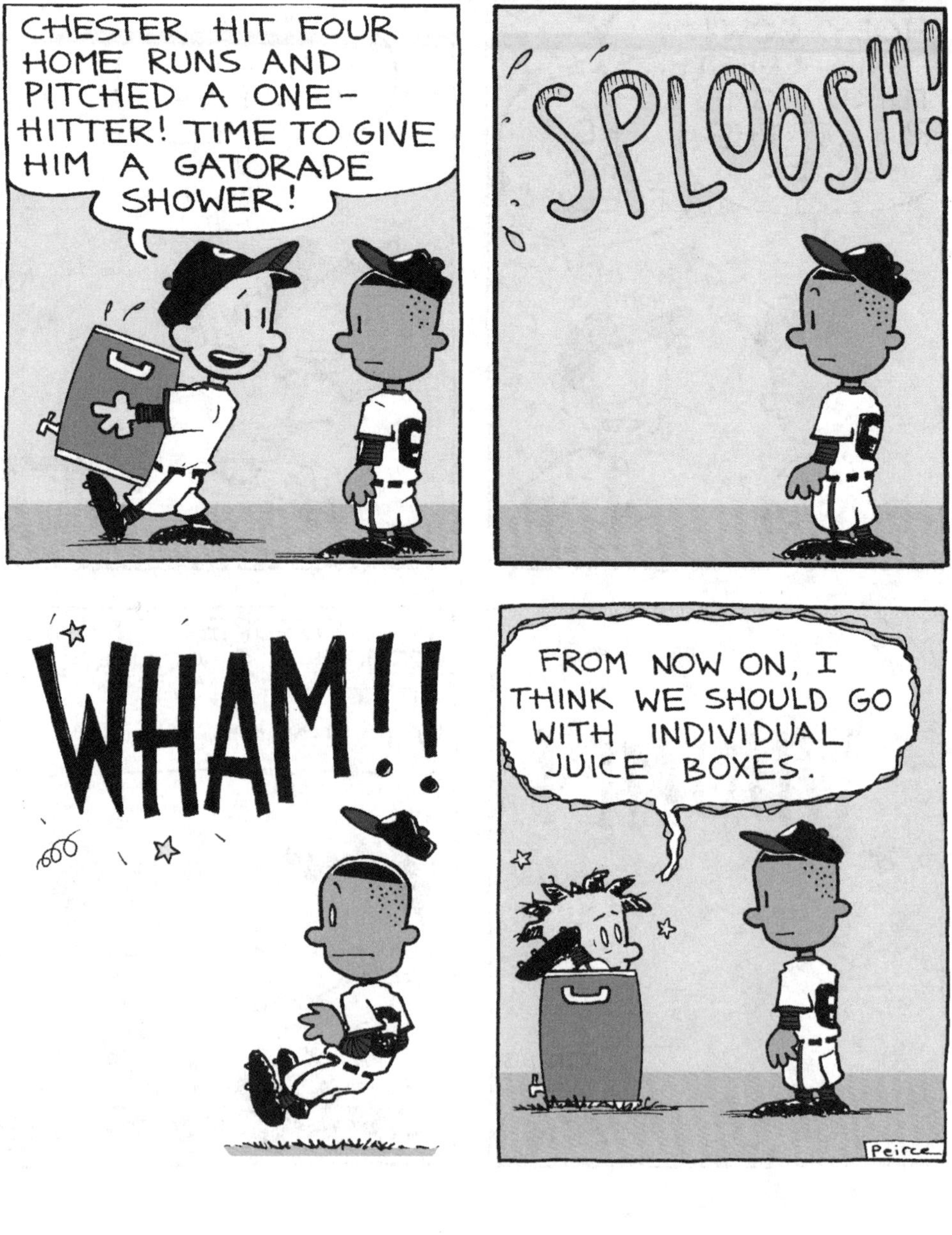
CHESTER HIT FOUR HOME RUNS AND PITCHED A ONE-HITTER! TIME TO GIVE HIM A GATORADE SHOWER!
SPLOOSH!
WHAM!!
FROM NOW ON, I THINK WE SHOULD GO WITH INDIVIDUAL JUICE BOXES.
Peirce

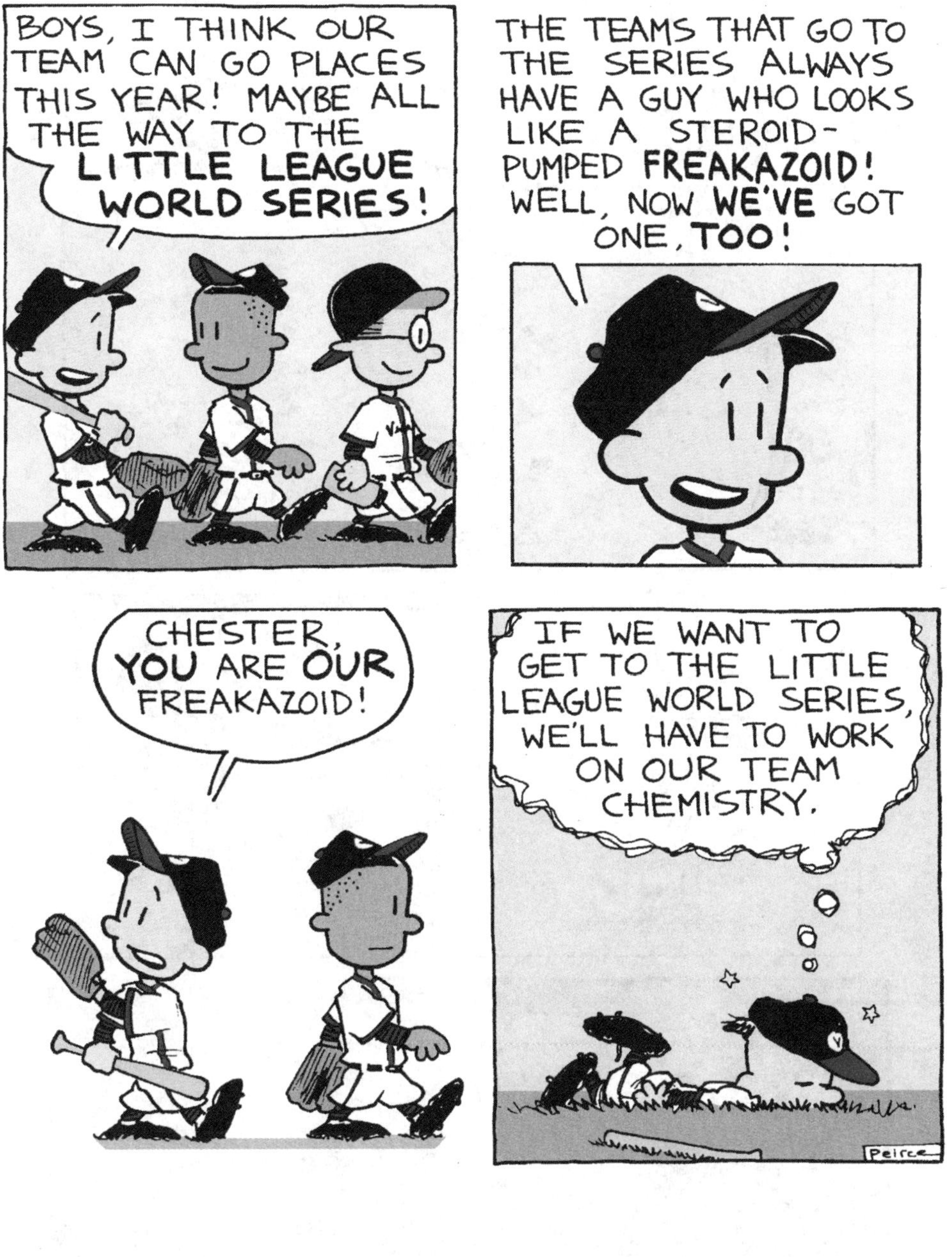
BOYS, I THINK OUR TEAM CAN GO PLACES THIS YEAR! MAYBE ALL THE WAY TO THE **LITTLE LEAGUE WORLD SERIES!**
THE TEAMS THAT GO TO THE SERIES ALWAYS HAVE A GUY WHO LOOKS LIKE A STEROID-PUMPED **FREAKAZOID!** WELL, NOW **WE'VE** GOT ONE, **TOO!**
CHESTER, **YOU** ARE **OUR** FREAKAZOID!
IF WE WANT TO GET TO THE LITTLE LEAGUE WORLD SERIES, WE'LL HAVE TO WORK ON OUR TEAM CHEMISTRY.
Peirce

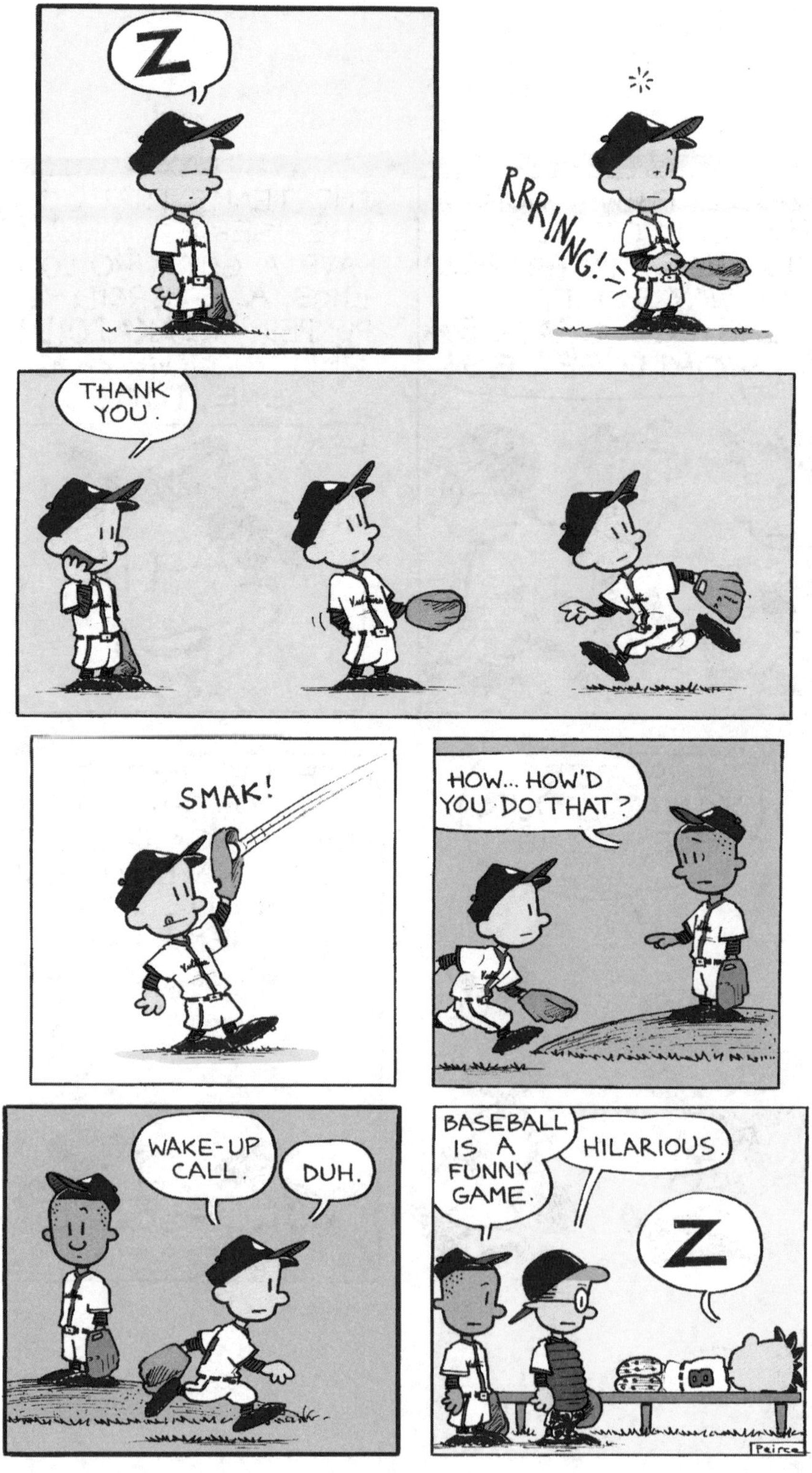
Z
RRRINNG!
THANK YOU.
SMAK!
HOW... HOW'D YOU DO THAT?
WAKE-UP CALL.
DUH.
BASEBALL IS A FUNNY GAME.
HILARIOUS.
Z
Peirce

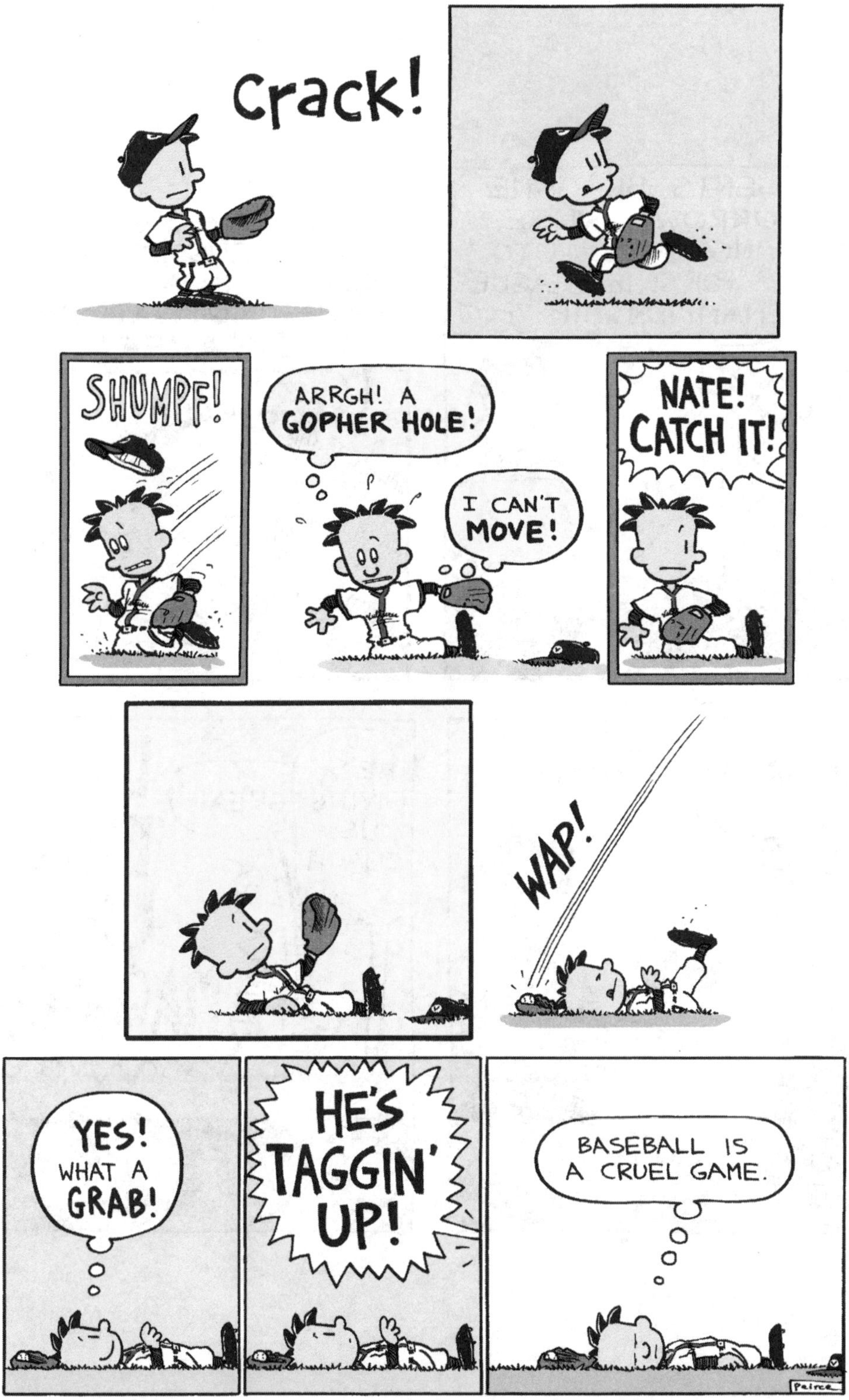
Crack!
SHUMPF!
ARRGH! A GOPHER HOLE!
I CAN'T MOVE!
NATE! CATCH IT!
WAP!
YES! WHAT A GRAB!
HE'S TAGGIN' UP!
BASEBALL IS A CRUEL GAME.
Peirce

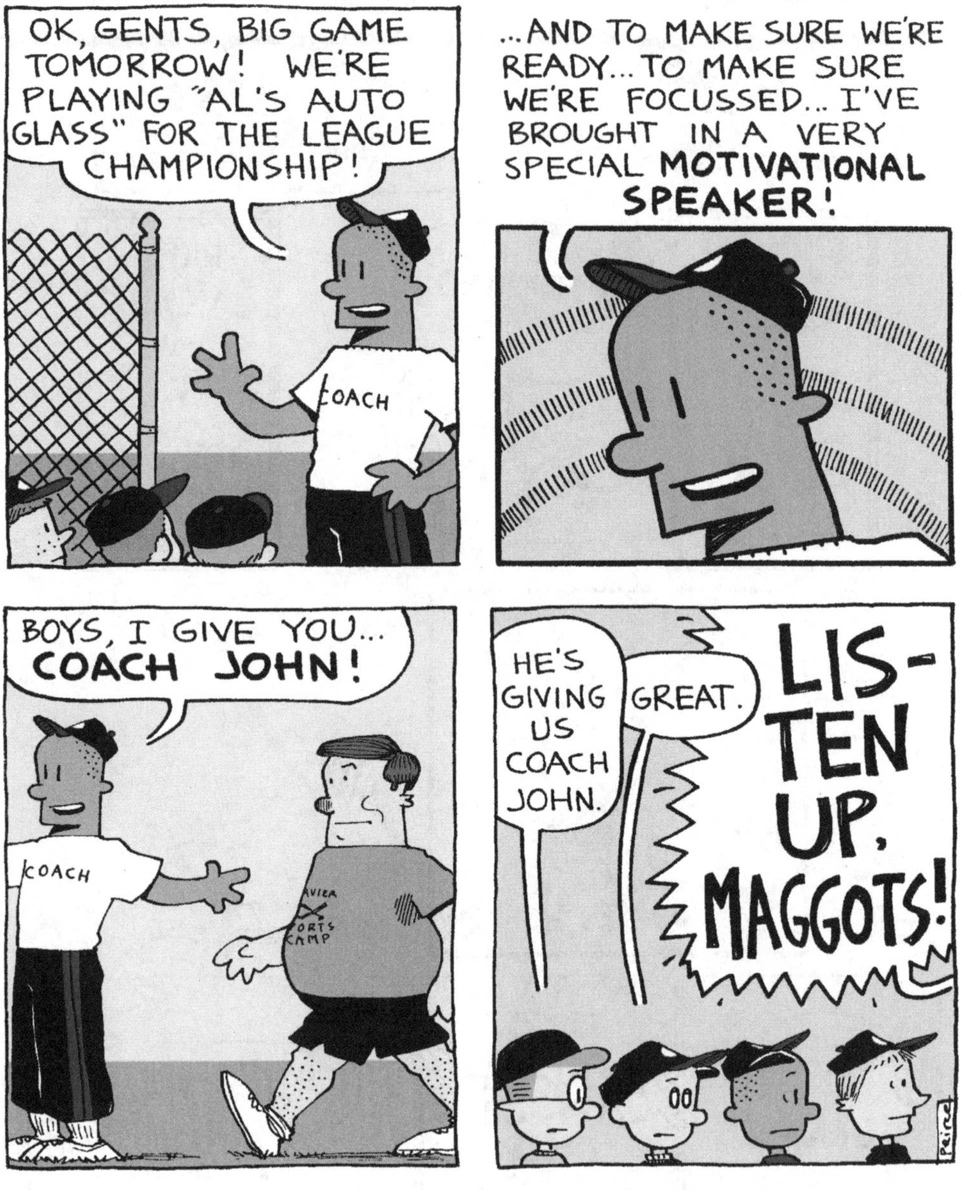
OK, GENTS, BIG GAME TOMORROW! WE'RE PLAYING "AL'S AUTO GLASS" FOR THE LEAGUE CHAMPIONSHIP!
COACH
...AND TO MAKE SURE WE'RE READY... TO MAKE SURE WE'RE FOCUSSED... I'VE BROUGHT IN A VERY SPECIAL **MOTIVATIONAL SPEAKER**!
BOYS, I GIVE YOU... **COACH JOHN**!
COACH
HE'S GIVING US COACH JOHN.
GREAT.
LIS-TEN UP, MAGGOTS!
Peirce

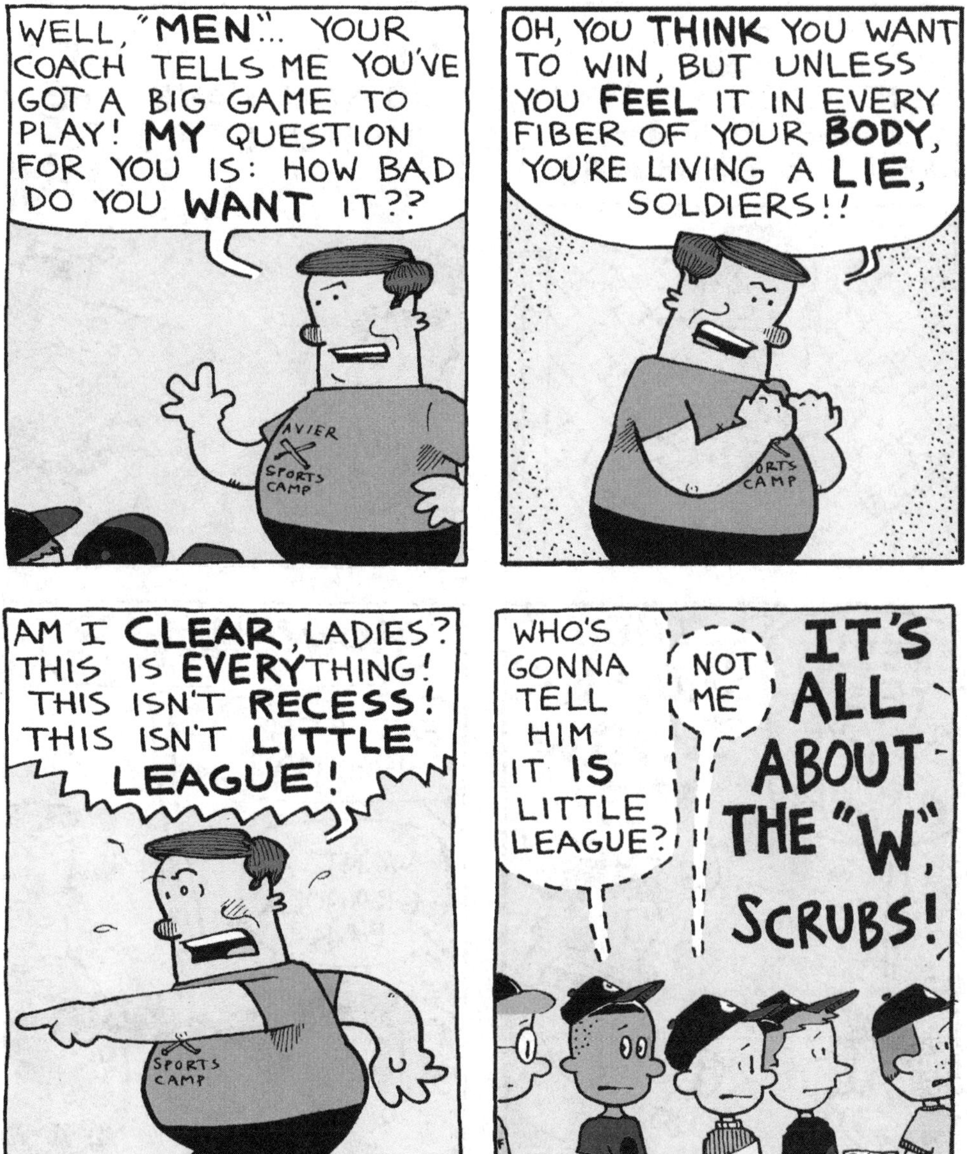
WELL, "MEN"... YOUR COACH TELLS ME YOU'VE GOT A BIG GAME TO PLAY! MY QUESTION FOR YOU IS: HOW BAD DO YOU WANT IT??
XAVIER SPORTS CAMP
OH, YOU THINK YOU WANT TO WIN, BUT UNLESS YOU FEEL IT IN EVERY FIBER OF YOUR BODY, YOU'RE LIVING A LIE, SOLDIERS!!
AM I CLEAR, LADIES? THIS IS EVERYTHING! THIS ISN'T RECESS! THIS ISN'T LITTLE LEAGUE!
SPORTS CAMP
WHO'S GONNA TELL HIM IT IS LITTLE LEAGUE?
NOT ME
IT'S ALL ABOUT THE "W", SCRUBS!
Peirce

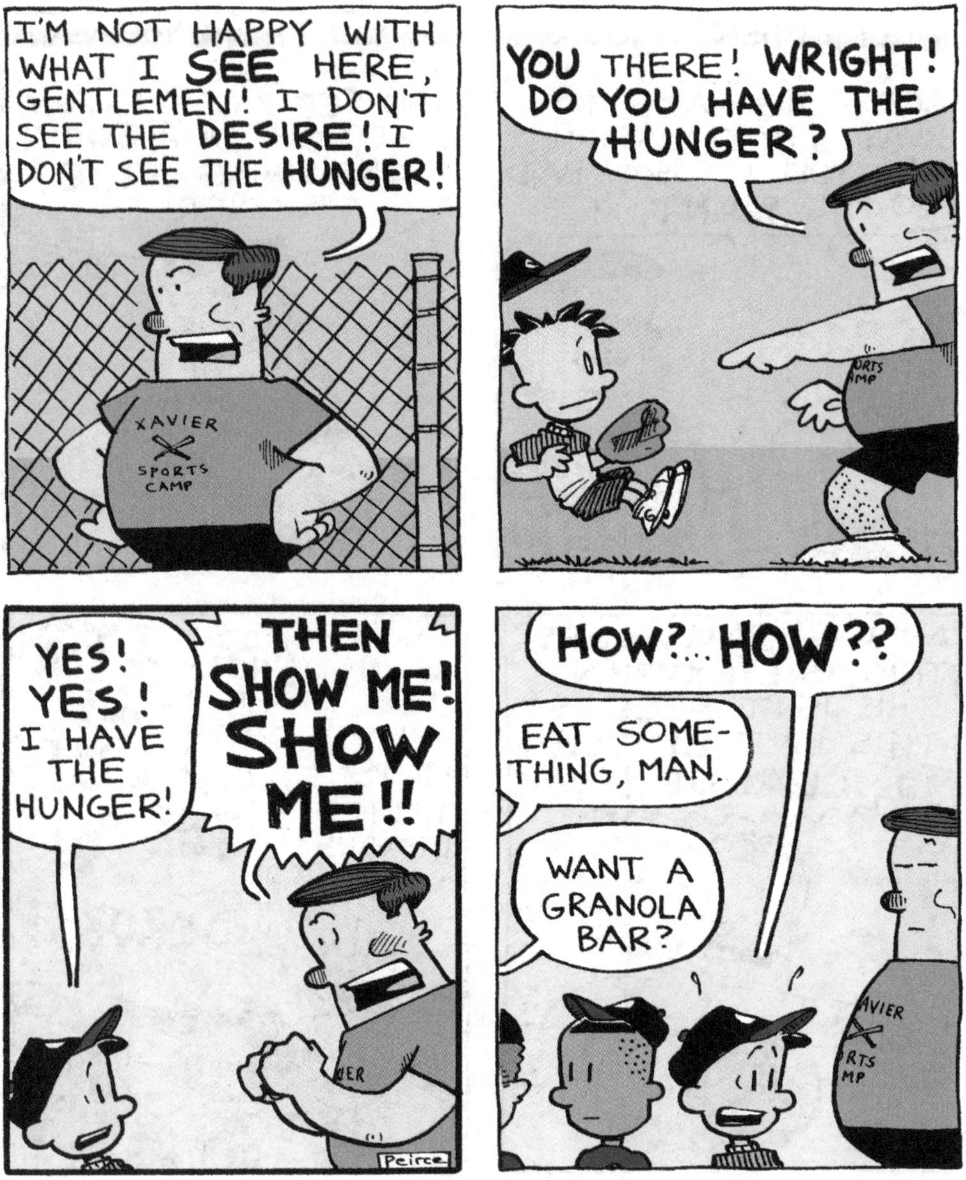
I'M NOT HAPPY WITH WHAT I SEE HERE, GENTLEMEN! I DON'T SEE THE DESIRE! I DON'T SEE THE HUNGER!
XAVIER SPORTS CAMP
YOU THERE! WRIGHT! DO YOU HAVE THE HUNGER?
YES! YES! I HAVE THE HUNGER!
THEN SHOW ME! SHOW ME!!
HOW?... HOW??
EAT SOME-THING, MAN.
WANT A GRANOLA BAR?
Peirce

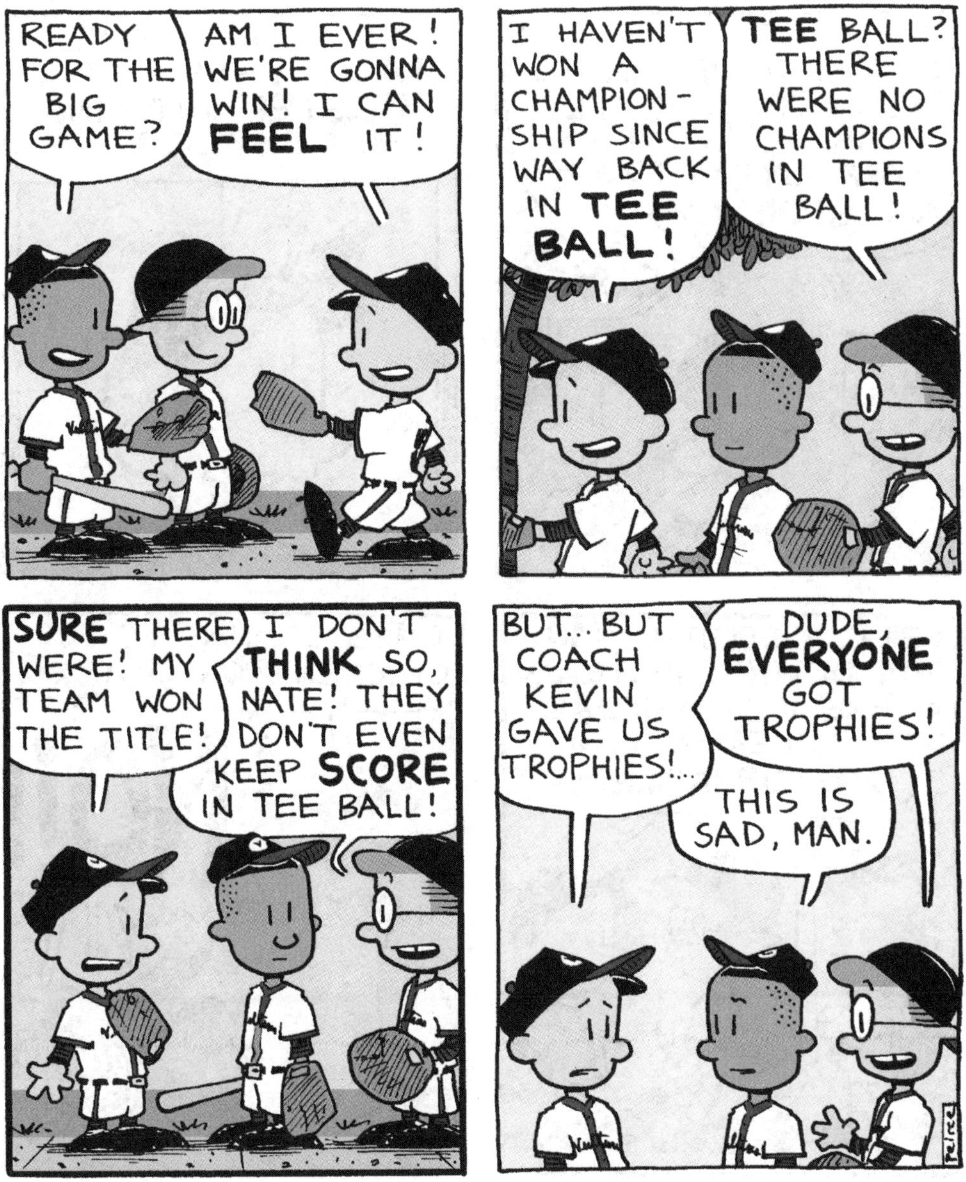
READY FOR THE BIG GAME?
AM I EVER! WE'RE GONNA WIN! I CAN **FEEL** IT!
I HAVEN'T WON A CHAMPION-SHIP SINCE WAY BACK IN **TEE BALL**!
TEE BALL? THERE WERE NO CHAMPIONS IN TEE BALL!
SURE THERE WERE! MY TEAM WON THE TITLE!
I DON'T **THINK** SO, NATE! THEY DON'T EVEN KEEP **SCORE** IN TEE BALL!
BUT... BUT COACH KEVIN GAVE US TROPHIES!...
DUDE, **EVERYONE** GOT TROPHIES!
THIS IS SAD, MAN.
peirce

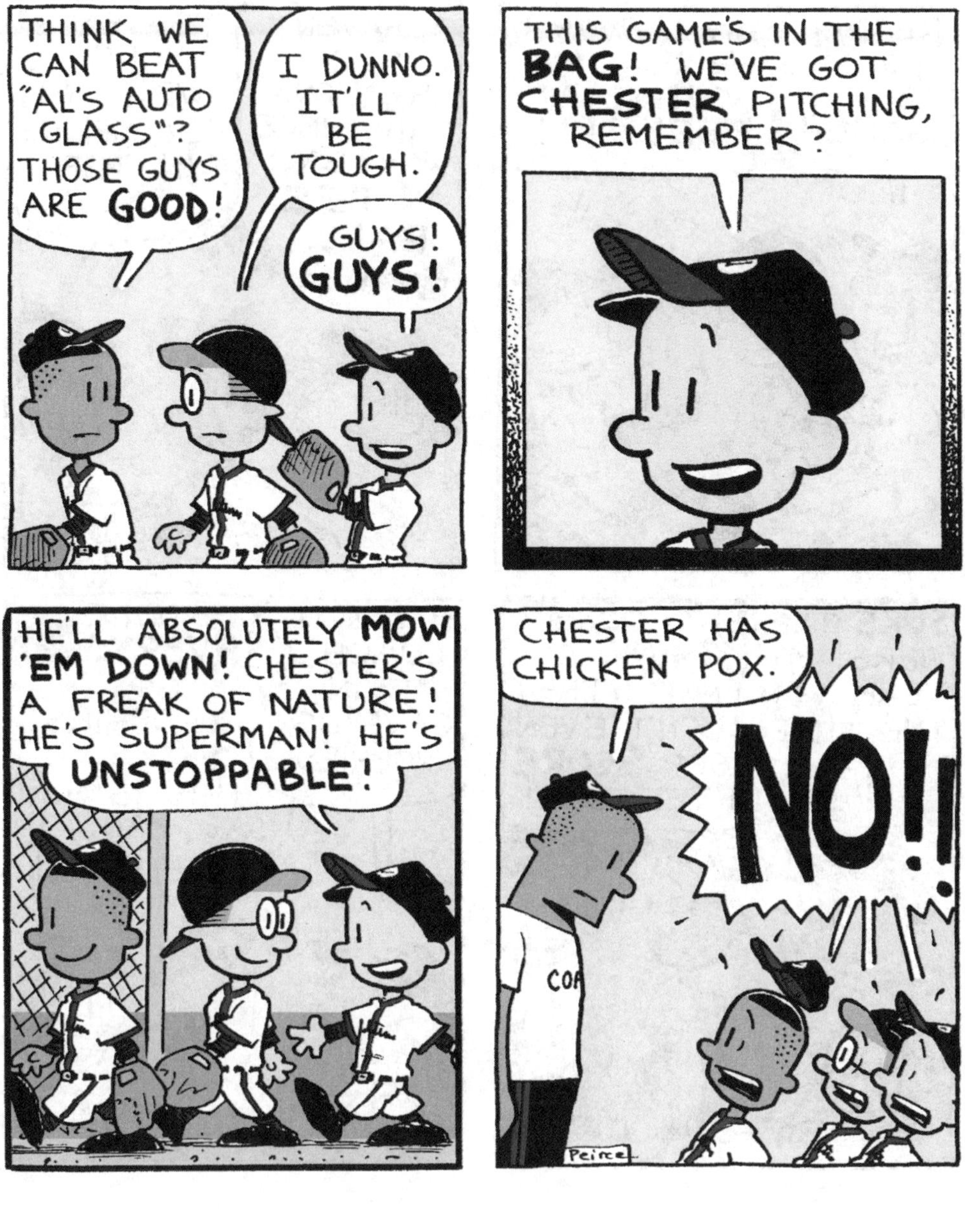
THINK WE CAN BEAT "AL'S AUTO GLASS"? THOSE GUYS ARE GOOD!
I DUNNO. IT'LL BE TOUGH.
GUYS! GUYS!
THIS GAME'S IN THE BAG! WE'VE GOT CHESTER PITCHING, REMEMBER?
HE'LL ABSOLUTELY MOW 'EM DOWN! CHESTER'S A FREAK OF NATURE! HE'S SUPERMAN! HE'S UNSTOPPABLE!
CHESTER HAS CHICKEN POX.
NO!!
Peirce

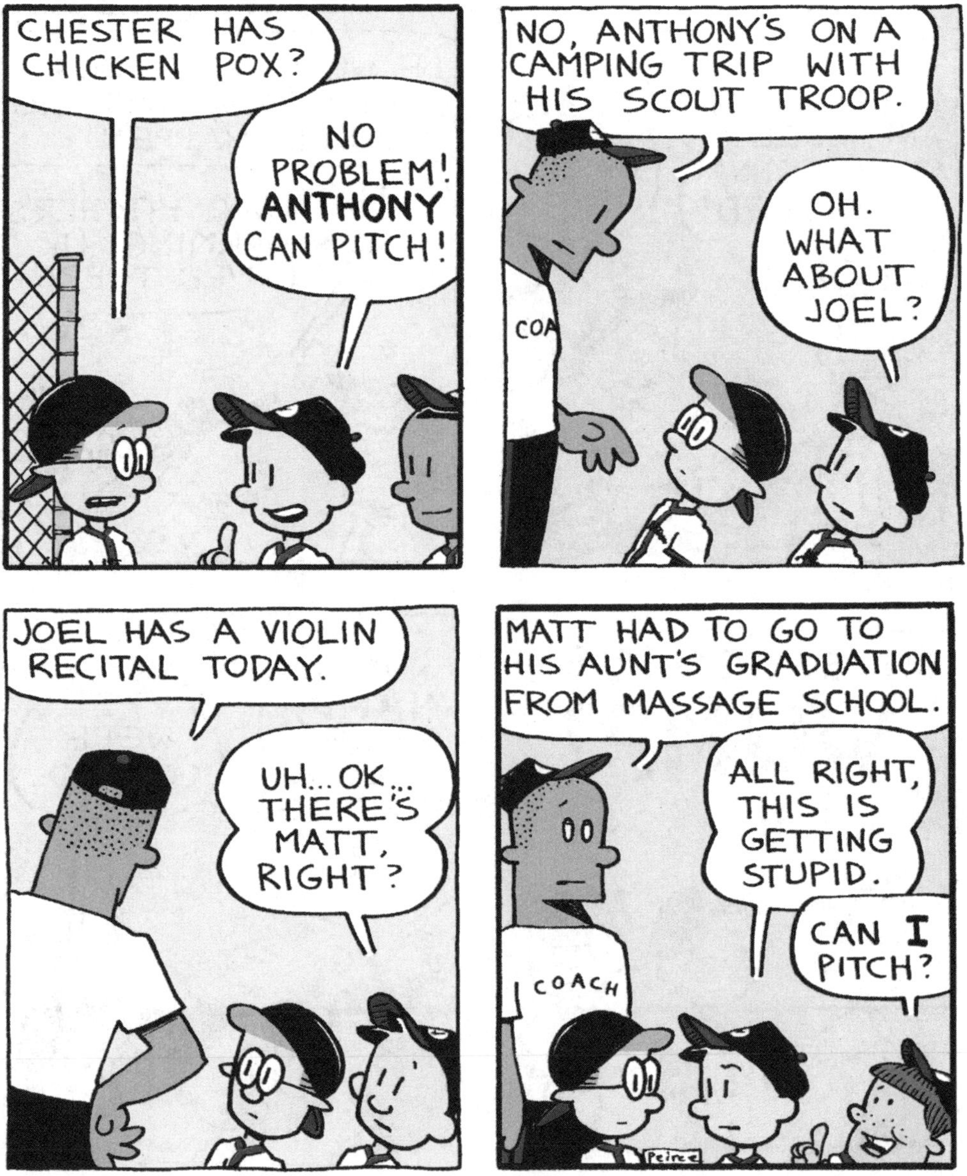
CHESTER HAS CHICKEN POX?
NO PROBLEM! **ANTHONY** CAN PITCH!
NO, ANTHONY'S ON A CAMPING TRIP WITH HIS SCOUT TROOP.
OH. WHAT ABOUT JOEL?
JOEL HAS A VIOLIN RECITAL TODAY.
UH... OK... THERE'S MATT, RIGHT?
MATT HAD TO GO TO HIS AUNT'S GRADUATION FROM MASSAGE SCHOOL.
ALL RIGHT, THIS IS GETTING STUPID.
CAN **I** PITCH?
COACH
Peirce

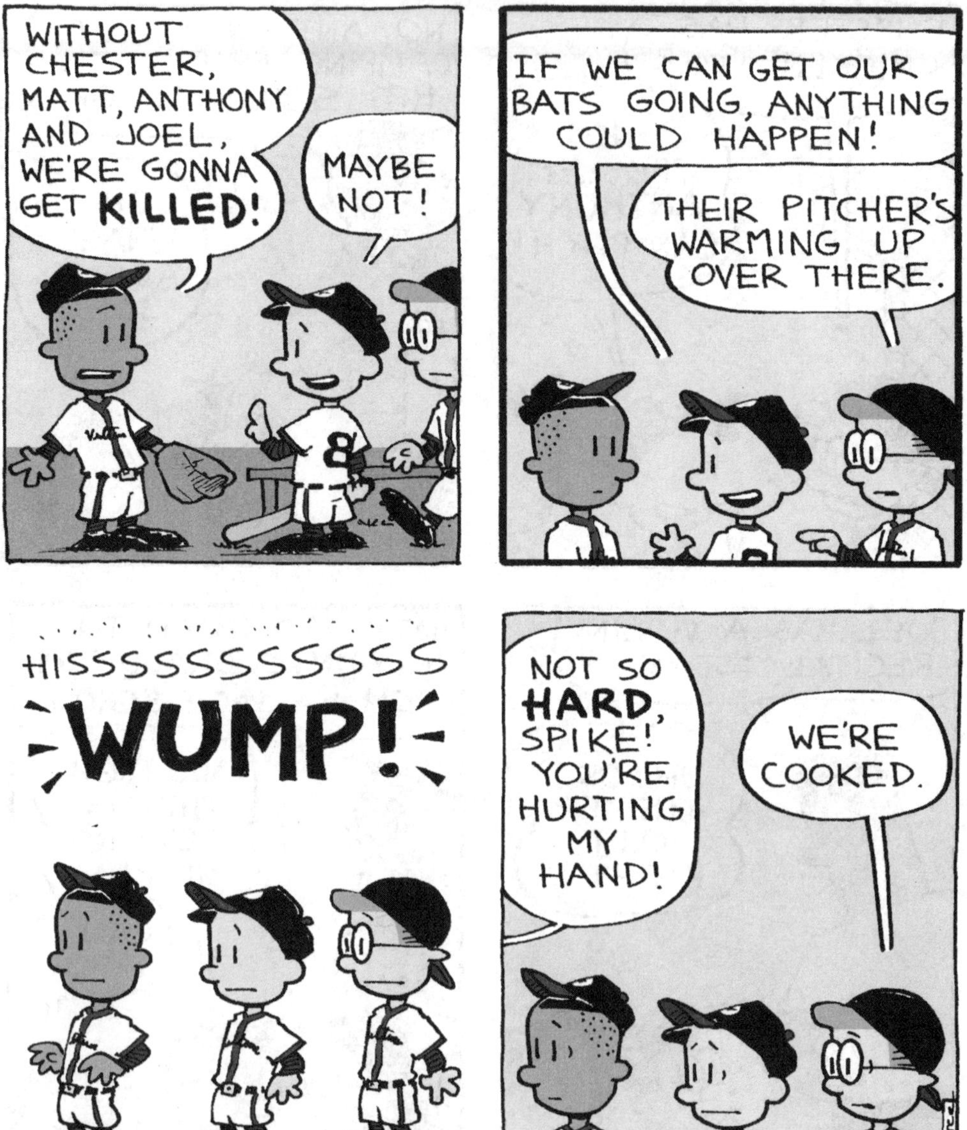

WITHOUT CHESTER, MATT, ANTHONY AND JOEL, WE'RE GONNA GET **KILLED**!
MAYBE NOT!
IF WE CAN GET OUR BATS GOING, ANYTHING COULD HAPPEN!
THEIR PITCHER'S WARMING UP OVER THERE.
HISSSSSSSSSSSS
WUMP!
NOT SO **HARD**, SPIKE! YOU'RE HURTING MY HAND!
WE'RE COOKED.

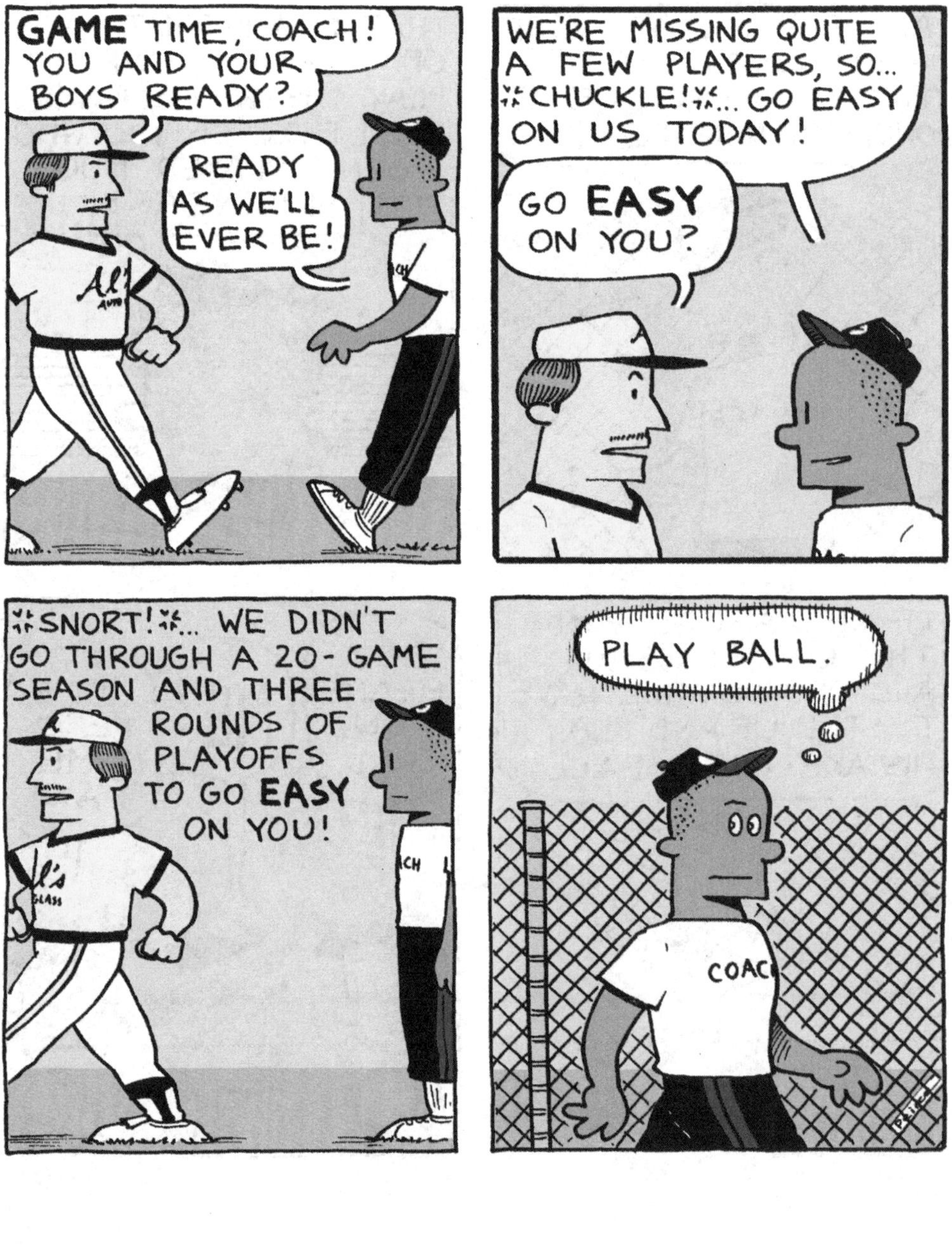
GAME TIME, COACH! YOU AND YOUR BOYS READY?
READY AS WE'LL EVER BE!
WE'RE MISSING QUITE A FEW PLAYERS, SO... *CHUCKLE!*... GO EASY ON US TODAY!
GO EASY ON YOU?
SNORT!... WE DIDN'T GO THROUGH A 20-GAME SEASON AND THREE ROUNDS OF PLAYOFFS TO GO EASY ON YOU!
PLAY BALL.
COAC

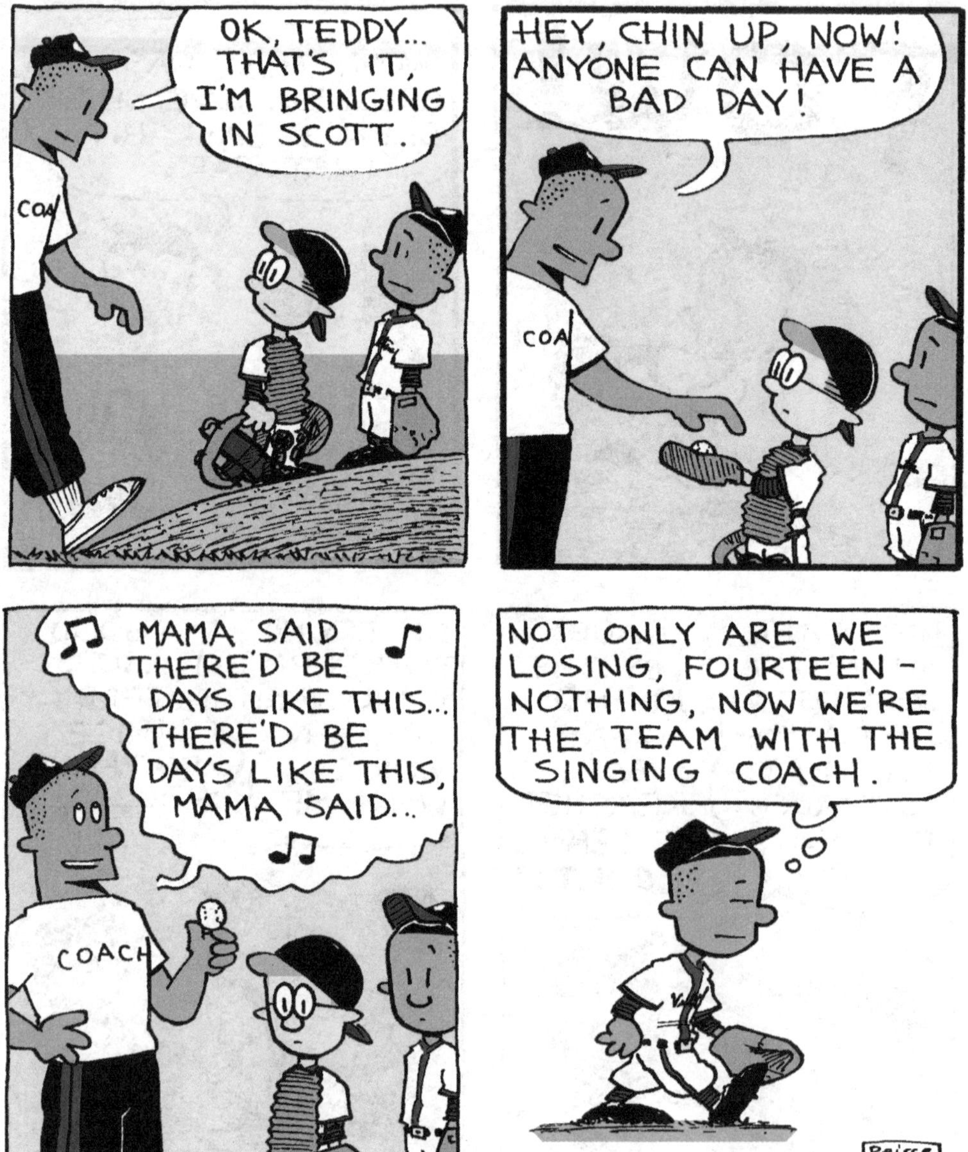
OK, TEDDY... THAT'S IT, I'M BRINGING IN SCOTT.
COA
HEY, CHIN UP, NOW! ANYONE CAN HAVE A BAD DAY!
COA
MAMA SAID THERE'D BE DAYS LIKE THIS... THERE'D BE DAYS LIKE THIS, MAMA SAID...
COACH
NOT ONLY ARE WE LOSING, FOURTEEN-NOTHING, NOW WE'RE THE TEAM WITH THE SINGING COACH.
Peirce

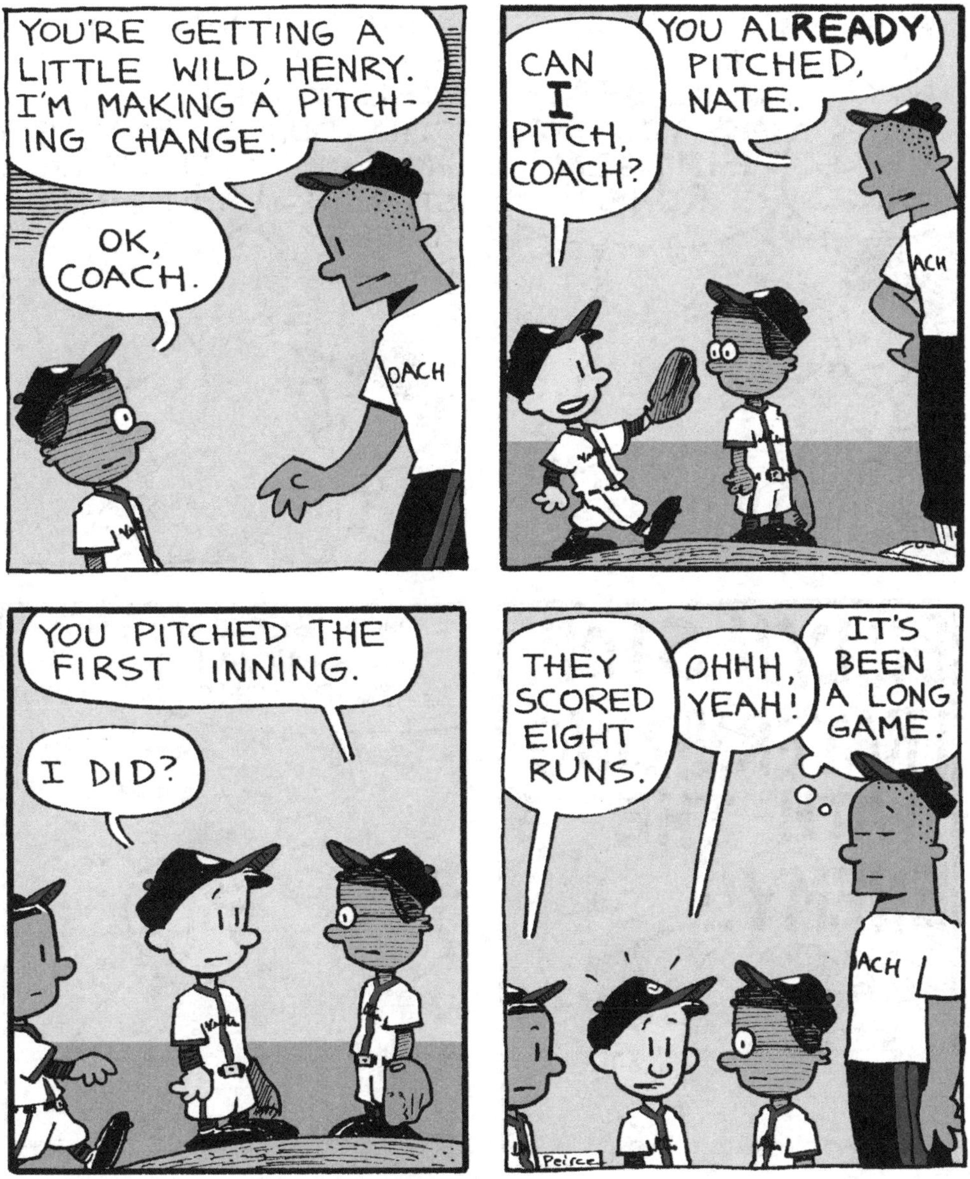
YOU'RE GETTING A LITTLE WILD, HENRY. I'M MAKING A PITCHING CHANGE.
OK, COACH.
OACH
CAN I PITCH, COACH?
YOU ALREADY PITCHED, NATE.
ACH
YOU PITCHED THE FIRST INNING.
I DID?
THEY SCORED EIGHT RUNS.
OHHH, YEAH!
IT'S BEEN A LONG GAME.
ACH
Peirce

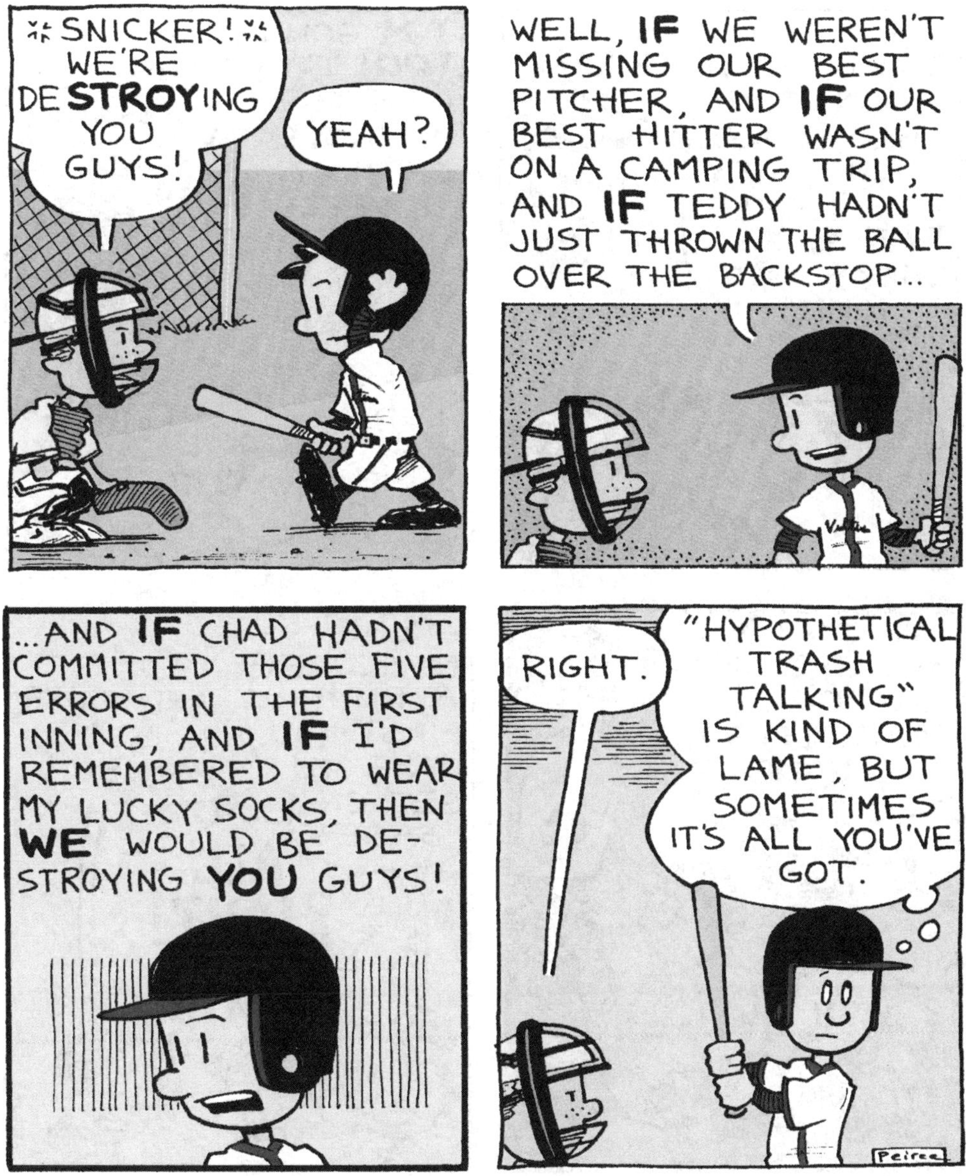
SNICKER! WE'RE DE**STROY**ING YOU GUYS!
YEAH?
WELL, **IF** WE WEREN'T MISSING OUR BEST PITCHER, AND **IF** OUR BEST HITTER WASN'T ON A CAMPING TRIP, AND **IF** TEDDY HADN'T JUST THROWN THE BALL OVER THE BACKSTOP...
...AND **IF** CHAD HADN'T COMMITTED THOSE FIVE ERRORS IN THE FIRST INNING, AND **IF** I'D REMEMBERED TO WEAR MY LUCKY SOCKS, THEN **WE** WOULD BE DE-STROYING **YOU** GUYS!
RIGHT.
"HYPOTHETICAL TRASH TALKING" IS KIND OF LAME, BUT SOMETIMES IT'S ALL YOU'VE GOT.
Peirce

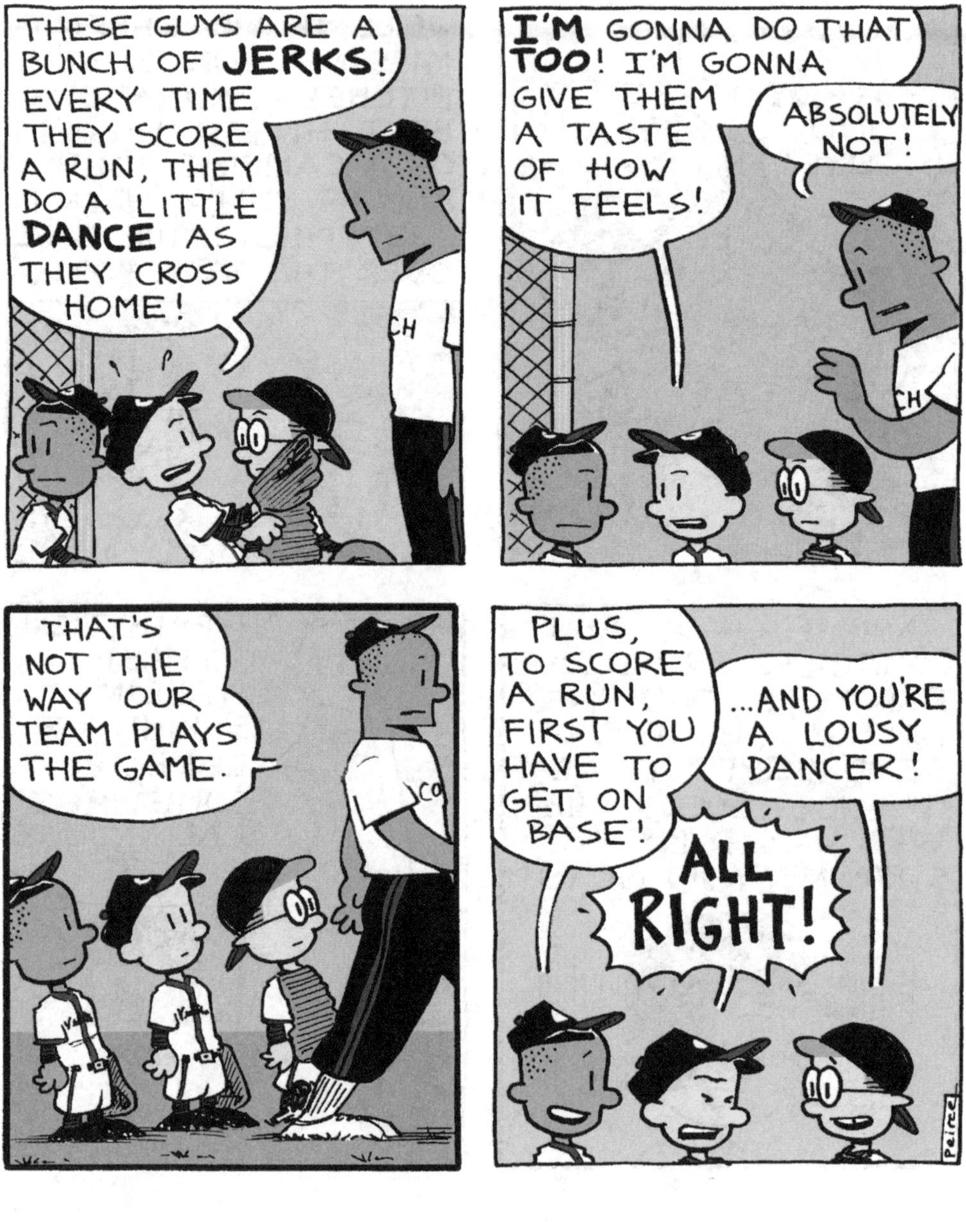
THESE GUYS ARE A BUNCH OF JERKS! EVERY TIME THEY SCORE A RUN, THEY DO A LITTLE DANCE AS THEY CROSS HOME!
I'M GONNA DO THAT TOO! I'M GONNA GIVE THEM A TASTE OF HOW IT FEELS!
ABSOLUTELY NOT!
THAT'S NOT THE WAY OUR TEAM PLAYS THE GAME.
PLUS, TO SCORE A RUN, FIRST YOU HAVE TO GET ON BASE!
...AND YOU'RE A LOUSY DANCER!
ALL RIGHT!
Peirce

143

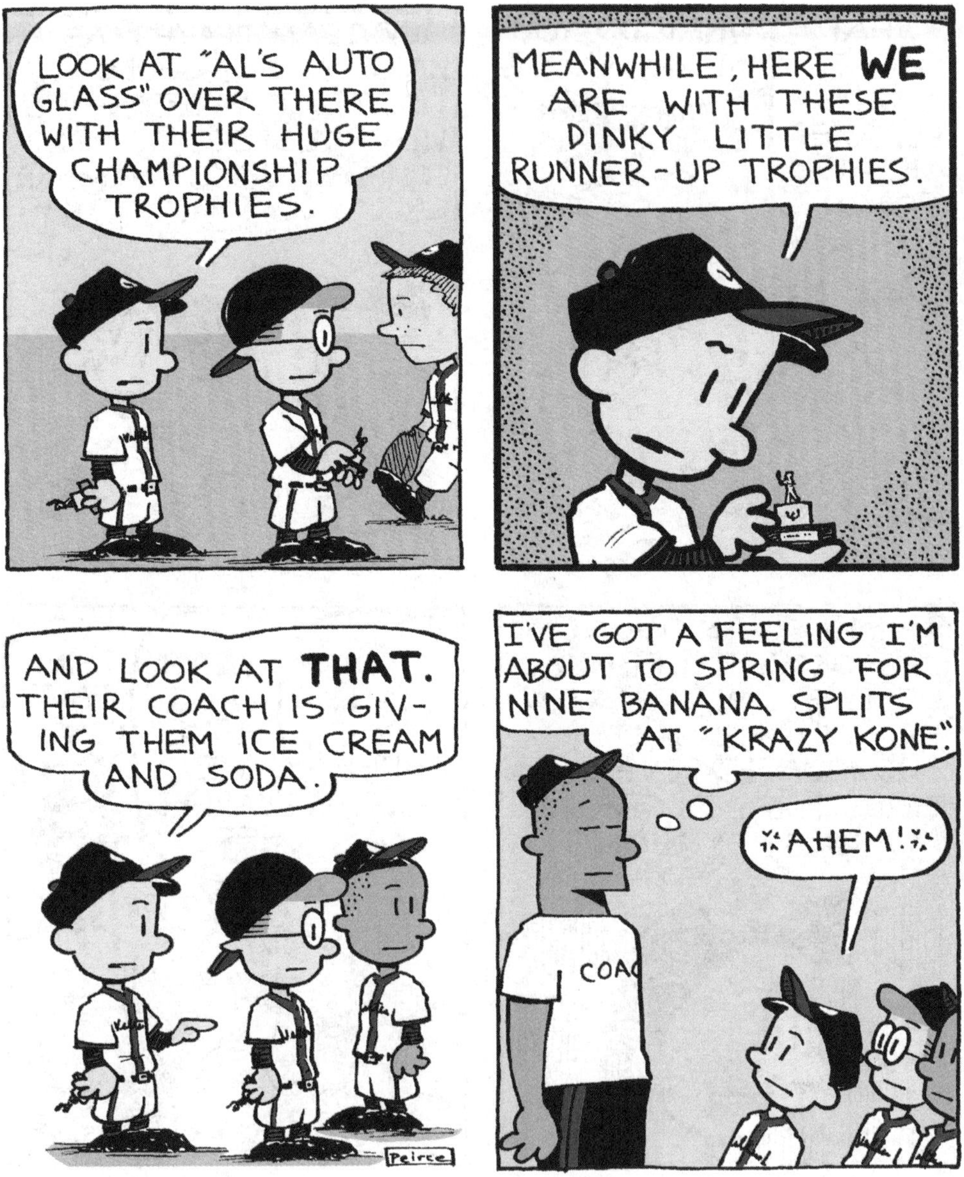
LOOK AT "AL'S AUTO GLASS" OVER THERE WITH THEIR HUGE CHAMPIONSHIP TROPHIES.
MEANWHILE, HERE **WE** ARE WITH THESE DINKY LITTLE RUNNER-UP TROPHIES.
AND LOOK AT **THAT.** THEIR COACH IS GIVING THEM ICE CREAM AND SODA.
I'VE GOT A FEELING I'M ABOUT TO SPRING FOR NINE BANANA SPLITS AT "KRAZY KONE."
AHEM!
COAC
Peirce

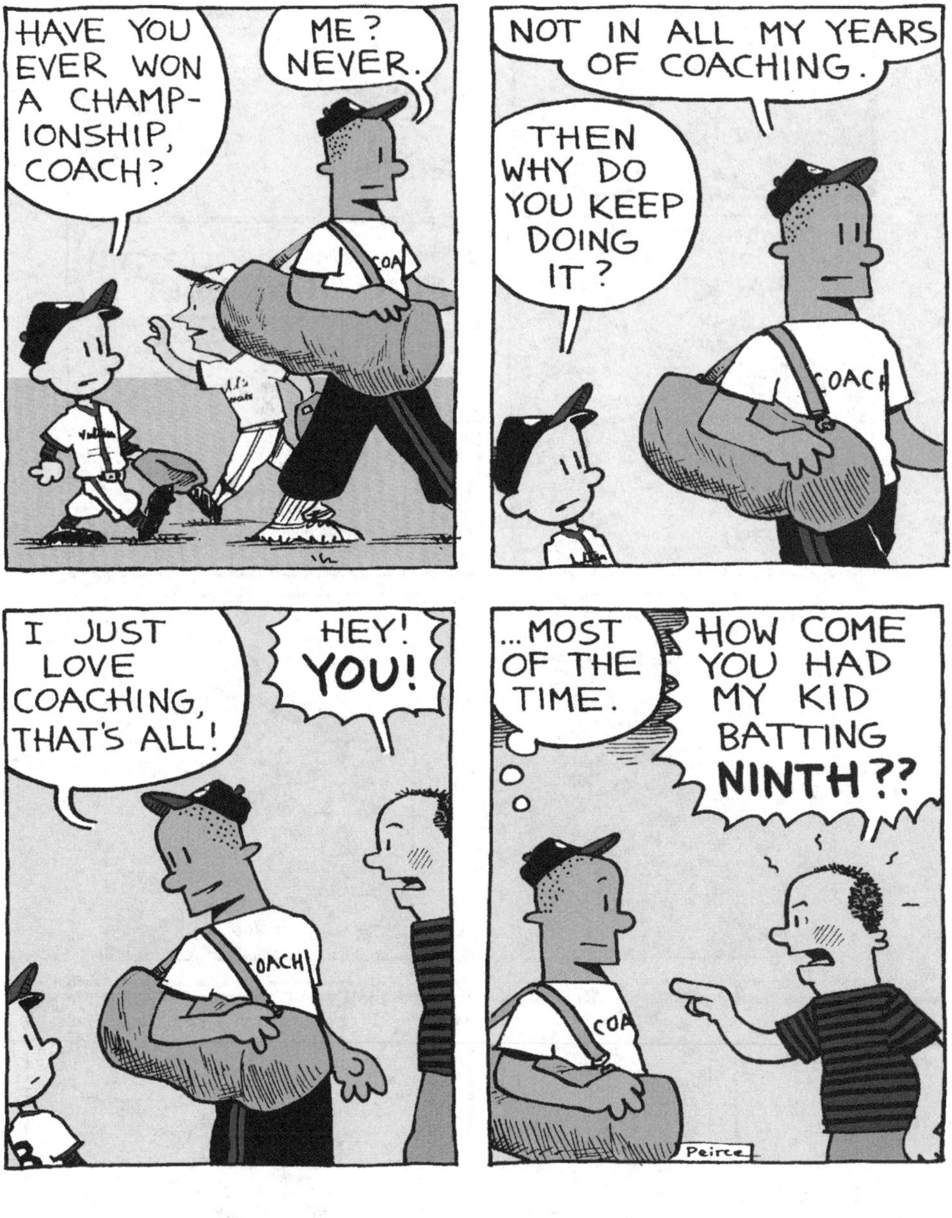
HAVE YOU EVER WON A CHAMPIONSHIP, COACH?
ME? NEVER.
NOT IN ALL MY YEARS OF COACHING.
THEN WHY DO YOU KEEP DOING IT?
COACH
I JUST LOVE COACHING, THAT'S ALL!
HEY! **YOU!**
COACH
...MOST OF THE TIME.
HOW COME YOU HAD MY KID BATTING **NINTH??**
Peirce

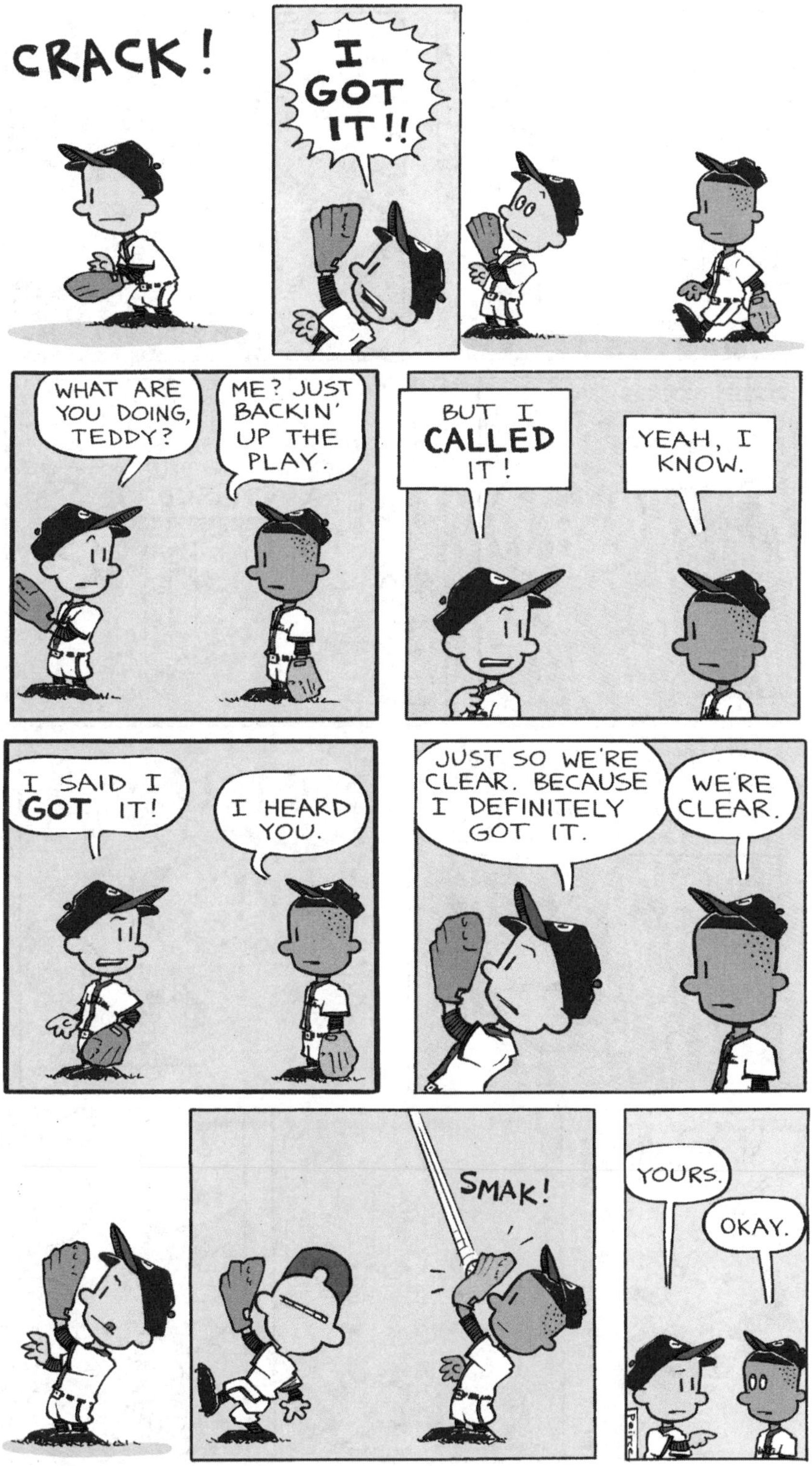
CRACK!
I GOT IT!!
WHAT ARE YOU DOING, TEDDY?
ME? JUST BACKIN' UP THE PLAY.
BUT I CALLED IT!
YEAH, I KNOW.
I SAID I GOT IT!
I HEARD YOU.
JUST SO WE'RE CLEAR. BECAUSE I DEFINITELY GOT IT.
WE'RE CLEAR.
SMAK!
YOURS.
OKAY.

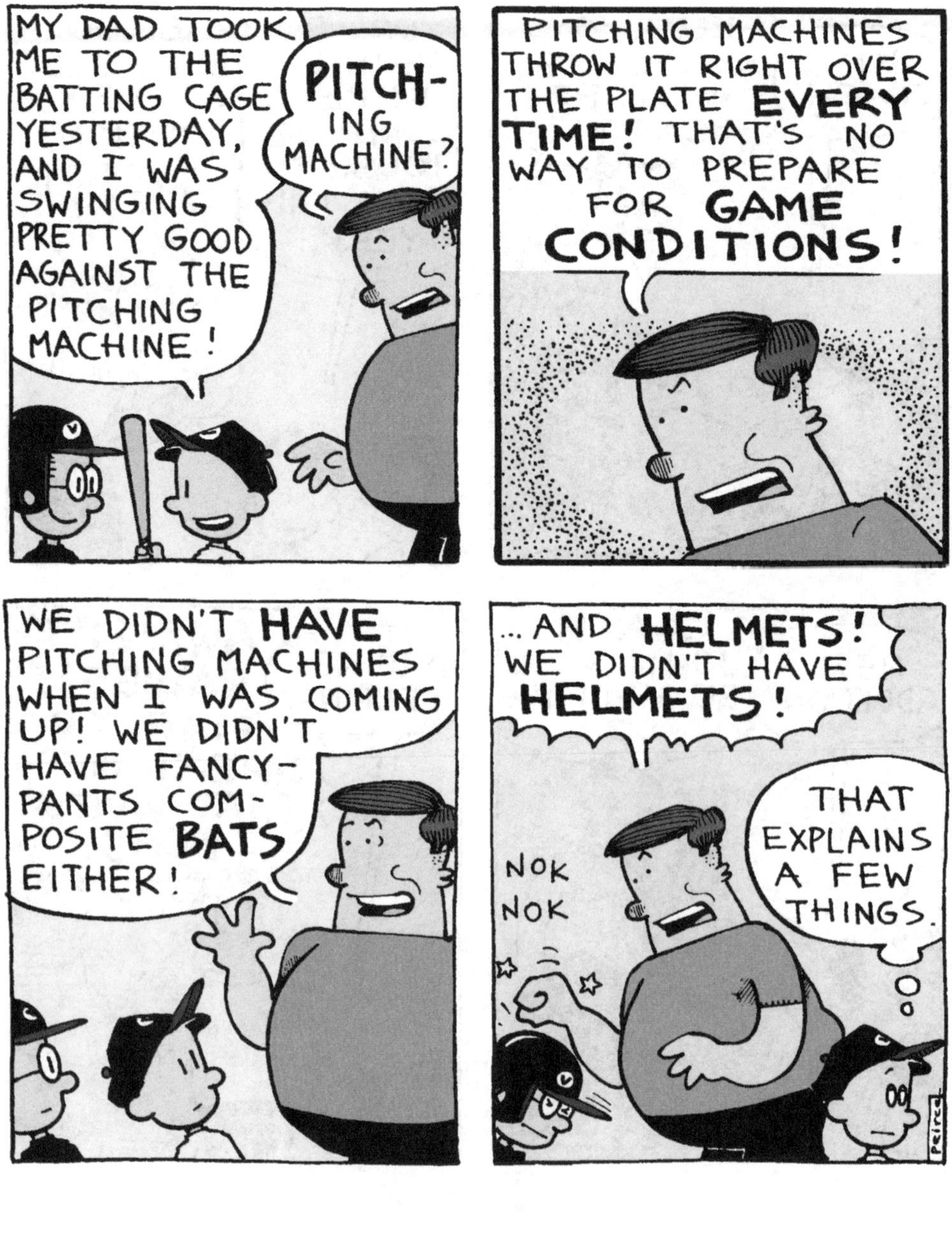
MY DAD TOOK ME TO THE BATTING CAGE YESTERDAY, AND I WAS SWINGING PRETTY GOOD AGAINST THE PITCHING MACHINE!
PITCH-ING MACHINE?
PITCHING MACHINES THROW IT RIGHT OVER THE PLATE EVERY TIME! THAT'S NO WAY TO PREPARE FOR GAME CONDITIONS!
WE DIDN'T HAVE PITCHING MACHINES WHEN I WAS COMING UP! WE DIDN'T HAVE FANCY-PANTS COMPOSITE BATS EITHER!
...AND HELMETS! WE DIDN'T HAVE HELMETS!
NOK NOK
THAT EXPLAINS A FEW THINGS.
Peirce

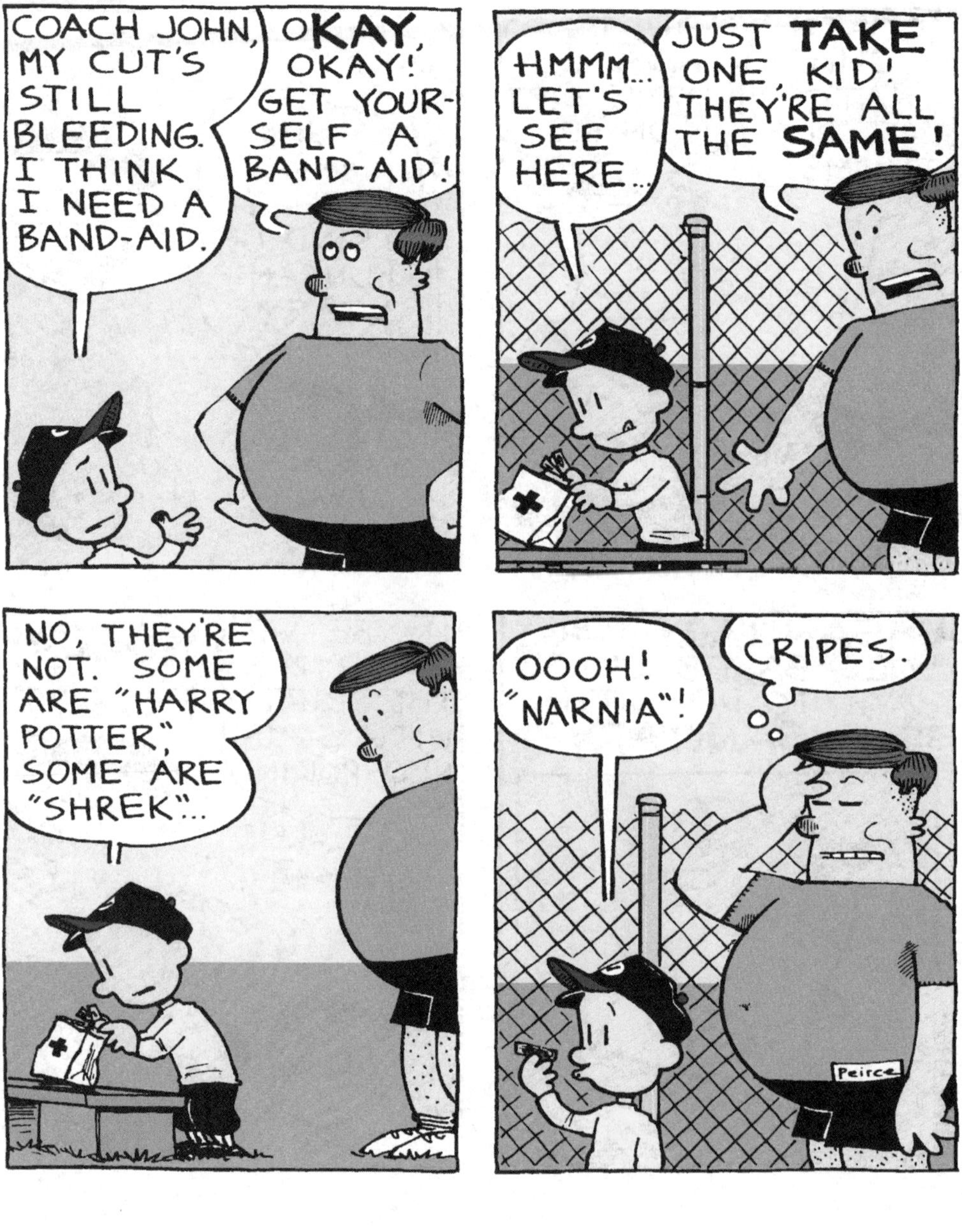
COACH JOHN, MY CUT'S STILL BLEEDING. I THINK I NEED A BAND-AID.
OKAY, OKAY! GET YOURSELF A BAND-AID!
HMMM... LET'S SEE HERE...
JUST TAKE ONE, KID! THEY'RE ALL THE SAME!
NO, THEY'RE NOT. SOME ARE "HARRY POTTER", SOME ARE "SHREK"...
OOOH! "NARNIA"!
CRIPES.
Peirce

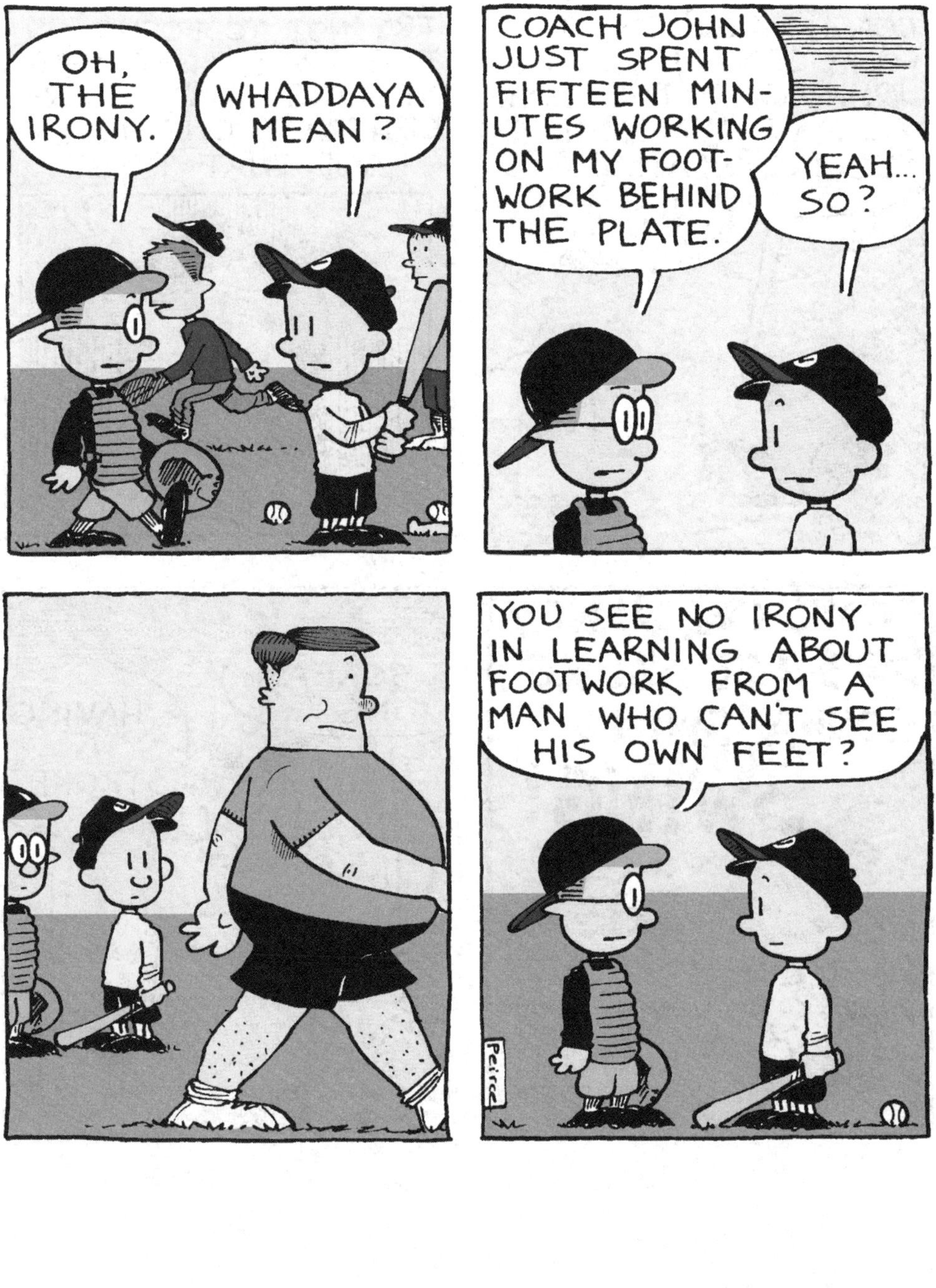
OH, THE IRONY.
WHADDAYA MEAN?
COACH JOHN JUST SPENT FIFTEEN MIN-UTES WORKING ON MY FOOT-WORK BEHIND THE PLATE.
YEAH... SO?
YOU SEE NO IRONY IN LEARNING ABOUT FOOTWORK FROM A MAN WHO CAN'T SEE HIS OWN FEET?
Peirce

158

GOAL!

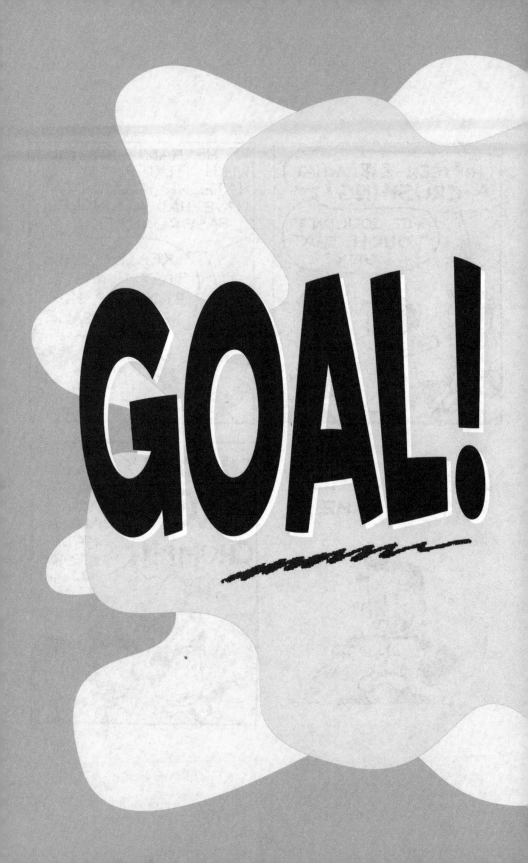

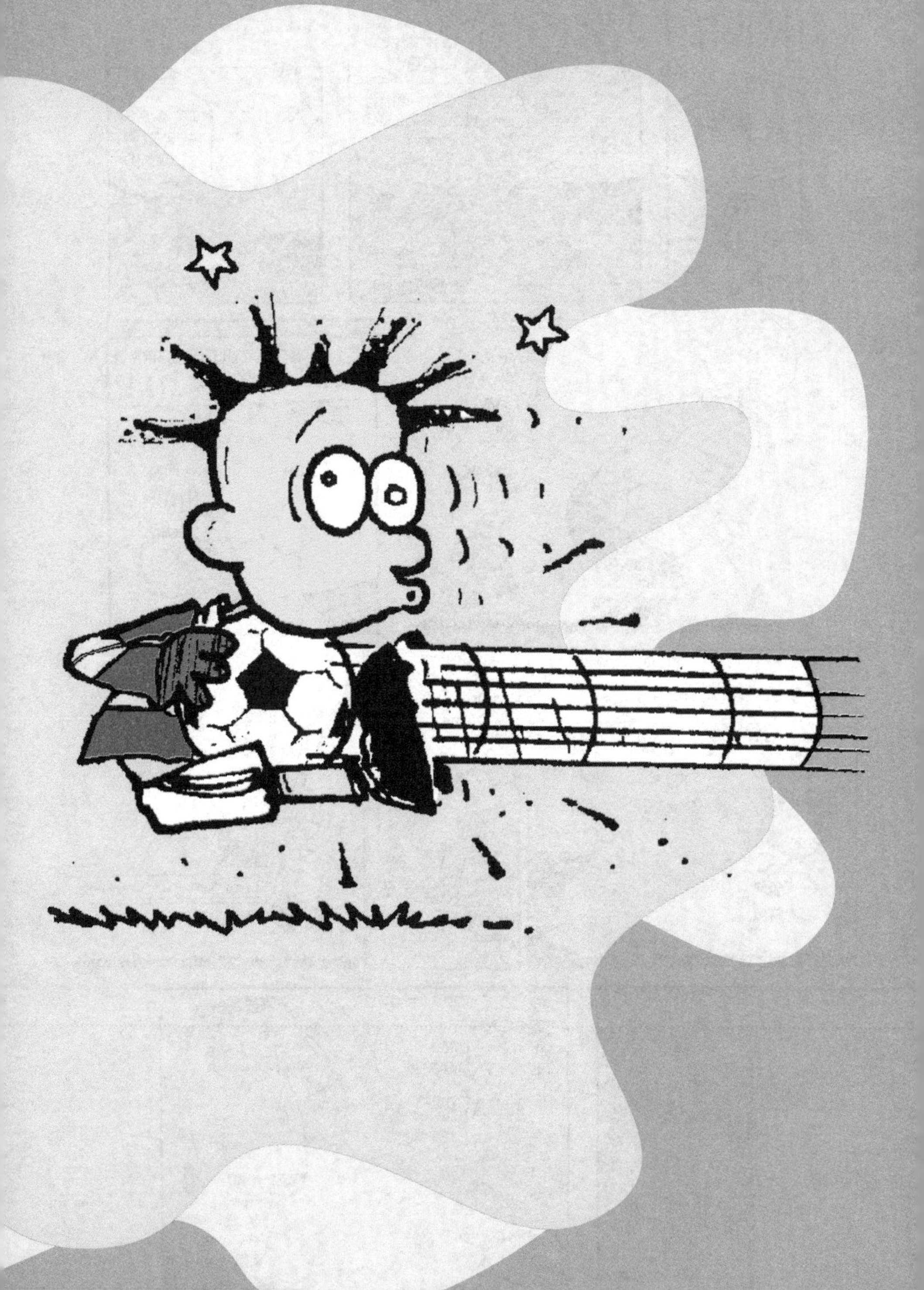

166

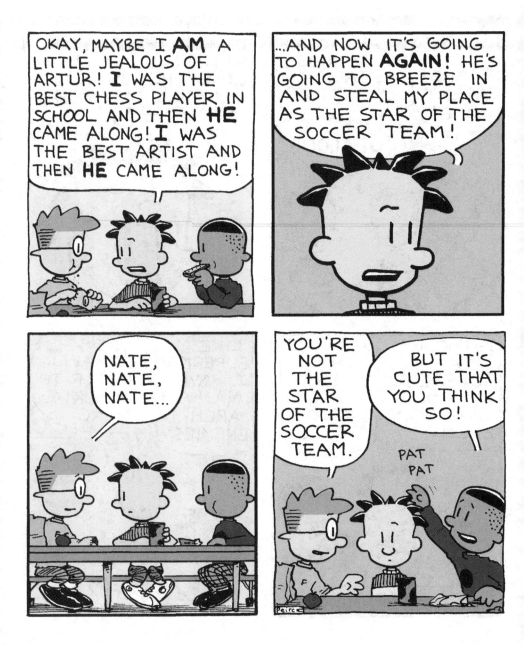

179

181

183

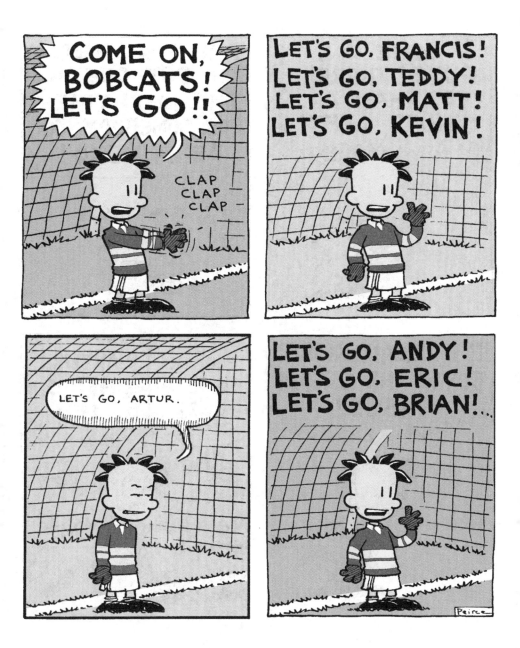

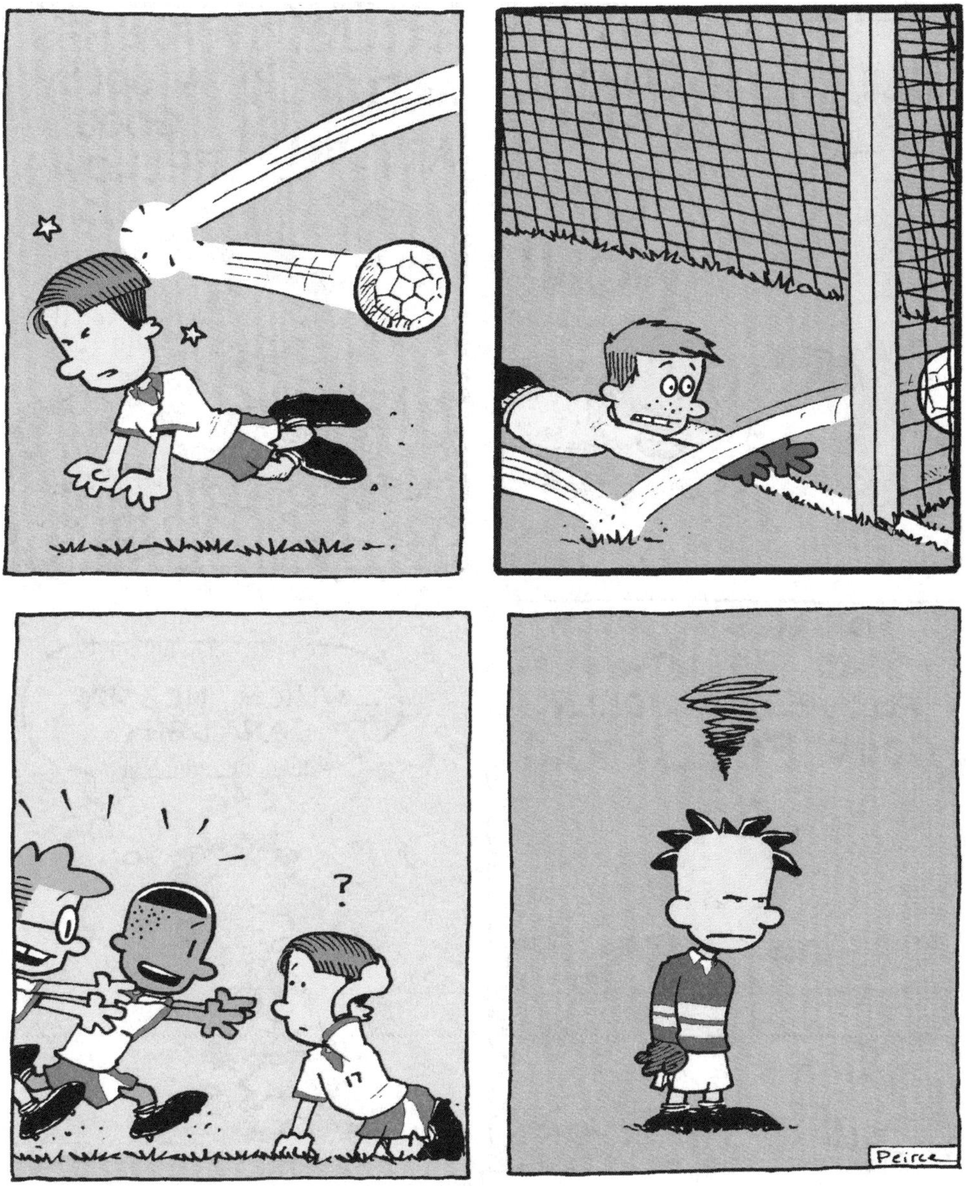
?
17
Peirce

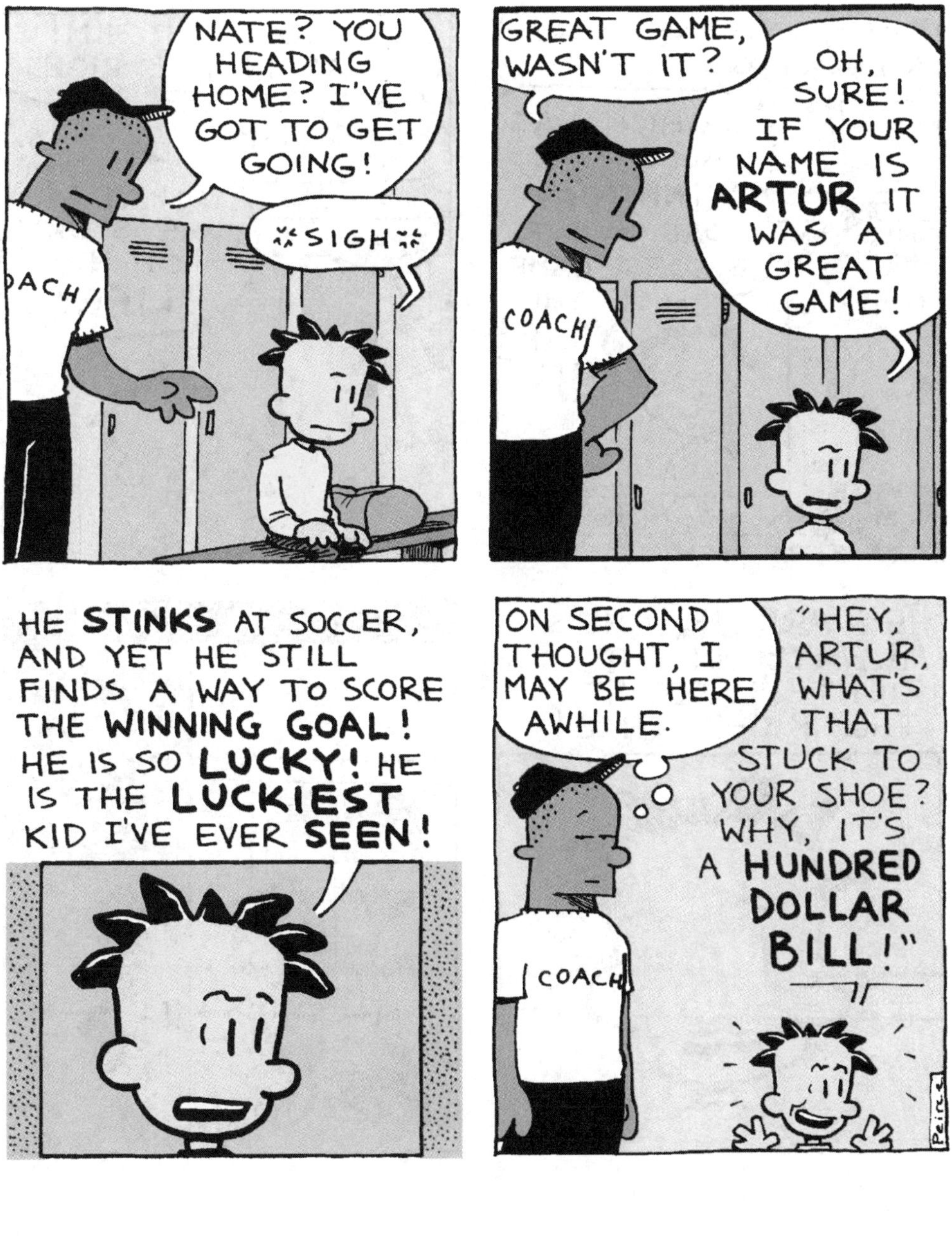
NATE? YOU HEADING HOME? I'VE GOT TO GET GOING!
SIGH
GREAT GAME, WASN'T IT?
OH, SURE! IF YOUR NAME IS ARTUR IT WAS A GREAT GAME!
HE STINKS AT SOCCER, AND YET HE STILL FINDS A WAY TO SCORE THE WINNING GOAL! HE IS SO LUCKY! HE IS THE LUCKIEST KID I'VE EVER SEEN!
ON SECOND THOUGHT, I MAY BE HERE AWHILE.
"HEY, ARTUR, WHAT'S THAT STUCK TO YOUR SHOE? WHY, IT'S A HUNDRED DOLLAR BILL!"
COACH
Peirce

194

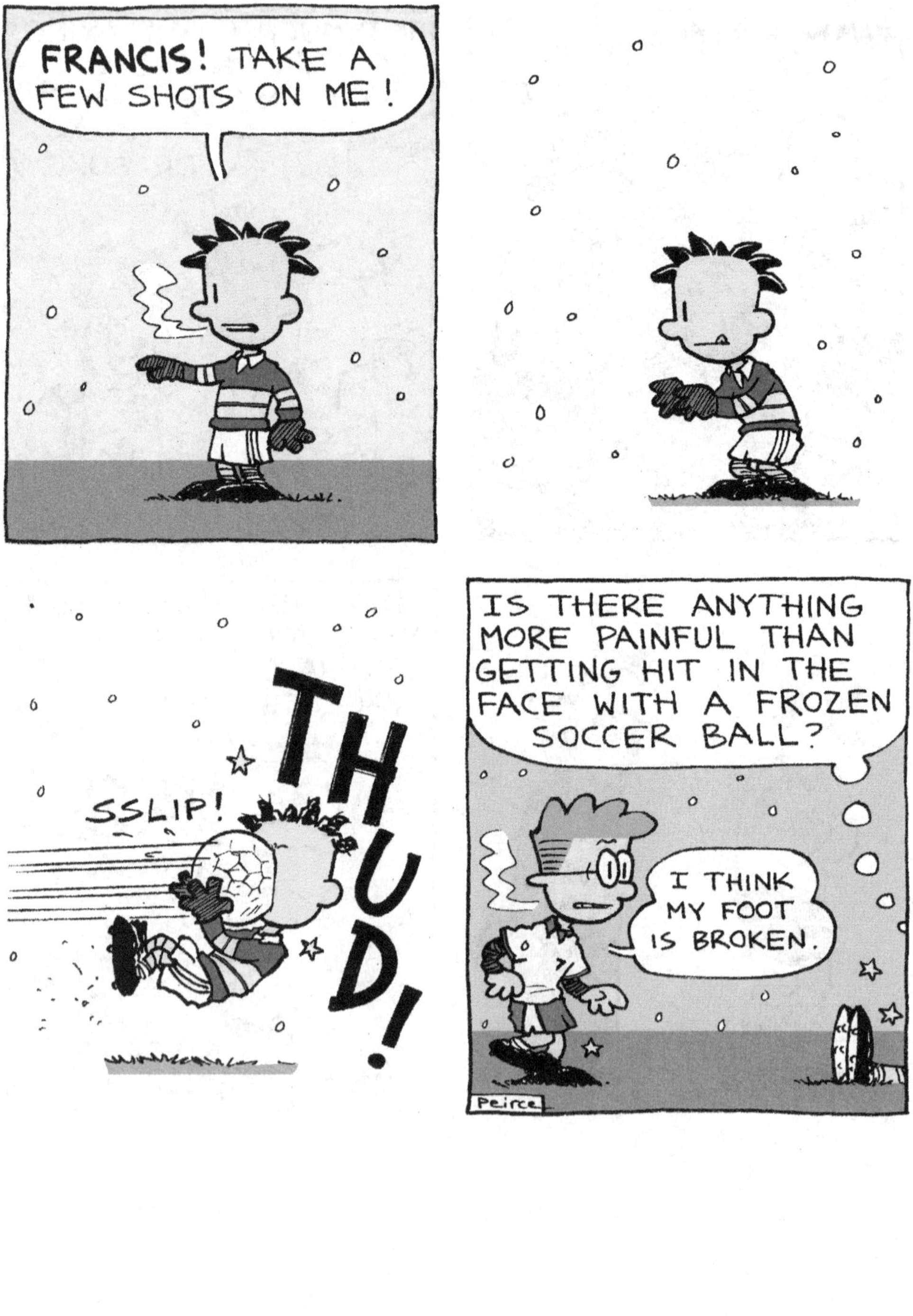
FRANCIS! TAKE A FEW SHOTS ON ME!
SSLIP!
THUD!
IS THERE ANYTHING MORE PAINFUL THAN GETTING HIT IN THE FACE WITH A FROZEN SOCCER BALL?
I THINK MY FOOT IS BROKEN.
Peirce

204

212

AWRIGHT, LADIES, YOU KNOW WHY YOU LOST YESTERDAY? YOU GOT **OUTMUSCLED!!**

TO WIN, YOU HAVE TO LEARN HOW TO PLAY AGAINST TEAMS THAT ARE **BIGGER** AND **STRONGER!**

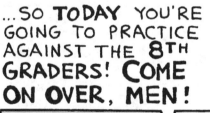

...SO **TODAY** YOU'RE GOING TO PRACTICE AGAINST THE **8TH** GRADERS! **COME ON OVER, MEN!**

STOMP! STOMP! STOMP! STOMP!

"MEN" IS RIGHT.

IS IT TOO LATE TO SWITCH TO CROSS-COUNTRY?